KISSING LADY PHOEBE

Phoebe had no idea what she was doing. She'd never before been affected like this. His eyes and body willed her closer. She ignored the small voice urging caution. Her pulse thrilled and there was no more space between them.

"I have never been kissed before," she said. "I don't know what to do."

"I'll teach you."

Marcus placed his hands on her small-waist, reveling in the feel of her body. Her hands held his face tenderly. They were so small. She was so petite. He moved his lips on hers, teasingly, asking Phoebe's to respond. She did, innocently, tentatively at first. He waited until she was comfortable returning his kisses before kissing her more firmly . . .

Books by Ella Quinn

The Marriage Game
THE SEDUCTION OF LADY PHOEBE
THE SECRET LIFE OF MISS ANNA MARSH
THE TEMPTATION OF LADY SERENA
DESIRING LADY CARO
ENTICING MISS EUGENIE VILLARET
A KISS FOR LADY MARY
LADY BERESFORD'S LOVER
MISS FEATHERTON'S CHRISTMAS PRINCE
THE MARQUIS SHE'S BEEN WAITING FOR

The Worthingtons
THREE WEEKS TO WED
WHEN A MARQUIS CHOOSES A BRIDE
IT STARTED WITH A KISS
THE MARQUIS AND I
YOU NEVER FORGET YOUR FIRST EARL
BELIEVE IN ME

Novellas
MADELEINE'S CHRISTMAS WISH
THE SECOND TIME AROUND
I'LL ALWAYS LOVE YOU

Published by Kensington Publishing Corporation

ELLA QUINN

The SEDUCTION *Of* LADY PHOEBE

ZEBRA BOOKS
KENSINGTON PUBLISHING CORP.
www.kensingtonbooks.com

ZEBRA BOOKS are published by

Kensington Publishing Corp.
119 West 40th Street
New York, NY 10018

All Kensington titles, imprints, and distributed lines are available at
special quantity discounts for bulk purchases for sales promotion, pre-
miums, fund-raising, educational, or institutional use.

Special book excerpts or customized printings can also be created to fit
specific needs. For details, write or phone the office of the Kensington
Sales Manager: Attn.: Sales Department. Kensington Publishing Corp.,
119 West 40th Street, New York, NY 10018. Phone: 1-800-221-2647.

Zebra and the Z logo Reg. U.S. Pat. & TM Off.

First Kensington Books eBook Edition: September 2013
First Zebra Books Mass-Market Paperback Printing: November 2019
ISBN-13: 978-1-4201-4728-5
ISBN-10: 1-4201-4728-5

ISBN-13: 978-1-4201-4730-8 (eBook)
ISBN-10: 1-4201-4730-7 (eBook)

10 9 8 7 6 5 4 3 2 1

Printed in the United States of America

This novel is for my husband, who really didn't know what he was getting himself into when I said, "Honey, I think I'm going to write a Regency romance."

And he answered,
"You can do it."

Acknowledgments

Writing may be a solitary profession, but it takes a team to birth a book. To my mother-in-law, who read, critiqued, and is always ready with help or suggestions.

To my lovely agent, Elizabeth Pomada of Larsen-Pomada Literary Agents, who recognized a diamond in the rough, and loved my books as much as I did, and my editor, John Scognamiglio, who loved them enough to buy them. To Claire Cavanaugh, who taught me how to edit. To the wonderful Delilah Marvelle, who taught me how to write a blurb and synopsis. The Beau Monde Chapter of Romance Writers of America, whose members are always there for advice, research, and support, and the members of the Compuserve Writers Forum who didn't laugh at me when I posted a message stating, "I just wrote a 100,000-word Regency, now what do I do?" No acknowledgment would be complete without mentioning my critique groups, Regency Romance Critiquers and Rom-Critters, without whom I never would have figured out what head-hopping was or any number of other things. They have been with me through good times and bad.

Chapter One

Late June 1806, Worthington Hall, England

Lord Marcus Finley poured his third glass of brandy and strolled back to the library window. The sunlit terrace and lawn provided a stark contrast to the dim, wood paneled room in which he stood contemplating his bleak future and imminent banishment to the West Indies.

His gaze was drawn to the petite figure of Lady Phoebe Stanhope. The sun caught her reddish-blond curls, creating a halo effect as she laughed and played with the Worthingtons' young girls. Simply seeing her joy eased some of his pain.

Everything about Lady Phoebe was perfect, from her curls and deep sky-blue eyes to her small feet and neatly turned ankle. There was a connection between them. He'd felt it. She was the only one who had tried to understand him. He wanted to marry her, but it seemed impossible now. Why had he met the only woman he'd ever want just days before he left?

He wondered what their children would have looked like.

Another rush of anger swept through him, and he forcibly loosened the fingers he'd tightened around his glass.

"Marcus, there you are."

He turned as his friend, Lord Mattheus Vivers, heir to the Earl of Worthington, strode toward him. Vivers was the only reason Marcus was at the house party.

His friend pointed at the brandy. "That's not going to help, you know."

Marcus stared at the glass for a moment, watching the sun catch the amber shades of the liquid before downing the drink. "I'm going to hell in any case. What does it matter how I do it?"

Vivers rubbed a hand over his face. "When was the last time you were completely sober?"

"When my father told me I was being banished—and to where." Marcus turned back to the window, his anger consuming him. Even his brother, Arthur, hadn't defended Marcus. That had been the worse betrayal.

Vivers joined him at the window. "What's so interesting out there?"

Marcus went back to the view of Lady Phoebe. "My last unshattered dream."

Vivers glanced out. "Lady Phoebe Stanhope? Give it up."

Scowling, Marcus replied, "Why? I may be a second son, but I'm still eligible. Once I reach my majority, I have the inheritance from my mother's aunt."

His friend ran a hand through his hair, disordering its fashionable style. "Very well, I'll list the reasons. You're a minor and need your father's consent to wed, the same father, by the way, who is banishing you to the West Indies before you embroil yourself in a scandal here that can't be smoothed over. The most important is she is not yet out."

Marcus's stomach clenched as if he'd been punched. "What do you mean she's not out?"

"Not. Out. Not old enough to be on the Marriage Mart,"

Vivers enunciated clearly. "At twenty you're five years too young yourself. Do you really imagine that her father would consent to you marrying her? Ladies marry at twenty, not gentlemen."

Marcus shook his head, trying to clear it. Why was she at this house party then? Was this some joke fate was playing on him? Or was it more punishment? "How old is she?"

"I don't really know," his friend shrugged. "Sixteen or seventeen, maybe. She has a great deal of countenance, so it's hard to be certain. It's a shame you won't be here when she does come out," Vivers mused. "I don't expect she'll last long on the Marriage Mart."

Marcus felt like he was dying. By the time he was five and twenty, she would be married and have children. "Perhaps Lady Phoebe would go with me to the West Indies. God knows I love her."

"We'll have dinner at the tavern and attend the cockfight," Vivers said. "That will put you in a better frame of mind. She leaves early to-morrow. Better if you don't see her."

Marcus poured another glass, tossed it off. "There must be something I can do."

He went to add more brandy to his glass, but Vivers snatched the tumbler from Marcus's hand.

"You've had more than enough to drink. Good God, man. Get it through your head. You cannot marry her. Now go to your chamber, and sleep it off before you do something stupid."

Vivers left, and Marcus went to follow. He wobbled a bit as he took a step.

Lady Phoebe was waving as she made her way to the house. He would intercept her and make his case. This was his last chance to win her. In nine days he'd be on a ship to the West Indies, but first he'd take her to Gretna Green.

* * *

Phoebe entered the house through a side door. She'd thought Lord Marcus would join them outside and wondered if he was off with Lord Mattheus. Lord Marcus was so nice—no, better than nice—and handsome. Her stomach felt like it had butterflies whenever she thought of him. He'd touched her hand once and it tingled. She couldn't even breathe when he was near, his presence filled her with such joy and her heart pounded when they spoke. Phoebe was sure she was in love. Nothing else could be so magical.

She hesitated, remembering what Lady Worthington had said. That Lord Marcus wasn't at all the thing, and that he was being banished before he caused a large scandal. But if that was true, surely Phoebe would not have fallen in love with him. The only thing to do was to ask him about the rumors.

An hour later, dressed in a very pretty gown of sprig muslin, Phoebe made her way toward the drawing room, passing through the picture gallery. The afternoon sun lit one-half of the wide corridor. Long mullioned windows were flanked by red and gold brocade hangings and red velvet-covered benches sat against the outside wall.

Centuries of portraits of somber-faced Vivers hung on the inside paneled walls. As she approached the ancient, carved, double doors leading to the grand staircase, something moved. She stopped.

Lord Marcus staggered slightly as he strolled out from the corner. "I've been looking for you, my dear." His words were slurred as if he was drunk.

"Lord Marcus, have you been drinking?" A chill ran through her as she remembered what Lady W had said.

"Just a mite," he said. "Liquid courage and all that. I have something important to discuss with you."

She raised her chin and moved to go around him. "I have nothing to say to you, my lord."

"But I have a lot to say to you, m'dear." He held out a hand to block her exit. "Come to me, Phoebe."

Her initial trepidation turned to rage. She narrowed her eyes and used her coldest tone. "How *dare* you address me in such a manner? Out of my way and let me pass." How could she have been so wrong, and now what was she to do?

Lord Marcus's arm snaked out to grab her. "I've a better idea."

Phoebe jumped back and tried to run around him, but he caught her. The strong scent of brandy assailed her nose. Her heart thudded wildly. What a mistake she had made. Lord Marcus was nothing like she'd imagined. She had to get away from him.

His arm tightened around her. He took her jaw in his hand and turned it to face him. "I love you, and I want you to be mine."

His gaze burned hot. She shook her head back and forth, trying to avoid his lips and his fingers brushed her breast. A jolting thrill went through her followed by overwhelming panic. What had he done to her?

For the first time in Phoebe's life, she was truly afraid. Desperate, she broke his hold and drove her fist into his nose.

Blood spurted out. Lord Marcus reeled back and fell to the floor with a grunt.

She stood over him, shaking with anger. "You rogue— you have the privilege and wealth of a gentleman, and what do you use it for? Nothing. I didn't want to believe the stories, but you've proven them true. You treat people with contempt and wonder why you're not respected. Until you learn to put others first and use your power and affluence to help people rather than hurt them, you will remain the poor excuse for a man you are now. Leave this house now. I never want to see you again."

Phoebe turned on her heel then strode swiftly away. She'd

not give him the satisfaction of seeing her run—or realizing how much his behavior had devastated her. She'd thought she loved him. How could she ever trust her judgment again?

Once Phoebe reached her room, she rang the bell for her lady's maid.

Rose entered from the dressing room and dropped the garments she was carrying. "Oh, my lady, you're so pale. Why do you have blood on your gown? Are you hurt?"

Phoebe blinked back the tears. She would not cry further over Lord Marcus. He wasn't worth it. "I'm not injured," she said, hating the tremor in her voice, "but I cannot go down to dinner."

"Don't you worry," Rose said. "I'll send a message to her ladyship that you're not joining them and order you some warm milk and toast brought up."

Rose helped her mistress undress and into her nightgown, all the while listening as Phoebe poured out the whole tale.

"My lady," Rose said, "you must tell your mamma what happened. That young man should be punished."

Phoebe shook her head. "No, I don't want anyone else to know. I'm so ashamed. Oh, Rose, what did I do to encourage him to treat me so badly?"

The maid combed Phoebe's hair and made soothing noises. "You didn't do nothing, my lady, and don't you think it. Lord Marcus Finley is young, wild, and headstrong as they come. A bad apple. Heard all about him at the table in the servants' hall. From the tales his groom told, his lordship doesn't have any business being around decent folks until he mends his ways."

The milk and toast came, and Rose made Phoebe drink and eat before finally tucking her desolate mistress into bed and pulling the hangings closed.

Phoebe lay in the darkness trying to push Lord Marcus

Finley out of her mind. He was a vile rogue and an arrogant troll. Thank God, he was being sent to the West Indies. She would never have to ever see him again.

Eight years later. June 1814, Newhaven, Sussex, England

Guy, the Seventh Marquis of Dunwood, watched as the American-made schooner approached the dock. A tall, tanned, young man in his late twenties stood at the bow, a line in hand ready to throw to one of the dock hands on the pier. He looked more like a seaman than a well-born gentleman.

His youngest son. The one, Guy thought ruefully, he hadn't recognized two years ago, when Marcus had come to visit.

The line sailed through the air and looped perfectly around a piling. After tying it off, Marcus walked back and addressed the captain before disappearing from sight.

Not more than a half an hour later, Dunwood greeted his son. "Welcome home. You could have returned earlier."

The good humor drained from Marcus's eyes. "Not and have made provisions for Lovet's family. They were left in bad straits when he died."

Dunwood would never understand the reason his son saw the need to care for those who were not his dependents. Apparently the West Indies had more of an impact on him than Dunwood thought it would. Well, what Marcus did with his private fortune was no bread and butter of Dunwood's. Rather than argue, he asked, "How is the new steward doing?"

His son's broad shoulders relaxed. "Well indeed. He used to work for the Spencer-Jones family, but when their third oldest son married, the property my new steward was managing went to the son. The man came highly recommended. I made the offer before anyone else could beat me to it."

"Good. I'm glad you were able to find someone." Dunwood started toward the two large coaches near an inn. "Where are your trunks?"

"I've only one. Covey, my man, will see it stowed," Marcus said. "How are Arthur and the girls faring?"

"Your brother is doing as well as can be expected, as are his daughters."

Marcus glanced around to see Covey wave to him. The last time he'd visited his brother, Arthur was hale and hearty. Now he was dying of consumption. His wife had passed a few years ago leaving him two daughters, but no heir.

As a result, Marcus had been recalled from banishment. He wondered how difficult it was going to be, after all the years of being his own master, to live with his father and be under Dunwood's rule.

Glancing around the small town, Marcus felt as if he were in a foreign country, but he'd been gone long enough. He looked at his ship, the *Lady Phoebe*, tied up at the dock. Perhaps too long.

"After you've spent a few days visiting your brother, I'll take you to London." His father's lips formed a *moue*. "You need to call on Weston and Hoby to see about your clothing before the Little Season begins. One of your first jobs will be finding a wife."

Marcus nodded. At long last he and his father agreed about something. "I'll make it a priority."

Last week in August 1814, Cranbourne Place, England

Phoebe walked briskly into the large, sunny breakfast room, the train of her pale green nankeen riding habit draped over one arm.

She greeted her brother, Geoffrey, the sixth Earl of Cranbourne. "Good morning."

When he looked up from his news sheet and met her gaze, Phoebe saw the fatigue etched in his face.

"Oh, you poor dear," she said. "Is it the baby?" Miles was Geoffrey and his wife, Amabel's six-month-old son.

"Yes," Geoffrey replied. "He's getting his first tooth. I dare say, had I'd known he would be in this much pain, I would have recommended to him that he not bother."

Grinning, Phoebe said, "I am sure he would have appreciated the advice."

Geoffrey handed her a section of the news sheet, and they sat in companionable silence until her sister-in-law joined them.

After pouring a cup of tea, Amabel asked Phoebe, "When do you leave for Town?"

She swallowed a piece of toast. "Next week."

"I do wish I could go with you," Amabel said.

"What a whisker!" Phoebe smiled. "You have no desire at all to go to London and dance attendance on me, and, indeed, I have no wish for you to have to do so. I am quite content to stay with my aunt St. Eth. I much prefer the political parties the St. Eths attend."

Her sister-in-law pulled a face. "But they are so dry."

Phoebe laughed when Amabel wrinkled her nose. "I know, for you the subject is a dead bore, but I enjoy it extremely."

Her sister-in-law frowned. "My dear, how will you ever find a husband if you are attending only political parties?"

"It is not as if there are *no* unmarried gentlemen at the parties," Phoebe retorted. "Besides, I daresay I have met every unmarried gentleman the length and breadth of England. Not one has given me the smallest desire to marry. Perhaps I shall set up a salon and become a famous bluestocking."

Her sister-in-law's mouth dropped open in shock. "You cannot mean that!"

Phoebe tried to hide her exasperation. "I know you've tried very hard to bring about a match for me. I wish you would not persist. I shall marry when I find a gentleman I can love and not before."

"But you must marry," Amabel said. "You are almost twenty-four, and you are much too beautiful to become a spinster."

"I am well aware of my age," Phoebe said as mildly as she could. "I'm not on the shelf yet."

After taking a sip of tea, Amabel said airily, "I have invited my brother to visit us."

Phoebe creased her brows. "Evesham? I thought he was too ill to travel."

"No, Arthur is indeed too ill," her sister-in-law said. "I have invited my other brother, Marcus. He shall arrive in three days' time."

"Lord Marcus?"

Amabel hesitated before continuing, "He needs to marry now, and I immediately thought of you."

At the mention of Lord Marcus Finley, Phoebe's stomach clenched, and the humiliation she had not felt in years burbled within her, feeding her anger.

She took a breath and calmly but firmly said, "I have met Lord Marcus, we did not suit. Amabel, pray excuse me. I have just remembered something I must do."

Phoebe rose and left the room. Upon entering her chamber, she closed the door with a snap. The control with which she had been holding herself threatened to unravel. Lord Marcus Finley was back.

Myriad feelings of fear, hurt, and despair assailed her. It confused her to feel almost as raw as she had eight years ago when he'd shattered her childish romantic ideas. She had pushed him out of her mind then and, other than the bad dreams, had not purposely thought of him since.

She'd hoped never to hear his name again and certainly

did not want to meet him. She'd learned to protect herself, but still mourned the loss of her innocence he'd stolen. She would not weep over Lord Marcus. No good could come of thinking of him. Forgetting that day had been easier when he had been safely across the ocean.

Phoebe breathed deeply and strode to her writing desk, a beautiful cherry secretaire. She furiously mended her nib then took a piece of hot-pressed paper, dipped the pen in the standish, and wrote her first letter to her aunt, the Marchioness of St. Eth.

> *My Dearest Aunt Ester,*
> *I was very happy to receive your letter informing me that you are now in residence at St. Eth House. Dear Aunt, I am in sore need of replenishing my wardrobe, and I trust it will not be too inconvenient for me to come to you on Thursday. I look forward to being with you soon.*
> > *Your devoted and loving neice,*
> > *P*

She penned a letter to the inn she intended to stay at and then wrote a note to Amabel. An hour later she knocked on the door of Geoffrey's study, entered the room, and began to pace.

He raised his brows. "Something has you in a bother. Is this about Amabel's brother?"

"Yes." Phoebe walked some more before turning to him. "Geoffrey, I cannot see him again, I choose not to. I—I am sorry, but I have decided to bring forward my trip to London to to-morrow."

"Do you wish to tell me what this is about?" he asked with grave concern. "Shall I defend your honor?"

"No." She stopped as her throat caught. "I don't wish to talk or even think about it."

"If you change your mind, I'm here to listen." He paused. "I suppose you need my baggage coach?"

Phoebe smiled gratefully. "You are the best of brothers, but no, thank you. My excuse to Aunt Ester will be that I must shop. I shall take only what I can carry in my coach."

Phoebe handed him her missives. "Will you frank these for me? I want them to go by express post."

"Yes, of course." He took the letters, sealed them with wax and his signet ring before scrawling his title across them, and gave them back to her. "Tell Wilson I said to have one of the grooms ride to Town immediately. What time do you plan to leave?"

"Quite early, I think, before Amabel is down to breakfast," Phoebe said quietly and left the room.

She found her maid in the dressing room. "Rose, we are leaving in the morning and will take only one carriage. I would like to depart at seven o'clock."

"May I ask, my lady, if this is to do with Lady Cranbourne's brother?"

Phoebe sighed. "I take it the news of his impending visit is all around the servants' quarters?"

Rose nodded.

Phoebe answered her frankly, "Yes, that is the reason."

Her maid's face became militant. "Everything will be ready to leave at first light, my lady. There is no reason in the world why you should have to see that Spawn of Satan again!"

Early the next morning, Geoffrey handed her into the coach. "I'll see you when I come up for the legislative session votes," he said. "Give my love to Hermione and Edwin and Aunt and Uncle St. Eth . . ."

Phoebe laughed. "Yes, yes—and William and Arabella and Mary," she added. "I shall. Thank you for being so understanding. I cannot imagine Amabel will be happy about this."

"No, probably not." He smiled wickedly. "Of course, not having married a harridan like m'sisters are, I know she won't fly up into the boughs."

Phoebe punched him playfully. "No, *you* certainly do not live under the cat's paw. She spoils you."

Geoffrey grinned ruefully. "So true. Is Marcus Finley that bad, love?"

"He is a disgusting, vulgar scamp!" she replied angrily.

"Oho, you did take him into dislike!"

"Yes." And now she must find some way to avoid him permanently.

Chapter Two

After waving farewell to her brother, Phoebe sat back against the plush squabs and tried to allow the coach's sway to comfort her. The vehicle was in the newest style, light, and well sprung. The outside was a dark green with gold piping, and the inside cushions were in her favorite shade of apple green. Across from Phoebe, Rose's eyes drifted closed.

Phoebe sighed, settling in for a quiet journey. At least she had made her escape before Lord Marcus arrived. Perhaps with his brother being so ill, Lord Marcus would not come to Town for the Little Season. On second thought, based on what she knew about him, he probably would be in London, if for no other reason than to visit the gaming hells and impures. She ruthlessly shoved him from her mind.

Her first day of travel passed much as she'd expected. The weather was fine and warm, and the roads dry. After a time she began reading *Patronage*, the latest novel to have come her way.

She arrived at her sister Hermione's home in the mid-afternoon. Her nephew William's shrill voice floated on the air. Phoebe leaned out the window, smiled and waved to her nieces and nephew as the children came running to-ward the drive.

William shouted, "Mamma, look, Mamma look, it's Aunt Phoebe!"

Laughing, she descended from the coach. William and Arabella, five-year-old twins, took Phoebe's hands, and Mary, age three, grabbed onto her skirts.

Phoebe hugged and kissed them all. "My loves, I am very happy to see you as well, but you must allow me to greet your mamma."

Phoebe disentangled a hand and held it out to her sister. Hermione and her twin, Hester, were a few years older than Phoebe, but younger than Geoffrey.

Her sister embraced Phoebe, and Hermione's eyes twinkled as the children tried to pull their aunt away. "Not that I am not delighted to see you, my dear. But what, may I ask, brings you to me a week early and with no notice?"

Phoebe pulled a face. "*Amabel* is matchmaking again."

Answering an insistent tug on her skirts, Phoebe picked up little Mary.

Hermione shrugged. "Amabel has been trying to arrange a match for you since the first Season after she and Geoffrey married, when you fagged her to death."

"Yes, but this time she has gone beyond the line of what I can endure." Phoebe pressed her lips together. "Though to be fair, she doesn't know what she did."

Her sister raised an enquiring brow.

Phoebe briefly closed her eyes. Hermione had seen her leave the gallery that day, but they had never discussed it.

"Amabel invited her brother, Lord Marcus Finley, to meet me in two days." Phoebe adjusted Mary on her hip. "I told him eight years ago at Worthingtons' estate, when we had that unfortunate contretemps, that I never wanted to see him again and nothing has changed."

Hermione nodded. "I remember how upset you were."

Holding Mary closer, Phoebe said, "Now that he has returned for good, I know I'll not be able to avoid meeting him at some point, but I do not wish to be placed in the position where I must be alone with him. That's exactly what would have happened had I stayed at Cranbourne Place."

Phoebe was distracted by her niece, whose bouncing had become insistent. "What is it, my love?"

Mary took Phoebe's face between her small chubby hands. "Don't be 'set," Mary said, and kissed Phoebe. "It be all wight."

She held her closer. "Yes, sweetheart, I'll be right as a trivet. Aunt Phoebe just needs to escape the troll."

Hermione frowned. "That was a piece of high meddling on Amabel's part to be sure. My dear, what *will* you do when you see him again? As Dunwood's heir, Lord Marcus is bound to be at many of the same events you will attend."

Her sister was right, Lord Dunwood was very politically active, as was her uncle, Henry, the Seventh Marquis of St. Eth. Phoebe raised one brow and haughtily looked down her nose. "If we meet, I shall, of course, be civil," she said icily.

Her sister burst into laughter. "Oh, yes, that look should send him to the right about."

Phoebe responded, "Well, I certainly hope it does. The last time I had to punch him in the nose to dissuade him. It's a shame I am too young to set up my own household."

"Oh, Phoebe!" Hermione's eyes widened. "Do you wish to set the *ton* on its ear?" She tapped her cheek, appearing as if she were deep in thought. "Hmm. I have just the thing. You could find a husband."

"Et tu, Brute?" Phoebe tried to look hurt, but couldn't stop the laugh. "Marriage to just anyone won't solve anything."

"Phoebe, we just have your best interests at heart. Surely there must be someone."

"Well, Hermione, at least you *do not* try to make matches for me."

"No, and I will not do so," her sister responded. "You will know when you meet the right man, without any assistance from me or anyone else."

Suddenly wistful, Phoebe raised her gaze to her sister's. "Do you truly think I shall know?"

"I do indeed. You need only remember what Mamma told us. That when you find the gentleman of your heart, it will be as if he is the only person you can see."

Hermione's husband, Edwin, the Earl of Fairport, said from the portico, "What is this? *Et tu, Brute.* You've only just arrived, and you're already discussing the classics? You've become very blue, my dear sister."

"No, silly." Hermione laughed as Edwin approached. "We are discussing marriage."

His gray eyes twinkled. "But what, I ask, does the betrayal of Julius Caesar have to do with marriage?"

"Not Julius Caesar," Hermione said, "Amabel."

"You have lost me." Edwin hugged and kissed Phoebe.

His wife fondly patted his arm. "We will explain it later."

He nodded toward Phoebe's horses, about to be led to the stables. "Is that the team you had off Marbury?"

"Yes, do you like them?"

"Don't I just." He signaled to the groom to stop and began to look them over.

Hermione took Edwin's arm and pulled him toward the steps. "Oh, no, you are coming into the house, else the two of you will be discussing horses and carriages until dinner."

She glanced back at Phoebe. "And you, my dear, you must spend some time with your nieces and nephew, if we are to have any peace at all."

Glancing at his children, Edwin asked dryly, "Why is it,

my normally well-behaved children suddenly become heathens whenever their aunt Phoebe arrives?"

Arabella and William vociferously denied being heathens rather than only very happy to see their aunt.

"For you know, Papa," William said, "she is the most fun of all our aunts, and she's always interested in playing games with us and knowing what we are doing."

"What I know, you young cawker," retorted his father fondly, "is that *my* definition of heathen and *yours* bear little in common."

Giggling, Phoebe allowed herself to be tugged by William and Arabella's small hands into the children's parlor at the back of the house. With Mary on her lap, she sat on the comfortable sofa and enthused over William's drawings and Arabella's watercolors.

All too soon, it was time for the children to return to the nursery. Upon being assured that their Aunt Phoebe would come bid them good night, the children obediently followed Nurse out of the parlor.

Edwin and her sister immediately turned the discussion to the reason for Phoebe's early visit.

Phoebe's heart raced at the mention of Lord Marcus Finley's name. "Please, can we not discuss him? I'd much rather talk about the pending legislation concerning the trade issues."

Her brother-in-law gave her a curious look, but diplomatically changed the topic.

Once in her room, Phoebe tried to block out the memory that continued to return since her discussion with Amabel. She could still smell the brandy and feel his hands as they brushed her breasts. She shuddered, remembering the strange feelings when he'd touched her and the sudden fear she'd felt. Why did *he* have to come back?

After dashing a tear from her cheek, she dipped a cloth

into the water basin and applied it to her face. If she appeared in the drawing room looking as if she'd been weeping, Hermione and Edwin would just ask more questions.

Edwin entered his wife's dressing room to try to get to the bottom of his sister-in-law's distress. "My love, what happened between Phoebe and Lord Marcus?"

Hermione shook her head. "I am not precisely sure, other than it happened at the house party where you and I were betrothed. One minute Phoebe was asking me about love, and the next time I saw her she was leaving the gallery in a tearful rage. When I looked down the corridor, Lord Marcus was lying on the floor."

"On the floor? Doing what?" Edwin asked.

"Bleeding."

He motioned for her to continue.

"From the nose, I believe. Phoebe punched him."

"What the deuce did the man do?"

"I have no idea," Hermione said. "Phoebe would never discuss it, and she made an excuse not to come down for dinner. When we left the next morning she acted her normal steady self. Frankly, I was so caught up in our wedding plans, I forgot all about it."

"Hmm, his peculiar behavior makes much more sense now."

His wife leaned back to gaze at him. "What makes more sense?"

"You will remember I went to Town to get the documents needed for the settlement agreement?"

She drew her brows together. "Yes."

He continued. "Finley came back to London like the devil was chasing him, sporting a swollen nose and a black eye. Made an addle-pated fool of himself. He was well in

his cups when he admitted a woman had planted him a
facer. Though he had sense enough to keep her identity a
secret."

Edwin chuckled at the memory of that night. "Finley
was, by all accounts, quite dazzled by her. Called her his
Vision. Of course, it was all over Town by the next day. His
behavior was shockingly outrageous."

Edwin glanced at his wife. "But Finley had never before
behaved toward any female, lady or not, in a way that
would have caused that sort of reaction."

"Indeed?" Hermione said tightly. "I thought he was just
some young blood trying to take advantage of a girl not yet
out. How do you know he was dazzled? *I* never heard anything."

Edwin grinned. "Well, my love, you could hardly have
expected to have been told. After all, it's not the sort of
thing one discusses with a lady. Besides, none of us knew
who the female was."

He kissed his wife. "Finley has changed a great deal
since then. I met him a couple of years back, and can say,
without a doubt, that the West Indies was the making of
him."

Edwin glanced down. "Socially and politically, it would
be a good match. Phoebe could do much worse."

Hermione placed her hand on Edwin's cheek and kissed
him. "Be that as it may, my love, I shall own myself surprised if Phoebe can be brought to *unbend* enough to do
more than be polite to him. Do you honestly believe she'll
allow Lord Marcus close enough to *woo* her?"

Raising a brow, Edwin responded, "She may not recognize him. I almost did not, and I've had a much longer acquaintance with him than Phoebe."

"Well," his wife retorted. "I do not believe she will
allow him within ten feet of her."

Edwin pressed his lips to his wife's temple. "When do we go to Town? I think we are going to be entertained this year."

"How *incorrigible* you can be." Hermione narrowed her eyes. "I don't know what you expect to happen. As you well know, Phoebe has never given the vulgar food for speculation."

"Yes, all very true"—he nuzzled Hermione's ear—"but the same can't be said of Finley. Although he is expected to take over the title, which will help restore him to respectability. Still, I would dearly love to watch this courtship develop. For a courtship it will be. That, I would wager on."

"I think you very vulgar, my lord," Hermione said with an exaggerated sniff.

"Oh no, my love, not vulgar. I just like a little sport now and then." Edwin lifted his wife and kissed her soundly. "And everyone deserves to be as happy as we are."

"Edwin, put me down. You know how scandalized Tuttle will be if I must call her in to dress my hair again."

He continued kissing Hermione, aware that hidden behind his wife's maid's brisk exterior, Tuttle had an incurably romantic disposition, and one of the joys of her life was to repair the depredations his lordship made upon his lady's toilet. "I've been scandalizing her for years."

"I'm lucky she hasn't left," Hermione mumbled, returning his kiss.

The following morning, Hermione and Edwin accompanied Phoebe to her coach.

Hermione hugged her sister. "We will see you in Town soon, my dear. I shall write Aunt Ester with our date."

Edwin looked up at the cloudless sky. "It seems you'll

have a good day to travel. When do you plan to arrive in Littleton?"

Phoebe glanced up as well. "We should reach the town in the late afternoon. We'll travel by easy stages to spare the blacks."

"Are you staying at the White Horse Inn?" he asked.

"Oh, yes, always," she replied. "The landlord and his wife are so *very* accommodating, and their head groom allows Sam, my groom, to have his way. That is imperative."

Edwin broke in with a shout of laughter. "Of course, it's the horses with which you are most concerned."

"Well, they *are* important." Phoebe glanced fondly at her team. "I find it much easier giving my custom to the same inns and coaching houses. Besides, I like the consistency."

"Yes. The better to insure Sam can take over their stables. What a piece of work you are."

Phoebe's eyes twinkled, but she had the grace to blush. Hugging Edwin, she said, "I'll look forward to seeing you in Town."

"Indeed, it promises to be a very interesting Season." He smiled enigmatically as he handed her first, then Rose, into the coach. He wondered how soon he and Hermione could be ready to leave for London.

He waited until Phoebe's carriage was down the drive before escorting his wife back into the house. "Will you write your sister, Hester?"

"I think I shall."

Retreating to their respective desks, Edwin penned a letter to his brother-in-law, Geoffrey, explaining that he knew Phoebe had refused to meet Finley, but that the man had changed appreciably. Edwin urged Geoffrey to stay safely ensconced at Cranbourne Place until he had reason to come to Town as his wife might be tempted to meddle.

Hermione picked up her pen, made sure it was sharp, and took a sheet of her elegant writing paper.

My Dear Sister,

You will remember in what a rage Phoebe was at Lord Marcus Finley during Lady W's house party. However, E seems to think that there is hope for Lord M yet, as P has never *remained so angry at anyone for so long a time. E is convinced that Lord M will try to court her. I beseech you—come to Town in support of our Sister. At the very least it will be diverting!*

All my love,
H

Chapter Three

The carriage bowled south along the Great North Road. Lately, Phoebe couldn't stop thinking about Lord Marcus and, last night, the bad dreams she'd had eight years ago returned.

Phoebe was so looking forward to walking off her agitation with her customary stroll around the small market town of Littleton before dinner. She would visit the old Norman church and walk past the picturesque little cottages, which always delighted her.

As she foresaw, they arrived in Littleton in the late afternoon.

Phoebe sat forward and blinked, unable to believe what she was seeing. The town was full of men, all shapes, sizes, and stations.

An amazing number of conveyances, phaetons, gigs, and curricles, along with other more modest vehicles, lined the roads.

"Oh, no." She sat back against the seat so as not to draw attention to herself. "I won't be able to have my walk now."

Rose stirred from her nap. "What is it, my lady?"

Sighing, Phoebe replied, "It appears we've arrived in the

midst of some sort of sporting event or the other. There is no other reason I can think of for there to be so many men in Littleton. I'm happy I sent an express changing our dates."

Rose shifted on the seat. "Even if you'd not, Mr. Ormsby would have made sure you got your chamber."

Phoebe smiled. "You are right, of course. Mr. Ormsby and his wife are very good to us. I shall have Sam escort me in. I do not at all relish walking through this crowd of, um, gentlemen."

The inn's ostlers shouted, over the commotion of other arriving vehicles, to her coachman, directing him ahead of the other carriages attempting to gain access to the White Horse.

Phoebe's conveyance drew to a stop in front of the large rambling white building. After her groom handed her down, Phoebe signaled for him to follow her into the building.

Mortified and very much aware of the proprieties, Phoebe looked straight ahead toward the open inn door.

A young buck stepped in front of her, leaned forward, and leered. Phoebe was tempted to punch him in the nose, but that would only cause the type of scene she was hoping to avoid. Mentally gritting her teeth, she raised one haughty brow and fixed him with a cold look of disdain.

He sketched a hasty bow and begged pardon, moving quickly out of her way.

Sweeping past him, then through the throng of men in the hall, she ignored anyone trying to catch her eye.

The innkeeper, Mr. Ormsby, a thin man, just over medium height with stooped shoulders, came forward to greet her.

Phoebe held out her hand to shake his. "Good afternoon, Mr. Ormsby. You seem to have quite a crowd to-day."

Mr. Ormsby bowed and pulled his forelock before taking a couple of her fingers and shaking them. "Good afternoon, my lady. There's a prize-fight in the area, and we're full up, even the stables. But you're not to worry. We have your usual accommodations."

He lowered his voice. "I mislike this crowd of gentl'men, my lady. You might want to make sure you keep your room door locked up tight, and your maid on a trestle in with you.

"These gents may look harmless now, but once they get to drinking . . . Well, me and my missus want to make sure that you're safe in our inn."

Phoebe nodded. "Yes, indeed, Mr. Ormsby. You are correct. I shall forego my usual parlor if you will serve dinner and breakfast in my chamber."

"It's a right good idea, and will make my missus much happier." Mr. Ormsby drew his bushy gray brows together. "For I have to tell you she's been a mite worried about you a-comin' with this crowd in town. I'll have my son, Jamie, get your maid from the carriage, then he'll take your lay'ship and Miss Fitchley to your room."

Phoebe smiled grimly. The innkeeper's arrangements were the best she could do. "Thank you, Mr. Ormsby."

Once settled, Phoebe paced the large chamber. "What bad luck." She glanced at Rose. "I hope you don't mind sleeping on that trundle bed."

Rose pulled the lace curtain aside and gazed out the window of their second-story room. "I'll make do, my lady. Look at that crowd. They're setting up the tables outside for them."

"Rose, please stand back so no one can see you." Phoebe rubbed between her eyes. "We do not wish to encourage visitors at our door. At least half a dozen gentlemen—and ne'er-do-weels—must have seen where we are. Oh, this is so aggravating."

Phoebe stopped pacing to consider the pugilist match responsible for the overcrowding. She really would have liked to see the bout. "I wonder who is fighting. It must be Figg or someone like that, to account for this many people. I do wish ladies were allowed to attend those types of events."

"My lady."

"I know I cannot." Phoebe paced again. There were so many things ladies could not do—especially unmarried ladies—it was frustrating.

Mrs. Ormsby, a plump, cheerful matron of indeterminate age, knocked and called through the door. Phoebe opened it and greeted her.

The older woman's face was flushed with pleasure and the crimped, graying curls under her mop cap bounced as she took one of Phoebe's fingers.

"My lady, I've come to see about yer dinner. I have a nice clear soup, and a capon I'm roasting for ye. It's garnished with a rosemary sauce, just as ye like it, removed with French beans and mushroom fritters. Cheese and fruit are for your dessert. Miss Fitchley"—Mrs. Ormsby turned to Rose—"we was looking forward to having ye dine with us. I can have one of my sons escort ye down, if it would suit ye."

Rose glanced at Phoebe.

"You go have your dinner as you usually do," Phoebe said. "Just because I am confined to the room doesn't mean you need be. I shall go on tolerably well."

Her maid smiled. "My lady, if you don't mind, I'd rather remain here with you."

Phoebe sighed softly. She didn't want to ruin Rose's fun, but was relieved she wouldn't have to spend the evening by herself. "If you are sure that is what you want to do, I cannot say I will be unhappy for the company."

Rose remained firm in her desire and Mrs. Ormsby bustled back out of the room.

By the time Phoebe washed and re-dressed, dinner had arrived. In addition to the dishes discussed, a bottle of good red wine had been sent.

The landlady returned after dinner. "Miss Fitchley, it was a good thing you decided to stay with her ladyship," Mrs. Ormsby said, as she cleared the dishes. "I've all my sons servin' outside, and in the tap as well. I won't allow my girls out amongst those men. For gentlemen I will not call them, even if some of 'em be quality-like."

Rose smiled sympathetically. "I don't envy you, Mrs. Ormsby. I am quite happy to keep my lady company."

Nodding, Phoebe said, "I quite agree with Rose—I don't envy you at all. What a lot of noise they are making for us to be able to hear it up here."

"If it was *only* noise, my lady, that I have to worry about," Mrs. Ormsby said with an arch look, "but I won't say more on that head. I shall wish ye a good night."

Marcus Finley arrived at the White Horse Inn with his friend Robert, Viscount Beaumont, who had reserved rooms there. Marcus found chambers across the street at the Red Unicorn. They met later to dine in a private parlor Marcus hired.

"Quite good ordinary they have here." Robert sat back in his chair, crossing one highly polished boot over the other. "The brandy is as good as any I've had. Must be French, though I don't wish to know how the landlord came by it."

Marcus grinned. "Yes, it's very good and probably smuggled."

Silence fell for a few moments, then Robert sat straight up in his chair. "Marcus, my boy, I saw the most beautiful gal I've ever seen in my life at the White Horse."

Marcus lounged in his chair, lifting a brow in inquiry.

Robert was known to be a favorite with the many disenchanted matrons of the *ton*.

"And where did you find this paragon of nature?" Marcus asked in a languid drawl. "In the tap?"

"No, no, my boy, not a game-pullet. Not at all. She was *a lady*."

Marcus raised his quizzing glass and regarded his friend more closely. "Married?"

"No. Put that thing away, you know I don't like it. Besides, there's nothing wrong with me. *She is a well-bred, unmarried lady*. Beautiful, I tell you. Tiny. Has a good figure, quite a neat ankle, and the most gorgeous gold-red hair. Perfect in every way."

Marcus's fingers tightened around his glass. Robert's conquests were legend, but they didn't extend to well-bred innocents. A terrifying thought began to fill Marcus's mind. It couldn't be Phoebe. She was at Cranbourne Place.

He fought to keep his face calm, his gaze focused on his friend. "Who is this lady, do you know?"

"Yes, got my groom to ask one of the ostlers. Stupid fellows, those ostlers, giving out that kind of information," Lord Beaumont ruminated, definitely on the go. "Yes, now that I think on it, I believe I shall have a word with the landlord. The servants ought not be giving that sort of thing out."

Marcus tapped his fingers on the table. "Her *name*, Robert?

"Her name?" Marcus repeated and waved an impatient hand to encourage his friend to continue.

"Oh, yes," Robert finally said. "*Lady Phoebe Stanhope*. Heard of her of course. Never seen her before. Don't, as a rule, attend those types of events. Not much for the Grand Strut you know. Must avoid the matchmaking mamas. M'grandmother's been after me to marry. Lady Phoebe is a devilish good-looking gal. I may have to make a push."

Marcus fumed. Lady Phoebe. His *Vision*. Friends or no, he would be damned if he'd let Robert anywhere near her.

Marcus poured another brandy and deliberately turned the conversation to the fight the next day. Shortly afterward, he realized that if he did not get Robert back to the White Horse, his chances of seeing the match would be slim.

Marcus summoned his groom, Covey. "I must help Beaumont to his chamber. Lady Phoebe Stanhope is here. Find out what the devil she's doing in Littleton at a time like this."

Frowning, Marcus added, "I cannot think of a more uncomfortable position for her to be in. She must be the only lady of quality here."

Afterward, Marcus helped his friend across the street and up the stairs of the inn, to his room where he handed Robert to his valet.

"Henley, try to make sure that he's in the taproom by eight o'clock. I want a good place in which to watch the fight."

The valet bowed. "Yes, my lord, I shall do my best."

As Marcus turned to leave, someone began pounding on a door at the far end of the hall. From the almost unintelligible words of love coming from the young blood attempting to lay siege to the chamber, it appeared the young man was in his altitudes, and he'd found Phoebe. At least Marcus didn't think the idiot would be reciting bad poetry to anyone else. Damn.

Much to his disgust, Marcus recognized something of his own prior behavior toward Phoebe in the drunken young man. With long strides, Marcus quickly covered the distance to her door. Taking the other man by his coat collar, Marcus picked him up, and shook him. Hard. In a low, fierce growl, he said, "You, my lad, are leaving with me now, and you will not return to bother this lady again. If you do, I shall take great delight in breaking every bone in your body."

Through the fellow's alcoholic haze, he tried to focus on his tormentor. Marcus received a grim satisfaction at the fear in the blood's eyes. Marcus slowly lowered the younger man until his feet touched the floor, then Marcus guided the buck down the hall to the stairs and out the front door, handing him over to one of the ostlers still on duty.

Marcus scowled. "Take this fool, and do not allow him back in the inn."

The ostler eyed Marcus cautiously. "But, my lord, he's stayin' here."

He fixed the ostler with a cold, hard glare. "I don't give a damn where he is staying. He was bothering a female guest. *You* will not allow him back in the inn, or you'll answer to me."

"Of course, my lord. I'll put him in the barn."

As the ostler started off, Marcus asked, "Where's the landlord?"

"I don't know, my lord."

Marcus scowled as the ostler hurried off with his charge. When his groom, Covey, called out, Marcus glanced over.

"What did you discover?" he asked curtly.

"Seems as if it were just bad luck, my lord, her la'ship being on her way to London. Stays here a lot she does. She was supposed to have arrived next week but came early."

"Did her servants tell you anything?"

"Close as clams. Don't tell no one nothin'. Got the information from one of the ostlers. She's travelin' with a groom, coachman, and maid."

"Those damn ostlers talk too much," Marcus responded savagely, striding back to the inn and to the hall outside of Phoebe's chamber. If the innkeeper couldn't protect her, he would.

* * *

Phoebe had remained calm, her small Manton-made pistol in hand, and had listened as a man with a deep, very definitely cultured voice with a strong note of command, firmly ordered the male beating on her door to stop and leave. She thought she had heard something about breaking bones and grinned at the remembrance. His threat must have worked.

The pounding had stopped immediately. Then two pairs of feet, one firm with a long stride, the other stumbling, made their way down the hall to the stairs. After a long silence, Phoebe sighed with relief, then whispered to Rose, "I believe we've been saved, but I wonder by whom?"

"I don't know, my lady, but I'm glad someone did."

Rose returned to her cot, and moments later Phoebe heard soft breathing. *How did Rose drop off to sleep like that?*

About ten minutes had passed when she heard a soft knock on her door and the low voice she recognized as the gentleman who'd saved them earlier.

"Don't open the door, my lady. I wanted you to know I'll be sleeping out here for the remainder of the night. I didn't want you to be frightened in case I snore."

Fascinated, Phoebe wondered who it could be. He called her "my lady." Was she acquainted with him? She walked silently to the door, meaning to thank him, but instead she asked with a slight giggle, "*Do* you snore?"

There was humor in his voice. "I've never been told I do, but I think it a distinct possibility. Many men snore, you know."

Well, she didn't. After all, there was no reason she would. "Oh, I really hadn't considered."

"No, I suppose not. Well, good night."

Ear against the door, she heard him move to the floor. He really was going to give up a soft bed to sleep on a cold, hard floor, for her. "Won't the floor be too uncomfortable?"

His voice was low and deep. "I've slept in worse places."

She cast about for something she could do to stop him from making such a sacrifice. "I'm sure the landlord would send someone up."

"They're all asleep by now." He paused and, when he continued, his tone was gruffer. "I'd consider it an honor to be allowed to protect you."

Phoebe placed her hand on the door and tried to picture the man on the other side of it. His voice washed over her like a warm wave, making her feel safe. That was curious. Usually she was defending herself from men.

How very kind of him. A small niggling in the back of her mind suggested she'd heard his voice somewhere before, but she couldn't place it. If only he would have asked to be introduced. "I can hand you a blanket or pillow."

"No," he said emphatically. "Do not open the door. I would not want anyone to get the wrong idea."

Her heart beat faster. Not only was he kind, but he was honorable. "Thank you."

"No, don't thank me. It is my pleasure, my lady."

Phoebe smiled. "But I *will* thank you for saving me, and I am honored to have your protection. Are you sure you won't be too uncomfortable?"

"I'll tell you if we meet again, my lady, but now, you should try to sleep."

If they meet again. Perhaps he was only being nice. "Very well. I bid you a good night."

"Good night, my lady."

Phoebe thought about the gentleman sleeping in the hall and wondered who he was. She expected sleep to elude her, but the next thing she knew she awoke to the sounds of carriages and horses being readied and the inn awakening with calls for breakfast, coffee, and ale.

The unknown gentleman came immediately to mind.

Her maid turned from the door with a pitcher of water in her hands.

"Rose, did you see him? The man who protected us last night?"

"You could say that, my lady." She grinned. "I tripped over him."

Phoebe was almost breathless with excitement. "Tell me, what did he look like?"

Rose shrugged. "He looked like he sounded. He's a large man, tall. He has broad shoulders, well set up. Dark hair. Looked to be about thirty or so. Very fashionable attire, though a bit wrinkled this morning."

Rose set the jug down and took one of Phoebe's gowns to shake out. "He was very pleasant as well. He apologized for causing me to trip, and said I should let you sleep as you couldn't leave until after the fight crowd had departed. I asked him to send a maid with water to us, and he did."

Phoebe's heart thudded. "Did he tell you his name?"

"No, my lady."

"Oh." She felt as if her whole face fell. So disappointing. She hadn't realized how interested she was in discovering his identity.

A knock on the door heralded Mrs. Ormsby. Wringing her hands in her apron, she wore a worried look on her normally jovial face. "Oh my lady, we're so sorry. We ain't never had nothin' like that happen afore. We run a respectable house here. If it weren't for that nice gentleman . . . What with the ruckus, we couldn't hear anything. In any event, he told the ostler, Harry, not to let that young man back in the house, and you may be sure we didn't. Please don't take it amiss, my lady."

Phoebe set about soothing her. "No, indeed, Mrs. Ormsby. I don't blame you at all." Phoebe paused and held her breath. "The gentleman who slept outside my door last night, do you know who he was?"

"No, my lady. I'm sorry. He wasn't stayin' here."

Mrs. Ormsby left and Phoebe tried to reconcile herself to not learning her gallant's name.

After breakfast, she was reading, waiting for the town to empty, when she heard a knock on a door down the hall and the deep voice of the gentleman who had saved her.

She opened her door a small crack, just enough to see the back of a large man dressed in a coat of dark blue superfine, cut to perfection across his broad back. He also wore buckskin breeches, and glossy Hessian boots.

A small quiver ran through her. She quietly closed her door and wished it was proper for her to ask his name.

Finley knocked on Beaumont's door again, sore and tired, but feeling elated. Marcus had returned to his room at dawn. Now at nearly eight o'clock he returned to the White Horse. After glancing briefly into the taproom to find Robert, Marcus had made his way up to the second floor taking the steps two at a time. He knocked on his friend's door, once more.

Henley opened it and bowed. "My lord, Lord Beaumont will be down presently. We are having a little difficulty rising this morning. However, I daresay, if you could be patient for ten or so minutes, his lordship will join you in the taproom."

Marcus heard the click of a door opening down the hall and a tremor slid down his back. *Phoebe*. She was the only one who affected him like that.

Damn, he did not want her to see him yet. He froze in place and forced himself not to turn. "Henley, you may tell your master that I will wait ten minutes, no longer. If we are any later than that, we'll be so far back in the crowd we shall not be able to see the fight."

Marcus felt rather than heard Phoebe's door shut. Letting out a breath he'd not realized he was holding, he turned and went downstairs to wait.

Robert joined him twelve minutes later.

The morning was clear and sunny, promising another warm late summer day. Marcus maneuvered his curricle skillfully through the crowd until they were close enough to the ring, which had been set up in a fallow field.

Matt Vivers, now the Earl of Worthington, and Lord Rutherford, both long time friends of Marcus's, were also present.

But Marcus may as well not have been there at all for all the attention he paid to the fight. He spent his time trying to decide whether to return to Town or continue on to his sister's to see what she knew of Phoebe's plans.

Phoebe. He'd received so many letters from his family and other mutual friends, Marcus had trouble thinking of her as Lady Phoebe. She must have left Cranbourne Place to avoid him. What a worthless fellow he'd been eight years ago. His lip curled in self-derision. No wonder she'd run. She had no idea how her words had affected him. How he'd striven to become a man worthy of her hand.

His family and friends had warned him that with his fortune, birth, and the potential of inheriting the title, he would be constantly pursued by all the matchmaking mamas. But there was only one lady he wanted. The only woman to have held his interest.

Even after all his years away, her image was still sharp in his mind. An oval face, a straight little nose that escaped the aquiline, and a determined chin. Her grace and beauty had first captured him, but more than anything during his time away, he remembered her intelligence and kindness.

Phoebe had been caring and understanding to everyone. She would help the one young matron who clearly felt uneasy in the august company that weekend and respond, with an uncommon ease of breeding, to the shrewish girl, newly out. Phoebe was the only person who'd reached out to try to understand him. He'd felt such a connection between them, and then he'd ruined it by getting drunk and treating her like a trollop.

He remembered the exact moment when the compassion in her lovely blue eyes had turned to mistrust, fear, and then anger. His hand had touched her breast. Marcus groaned. She would never set her cap at him, and, based on her escape, he'd have a devil of a time getting close to her.

Still, he would not rest until he had convinced her he'd changed. He couldn't live his life without her as his wife. He would go to his sister's and discover what she knew of Phoebe's flight to London. Perhaps it would give him some clue as to how to approach her without getting a black eye or bloody nose in the process.

Chapter Four

Marcus arrived at Cranbourne Place late on the day of the fight. As he jumped down from his curricle, Amabel, his sister, appeared at the door, clearly delighted to see him. She was as fair as he was dark.

She wore a gauzy white day gown that seemed to float around her as she gracefully descended the stairs of the portico and held out her hands in greeting. They'd exchanged letters and portraits over the years, but the last time he'd seen her she'd still been in the schoolroom and wore braids down her back.

"Marcus, do please come in. I am so glad you are here. How have you been? You are not too tired, are you? Do you wish to rest? But no, you have too much energy. You must tell me everything."

He chuckled. "What a goosecap you are, Amabel. I suppose I can't muss your hair now that you wear it in such a fashionable style. I'll tell you everything as soon as you give me a cup of tea, and we may be comfortable."

She tucked her arm in his and led him into the house. A large man stood in the entrance. Geoffrey, Earl of Cranbourne, his brother-in-law, was easily as tall as Marcus, in his mid-thirties, and dressed for the country in buckskin breeches, a loose shirt, waistcoat, and hunting jacket.

From under lowered brows, the earl gave Marcus a hard look. "Lord Marcus, welcome. I am pleased to finally meet you. You may come with me, sir. We need to discuss the reason my sister found it necessary to leave her home rather than meet you."

Marcus regarded his brother-in-law for a few moments, before saying to his sister, "Amabel, please excuse us. Cranbourne is right, I do need to explain. Better to have it done."

Marcus bent down to give her a peck on the cheek, and followed his brother-in-law to the study.

Cranbourne sat behind his large walnut desk and motioned Marcus to a chair on the other side. They spent a few moments taking each other's measure, while Cranbourne's butler served tea.

Once alone, Marcus broke the silence. "What has Lady Phoebe told you?"

"Phoebe has told me nothing other than she does not wish to meet you. If you are granted the opportunity to know her better, you'll find she keeps her own counsel."

Cranbourne gave Marcus an unfriendly stare. "I would hear from you, sir, without any roundaboutation, what happened between you."

They locked eyes. If Phoebe fled because of him, her brother deserved to know the truth.

"I do not attempt to excuse my behavior. It was inexcusable. I was young, just on the Town, immature, thoughtless, and reckless. There were few vices in which I did not indulge. Not quite a Peep o' Day Boy but very close. Too close for my father, which is the reason I was banished."

Marcus glanced away. This was harder than he'd imagined it would be. "I thought that anything or anyone was mine for the taking. Lady Phoebe and I were at the same house party eight years ago, not long before I was to set sail to the West Indies. I was in the drawing room when I first saw her enter with your mother and sisters."

He lowered his voice to a whisper. "To say I was stunned by her would be a gross understatement. I felt as if I was seeing a vision. Her beauty jolted me as I'd never been jolted before or after."

Thinking back, reliving the moment, his tone became soft and wistful. "I'd never seen anyone as lovely, as assured, with as much countenance and kindness." Marcus paused and continued more briskly, "In my arrogance and stupidity, I thought I could lift my finger, and impress her enough that she would, if I desired it, be mine."

He gazed at Cranbourne, whose countenance had hardened.

Marcus's voice was heavy with sarcasm. "You, I expect, will be amazed to discover that she was not at all impressed with me as a drunken lout."

His brother-in-law's expression hadn't changed and he motioned Marcus to carry on.

Taking a sip of tea, he cleared his suddenly aching throat. He'd relived that weekend, that day, so many times over the years. If only he had behaved differently.

"In the end, I behaved badly. I failed my family, again, but more importantly I failed Lady Phoebe. A woman I respected and adored."

"What exactly did you do to my sister?"

Firming his jaw, Marcus met Cranbourne's gaze. "I waited until she was alone in the gallery—by then I knew she wasn't out, and that it would be infamous to approach her, but I revealed myself as she tried to walk past. I caught her around the waist and tried to kiss her. What I didn't know was that she'd been trained to defend herself."

Marcus finished the cup, placing it on a table. "She broke my hold, and delivered one of the most punishing rights I have ever had the privilege to receive. Once I was sprawled on the floor, she used me to sharpen her tongue."

He paused, then continued with self-deprecatory humor. "There I was, twenty years old, a man, or so I thought, being bested by a tiny chit of a girl. Imagine, if you would, my consternation. First that she'd knocked me down, and yet, rather than fleeing, she stood there, in a high dudgeon, completely unafraid, telling me explicitly everything that was wrong with me. When she'd finished, she ordered me to leave the house that day, and never to darken her path again. I was still lying on the floor, amazed, when she walked away, her back straight. She was magnificent. If I hadn't already loved her to distraction before, my fate would have been sealed then."

Marcus picked up the empty cup and fiddled with it before putting it back down. "I made my excuses to my hostess and left the house as soon as I could, tail between my legs, sporting a rapidly swelling nose and eye. I never saw Phoebe again, but I've never forgotten her."

His brother-in-law would probably insist Marcus leave, but for the first time in eight years, he'd confessed. He hid his sigh of relief.

The gravity in Cranbourne's expression hadn't lifted. "If my sister told you she did not wish to see you again, then what are you doing here now?"

Marcus sat up straighter. "When Amabel invited me, I thought Lady Phoebe knew about the invitation. That she'd forgotten the incident, or it had faded, at least enough for her to consider meeting me again."

Marcus stopped and looked up at the carved wood lintels in the ceiling before continuing sadly. "It appears I was mistaken."

His brother-in-law rose, stepped to the sideboard, and poured two glasses of brandy. Cranbourne took one and offered the other to Marcus before taking a chair. His brother-in-law regarded Marcus for a long time before Cranbourne's countenance lightened.

"It doesn't surprise me Phoebe gave you a bit of home brew and good bear garden jaw. My parents trained all m'sisters to protect themselves. Got devilish sharp tongues as well."

The earl took a sip of the brandy. "You may have been the first man to make a cake of himself over Phoebe, but you certainly were not the last. She's not only a well-looking girl, but an heiress as well. Several gentlemen have tried what you did with Phoebe. I can't remember her ever holding a grudge against any of 'em. I find that interesting."

Marcus stiffened. "Others tried to kiss her as well?"

Cranbourne grinned. "Of course, they don't do it again. For the most part, they've found sporting a black eye or a bloody nose at the hands of a female is more than enough humiliation to put an end to that nonsense."

That bit Marcus hadn't heard. Phoebe having to defend herself was his fault. If he'd treated her differently, she would have been his and no man would have been allowed to forget it. He placed his untouched glass of brandy on a table.

There was something his brother-in-law hadn't told him. "You said she wouldn't meet me, but there was more, wasn't there?"

Cranbourne smiled with unholy amusement. "Ah, yes, there *was* something about you being an arrogant troll. But even I can see that no matter how poorly you looked before, you have much improved."

The tension in the room eased, and Marcus gave a bark of laughter. "She was in the right of it. I have no doubt I was indeed an arrogant troll." He took a sip of the brandy. "Just how well trained are your sisters in the defensive arts?"

Cranbourne's eyes lit wickedly. "As well as if they'd been boys. Boxing, wrestling, short sword, and pistols. My father always told them they had an advantage and a disadvantage. No man would think a mere female capable of defending herself, which gave them an advantage. The disadvantage was they would always be smaller and physically weaker than any male. Father taught them to do what they needed to protect themselves. I carried on with Phoebe's training after his death."

How different that was from Dunwood's views and the way Amabel had been raised. "But, how did it come about—your parents' interest in educating their daughters beyond what is considered usual?"

Cranbourne sat back in his chair. "You may well ask. M'mother was a great admirer of Mary Wollstonecraft, Jeremy Bentham, and the Marquis de Condorcet. All of whom espoused the rights of women. My father said he was just being practical. Can't have three beautiful heiresses not be able to protect themselves. He was right."

That was fascinating. Marcus had heard of ladies being raised like that. He hadn't known Phoebe was one of them. He needed to know more, to hear more about her. "Other than stopping wayward kisses, have your sisters had to defend themselves?"

Cranbourne replied proudly, "Oh, yes. Fairport, my brother-in-law, told me they were waylaid by Gentlemen of the Road last year. He and the other men were kept outside of the coach. The highwaymen left Hermione inside, thinking to use her as a hostage. Naturally, the leader thought, as a female, there was little Hermione could do."

Cranbourne chuckled. "Unfortunately for him, Hermione still had her own pistol, and the second set of coach pistols she'd hidden beneath her cloak. She shot the leader as he leaned into the window, then held his two accomplices at bay until Fairport and the others could tie them up."

Cranbourne picked up his glass and took a sip. "None of my sisters have any fear. Phoebe is the worst of 'em. Set up her own stable when I married, and she will never have outriders. A year or so ago, a gentleman, or a man dressed like one, decided to have a try at her. A couple of thugs were with him and they stopped Phoebe's coach. She put a ball in one of the thugs and another in the gentleman. Unfortunately, they were able to get away. It was a shame she couldn't bring herself to kill them. Her groom shot the third man dead."

Cranbourne frowned darkly. "I wish I knew who the main blackguard was. He had a kerchief over his face, but Phoebe's abigail saw his eyes. She said she'd recognize him again." He paused for a few moments. "Not that it'll do us much good, unless he is walking near the house or in Bond Street one day."

Marcus had heard what he'd thought was a complete account of Phoebe over the years, but no one had given him the information his brother-in-law had, and Marcus wanted desperately to know all about her.

"Inasmuch as the *ton* loves scandal and gossip, one would have thought that there would be some talk of such events. My mother and friends keep me up to date on all the *crim cons*, but I've heard nothing."

"You won't," Cranbourne said. "M'sisters are very high-handed about all of it, *and* they carry it off. Refuse to discuss anything that happens. I've seen them, if asked, raise a brow and state that they do not feel it necessary to provide food to the vulgar. So any talk goes off quickly."

Marcus frowned. He'd dearly love to know who the men were who had tried to kiss Phoebe, but knowing what she wanted now was more important. "Lady Phoebe obviously has not been interested in any of the gentlemen who have shown an interest in her, which I understand to be most of the *ton*'s bachelors. Do you know the kind of man she's looking for?"

Cranbourne heaved a sigh. "No, none of us can figure it out, and there is no changing her mind to settle for less than what she wants. There is also the family tradition to consider."

Marcus shook his head. *Tradition?*

"In our family, we marry only for love. Phoebe needn't wed unless she wishes to do so and none of us will push her into it."

After Cranbourne had his brother-in-law shown to a bedchamber, he joined Amabel in her dressing room. His news would not be easy for her to hear, but she'd be anxious for word.

After he'd related what her brother had told him, she sat silently for several seconds, as if unable to comprehend what Geoffrey had said.

"Good God! I've never been more shocked!" Amabel dropped her face in her hands for a moment. "No wonder Phoebe left. What a horrible thing to have done to a young girl. I can scarcely believe it of Marcus. But why did she not tell us?"

"My love, you could hardly expect her to tell *you* the whole about your brother." Cranbourne rubbed Amabel's shoulders. "Phoebe would not for the world cause you pain. Which, I have no doubt, would have happened."

"Oh, yes, I would have been mortified." Amabel grimaced. "But I never knew any of this. Why did no one tell me? Surely she would have confided in someone."

Geoffrey felt his lips curve up. "You know as well as I, no one would have spoken of it to you when you were younger, and by the time you came out, Marcus had been gone for a while." Geoffrey hugged Amabel. "Of course, it was very wrong of him, but I think Marcus had the worst of it. He is fully sensible that his behavior was untenable, and thinks just as he ought concerning the matter. He didn't try to excuse his conduct, at all. I am convinced it was an aberration of youth, and I am in agreement, my dear, with your opinion that he is a good man. Whether Phoebe will ever agree, remains to be seen. I'll not push her, and I hope you will not either."

Amabel glanced quickly up at him. "Oh, no, Geoffrey, I could not do so now that I know what happened. I only hope this has not caused a rift between Phoebe and me."

Geoffrey drew her to him. "I don't think it could, my love. Phoebe is very attached to you. She knew you had no idea what had happened. I do, however, think this must end your attempts at matchmaking."

His wife's pretty lips turned down. "Yes, I suppose it must. What a mull I've made of it."

Amabel and Cranbourne greeted Marcus when he joined them shortly afterward in the drawing room.

Marcus saw the chagrin in Amabel's face. "I am sorry, my dear, to have been such a scamp. Can you forgive me?"

She smiled wanly. "It was all so long ago, but really, there is nothing for *me* to forgive. You were always so charming to me as your little sister. The situation with Phoebe, however, is a different matter."

"I shall try to rectify that."

"Thank you." Amabel straightened and smiled more brightly. "We will not have much time together now. I know Papa will want you back in Town."

Marcus grinned. "Yes, *you* are not the only one trying to matchmake. Papa has arranged introductions to every unmarried young lady he knows of."

Cranbourne's eyes sparkled with mischief. "You will have to watch you do not raise false hopes in the innocent breasts of all the young ladies setting their caps at you, and beware of traps. I have to say, one of the best parts of being betrothed was that the ladies stopped pursuing me."

"Geoffrey," Amabel said, shocked.

"No, no, my dear, don't eat me. You never chased me, but allowed me to hunt you. It was most invigorating."

She blushed hotly. "Geoffrey, you should not speak in that vulgar way."

Marcus grinned at his sister and brother-in-law who clearly loved each other and wondered if his hunt would be as successful.

The next day, after admiring his nephew, Miles, and joining his sister and brother-in-law for an early luncheon, Marcus took his leave. Once he cleared the Place's gates, he sprung his horses.

Covey, his groom, said, "And what may I ask, my lord, is we doing going down this road like we got Davy Jones a-chasin' us?"

Marcus listened in good humor to the rest of his groom's harangue. Covey had begun as a stable boy, and by the time Marcus was old enough to sit his first pony, Covey had been assigned as the second son's groom.

Covey had traveled to Jamaica with Marcus, even though it meant leaving his large family behind in England. Once on board the ship, his groom's duties expanded to more of a general factotum, taking care of Marcus, his clothing, his horses, and his back, when necessary.

"You know I must return to Town. My father doesn't want me gone that long."

His groom glanced over, disbelief written plainly on his face. "What are you up to, my lord? Iffen' you wants to get back to Town, you'd better slow them horses or we may not make it at all."

Stifling a chuckle, Marcus retorted, "After all we've been through, don't tell me you're turning into an old woman on me?"

"No, my lord, but give over, do. If you tip this here curricle, we'll be a lot later gettin' back than if you'd kept a decent pace."

Marcus kept his horses well up to their bits but smiled to himself.

As he didn't acknowledge Covey's last remark, his hard-put-upon henchman lapsed into disapproving silence.

They arrived at Dunwood House, on Grosvenor Square, late that evening. The lights were still lit, which meant his father had not returned home. Marcus had stopped only to change horses and eat a bite during the pauses.

Wilson, his father's butler, opened the door and summoned footmen to take the curricle to the stables. "Good evening, my lord. His lordship is at his club, if you wish to see him immediately."

Handing the butler his hat and greatcoat, Marcus replied, "No, thank you, Wilson. We drove straight through. I need to wash off the dust. Please order a bath and inform Cook that I'll dine in my chamber."

Later, as Marcus soaked in his bath, his mind turned to Phoebe. He must find some way to make her look at him without disgust in her lovely eyes. He'd not felt so helpless in years. There must be some way to show her he'd changed, but how did one win the hand of a woman who refused to even meet him?

Chapter Five

Phoebe arrived at the London residence of her aunt Ester, Marchioness of St. Eth, just past noon.

St. Eth House, built in the last century, was one of the larger residences gracing Grosvenor Square and one of the few free standing houses, the others being connecting townhouses. Since Phoebe's mother had died, Phoebe had spent almost every Season there.

Her apartment was in the front, overlooking the Park and one of the small side gardens. It consisted of a bedchamber, decorated in various shades of earthy greens, anchored by a four-poster bed, a dressing room, a small parlor with a pretty desk, a sofa, and two comfortable chairs.

Ferguson, St. Eth's butler, bowed her through the door. "My lady, may I say it is a pleasure to have you with us again."

"Thank you, Ferguson." Phoebe waited as he removed her pelisse. "It is good to be back."

François, her aunt's *chef de cuisine*, sent a cold collation of meats, cheeses, and fruit to Phoebe's parlor. After she'd eaten and washed, Phoebe changed into a simple, pale yellow twill walking gown and lightweight paisley spencer in coordinating greens and yellows.

Greeting the butler, she said, "Ferguson, I am going to Bond and Bruton Streets to shop. I'll need a footman. Is Jim available?"

"Yes, my lady, I'll call for him. Would you like a carriage, my lady?"

"No, thank you, Ferguson. I have been too much cooped up in the coach for the past few days, and am in great need of a walk."

Her first stop was at Madame Lisette's in Bruton Street. Madame had been Phoebe's modiste since her come out.

"Bonjour, Madame," Phoebe called, entering the shop.

A small, dark-haired lady stepped out from the back.

"Mon Dieu, Milady Phoebe, but you are in Town early, *n'est-ce pas?"*

"Yes, I am a week early I'm afraid, and in immediate need of gowns. I hope that does not pose a problem?" Since Phoebe replenished her wardrobe each Season, she trusted Madame would have some of the clothes ready.

"Mais non. I will have more for you in a few days *naturellement. Bien,* I show you what I have completed, milady." Madame disappeared behind the drapes to shortly emerge, followed by two young women carrying an assortment of gowns.

Phoebe selected what she would need in the next few days and stood for the fittings. After making arrangements for most of the boxes to be delivered to St. Eth House, she went on to Bond Street, returning to Grosvenor Square just as her aunt Ester arrived.

Her aunt was so much like Phoebe's mother. A handsome, elegant woman, her aunt shared Phoebe's sparkling blue eyes and gold-red hair, albeit faded with age. Aunt Ester had all the height Phoebe lacked. As always, the marchioness was dressed in the first stare of fashion in an aubergine silk carriage gown that had two embroidered flounces at the bottom and long sleeves that buttoned tightly at the wrist.

Ester smiled as Phoebe walked up the paved path to the house. "Oh, Phoebe, my love, I am so glad you have arrived."

Taking in the sight of the footman burdened with boxes, Ester asked, "Shopping already?"

Phoebe embraced her aunt. "I am so very happy to be here. Aunt Ester, you will not believe how shabby my wardrobe has become. I decided to begin immediately, and I still have *much* more shopping to do."

Ester, knowing Phoebe as she did, did not believe for a moment her niece had allowed her wardrobe to become in such poor repair, or so out of date, as must needs this sudden bolt to Town.

Leading the way to the light airy hall paved with cream and blue tiles, Ester and Phoebe divested themselves of bonnets, gloves, and the packages Phoebe carried. Ester ordered tea to be served in the morning room at the back of the house.

Phoebe crossed to a comfortable side chair, set to one side of a sofa upon which Ester usually sat, and sank gracefully onto it.

As Ester poured tea, she studied her niece for a few moments. Phoebe was the closest thing Ester had to a daughter and something was not right. "I shall tell you, that I do not believe for a minute that Banbury tale about your clothing. What has brought you to Town so suddenly?"

Phoebe returned her aunt's gaze and sighed. "I left to avoid meeting Lord Marcus Finley, whom I met eight years ago and still hold in great dislike. Amabel invited him to the Place to meet me, and he was due to arrive three days later. To-day in fact."

Ester sat up sharply. "But where was Geoffrey? What had he to say to all of this?"

Shaking her head, Phoebe replied, "I only told Geoffrey that I needed to leave. He was very understanding. Neither Geoffrey nor Amabel are aware of the reason that I do not wish to meet Lord Marcus. I did not tell Amabel, as I don't want there to be constraint between them over her brother. Geoffrey trusts me to do what is right and proper. I wrote Amabel to assure her that my leaving had nothing to do with her.

"I do not believe," Phoebe continued grimly, "Lord Marcus will be surprised that I am not there to greet him. I cannot believe he'd think I would wish to see him again."

Ester frowned. Phoebe had never run away from anything. "*When,* my dear, did you meet him? You were not even out when he left for the West Indies."

Phoebe told her aunt of their meeting eight years ago.

"Well, we certainly shan't encourage Lord Marcus." Ester patted her niece's hand. "I am happy you understand you will not be able to avoid him forever, though indeed, you need not be more than civil."

Pursing her lips, Ester continued, "It is a shame your mother died when she did. You have been left very much to your own devices since then. I always believed Geoffrey was wrong in allowing you to become so much of your own woman at such a young age. He encouraged you to take over the management of the household when you were only seventeen. Since he married Amabel, you have been even more on your own."

Phoebe opened her mouth to protest, but Ester held up a hand. "It is not that I am criticizing Geoffrey, well only a little, but I am not criticizing you at all, my dear. You showed superior sense, especially for as young as you were. Still there is no denying you have been allowed to take your life into your own hands as no other young lady of my acquaintance has been allowed to do."

Ester stopped to refill her cup. "I was very happy when you so easily turned over the household to Amabel and did your duty by her in showing her how to get on. Fortunately, because of your very correct behavior, you have never been thought eccentric, for *that* would not do."

Phoebe absently nibbled on one of the small tea cakes. "The situation is not as bad as that. I get on well with Amabel, except, of course, when she tries to arrange matches for me. She and Geoffrey are both always happy to have me at the Place, and I am very fond of them. I just think they need time to themselves, especially now with Miles. Amabel *truly* does not wish to go into Society anymore." Phoebe shrugged lightly. "When I am there, well . . . I think she feels obligated to find me a husband."

Ester replied tartly, "I have no sympathy for Amabel. If she'd left well enough alone, rather than insisting she chaperone you once she became Lady Cranbourne, she would not now be so unhappy with the result."

Taking Phoebe's hands, Ester said, "I *do* have sympathy for you, my dear. You are almost twenty-four, Phoebe, what *will* you do?"

That is what she had been starting to wonder. Because of her age, she was in a No Man's Land. Too young to set up her own household and too old to be treated like a young miss. "I don't know. I'd like very much to marry. If only there was a gentleman for whom I felt *affection*.

"Unfortunately"—she couldn't keep the discontent and disappointment from her tone—"I've never met a man for whom I feel more than friendship. Mamma said I would know. She said when she first set eyes on Papa it was as if she could see *him* as she'd never seen any other man."

Phoebe played with her empty cup. She desperately

wanted the type of love her mother, aunt, and sisters had. "I have not yet felt that, and I want to. I will not marry just for position. I have quite a healthy competence. If I do not meet someone, I have been thinking I will set up my own household."

Aunt Ester nodded. "Rather more than a healthy competence, my love. You are very well off. But, my dear, how do you plan to meet such a gentleman when you never allow any of them close to you?"

Phoebe's thoughts drifted back to Lord Marcus Finley, a man she'd thought held so much promise, before he'd turned on her. What he'd done—how he'd treated her—had haunted her for years. "I don't know. I don't know if I trust myself to pick the right gentleman."

Her aunt passed Phoebe another biscuit. "Nevertheless, you are much too young to think of setting up your own house."

Phoebe glanced up and grimaced. "I know, but where am I to live now that Lord Marcus is back? With his being Amabel's brother, I may need to remove myself from the Place. Perhaps Aunt Clara will take me until I am of sufficient age. I do *so* wish the man had not returned."

"If it comes to that," Aunt Ester said firmly, "you will live with us. With your interest in politics, no one will think it strange."

Phoebe was thankful when her aunt turned the conversation to Phoebe's wardrobe. The only person she had told about *that day* was Rose. Hermione and, by extension, her twin Hester, knew Lord Marcus had behaved badly, and that Phoebe had been angry, but she'd never told anyone else. Nor could she explain how she felt less than a lady anytime a gentleman tried to kiss her.

Much later, Phoebe and her aunt were sitting with their heads together over the latest fashion plates, when the door opened. Phoebe glanced up to see Uncle Henry, Marquis of St. Eth, enter. She smiled noticing there was just a bit more silver in his dark hair than the last time she'd seen him. His green eyes sparkled, however, as he gazed at the two of them.

He greeted his wife by kissing her briefly on the lips before addressing Phoebe. "What a pretty picture the two of you make. Well, my girl, you are in looks, I will say."

Phoebe rose and curtseyed, before offering her hand, and her cheek. "Thank you, sir." Her demure tone belied her roguish smile. "You are very good to notice."

He laughed. "Minx. What plans have you two concocted whilst I've been out, and how am I involved?"

Aunt Ester's gaze rested lovingly on him. "We have no plans this evening, my dear, but to-morrow we have the Fancotts' ball. Then there is a very good play Phoebe has expressed a desire to see, dinner with the Stavelys . . ." Aunt Ester went on.

Her uncle's eyebrows rose as his wife recited the list of invitations she'd so far received. "I had no idea so many were already in Town."

"I don't know how it is, my love," Aunt Ester said, "but there does seem to be a lot to do for so early in the Season. Phoebe told me we can expect Hermione and Edwin in a week or so."

Aunt Ester glanced quickly at the clock and shooed them out to dress for dinner.

As Phoebe was changing, she remembered the gentleman at the inn, and wondered again who he was and if she would see him in Town. How strange it would be if he turned out to be the one. Running away from Lord Marcus Finley might have been the best thing she'd ever done.

*   *   *

The next morning, Henry entered the breakfast room to find Ester there before him. "I take it you and Phoebe plan to spend the morning visiting the shops?"

"No, not to-day," his wife replied. "Phoebe's excuse in coming to Town so quickly was to refurbish her wardrobe. She brought only what she could carry in her coach. Although she called upon Lisette yesterday—I believe in an effort to make me believe her story—if Phoebe is to have enough to carry her through the Season, she will need to make many more purchases."

Henry had taken his place at the table and Ester poured his coffee. "To-day, we have a full schedule of morning visits and afternoon teas so it will be known Phoebe is in Town. Shopping will have to wait until Saturday."

Henry added sugar to the cup and said, "I did not like to ask it in front of Phoebe. Did she tell you what brought her here in such a rush?"

"Yes. It appears there is a bit of a contretemps surrounding Lord Marcus Finley." Ester went on to explain what Phoebe had told her.

Henry's countenance hardened. "That young man has much to answer for."

A few minutes later, Phoebe swept into the room.

"Dear Uncle Henry." She flashed him a saucy smile. "Do you have room in your stables for my phaeton and horses? The phaeton is at Cranbourne House, but, of course, as Amabel does not come to Town for the Little Season, Geoffrey will only be up when he must needs. Understandably, that will not leave any of the stable staff in residence. If at all possible, I prefer to have the horses and the phaeton in the same location, but if it is *too* much of an imposition, I will have Sam and John Coachman care for them at Cranbournes' stables."

Henry laughed. "In addition to your traveling coach? What a way to start the morning. You are very lucky, my girl, that I am not one of those gentlemen who refuses to discuss anything at the breakfast table." He sat back in his chair. "I take it you are referring to that high perched phaeton you bought last year, and your matched blacks? Yes, you may stable them here. I didn't have an opportunity to see them and am looking forward to going over their points with you."

After motioning for more coffee, Uncle Henry said, "Robert declared them to be a 'bang-up pair. Real blood and bone.' He was quite envious, you know, to have his cousin—his *female* cousin—driving such a rig. He besieged me to buy him a phaeton and pair. I told him when he could handle the ribbons as well as you, my dear, I would take it into consideration. *That* put him on his mettle."

Phoebe laughed musically. She took a piece of toast and accepted the cup of tea her aunt handed her. Glancing at her uncle, she smiled widely, a wicked gleam in her eyes. "But, my dear, dear Uncle Henry, what you do not know is that I have not only a pair, but a team. *Perfectly matched.*"

"Have you, by God? I'm very glad Robert is not here. I cannot wait to see them. How did you come by a matched team?"

She'd taken a bite of her toast and swallowed. "I had them off Marbury last year when he was forced to reduce his stable. As you can imagine, he was loath to lose them, but with his pockets to let, he had no choice."

"He must have been happier that you bought them than anyone else," Henry remarked.

Phoebe nodded with a wry smile. "Well, yes, he knew that I, at least, would take good care of them."

"Do you plan to ride this Season or will you only drive and walk?" Henry asked.

Phoebe's forehead wrinkled. "I should like to ride as well, but didn't bring old Jessie with me. I hoped that you could mount me. I need to find a new hack, but wish to take

my time looking around." Phoebe frowned. "It's really too
bad ladies are not allowed to go to Tattersall's. It makes
buying one's cattle so much more difficult."

"I have just the horse for you," Uncle Henry said. "A
very pretty, spirited mare, fast as the wind, I bought at Tattersall's last month. She is a sweet goer with a lively disposition. I think you will like her very well indeed. She
should be just the thing."

Phoebe smiled. "Thank you so much. You are quite the
best uncle in the world."

Henry thought, not for the first time, how much Phoebe
would bring to a marriage, if only she could find the right
man. Damn Marcus Finley for scaring her so young.

Saturday morning, Phoebe and her aunt visited Madame's.
Phoebe's purchases included new walking and carriage
gowns, which naturally required new hats to match.

As she left the milliner's shop in Bond Street, looking
down to fasten her gloves, she was knocked off her feet. A
pair of powerful arms grabbed her from behind to steady
her, then, as if she were a rag doll, she was suddenly pulled
back against his equally strong hard male body.

Phoebe gasped as the tremor ran down her spine. Her
senses seized with some emotion she did not immediately
recognize, and she was overcome with a strange desire to
melt against the person holding her.

A deep voice, one she'd heard before, lightly cursed in-
considerate boys. At the same time the man appeared to deliberately release her.

Which, to Phoebe's surprise, was not at all what she
wanted.

She turned, to thank her rescuer, and gazed up into the
most beautiful pair of blue eyes she'd ever seen. The shade

reminded her of the color of the water in paintings of the tropics. Turquoise.

The effect was enhanced by his deeply tanned visage, as he stared down at her. Small lines creased the corners of his eyes, and he smiled with perfectly molded lips.

Phoebe's breath came fast and she tried to slow her heart, which had decided to dash off madly. Dragging her gaze from his lips, she took in his lean, rugged face, and aquiline nose. A lock of dark sable hair fell over his broad forehead. His eyes warmed the longer he looked at her. He was magnificent.

Phoebe's arms and back tingled with the memory of his touch.

Why was it she'd never noticed him before?

Marcus had been approaching a milliner's shop when a youth, running unheedingly down the street, almost hit him. Just at that moment, a young lady stepped out of a shop door. The lad bumped into her, perilously knocking the woman off her feet. Marcus immediately reached out to keep her from falling and almost dropped her altogether.

The moment Marcus touched her arms, his hands shook with a tremor so violent he'd pulled her sharply against his chest, causing an even greater vibration to pass through him. He didn't even have to look at her to know it was his Phoebe.

Bracing himself for her shock and anger at finding herself in his arms, he slowly, deliberately released her. Lady Phoebe stared up at him and he was lost in her eyes, an intense sky blue. He smiled down and couldn't let go of her gaze.

Phoebe's soft feminine curves still made his hands tingle, even though he was no longer touching her.

She returned his smile with one of her own. "Thank you so much for rescuing me. I was quite knocked off my feet."

Still lost in her, he blinked. She wasn't running away, and she hadn't hit him. Good Lord, she hadn't recognized him. He wasn't about to set her straight, not yet at any rate. "It was entirely my pleasure. I am not often able to rescue a damsel in distress."

Phoebe's chuckle was soft and breathy. "No, I suppose not, at least not in Bond Street. You must be my knight-errant."

A position he would gladly hold. "Milady." He bowed, bringing her hand to his lips. Her fingers fluttered as he pressed a soft kiss on them. He continued to hold both her gaze and her hand after he'd kissed it. This was too good to be true. She didn't know him. He longed to take her into his arms again. Tell her she belonged with him. But that's how this whole conundrum began.

Ignoring propriety, she said, "I am Lady Phoebe Stanhope."

Just at that moment an older woman arrived. "Phoebe, what . . . ?"

"Oh, Aunt Ester."

He held Phoebe's gaze and though she spoke to her aunt, she looked at him. "I was almost knocked off my feet by—by a—a . . ."

His smile deepened. "A reckless boy."

She'd given him her name, but if he told her his, she'd leave him.

Nodding, Phoebe kept her eyes on his. "Yes, very reckless, and this very kind gentleman rescued me from falling."

If Lady Phoebe would allow it, Marcus would ask nothing more than to spend the rest of his life protecting her.

* * *

Ester regarded the man warily. Unlike Phoebe, who only seemed to be interested in his eyes, a particularly intense shade of blue. Ester sent an appraising glance over him, taking in the fashionable cut of his coat, his perfectly tied cravat, waistcoat, pantaloons, and his gleaming Hessian boots.

She also noticed he did not weigh himself down with the fobs and rings of a dandy. Rather, his only jewelry was an unusual tiepin in his cravat, a quizzing glass, and a large gold signet ring.

But she may as well not have been present as far as he was concerned. He was paying attention to nothing other than Phoebe, and Phoebe was not behaving any better. Ester couldn't believe her niece had actually given her name to a strange man who hadn't even asked to be introduced.

Glancing discreetly around, Ester was relieved to see no one they knew nearby. Indeed, the area was blessedly empty.

Ester turned her attention back to Phoebe and could scarcely believe her eminently sensible niece, who *always* paid attention to the proprieties, was standing in the middle of Bond Street *much* too close to a gentleman she'd never before met. Worse, Phoebe was staring at him, smiling!

Ester didn't know whether to laugh or be shocked. How long would the two of them remain there entranced with each other? Clearly, the answer was too long. If she didn't do something and quickly, they were going to create scandal.

Ester cleared her throat. "Well, sir . . ."

Ester waited for him to ask to be allowed to introduce himself. When he didn't, she raised a brow and peered pointedly at him for a moment. Still, the expected response did not come. Flustered, she took Phoebe's arm. "I am very thankful you were here to rescue my niece from harm. Phoebe, my dear, we *must* be going."

Phoebe didn't look away, just frowned slightly. "Yes, I suppose I must go. Thank you again, sir."

"Your gratitude is unnecessary. I am always at your service, milady." The man reluctantly allowed Phoebe's hand to slip from his grasp as Ester dragged her niece away.

Phoebe vibrated with excitement as she walked back to the St. Eth's town carriage. "Aunt Ester, it was him."

"Him who, child?"

"The gentleman. I felt it! That feeling!"

Ester paused before continuing on faster than before, her arm firmly entwined in Phoebe's. "Wait until we are home, then we can discuss it. We would not wish to be overheard."

Despite Ester's warning, Phoebe's exhilaration seemed to burble out of her.

Finally, ensconced in the morning room, Ester poured them each a cup of tea and searched her niece's bliss-filled face. Oh dear. Phoebe in love was going to prove to be a challenge.

Ester had never seen her niece so pent up. The thought occurred to Ester that she might be in need of something more potent than tea by the time this tale was told. "Now, my love, pray, what has happened to-day with that young man? The whole story, if you please."

Phoebe took a breath. Her eyes were wide and her cheeks flushed. "You know I was leaving the shop just before you, and I was struck off my feet. The gentleman caught me up into his arms, and I felt—*The thrill. The shiver.*—and I think he experienced it as well. Oh, Aunt Ester, I am sure he is the same gentleman who rescued me at the inn! Don't you see, this is fated."

Ester suddenly realized there was much more to this tale than she'd originally thought. What had Phoebe been up to? "He rescued you at the inn? What inn? Why did you require rescuing? Phoebe, I think you had better start at the beginning, and do not leave anything out. What a feather-brained creature you have become."

Phoebe told her aunt the story of the gentleman protecting her from unwanted attention, then sleeping outside of her chamber, guarding her honor. "So you see, Aunt Ester, he has twice saved me, and I don't even know his name."

"Yes, I did notice that he failed to request an introduction," Ester replied dryly, hoping to dampen Phoebe's ardor a bit. "Oh, my dear child, I do hope he is . . . well, that he is of our class. It would be awful if he were not, when you have your heart set on him."

Concern shadowed her face. "Aunt Ester, he did look like a proper gentleman. Don't you think?"

Ester seriously doubted Phoebe noticed anything other than his turquoise eyes. "Yes indeed, he was very properly dressed, and well looking. Oh, how awkward this is. Such a shame he was not with someone we know or did not make himself known. If it is as you say, and he is able to travel in our circles, he will find you. Believe me—the man knows who you are even if we do not know who he is."

Phoebe opened her mouth to protest.

Ester held up her hands. "I know, I know. It is hard for you, my dear, to restrain yourself. Nevertheless, you cannot always take the bit between your teeth. *You* searching openly for *him* will only make you look a fool, and I have never known you to be that."

Phoebe's face fell. "No, indeed, you are right. I would not want that at all."

"Then it's settled. It will do him good to search for you, as is proper, and gentlemen like to be the hunters." Ester could only hope Phoebe would listen and that the gentleman *would* seek her out, or there would no doubt be a scandal.

Phoebe lay in bed that night thinking of her rescuer's eyes, so clear and blue. Yet there was something more, a happiness emanating from them as if he was glad to be with her. The memory of his body against hers and his hard muscular arms as he caught her from falling made her shiver with delight. She'd never known a man's chest could feel like a warm rock. It had been Heaven.

Phoebe touched her hand where he'd kissed it and the place tingled again. How would his lips feel on hers? She'd never wondered about that before, had never wanted a man to kiss her.

His lean face was more rugged than the typical *ton* gentlemen's, though it may have been due to his deep tan. Phoebe sighed. How wonderful it had felt to be protected and wanted.

Aunt Ester had to be right. He would seek her out. A sudden fear that she could be wrong about this man took hold, dampening her joy.

Was she any more capable now at judging a man than she was eight years ago? She wished there was someone she could confide in. Phoebe suddenly felt alone and frightened, and unsure she could protect her heart.

Chapter Six

Marcus couldn't believe his luck. Phoebe hadn't recognized him. How good it felt to hold her in his arms, even if it was for only a moment.

It was clear her aunt was not at all happy he'd not done as he should have and requested an introduction. But how could he and ruin the moment?

What would Phoebe do? How would she react when she discovered that he was her nemesis? A plan took hold in his mind. Would it be possible for him to captivate her before she knew who he was, so that hopefully she'd no longer care what he'd done in the past?

With renewed optimism, he shuffled through the invitations that until then had not held much interest. Marcus wondered which balls Phoebe would attend, when he'd meet her again, and how he would keep his identity a secret.

Three evenings later Marcus kept to the sides of the large ballroom, trying to avoid being introduced to any more young ladies in need of husbands, as he searched for Phoebe. His frustration grew when it was forcibly borne upon him he didn't know her aunt's name or direction, and there wasn't anyone he could ask without engendering questions he didn't wish to answer.

This was the second ball he'd attended that evening, the fourth in the three days since they'd met. His height allowed him to see over most everyone's heads, but there was no sign of Phoebe's unique red-gold hair.

Marcus was beginning to despair of ever seeing her again. He may as well have attended the political dinner with his father, from which he'd begged off. Disappointed, Marcus left and made his way home.

The next morning after breakfast, Marcus joined his father in the study to work on a bill his father was proposing.

"You should have come to the dinner at Abemarle House last evening, Marcus," Papa said. "You could have met some of the younger members of the party. Lord St. Eth told me Fairport would be in Town soon. You remember him, don't you?"

Marcus listened absently. "Yes, a friend of Arthur's."

If Marcus wasn't looking for Phoebe, he'd rather be with his brother. How much more time would he have with Arthur before he died?

His father nodded. "St. Eth had his niece with him. Now there is a charming young lady with a great deal of sense. A pretty little thing, Lady Phoebe Stanhope, Cranbourne's sister, you know. We've only met her a couple of times. Never seems to be around when we've visited your sister. She will make a very astute political hostess someday, if the right man snaps her up. Just the sort of lady you should be looking for." His father paused for a moment. "Now that I think of it, wasn't that the reason Amabel invited you to visit?"

Marcus had been letting his father's prattle wash over him until he heard Lady Phoebe's name. His heart beat more rapidly as he attempted to maintain a languid drawl. "Yes, Papa. Only Lady Phoebe wasn't there. Between your recommendation and Amabel's, Lady Phoebe does indeed sound like a female I would like to meet. Do you happen to know which balls and so forth she'll attend?"

His father lifted his head from his papers and frowned, finally focusing his eyes on his son. "As Lady Phoebe is staying with her aunt and uncle, the Marquis and Marchioness of St. Eth, I imagine Lady Phoebe will attend the more political events."

Dunwood put his papers aside. "Since you seem interested in the connection, and your mother has arrived, we'll attend Lady Trevor's ball to-morrow evening. I'll tell you that you should attend. You may accompany us. There will be a political meeting before the dancing begins."

If there was a chance Phoebe would be present, Marcus planned to be present, though, it might be more difficult to hide his identity from her at that type of entertainment. Even so, with Beaumont's interest in Phoebe, Marcus was running out of time.

Later that evening, Isabel, Marchioness of Dunwood, looked up from her book when her husband walked into her bedchamber. "You look pleased, my dear."

"I am. I think Marcus will finally take my advice concerning an eligible lady," Lord Dunwood said proudly. "He seemed very interested when I told him about Lady Phoebe Stanhope."

"I wonder where he met Lady Phoebe," Isabel softly mused.

"Do you, indeed, think he *has* met her before?" her lord said with some little skepticism. "He's never mentioned her, and he said nothing to lead me to believe he had. She was my recommendation."

Isabel smiled softly. "My love, when have you ever known Marcus to be interested in a lady because *you* say she's interesting? You have, I daresay, suggested a great many young women to him since he's returned, and he has shown no interest at all in any of them—except this one. Of course he's met Lady Phoebe before." Isabel tapped her chin. "But how and where? A mystery."

Phoebe's frustration was reaching new heights. Though they'd remained home on Sunday, there had been two evenings of balls and dinners since then. At none of the events had she seen her knight-errant. She rose and paced, skirts swishing around her ankles, the only sound in the morning room other than her aunt opening mail.

"Aunt Ester, where could he be?" Phoebe stopped. The terrible thought that he might not be a member of the *ton* crossed her mind, again, only to be immediately dismissed. Life could not be that cruel.

"I don't understand why we haven't seen him."

"Remember, my dear," Aunt Ester replied calmly, "we have gone only to political parties. Perhaps he is not in those circles."

If only they'd had a bit more time together before Aunt Ester arrived, perhaps he would have asked for her direction. Had she given him a disgust of her by being too forward and telling him her name?

But no, he'd not wanted to release her hand when Aunt Ester took her away. If only Phoebe could think of something to bring about another meeting. But there was nothing. She tried to keep the discontent from her voice. "I know I'll meet him again. Though I do wish it were not taking so long."

"My dear," Aunt Ester said, looking up from her mail, "I received a letter from Hester. She and John are coming to Town. They'll break their journey with Hermione and Edwin, and then they will all travel here together."

That was good news at least. Phoebe exclaimed, "Oh, Aunt Ester, if anyone is able to help me find my knight-errant, my sisters will."

Later that evening, Ester snuggled in bed with Henry and discussed the past few days. She'd not had a chance to tell him about Phoebe and didn't know what he'd make of the young man with whom Phoebe was so enamored. She frowned. "It appears, my love, Phoebe has found an interest in a gentleman."

He put down the papers he was reading. "What delightful news. Who is it and why are you not happy about it?" Henry met her frown with one of his own. "Don't tell me he's a Tory."

When she'd finished, Henry asked, "You say, my dear, he looked a gentleman? You know it would not do for her to pick someone ineligible."

"Yes, Phoebe knows it as well. Dress, countenance, a well-bred air. His manners seem to be a little lacking. Although I looked at him most pointedly, he refused to give his name. Other than that, most definitely a gentleman. Though I must say, he was so taken with Phoebe he didn't seem to notice I was present."

"Hmm, interesting," Henry mused. "Now all we have to do is find him."

"Henry, pray, do not say that to Phoebe," Ester said. "Given the least encouragement, she will go off on her own searching for him. I've convinced her, for the moment, he must seek her out. Which I am sure he will do."

Henry chuckled. "After what you told me I don't doubt it. That, of course, should make it easier."

Henry drew Ester closer to him. "I received a letter from Fairport. He predicted this Season would prove interesting. It is his opinion that Lord Marcus will be hunting Phoebe."

Ester stiffened in disapproval. With what Phoebe had told her about her last encounter with Lord Marcus, Ester could not be happy about that prospect. "Well, I wish he would not."

"I have to agree with you, my love. We must hope he'll be cut out by this new gentleman of hers. I, like you, will be interested to see who he is. He cannot have been in London long or she would have previously met him."

Ester suddenly sat up. "Of course, Henry, you're right. I wonder why I didn't think of that."

"I do have my uses," Henry murmured.

Ignoring him, she said, "I don't think he's been on the Town before at all. Their attraction seemed strong enough that I don't think they *could* have even seen each other before and one not noticed the other."

She snuggled back against him, enjoying his warmth. "Hmm. If he has not found Phoebe by the time Hermione and Hester arrive, Hester shall take her to the entertainments we do not attend."

"By the by," Henry asked, "do you think Hester's husband, John Caldecott, would be interested in running for the House?"

"My love!" Ester narrowed her eyes in exasperation. "*You* will have to speak to John on your own. We ladies are trying to bring about a marriage, which is just as important as Parliament and much more interesting."

Isabel, Marchioness of Dunwood, glanced up from her embroidery and smiled as Marcus entered her parlor. "Have you come to spend some time with me?"

His lips tilted up briefly but there was a bemused look in his face. "Yes, Mamma, if you'll have me."

He'd been settling in well, better than she had hoped.

But he held his cards close to his chest, and she wondered if he was happy.

She patted the place on the couch next to her. "Tell me, what, other than politics and estate business, have you been doing?"

He'd been gone so long, this difficult son of hers. Something was bothering him. She waited, wondering if he'd tell her.

His tone was subdued. "Mamma, I have a problem with which, I think, you may be able to help."

Perhaps she'd now learn more about Lady Phoebe. Isabel kept her budding excitement to herself and maintained a sober countenance. "Yes, my dear, of course I have time."

Marcus paced briefly before sitting in a chair next to her. "Mamma, before I left for the West Indies, I fell in love, but I made a botch of it. She was very angry with me for good reason."

She nodded encouragingly.

Marcus told her what he'd done to Phoebe eight years ago, what happened at the inn and in Bond Street, and about the attraction he was sure the lady felt.

"She didn't recognize me and then her aunt took her away."

The look in her son's face reminded her strongly of when he was a child and had been focused on a difficult task.

Isabel bit her lower lip to keep from grinning. "Marcus, what do you mean she took her away? What were you doing?"

He explained more fully.

"And does this lady have a name?"

"Her name is Lady Phoebe Stanhope."

Aha. The mystery is solved. "Her aunt acted most properly. And not a moment too soon from what you've told me.

What, by all that is holy, were the two of you thinking of standing so close together in *Bond Street*, of all places, with all the world looking on?"

Looking ridiculously guilty, he asked, "What am I to do?"

There were times when difficult did not begin to describe him. "I understand why you did not wish to introduce yourself. Still, you will have to pay the piper at some point."

Marcus raised one brow in an obvious attempt to regain his dignity.

She leaned forward and patted her son's arm. "There is no point in looking at me in that odious way. I am not at all impressed. Although I am very shocked at your *extremely* disgraceful behavior eight years ago, there is also no point in bemoaning what is so far in the past. You will, of course, have to *convince* Lady Phoebe. But, my dear, what a coward you are being, to be sure."

She picked up the glass of water on the table at her elbow and took a sip. What a task he'd set for himself. The object of his affection was famously inured to men. "Are you positive she is the only lady for you?"

He nodded. "She is the only lady I can love. She is the only lady I've ever loved."

Isabel let out a sigh. "Well then, we must discover if she can return your affection. I expect she will lead you a very pretty dance."

Phoebe arrived at the Trevors' ball with her aunt and uncle to find the rooms filling with guests.

Aunt Ester looked around. "A very good showing for as early in the Season as this is."

A man waved at Uncle Henry, and he excused himself to the ladies. "It looks as if we are having the meeting earlier than I'd thought."

"Don't worry, my darling," Aunt Ester replied, "I knew how it would be. You'll be back before the dancing begins. We shall find plenty to entertain ourselves with the other ladies. As long as you gentlemen watch the time, I'll be satisfied."

Uncle Henry took her hand and kissed it before taking his leave.

Phoebe spotted two ladies she knew. She'd been told that Lord Marcus was in Town. Fortunately, she'd not run across him at any of the entertainments she had attended. He was probably too busy visiting the gaming hells. "Aunt Ester, I see Mrs. Spencer and Mrs. Burwell over there, do let us join them," Phoebe said, referring to two middle-aged women on the other side of the room.

Phoebe and Aunt Ester strolled to the sofa upon which Mrs. Spencer sat with Mrs. Burwell. Both ladies greeted the new arrivals with pleasure.

"Lady Phoebe, it is so good to see you in Town," Mrs. Spencer said.

Phoebe smiled and shook their hands. "Thank you, ma'am, it is a pleasure to see you, as well."

"How long have you been here?" Mrs. Burwell asked.

"I arrived last week to do some shopping," Phoebe replied, sitting in a chair.

Her statement prompted a spirited discussion of the fashions, which lasted until Mrs. Spencer turned the topic to the latest *on dits*. "So much has happened during the summer. Have you heard poor Lord Evesham is consumptive, and Dunwood brought his younger son, Lord Marcus Finley, back from somewhere in the West Indies, I believe it was?"

She lowered her voice to a conspiratorial tone. "I remember when they sent him away. What a wastrel he was to be sure."

"Of course they would have heard," Mrs. Burwell said. "Have you forgotten Lady Phoebe's brother, Cranbourne, is married to Amabel Finley?"

"Oh, yes, I had quite forgotten," Mrs. Spencer replied. "Has anyone met Lord Marcus, do you know?"

Mrs. Burwell smiled condescendingly. "Mr. Burwell and I met Lord Marcus at the Drummonds' dinner party. He had a well-informed mind. Mr. Burwell was quite impressed, and I thought him a very handsome man."

Mrs. Burwell glanced at Phoebe. "Lord Marcus is here this evening. He will be one of the biggest catches on the Marriage Mart this Season."

Phoebe struggled to maintain her indifferent countenance. If anyone thought they could match her with Lord Marcus, they would be greatly disappointed. She would rather be a spinster than marry him. A vision of him on the floor, bleeding, entered her mind. Good. If he came after her, she would lay him out again.

"Be that as it may, my dear Mrs. Burwell, good looks and intelligence are not the only qualities he needs," Mrs. Spencer responded, apparently determined to have her say. "We will have to see how he goes on. He will probably have picked up all sorts of strange ways living in the tropics."

Phoebe followed the conversation concerning Lord Marcus only in the hopes one of the women would point him out to her so she could avoid him.

Her aunt turned toward the direction Uncle Henry had gone and smiled. "Ah, here come the gentlemen."

Phoebe glanced at Mrs. Burwell, feigning a nonchalance she did not feel. "Indeed, ma'am, it is fascinating about Lord Marcus Finley. Perhaps when you see him, you could point him out. I would be interested in how such a reputed reprobate looks."

Phoebe wanted to escape the room before he could approach her.

Mrs. Burwell squinted. "There he is, I believe, next to Lord Abemarle."

Phoebe glanced in the direction Mrs. Burwell indicated and saw a tall, slender gentleman with dark hair. She noted that Lord Abemarle and Lord Marcus were walking in their direction.

Catching her aunt's eye, Phoebe said in a low voice, "Aunt Ester, I believe I shall go to the ladies' retiring room."

Her aunt inclined her head as Phoebe moved quickly and discreetly away.

Phoebe reached the door leading into the hall where the ladies' retiring room was situated. Having been to the house many times before, she knew the library was a few doors down. Perhaps she could safely sit there for a few minutes, to regain her composure and steel herself to meet Lord Marcus Finley again.

The ball, although well attended, was not so crowded she could hope to avoid him. Eventually, she thought grimly, he would cozen some unsuspecting person to introduce him to her.

Chapter Seven

Phoebe entered the library and realized she was not alone. A tall, broad-shouldered man stood across the room with his back to the door looking out the window.

"Oh, I am sorry to disturb you. I thought the room would be empty." She turned to leave.

A deep voice that seemed like a caress responded, "Stay. Please."

Her heart leapt. Her knight-errant.

He walked toward her, stopping just a few feet from where she stood. Once more, his turquoise gaze captured and held her.

"I came in here to think, after the meeting," he said, then took a step closer to her. "Being new to the political world, I wanted to ensure I fully understood the problems and solutions being proposed before taking a position."

Unable to speak for a moment due to the strange occurrence of her heart jumping to her throat, Phoebe nodded. "I think that is an eminently sensible desire. There is always so much to learn at first."

Her chest tightened with excitement, and she couldn't believe he was here.

"Have you much experience in this sphere?" Her knight moved a bit closer.

"I believe I stay well informed as to the issues. When I visit my aunt and uncle I attend all the political dinners and other entertainments." When she glided nearer to him, a hurry of spirits coursed through her.

He narrowed his eyes curiously. "What made you seek out the library?"

"I was avoiding someone." Phoebe found herself even closer to him and wanting to be in his arms again. His deep, soft voice was like a warm wave, drawing her in. Did male sirens exist?

"I see." He closed the distance a little more.

She searched his face. Barely a foot separated them. If only he would reach out to her. "You were in Littleton for the fight last week."

"Yes, I attended with a friend," he replied, his tone, intimate.

Phoebe tried to steady her thudding heart. "I remember your voice. You rescued me from the young man pounding on my chamber door and spent the night guarding me."

She drew a ragged breath. Why was it so hard to breathe? "You didn't want to be thanked. You have now saved me twice from importuning young men."

His gaze seemed to focus even more intently on her. "Yes, I took him from your door. I thought, at the time, I didn't need to be thanked." His lips curled into a provocative smile. "I may have been mistaken. You may thank me, if you wish."

Phoebe had no idea what she was doing. She'd never before been affected like this. His eyes and his body willed her closer. She ignored the small voice urging caution. Her pulse thrilled and there was no more space between them.

Tilting her head up, she put one hand on his face, resting her fingers lightly on his cheek. "Yes, I would like to thank you."

He bent his head and lightly, very lightly, touched his lips to hers. They were warm and firm and so enticing.

Phoebe's lips tingled just as her hand had when he'd touched it, but that was through gloves. This was a great deal better. "I have never been kissed before. I don't know what to do."

A flame lit in her knight's eyes. "I'll teach you."

Phoebe took her cue from him, copying him, learning, returning his kisses more confidently. She never knew a kiss could be like this. She wanted so much to trust this man. To try to find the happiness her sisters and aunt had.

She tamped down her fear and tried to step nearer to him. His large warm hands held her firmly in place, but his lips incited her to respond and give him more. Heat rose within her. She felt a wanting she'd never experienced before, as if he was opening a new world to her. A world she needed to explore. Phoebe moved her hands to his shoulders.

Marcus placed his hands on her small waist, reveling in the feel of her body. Her hands held his face tenderly. They were so small. She was so petite. Her head didn't even reach his collar-bone. He moved his lips on hers, teasingly, asking Phoebe's to respond. She did, innocently, tentatively at first. He waited until she was comfortable returning his kisses before kissing her more firmly.

He kissed her more fully and sensed Phoebe's hesitation before she responded to him again, to his need. He stopped her from leaning in to him. That would be disastrous. The mere fact that she was here, touching him, threatened to fray his resolve. Her hands slid up to his shoulders and he almost groaned. It had been five years since he'd held a woman and kissed her.

Marcus wanted to pull her into his arms, but this was a long game. He could not allow them to go too far, too quickly. This time he would care for her as she deserved and treat her like the innocent she was. It wouldn't be safe to take the kiss any deeper.

Gradually easing back from Phoebe, he lifted his head.

She sighed. Her blue eyes, hazy with desire, gazed up at him.

He smiled. If he could, he'd keep her here all evening, but it wasn't possible. He needed to be concerned for her reputation and his.

As he murmured in her ear, she shivered. "Milady, I hear the orchestra starting. I was told the first set would be a waltz. Will you grant me this dance?"

Phoebe's voice was soft. "Yes, my knight, it would be my pleasure to dance with you."

Placing her hand on his arm, he led her into the ballroom just as the other couples were taking their places.

He was careful to keep the proper distance between them. Finally, his dreams were coming true. He'd ached for years to hold her and kiss her. Phoebe relaxed in his arms, as he twirled her around the floor.

She smiled up at him. "You waltz very well, my knight."

"Thank you, milady, as do you." But he knew she would. Was there anything she didn't do well?

Phoebe was so happy and satisfied that there was no reason to speak as she would normally have done while dancing. The warmth of his hand on her waist and the way his other hand engulfed hers sent a pleasant tingling sensation through her body.

Her knight must feel the same, as he said not a word. His eyes twinkled as he moved them gracefully around the floor. No man had ever looked at her like that, and Phoebe wondered what it meant.

Henry and Ester were twirling around the floor when Ester saw Phoebe and her "knight-errant."

"My dear, there is that young man with Phoebe. The one from Bond Street. Do you know who he is?"

Henry glanced at her wryly. "*That,* my dear, is Lord Marcus Finley."

She couldn't keep her eyes from widening. "Oh no."

"Indeed."

"Henry, she cannot know who he is."

"That, I think," he said dryly, "is rather obvious."

"It is no wonder he did not want to give me his name. *Oh my,* look at the way they stare at one another."

"I did notice they seem rather spellbound."

When Henry took Ester through the turn, she glanced at him. "What shall we do?"

Henry's hand tightened on her waist. "We wait. If Lord Marcus survives Phoebe finding out who he is, he may actually have a chance with her."

Ester gazed again at Phoebe and Lord Marcus, then back at Henry. "Do you think it possible, after what happened between them?"

Her husband answered, "I ask you, my love, when was the last time you saw such an attraction between two people? She'll be furious, to be sure. It will be up to him to try to convince her, and bring her around." Henry's eyes twinkled with humor. "We are about to discover, my love, the true depth of Lord Marcus Finley's address."

When the set ended, her knight released Phoebe, bit by bit, as if he didn't want to let her go. They stood where they were for a few long moments.

He broke the spell. "Where do you want me to take you?"

The question returned Phoebe to the world of the ball. Smiling shyly, she glanced at him from beneath her lashes. The library was her preference, but she could not return there with him.

He continued, "I should escort you to whomever you are here with."

"My aunt." She tried to focus on the proprieties, yet her mind drifted back to the dance and his kisses. "I suppose. I should return to my aunt."

Quirking his lips up, he replied, "Yes, of course. Who is your aunt?"

Phoebe raised her gaze, barely aware of the other guests milling around them. "My aunt, sir, is the Marchioness of St. Eth."

Phoebe searched the room and saw her uncle Henry escort her aunt to a sofa. He bowed then left. "She is over there with the lady in the purple turban and feathers."

Her knight brought her fingers to his lips. "Milady, I shall take you to your aunt next to the lady in the purple turban and feathers." Phoebe smiled at his silliness, but when Marcus glanced at the woman in question, he hid a groan. Lady Bellamny, his mother's old friend, was sitting with Phoebe's aunt. No prayers, no prevarication would save him now. Phoebe would learn his identity much sooner than he'd wished.

Would she allow him to explain how much he loved her, and how much he'd changed because of her?

Trying to delay the moment of her discovery, he allowed his gaze to rove over her, taking in every precious feature. Her skin was like warm cream, not the cold white of so many English ladies. She was more beautiful now than she had been at sixteen, more mature and elegant. She wore a dull gold silk gown. He wanted to groan as he took in the gown's low neckline that barely encased her ample breasts. Perfect mounds that he wanted to caress.

Phoebe's ears were adorned simply with pearl drops that tempted him to run the tip of his tongue over the outer swirl of her ear, to breathe in her fresh and woodsy scent.

Marcus couldn't bear the thought that Phoebe would

ever kiss another man. He'd never before felt such possessiveness. No other woman made his pulse race or called to
his soul. He wanted to tell her she was his—had always
been his.

Instead, he walked with her toward the lady with the purple turban and the feathers, feeling like he was walking off
a plank.

As they arrived at the sofa, Phoebe realized she did not
know her knight's name. Dancing with an unknown man
was the most scandalous thing she'd ever done, and she
couldn't bring herself to care. Yet, Lady Bellamny, whom
Phoebe had known all her life, remedied that oversight.
"Well, well, my dear Marcus," Lady Bellamny said. "It's delightful to see you, again. Lady Phoebe, I take it you have
already met the prodigal son."

Marcus? Phoebe stiffened. It couldn't be. *Lord Marcus
Finley?*

Lady Bellamny continued talking, and Phoebe felt as if
she were in a vortex, unable to think or act.

"I should probably call you Lord Marcus, now you are
out of short coats. How have you been, my boy? Your
mamma told me you were returned. I would not have
known you, if she hadn't pointed you out earlier. I'm so
sorry about Arthur . . ."

The reality of her knight's identity was finally sinking in.
*This was Lord Marcus Finley? How had she not recognized
him?* Phoebe smiled politely even as her stomach clenched.

Lord Marcus bowed over Lady Bellamny's hand. "I am
well, ma'am, and delighted to see you again. You look to
be in your usual good health."

Lady Bellamny's laugh jiggled her many chins. "I've
grown fat as a calf, but thank you anyway."

Phoebe barely heard Lord Marcus as he continued to

converse with Lady Bellamny. Phoebe wanted to run, yet she was frozen at his side.

Aunt Ester, with an expression of calm interest, caught Lady Bellamny's eye.

She was brought to her duty. "Allow me, my dear Lady St. Eth, to make Lord Marcus Finley known to you."

He bowed and took her hand. "My pleasure, my lady."

Ester glanced at Phoebe with concern. "Phoebe, my dear, it is a trifle warm in here. Let me take you to the terrace for some air."

She was ready to leap at the chance of leaving, when Lord Marcus said, "My lady, if Lady Phoebe will allow it, I would be honored to accompany her in your stead."

Phoebe couldn't breathe again. Very well, if that was the way he wanted it, they might as well end this farce now. She'd give him a piece of her mind and tell him never to approach her again.

"Please, stay where you are, Aunt Ester." Phoebe's voice was tight. "Lord Marcus may escort me."

Phoebe moved silently, as calmly as she could, beside him as he led her to the terrace doors. It cost her a severe struggle to maintain her countenance as her wrath bubbled up within her.

Lord Marcus bent his head and spoke. "Would you like to go where you may speak freely?"

She knew he meant rip up at him. "Yes, a place where we cannot be overheard would be best."

"As you desire, milady."

His deep voice washed over her again and she shivered, confusion added to her fury. She had never been so conflicted. That the man she thought fate had finally given to her to love could be Marcus Finley seemed a cruel joke. How *could* she be so attracted to him?

She'd let him—wanted him—to kiss her. How in God's name was she to forget what he'd done to her before? How he'd treated her that weekend. Could she ever truly trust him not to turn into a drunken lout again?

Lord Marcus escorted her down the terrace and turned the corner. He opened the door to an empty parlor, standing back to allow Phoebe to enter. A candelabrum cast a gentle glow over the room.

She swept past him, back straight, and he prepared for the worst. Closing the terrace door, he locked it and went to the door opening onto the hall, securing it as well before returning to her. It wouldn't do for anyone to walk in on them.

Marcus stood before Phoebe, waiting for the storm to break. He'd decided that if she wanted to plant him a facer, he'd let her. He didn't usually give his head over to another for washing, but if that was what he must do to break the coldness in her, do it he would.

For what seemed like hours but could have only been minutes, Phoebe stood staring at him.

Her face was white with rage. "You."

"Lady Phoebe—"

She cut him off with a curt wave of her hand. Her voice was suspended by tears. "How could you?"

She turned, blinking quickly as her eyes filled and threatened to spill over.

Marcus's gaze remained on her, studying her face. He prayed he could find a way to abate her wrath, to bring back the mood, the feelings they'd shared before she discovered who he was.

He stepped around to face her.

This time Marcus closed the distance between them and took her trembling hands. "Would it help if you hit me again?"

Phoebe raised her tear-filled eyes and shook her head.

Marcus had never pleaded before, not even when his father informed him he was being banished, but now, when his future depended on what he said, he'd beg. "Lady

Phoebe, please forgive me. I beseech you to believe I am not the same man who gave you such a disgust of me."

He looked up, praying for the right words. "If I could change the past I would. I would do *anything,* anything at all, to wipe that memory from your mind. There was no excuse, could be no excuse for my behavior. I don't know how I came to be so completely, so arrogantly stupid, but your words to me that day made a difference in my life. Set me on a new course."

Her hands were cold in his. Marcus wanted to take her in his arms and somehow, soothe her pain away. "Let me show you how much I've changed. How much I value you. But, if you find you cannot bring yourself to forgive me, to be in my company, I'll never approach you again. I only ask that you try."

Phoebe stared at him for a long time. She saw the very real contrition in his face, his eyes pleading. *Oh, his eyes.* They looked nothing like the clouded ones of so many years before. She was so very drawn to him. If his name were not Marcus Finley—but it was.

She dropped her gaze and her chest tightened, restricting her breathing.

She had never been afraid of anything before. She'd *never* been tempted to give her heart to anyone. It terrified her that it could be to *him.* Her gaze met his searchingly. There was a depth of feeling there she'd never seen in a man's eyes until now, at least not for her.

Phoebe knew if she didn't take this risk, she might never know love.

Trembling, she took a deep breath. Her questions tumbled out in a confused muddle. "Why? What do you want? What future could we have? What do you want from me?"

His mien was grave, pensive. "I love you. I want to marry you. There has never been any other woman for me since the moment I saw you. I need you in my life."

She looked away. Phoebe's heart was beating so rapidly she felt faint. She should be shocked by his words and was only surprised that she wasn't.

Part of her wanted to go to him, to have him hold her, to allow him to kiss her, so she could return his kisses. Another part of her, the part that held the hurt he'd inflicted years before, and she'd hidden deep inside, wanted him to pay, at least a little, for the harm he'd done.

Several minutes passed before she could meet his gaze again. No gentleman had ever made a claim such as his. "How could you love me? You don't know me."

His eyes warmed with the same look he'd had in Bond Street and in the library. "I do know you. I know your compassion and your kindness. I know you were the only person who tried to understand the desolate youth I was. There is no use telling me I can't be in love with you, when I am. It was the only good decision I've ever made."

She fought to hold back her tears and searched her reticule for her handkerchief. Before she found it, he'd tilted her head and, using his, gently dabbed the corner of her eyes.

"Pray excuse me," she said wetly. "I don't normally cry. I detest it."

He stroked her back lightly and waited while she composed herself. "Lady Phoebe, is it possible for us to have a new beginning?"

Phoebe shook her head. "I don't know. I don't know if I can trust you again, or forgive you."

But what if she did not even try? She'd never run away from problems before. Could she live with herself if she did it now when he was the only man to stir her heart? "You will need to convince me you've changed. The stories I've heard do not encourage trust."

But could she allow him to try to persuade her? Maybe, if she was in control of their meetings, and they proceeded very gradually. . . . "You—you will have to court me. I give you no promises. I will only give my hand where my heart already is."

Her heart, that errant organ, nudged to tell her it was his already.

Marcus let out a breath and brought one of her hands up to lightly brush his lips against it. "Thank you. I'll show you, I'll do anything I need to do."

Phoebe pushed her treacherous heart ruthlessly aside. "Don't thank me yet. I'm not promising you a happy ending. You have a lot of ground to make up. We shall take this slowly."

"I am still obliged to you. You're correct. Our courtship and feelings need to be right. I need to make them so."

Stunned that he'd acquiesced so easily, Phoebe could only nod. Lord Marcus was actually going to agree to what she wanted? "Yes, you do."

He straightened. "We've been gone long enough. Where do you want me to take you?"

Well, that was unexpected, his paying attention to propriety. Her voice sounded small to her as she struggled with her emotions. "I think I would like to go home."

"I shall escort you to your aunt."

"Yes, that would be best." Phoebe glanced at him. His eyes still held the same warmth and caring as before. But what would he be like in a week or two? Phoebe steeled herself. "If you do not have a prior engagement, you may meet me at St. Eth House at ten o'clock to-morrow morning."

"I shall be there." He kissed her hand. "I am different, you have made me so."

Phoebe drew back her hand from the warmth of his and prayed he was right.

Chapter Eight

When Marcus escorted Phoebe to her aunt, Lady St. Eth was alone on a small sofa. He bowed. "Lady St. Eth, would you like me to find St. Eth and send him to you?"

Aunt Ester regarded him shrewdly. "Yes, very kind of you to offer, Lord Marcus. I am feeling a little tired and would like to retire."

After he took his leave, Phoebe sat down and tried to smile. "I too am a little tired."

"My dear, are you all right?"

"I think so."

A few moments later, Uncle Henry came up. "I found our host and made our excuses."

The short drive home was silent. Aunt Ester and Uncle Henry exchanged glances. Phoebe knew she'd have to explain everything.

Once in the house, they went to the small parlor.

Uncle Henry poured Phoebe a sherry, pressing it into her hand. "Drink."

She obeyed and he refilled her glass.

Aunt Ester chafed her hand. "My dear, are you all right?

After what you'd told me I was never so astonished in my life to see you on Lord Marcus's arm."

Phoebe gazed at them both, chagrined. "Not as surprised as I."

Ester bit her lip. "I did see that you were quite taken aback when Lady Bellamny said his name."

Phoebe glanced at her aunt and uncle. They wanted the whole story and she wasn't sure she was ready to give it. "As you have already surmised, Lord Marcus is the man who rescued me both at the White Horse Inn and in Bond Street. I did not recognize him from before. He—he looks so different. He behaves so differently. I would never have guessed he was the same man I have hated all these years."

Aunt Ester abandoned subtlety. "*That* I understand. *How* did you happen to be with him tonight?"

Phoebe sighed and took a sip of sherry. "You'll remember Mrs. Burwell pointing out the man she thought was Lord Marcus? That's what he looked like years ago, rangy and petulant. I had not doubted it was he."

After taking another sip of sherry, Phoebe continued, "I decided to go into the library rather than the ladies' retiring room, and—and collect my thoughts, but Lord Marcus was already there. I only recognized him as the gentleman I'd been searching for. We talked a little, then heard the orchestra start up and returned to the ballroom.

"I thought he could protect me from Lord Marcus's attentions." She glanced at her aunt and uncle. "When he escorted me to you, as I requested, and Lady Bellamny said *he* was Lord Marcus, I—well, you of all people could see how upset I was. He very correctly offered to take me to a parlor where no one could overhear us talk, or rather could hear me confront him on his actions."

Phoebe grinned ruefully before continuing, "When he offered to let me hit him again, or rip up at him, I found, surprisingly, that was not what I wanted to do."

Uncle Henry's eyes were alight with laughter, but his tone was perfectly grave. "A brave man to offer to put himself once more through your castigation."

Aunt Ester glanced sharply at him, but Phoebe agreed. Lord Marcus could have left with another bloody nose. "Yes, that is what I thought. So I asked him what he wanted and he said"—her voice caught—"he said he loved me and wanted to marry me."

Her aunt gasped. "Oh, my child, what did you say?"

Phoebe raised her chin. "I told him I would promise him nothing. If he wanted to marry me, he'd have to court me properly and prove he has changed."

She smoothed her skirt. "I shall be in charge of this courtship. He agreed to be here at ten o'clock to-morrow morning. I'll take him for a drive in my phaeton."

Aunt Ester stared at Phoebe without saying a word for several moments. "Very proper. We all have a lot to consider, and I believe it's time to retire. This has been an extremely eventful evening indeed."

Henry stopped Phoebe as she was about to leave the room. "Did you tell Lord Marcus you were driving him?"

She managed a wicked little smile. "No."

Henry gave a short laugh as Phoebe left. "I must say, I admire Lord Marcus's address. I was surprised to see him return to the ballroom without so much as a black eye."

"Oh, my love," Ester said, "Phoebe never looked happier than when she was waltzing with him. I had despaired of her ever finding a helpmate. Now look where it has led. Why can't love be easy for her?"

Henry wrapped his arms around her. "I'll be interested to see how long he'll allow his future wife to control this courtship and how long Phoebe thinks it should last."

* * *

When Marcus reached his parlor in Dunwood House, he thought back to his meeting with Phoebe.

When she had discovered his identity, he'd been prepared to hear the worst and was surprised and chastened to see the shocked tears in her eyes. He'd known then, for the first time, how much he'd hurt her.

Phoebe's decision to allow him to atone was all he'd hoped to achieve and more. She would be his. He'd do anything to make it happen. But not only would he have to prove himself to her, he'd be paying penance for injuring her. He wondered how long it would be before they could marry.

A knock sounded on his door, and his mother entered. "So tell me what has happened."

Marcus glanced at his mother with a slight grimace. "I am to court Lady Phoebe."

"If she is allowing that, why so grim?"

"Lady Phoebe has made me no promises. She's still very angry and hurt. Mamma, I didn't know how much I'd harmed her. She won't make it easy. I am sure she'll test me, and, at least, I now know her feelings for me are strong, else she would never have agreed. I am to be at St. Eth House at ten o'clock to-morrow morning. The courtship is under her direction."

His mother smiled serenely. "Ah, my son, you will finally have a taste of having to run in someone else's harness. The question is, will you run willingly, and, if so, for how long?"

Marcus arrived at St. Eth House promptly at ten o'clock the next morning. He'd dressed with more care than usual and wore a dark blue coat, light tan waistcoat, knitted pantaloons, highly polished Hessians, and his cravat tied in the popular Mathematical. The only jewelry he wore was an onyx tie-pin, in addition to his gold signet ring.

After he'd given his hat and gloves to the butler, Marcus was shown to a small parlor.

"I will inform Lady Phoebe you have arrived, my lord." The butler sedately left the room.

Marcus received the distinct impression that no one in this household would hurry her to join him. As the minutes ticked by, his desperation grew. He'd heard she'd never allowed a man to court her before. What if she changed her mind and decided not to meet him?

Phoebe tripped into the parlor thirty minutes later, dressed in a very smart carriage gown of Pomona green, trimmed with dark brown ribbon, and a pretty chip hat.

She smiled brightly. "Good morning, Lord Marcus. So sorry to have kept you waiting."

Marcus bowed, took the hand she'd offered, and raised it. Her fingers quavered lightly as he pressed his lips against them.

She reminded him strongly of a skittish horse ready to bolt at the first provocation. He kept his tone low, soothing, and smiled. Let the games begin. "Good morning, Lady Phoebe, you look charmingly. What a fetching hat."

She took a breath and raised her chin, and said in a challenging tone, "Thank you. I thought we would take a drive around the Park."

Marcus stopped himself from narrowing his eyes. What the devil was she playing at? "I would be delighted to drive you around the Park. If you will allow me half an hour I'll bring my curricle around."

Phoebe gazed at him innocently, her eyes wide. "Oh, no, my lord, we shall take mine. I hear it being brought up. Perhaps, later, you may drive me in your curricle."

Her tone was too sweet. This was a test of some sort, but

of what? Bemused, he followed Phoebe out of the room and out of the house.

His eyes widened at the sight of a high perched phaeton standing in the street. The dashing carriage was well built and stylishly painted a fashionable dark green with gold trim. It had very large hind wheels. The body was hung directly over the front wheels, a full five feet above the ground.

Marcus knew it took great skill to drive one without turning it over, particularly as Phoebe had her horses harnessed to the phaeton's shaft random-tandem, rather than the more conventional side-by-side.

His jaw dropped but he quickly recovered himself as Phoebe stood ready to be assisted up the steps into the phaeton. The second he took her hand, her breathing changed, and, though she tried to hide it, that instantaneous connection between the two of them was there again, even through their leather gloves.

She briskly settled her skirts and he climbed up after her, trying to predict what other surprises she had for him. Marcus decided to behave with Phoebe in the same way he had when he'd faced the pirates. He'd show no fear.

Phoebe's attention was on her horses, and her rosy lips curved up. "This is the first time they've been out since we arrived. As you can see they are a bit fresh."

He watched the horses stamp and fling their heads. *Fresh,* she said. Humph. More like half-trained. They were damned fine beasts, though.

Meeting her gaze, Marcus gave her his most charming smile. "Lady Phoebe, what a grand rig. I don't think I've ever seen a better matched trio. They are complete to a shade."

"Thank you." Phoebe glanced lovingly at her horses. "I am very proud of them. They are actually part of a team."

He tried not to show his foreboding. Marcus wondered who the damn fool was who had chosen them for her. He didn't know many men who could handle that pair and he had real doubts about Phoebe's being able to hold them. "I'd love to see them all together sometime. Do you drive tandem often?"

Her dulcet tone belied the challenge in her eyes. "Yes, quite often. Does it bother you?"

"No, no, not at all," he lied. "You must be a very skilled whip."

"I am held to be. You must judge for yourself." Addressing the groom holding the pair, she said, "Sam, let go of their heads."

Sam jumped aside, and the carriage lurched forward as Phoebe gave her horses their office.

She didn't speak as she held them to a smart trot through the morning traffic.

Marcus noticed her light hands on the ribbons and how she held the whip at precisely the correct angle. Turning out of Grosvenor Square, she feathered the corner to an inch. Even though the traffic was heavy, he finally relaxed, admiring the way she maneuvered through it.

He saw two conveyances stopped in the road, effectively blocking any carriages from passing.

The drivers appeared to be engaged in an argument and were paying no attention to Phoebe's approach.

Marcus expected her to check her horses and allow one of the drivers to clear the way. When she did not, he tensed and itched to grab the reins from her. Was she trying to kill them?

His mouth dropped open in amazement as Phoebe, her blacks still traveling at a quick trot, skillfully drove the phaeton between the wagons. He glanced down. She'd cleared the other conveyance's wheel with not an inch to spare.

Marcus didn't know whether to be irritated, relieved, or proud. He glanced at Phoebe, whose attention was still fixed on the street.

"Lady Phoebe, that was famous driving," he said, after his heart left his throat. "You are every bit as good a whip as any man I've seen and better than most."

Phoebe gave him a sidelong glance. "Does that mean you're not concerned about my driving anymore?"

"I never was," he lied, again, though this time he didn't think he'd get away with it. "I have to admit I've never been driven by a lady, or in a high-perched phaeton behind such a high-couraged pair. I think I have gotten used to the experience very quickly."

"Really?" Phoebe went off into a peal of laughter. "I wouldn't have guessed by the look on your face."

"I don't know how *you* could have seen my face when your attention was on your horses," he exclaimed indignantly.

"Oh, I had time to glance."

"Vixen."

Her eyes danced mischievously. "Are you still sure you wish to marry me, my lord?"

There was no sweetness in her voice now. It was pure challenge.

"Yes, even more so now than before. By God you're a formidable woman. I'll take you to the West Indies with me, and let *you* deal with the pirates. You'll scare them to death, and we'll never have to bother with them again."

She laughed. "Never underestimate me, my lord."

They finally attained the Park and, with the exception of nursemaids and their charges, very few others were present. Marcus now had a good idea why they were driving at that hour of the day. Phoebe had no intention of allowing the *ton* to see his interest in her. The realization stung, but he said nothing beyond, "I thought the Park would be more crowded."

"No, not at this hour. During the fashionable hour it is, of course, very crowded—but not nearly as fun to drive."

Was that truly the reason? He shifted on the seat, resting his gaze on her countenance. "You are the most skilled whip I have ever seen."

Phoebe blushed and smiled. "Thank you."

Marcus longed to reach out and wrap one of the wispy curls escaping from under her hat around his finger. Instead his hand hovered near her neck. "How long have you been driving?"

She glanced at him wide-eyed and turned back to her cattle. "Since I was about ten years old. Papa thought that it was one of the accomplishments we needed to have to enter Polite Society. My sisters are quite notable whips as well. If I ever have daughters, I shall follow my parents' example."

His mother told him the Stanhopes were almost Radicals in their political and social views. Fortunately, Phoebe's ideas seemed to mesh with his. Once he'd gotten over the phaeton, that is.

Why had no one, over the years, told him how well she drove? Or had they—and he—only been interested in the fact she was still unmarried? "I agree with you. Ladies should be taught many more skills than Society currently deems necessary or desirable."

"I understand your family is part of the more conservative wing of the party," she said. "I know Amabel was raised much differently than my sisters and I." Phoebe glanced at him again. "When I marry, I expect to wed a man whose opinions are akin to my own."

Exactly his thoughts. Marcus tried to keep from smiling. "Indeed you should. You'd be very unhappy if you married a man who didn't agree with your outlook."

He kept his tone light. "Are there any other accomplishments you think our daughters should possess?"

She took a glimpse at him and swallowed. *"Our?"*

Marcus waited, pretending he hadn't said anything to shock her.

It didn't take her long to recover. Phoebe's lips tilted up. "Yes. As it happens, I also think girls should be skilled in boxing types of self-defense, the short sword, and pistols." She gave a short nod. "Papa always thought it was important for a woman to be able to defend herself if the need arose."

Marcus thought it was a shame that "Papa" was not still here. Marcus took the bit between his teeth. "I agree. However, some skill with a dagger would be helpful as well."

Though knives, of all sorts, were now thought to be weapons of the lower orders, and gentlemen were not, in the usual way, trained in their use. When he'd arrived in the West Indies, he'd quickly become proficient.

Dropping the ribbons for a brief moment, Phoebe almost lost her attention to her horses. *"Really?* Daggers?" She sounded excited. "How did you come to have such an idea?"

Marcus smiled slowly, pleased he'd intrigued her. "Living outside of England has given me a rather different perspective than most gentlemen. I've seen many times a blade was a handier weapon than others, particularly for women."

Settling his arm firmly on the back of the seat, he said, "It is not always easy to be a woman in this world. Many ladies of our class are so protected they've no knowledge of the evil that can befall females not so fortunately situated. Many gentlemen are afraid of losing control over the female race."

Phoebe nodded emphatically. "Very true, though, unfortunately, many ladies *are* aware of the evil and make no push to help those less fortunate than themselves." Phoebe tightened her lips. "You'd be surprised at how much women generally know. It is much more than most let on."

This was the Phoebe he'd first met. Passionate about the

problems of others. "So I've always thought. I suppose Society would fall apart if you ladies did betray such knowledge."

Phoebe gave a gurgle of laughter. "Yes, indeed, how shocking it would be. What is even more ridiculous is that no matter how *young* a *married* lady may be, *she* is allowed to have knowledge an *unmarried* lady, no matter her age, is not privileged to possess."

He allowed a teasing smile to play on his lips. "So tell me, Lady Phoebe, does that mean when you do marry you will finally learn this information, or that you will merely be able to acknowledge you know it?"

A haughty expression appeared on her lovely face. "When I do marry, which is not at all certain, I shall let you know."

"I'll hold you to it." Marcus watched her from the corner of his eye. Her breath hitched and he smiled to himself. "I am most interested to learn what you do and do not know."

Finally, she blushed. "This is a very improper conversation, and I have the feeling that you are aware of it."

"Do you really wish to engage in a proper conversation? I should think that'd be very dull," he drawled. "I would much rather hear what you think than what you feel you must say. I wish to learn more about *you*."

She glanced at him curiously. Unfortunately, as they were on a busy street a short ways from St. Eth House, he was not to discover her answer to-day.

Marcus wondered how much headway he'd made and how much longer it would be before she would trust him, for that was the first step toward love, and love him she would; otherwise, he was fated to go through life stuck in a loveless marriage, with a woman for whom he could feel no passion.

Chapter Nine

Phoebe had shocked herself at how bold she was with Lord Marcus. When he used that warm tone, it was as if he caressed her, and she became breathless. Why him? It was not as if other men hadn't tried the same thing. Why did she respond only to Lord Marcus? She wanted to glance at him, but had to mind her horses.

She'd driven her phaeton because it would limit conversation between them, but now he intrigued her. She'd no idea he could hold such radical opinions that were so close to her own. And, although he tensed when she drove between the wagons, he'd not tried to grab the ribbons, as many men would have. Nor had he become angry—another frequent male emotion.

Yet, mentioning *their* daughters in that wicked way. Phoebe tried to fight the blush threatening. Lord Marcus should not be so sure of himself.

Or was he trying to needle her? He'd been more familiar than most gentlemen would be, though he'd held the line of what was proper and not descended into the lewdness he had years ago.

Oh, bother. Why had she agreed to this ludicrous courtship?

When Phoebe brought the carriage to a halt, Lord Marcus jumped down and went around to help her alight, telling the footman who'd come out to go to the horses. He held her a bit longer than strictly necessary, his hands searing a ring around her waist, before walking her to the door Ferguson already held open.

For some reason she could not bring herself to go immediately inside. Glancing up, she said, "We do not attend more than one entertainment an evening. Tonight we will be at Mrs. Moreton's."

Marcus bowed before taking her hand. She'd expected him to kiss the knuckles as he had before. Instead, he turned it over and placed a kiss just above the edge of her glove. A tremor shot through her and she had to remember to breathe.

A light gleamed in his eyes. "I shall see you there, milady."

A shiver of excitement coursed through her at his reminder that he had protected her. Phoebe regained her chambers in total confusion. He *was* charming, dangerously so. She was starting to like him as a person, just a little. Yet that, in itself, was not a good basis for a marriage. Time would help her decide.

Still the fears and doubts she'd buried so long ago rose to the fore. Slurred words rang in her memory and a flush of panic. Dropping her head in her hands, she wondered if she could ever forget?

By the time Marcus arrived at the Moreton party, Phoebe was already talking with a group of men and women. He joined her and the discussion. Though he made a point of standing next to Phoebe, he was unable to draw her attention from the circle.

When he suggested a walk on the terrace, they all decided that was a splendid idea and decamped together. After everyone returned to the ballroom, another gentleman insinuated himself next to Phoebe. Marcus, not wanting to push her too soon, left the party irritated that he'd been unable to keep her next to him. Worse, he'd received no commitment from her to see him again.

Much to his disgust, more than a week passed before he could have any sort of private speech with her. He wondered if he'd been too forward and scared her.

The next two weeks were a little better. He'd been able to convince Phoebe to stroll with him around the rooms a few times. Though in such a venue, there was no opportunity for him to delve deeper into her feelings.

Most of the political entertainments they attended had no dancing, and Phoebe, he found to his perturbation, was much in demand.

He was at a standstill until she deigned to give him permission to call. Why had he agreed to this foolishness? The devil. He could be courting her forever at this rate.

Finally, at yet another entertainment, Phoebe asked him to present himself at St. Eth House the following morning, at ten o'clock. Once again, she selected the time when no one but nursemaids would see them, yet at least he'd be able to speak to her alone.

He arrived promptly on the hour and waited for fifteen minutes before she arrived.

Phoebe set the horses off and they reached the Park entrance shortly afterward. She was silent and tense and continued to keep her focus on her cattle rather than him. Finally she said, "The weather's been very nice."

He raised a brow. *The weather?* He glanced at the

cloudless sky. They were having what the Americans called an Indian summer, warm weather in autumn. "Yes, though to-day seems a little . . . chilly."

Phoebe glanced at him from the corner of her eye. "Really? I hadn't noticed."

Hiding his smile, he replied, "Perhaps it is my imagination? Have you been enjoying the Season?"

She shrugged lightly. "I usually enjoy the Little Season. It's not quite as hectic as in the spring."

What could he say to make her open up? Ah yes, he had it. "In Jamaica, we'd be starting to plant in about a month."

She slowed the horses and turned her head to him a little. "Why is that?"

"The summer is too warm for many plants and, of course, one wouldn't want to harvest during hurricane season, so we plant in November."

"How long is your growing season?" she asked with interest, slowing the horses to a walk.

"Until July, if we're lucky. After that, it becomes too hot again."

They'd completed the circuit and returned to Grosvenor Square.

When Marcus handed Phoebe down from her phaeton at St. Eth House, she glanced at him. "We shall attend Lady Buxted's party this evening."

Although Marcus had hoped to be able to spend more time with her that morning, he brought her hand to his lips. "I'll see you this evening, my lady."

Phoebe walked around the garden, lost in her thoughts. During the past three weeks since he'd kissed her, and she had agreed he could court her, she'd succeeded in keeping him at arm's length and controlling their conversations.

She sometimes had the impression he allowed her to do

so. There were no diversions into impropriety, but he'd given her a knowing look to-day, as if he knew what she was doing. She'd become breathless, waiting to see if he would go beyond the line she had set, but he had not.

Phoebe had to admit that controlling their conversations was not very much fun, even if it did make her feel safer, and she hadn't learned much about his life or what kind of man he was while discussing the weather and other unexceptional topics. His offhand remarks about Jamaica almost made her turn her phaeton back around the Park to pursue his comments further.

She'd not yet discovered whether she could trust him. She sensed his frustration building, but he had done nothing to challenge her.

To-day, when he'd lifted her down and held her too long, her heart had beat a hard tattoo. Phoebe wondered what it would be like to kiss him again, now knowing who he was. Maybe just once would be enough to rid her of her growing feelings for him.

But such an intimacy was a risk. If anyone saw them or he pressed her for marriage . . . Phoebe wished she wasn't looking forward to seeing him tonight.

Marcus entered Lady Buxted's house that evening and surveyed the room until his eyes lit on Phoebe. He was exasperated to find her once again surrounded by her court. Tonight her circle consisted of several gentlemen, most of whom he knew. How to arrange to detach her from them was his first concern. With great skill, Marcus slid between Phoebe and a Mr. Warwick, a tall, thin, young man with a good-humored countenance.

When Phoebe glanced up, Marcus captured her gaze.

She smiled politely. "Lord Marcus, how nice to see you this evening."

Her words were neutral, but the warmth in her eyes gave him hope. He smiled, letting her see his joy at seeing her again.

For a moment, they'd recaptured the feelings he knew they both felt and she was trying to deny. Keeping his eyes on hers, he possessed himself of her hand and brought it to his lips. "The pleasure, my lady, is all mine." Now, if he could only get her alone.

Phoebe's breath hitched, and Marcus turned to be introduced to Mr. Warwick, who seemed not to understand how it was he now stood next to Marcus rather than Phoebe.

Another gentleman, Lord Travenor, stood nearby. The man appeared about the same age as Marcus but much shorter with a barrel chest and undistinguished features. For a slight moment, Marcus noted a look of pure hate in Travenor's eyes when they were introduced. Marcus, unsure what he had done to garner such enmity, stared the man down and wondered why the name Travenor was so familiar?

Marcus nodded to Lords Wively, Huntley, and Rutherford, whom he'd known when he was at Eton and Oxford. He'd remained in correspondence with the gentlemen for years, and Marcus had easily picked up the threads of their friendship when he returned to England.

Rutherford was as tall as Marcus, but more loose-limbed. Huntley, not as tall, but well above medium height, had an athletic build, curling brown hair, and a deceptively open look in his intelligent face, which ladies seemed to love. Wively was tall and slender.

Once the men greeted each other, the talk turned back to the current bills likely to come up in the legislative session.

Phoebe, as Marcus expected, held her own in the discussions. He was impressed to note that not only did his friends listen to her with respect, but earnestly solicited her opinions as well. His father had been right. She would make an excellent political hostess.

Only Lord Travenor, who was not in the same intellectual league as the others, seemed not to hold Phoebe's opinions in high regard.

For the most part, she allowed his patronizing comments to wash over her, though how she seemed so unconcerned was a mystery to Marcus. He would have been happy to re-arrange Travenor's opinions—and face—for the man.

However, the gentlemen who formed Phoebe's regular court were not content to allow this interloper to attempt to discredit her without waging a defense.

During one of these spirited debates, Phoebe glanced up at Marcus under her lashes. "Will you not defend me as well, my lord?"

He responded in a low voice, "You don't appear to need my help. Does this always happen?"

"Only when someone like Lord Travenor joins our discussions."

Marcus could not like Travenor, something about him was off. "What do you know about him?"

Shrugging lightly, she replied, "Nothing, he just came into the title and is finding his way. Why?"

Marcus tried to shake off his strong sense of unease. "No particular reason." But there was. The man was a pompous bore.

Phoebe allowed the debate to continue for the next several minutes before, finally, she assumed a perplexed look. "Lord Travenor, I do not understand why you remain in our discussion when you hold everything I say in contempt."

Travenor puffed out his chest like a bantam rooster. "My dear Lady Phoebe, I am a plain man and know such flummery is nonsense. It is a well-known fact that a gentleman's understanding of these issues is superior to a lady's. It is for we gentlemen to guide you ladies and your thoughts to the proper outcome."

Phoebe's eyes were wide and innocent, her tone honeyed.

"Indeed, my lord, and what do you hope will be the 'outcome' this evening?"

Lord Travenor replied in a self-important manner, which made it clear he thought he had won his argument, "I would like to take you for a stroll on the terrace, my dear Lady Phoebe, where we may discuss topics more to your level of comprehension."

She smiled tightly. "Ah, now I begin to understand you, Lord Travenor. You seek to discredit my intellect in an attempt to seduce me."

Travenor's jaw dropped. He had not expected such a direct attack and did not have the social skills to deflect it. He said, rather disjointedly, "No, my dear Lady Phoebe, I have the utmost respect . . ."

She adroitly took control of the conversation. "Lord Travenor, I think my uncle, Lord St. Eth, would disagree with your contention that females, as a race, are inferior to males. In particular, as I am helping him to write the bill he is proposing this session. I understand you are new to politics at this level. I very much suggest you to take the advice given to me upon entering political circles. Listen more than you speak."

Travenor was seething, but Phoebe appeared not to notice. Marcus had to remind himself that he was in London, where cuts were made with the tongue and not with a blade. He wondered briefly if Travenor adhered to those rules. There was something distinctly under-bred about the man as if he'd be happier drinking Blue Ruin rather than champagne.

Phoebe glanced around. "Now, I find I wish to take a stroll on the terrace. Lord Marcus, will you accompany me?"

He bowed, offering his arm. "I would like nothing better, my lady."

Rutherford raised his brows and leaned into Marcus. "A signal honor. Don't try to kiss her or you'll find yourself on the ground. She's got the most punishing right I've ever had the misfortune to come across."

Marcus glanced at him, whilst Phoebe excused herself to the rest of her court. He smiled. "I know, and a devilish sharp tongue as well."

As they left, Rutherford murmured to Huntley, "Do you think she's finally been caught?"

Huntley whispered in return, "Well, she certainly hasn't strolled with anyone alone on the terrace since her second Season."

Rutherford responded, "I predict the betting in the clubs will begin soon."

Although Marcus overheard their comments, he resisted the temptation to look back at his friends. There would be no wagering if he had anything to say about it, but first he had to fix Phoebe's attention.

The evenings were still comfortably warm enough for there to be many guests on the terrace. Marcus led her away from the others until they were alone in the shadows, under a tree whose branches overhung the stone balustrade. A lingering scent of nicotina and night-blooming jasmine perfumed the air.

He stopped and she faced him, her back to the garden and his to the terrace. A sliver of moonlight came through thinning branches of the tree, casting a silver light to one side, but not illuminating them to anyone else on the terrace. They were, in effect, hidden in darkness.

Marcus searched Phoebe's face. "Do you come across many men of Lord Travenor's ilk?"

"Not so much anymore," she said, returning Marcus's gaze. "And the ones I do meet are usually newly up to Town. They've been lord and master of all their dependents with no

one to gainsay them. This allows those men to think they are
the only ones with an opinion worth valuing."

Marcus and Phoebe were standing mere inches apart.
"You didn't seem particularly upset by him."

"No, why should I?" A perplexed look appeared on her
lovely face. "He has no power over me. He is dazzled by a so-
phistication he does not see much, or at all, in the country. He
must live someplace where there are no great families, thus
giving him an inflated opinion of his own self-consequence."
Her perfect lips formed a *moue*. "Unfortunately, his manners
are deplorable. Only his title gains him entry to the *ton*. His
behavior is such that he shan't be welcomed for long."

Struck by her insight and calm, his brows drew together.
She had always possessed composure, now it was something more. She had matured far beyond her years since
he'd been gone. He keenly felt the loss of time with her and
wished, not for the first time, that he'd returned sooner. "I
have to think him a very stupid man who would try to win
you by disparaging your intellect."

Phoebe laughed softly. "Yes, there is that. Strangely
enough, he would not be the first to try that particular approach."

"Indeed?"

"It's not really very complicated, though it may well be
convoluted." Phoebe smiled. "Men like Lord Travenor,
who try to 'disparage my intellect' as you put it, have noticed that the gentlemen who make up my court respect my
opinions and do not try to woo me. Therefore, those men
attempt the opposite. Of course, none of them would ever
respect a female's opinion over his own."

She paused and glanced out at the moonlight and continued in a wistful, bittersweet tone, "I don't know how it
was, but even though I discouraged my usual court's romantic pretensions, we have remained friends. I suppose
one would now call them my *chevaliers*."

Marcus had never wished more that he'd behaved differently with her. It may not have stopped his father from banishing him, but perhaps she would have married him long ago. "Rutherford warned me not to try to kiss you as you had the most punishing right."

An interested twinkle appeared in her eye. "How did you respond?"

Though Marcus didn't remember either of them moving, he would swear they were now standing closer together. "I told him I knew and that you had a very sharp tongue as well."

Phoebe smiled teasingly. "It is well for you that you remember, my lord."

He frowned. "How many men have you had to hit?"

Her brows flew up in surprise. "Oh. What a question to ask. During my first couple of Seasons, too many. Of late, only a couple. Word must have got around."

They stood quietly for a moment, once again staring into each other's eyes. His gaze dropped to her lips. They were definitely nearer, and even though he was too late to have protected her in the past, he'd do it now.

Would Lord Marcus kiss her? Phoebe's lips tingled as if they, on their own, wanted contact with his. Her breathing quickened. She felt as if she were on a cliff, about to jump off. "Would you like to kiss me?"

"I would very much like to kiss you." He grinned. "Are you going to hit me if I do?"

He didn't wait for her answer before placing his hands on her waist and drawing her the last few inches to him. Phoebe went willingly. Her breasts were almost touching him, his heat radiated through her. She rested her hands on his chest, reveling in the feeling of hard muscles beneath her palms. How strong he was. As he had the last time, his lips touched hers. She sighed at the warm, feather-like touch. Responding slowly, returning his pressure, she would never have imagined she'd knowingly allow Lord Marcus Finley to hold her.

His lips firmed on hers, urging her to continue, this was better than the last time. As their mouths merged, Phoebe's skin warmed where the heat of Marcus's hands touched her through her thin silk gown, sending shivers of delight through her body.

Oh, how could she crave these sensations so much? It seemed as if their last time together made her anticipate this one and the excitement she'd had, the feelings she now desired in spite of her fears. His body tightened in response to her, lightning coursed through her veins, and her heart pounded so hard Phoebe was surprised no one could hear it. She pressed her mouth against his, responding to his intoxicating, addictive lips, as they moved firm and warm on hers. Putting one hand on his face, she leaned forward to caress the dark sable waves at his neck, but couldn't reach and tried to remove all the space between them.

He held her tightly in place. "No."

"But I want to put my arms around you."

He groaned. "Trust me. It's too soon."

Never had Marcus enjoyed such an innocent kiss so much. Phoebe's lips were soft and offered a tantalizing hint of champagne and honey, her hair smelled of citrus and something else he couldn't place. He ached to draw her into his arms as he responded to her hand moving on his chest, scorching him through the fabric of his waistcoat and shirt. He yearned to feel her soft curves against his.

His need for her raged, urging him to pull her into him, to brand her, make her his. But despite his desire or perhaps because of it, he kept his hands on her waist.

Marcus wanted more than her kisses. He wanted all of her forever.

He hid a groan as he fought the urge to take her further.

Not now, not yet, not here. Marcus finally realized they'd been gone long enough.

Deliberately, reluctantly, he broke the kiss, lifting his head.

Phoebe's gaze was questioning as she stared up at him.

"We've been gone long enough."

She blinked. "Oh, yes, of course. Strange, it didn't feel that long."

He tried to keep the smugness from his smile and bent his head, taking her lips one last time. His lingered as if to make their touch last until they could be alone again.

Phoebe put her hand on his arm. He covered it with his own, and they strolled back to the doors.

"Is that what you wanted to do at Lady W's house?" she asked tentatively.

He was without humor. "What I wanted then doesn't bear thinking of. I don't blame you at all for knocking me down. You were completely right to do both. That day changed me. You changed me."

She flushed, then said with a twinkle in her eyes, "You are not at all troll-like now. You have changed, or I wouldn't have kissed you."

Marcus stifled a laugh. "Has anyone ever told you that you're an incorrigible imp?"

Phoebe's eyes widened. "No, am I? How nice. So much better than boring."

"You? Boring? Unlikely."

She smiled. "Will you come to St. Eth House to-morrow morning at ten o'clock?"

Still in the morning. At least she'd asked him to come. "I'd be delighted."

When he'd arrived at the party that evening, Lord Thaddeus Travenor had stood against a wall, staring across the

ballroom at Lady Phoebe. Now that he was a lord, he vowed
he'd have her. There had been no hope before. Travenor's father had been held to have married far below his station and
he wasn't the first one to do so. That side of the family had
not been considered by the rest of the Travenors to be very
genteel, frequently marrying into the merchant and gentlemen farmer classes in the area around Bristol. Despite that,
Thaddeus had still managed to become heir to his cousin.

He snagged a glass of champagne from a footman. The
first time he'd had it, he'd almost spit the drink out. Why in
the bloody hell couldn't port or brandy be served? He
smiled. Four months previously, the former Lord Travenor's
body had been found with his throat slit. Mr. Thaddeus Travenor had inherited the title to the minor barony. There had
been quite a bit of speculation as to why Baron Jonathan
Travenor, a well-liked pink of the *ton*, was in Whitecastle, in
the early morning hours, but Thaddeus was not going to en-
lighten them on his "beloved" cousin's last moments. The
man died as he deserved.

Thaddeus had first seen Lady Phoebe in Bond Street over
two years ago. When he'd eventually inquired about her, the
baron had laughed at him. She, Jonathan told Thaddeus, had
spurned suitors with far greater rank and much greater address than Thaddeus would ever have.

Jonathan's lip curled in scorn as he'd said, "It would be
worse than Beauty and the Beast, at least the Beast had
manners." The baron refused to introduce Thaddeus to
Lady Phoebe or, indeed, foist him upon any of Polite Society, despite Thaddeus's position as the heir. The remarks
were Baron Jonathan Travenor's final words.

Thaddeus wanted Lady Phoebe and he didn't care how
he got her, so long as he did. He wanted her creamy skin
under his hands and to feel her body beneath his. He fanta-
sized about her until his obsession grew to the point where
he'd tried to abduct Lady Phoebe. But the attempt failed.

How was he to have known that she, a gently bred lady, would be so handy with a pistol? He'd got away with a ball in him, but fortunately he'd worn a mask. Still she hadn't dissuaded him. In fact, he wanted her more, desired her more after she'd shot him than before.

He knew how to treat a woman who tried to fight back, as he had no doubt she would. She'd be on her knees, naked. Rubbing his fingers together, he could almost feel her soft skin, and the silky texture of her hair. All women were whores at heart, and he'd school her, using the whip if he had to. He imagined her taking him into her hot mouth. Travenor's groin grew hard, and he downed the champagne.

Thaddeus had managed to join Lady Phoebe's circle, but struggled to keep his face calm when he was introduced to Lord Marcus Finley, the man who'd ruined him. He scowled. Lord Marcus would rue the day he was born if he thought he'd steal Lady Phoebe. That prig had taken one treasure from him, causing Thaddeus years of suffering, having to make and scrape. He wasn't going to give Lord Marcus a chance to take another prize.

Lady Phoebe was Travenor's, her money and her body, even if she didn't know it yet. He'd burned with rage when Lord Marcus walked off with her.

After grabbing another glass of wine, Thaddeus moved out onto the terrace. He had heard Lady Phoebe had never been kissed. Maybe it was because none of these *gentlemen* were men at all. Travenor glanced around. There were plenty of people, but no Lady Phoebe. Suddenly something sparkled at the far end of the veranda, and Lady Phoebe and Lord Marcus were walking toward the doors.

Lord Travenor's fists clenched and he started to shake with fury. He narrowed his eyes and was having a hard time keeping his face schooled in the calm, slightly bored expression he'd learned to assume in Polite Society. Something had happened between them. He stepped back into the room, and when Lady Phoebe entered, her lips were swollen, and her cheeks flushed. Well kissed and possibly more. He'd have to start making his move to get her soon.

Phoebe thought of nothing but Marcus during the carriage ride home. About his kisses, and her contradictory feelings, how they were changing, or were they? Once in the house, Ester signaled Phoebe to follow her to the parlor.

"Tea, my dear?" Ester asked.

"Yes, please, Aunt Ester."

Her aunt appeared troubled. "Phoebe, who was that short, rather undistinguished gentleman who joined your group this evening? I did not care for his look."

"Oh, Lord Travenor," Phoebe responded, waiting for her aunt to come to the point. "He spent most of his time denigrating my opinions and views. Did you know, Aunt Ester, that we poor creatures cannot possibly have a rational thought unless it was put there by a male?"

Ester gasped. "He dared not say that to you?"

Phoebe's eyes sparkled. "Indeed he did. His manners are atrocious. He joined us without benefit of an introduction. Rutherford and the others defended me, of course. The most outrageous part was, after being so stupid as to say what he did, he asked blithely if I would like a stroll on the terrace."

"What a very stupid man, to be sure. And very bad *ton*."

"Yes, indeed, I told him what Uncle Henry told me when you first began taking me to political parties. That he should listen more than talk." She paused. "Then I asked Lord Marcus to escort me for a walk on the terrace."

Aunt Ester gazed at Phoebe over the rim of her tea-cup. "I see. Did you enjoy your stroll with Lord Marcus?"

She would not tell her aunt they'd kissed, and she tried to

stamp down the heat rising in her face. "It was very pleasant. We walked the length of the terrace and . . . talked."

Ester gazed suspiciously at Phoebe as she lost her fight against her reddening cheeks. Her aunt must have suspected they had done more than converse.

Phoebe was relieved when Aunt Ester merely asked, "Do you meet him again in the morning?"

"Yes, he will be here at ten o'clock."

"My dear, do you know how you feel about him yet?"

Phoebe looked down. She never should have allowed him to kiss her, but she couldn't seem to stop herself. "I don't know. I've been pleasantly surprised by his awareness of political issues. He's very intelligent and interested in my opinions."

"Do you see him now in a more favorable light?"

Phoebe glanced at her aunt. "I just don't know. If it were not for that memory of the way he treated me before, I would"—she paused—"it would not be so difficult to decide how I feel. When I'm with him, it's different somehow. When he's not there, I remember the way he was, then I don't know what to do."

Ester leaned forward and patted Phoebe's arm. "Well, it is early days yet, my love. I understand your memories of him are not pleasant. That said, you must answer the question for yourself. Is it fair— to either of you—for you to ignore the man he is now, in derision of the youth he was?"

Phoebe frowned. "Yes, I see what you are saying. I wish I knew of a way to—to banish the memories from my mind."

Her aunt sat back and picked up her cup. "What other plans do you have for to-morrow? There is a drawing room at Lady Thornhill's. Would you like to join me?"

Grateful her aunt changed the subject, Phoebe responded, "Yes indeed, I always enjoy her gatherings. I have always thought that I would someday like to be like Lady Thornhill. She is such a famous bluestocking, and her drawing rooms include quite an amazing group of diverse people including artists, writers, politicians, and anarchists."

"I agree," said her aunt. "The conversation is all wit and elegance. Perhaps, you will entertain in the same fashion."

Phoebe smothered a yawn. "Aunt Ester, I'll seek my bed now, if you don't mind."

"No, no, my dear. You run along."

Needing to think, Phoebe bid her maid good night as soon as she was ready for bed and paced. If anyone had discovered Marcus kissing her tonight, she'd be betrothed, all choice taken from her—and it would have been her own fault.

She sunk onto the sofa and put her head in her hands, unable to believe she'd encouraged him. What would he think of her? That she was a loose woman? Would he treat her as he had before? Phoebe crossed her arms over her waist and rocked, knowing the worst thing was she'd enjoyed every moment and couldn't wait to kiss him again.

Chapter Ten

The morning dawned fair but considerably cooler than in the days previous. From her window, Phoebe saw her phaeton was being brought around as Lord Marcus climbed the steps.

She was descending as he said, "Good morning, Ferguson."

"Good morning, my lord. I shall send a message to Lady Phoebe at once, if you would like to step into the parlor."

"That won't be necessary, Ferguson," Lord Marcus said.

Phoebe watched as his gaze took her in. She'd dressed in a bronzy-gold carriage gown, cut in a military style, but plainly trimmed. Atop her head was a shako style hat. She knew she looked well, but she didn't think any other man viewed her the way he did—as if she was the only woman in the world.

Lord Marcus smiled and bowed. "Good morning, my lady. You're punctual this morning."

What was it about him that cheered her, even after her doubts of the evening before? She replied with mocking tartness, "Good morning, my lord. I usually am punctual, however, I didn't know if you were. It would not have done for *me* to stand around in the hall waiting for *you* to arrive."

His lips quivered. "Ah, now that you have so kindly explained your point to me, I find your reasoning entirely understandable."

She finished descending the stairs and he took her arm, and led her to the phaeton.

Upon reaching the Park, Phoebe slowed her blacks to a walk and cast Marcus a sidelong glance. There was so much she needed to know about him. "Lord Marcus, I do not wish to seem impertinent." She knitted her brows, trying to find the right words. "You said you were different and that I had a hand in that." Phoebe paused and tried not to rush her fences. "You appear to have changed in so many ways. I've wondered how that happened. What you've gone through in your transformation."

Lord Marcus stared ahead and was still for so long she began to think she'd made an error in asking and that he wouldn't answer. She felt it when his gaze rested on her again.

"You know what I was," he began and took a breath. "When I came down from Oxford, it was the first time in my life I had nothing to occupy me. I was always the second son, but I was quite a wealthy second son. My closest friends had estates to manage or learn to manage. I was left on my own, at loose ends and ripe for any lark."

His lips tightened. "I fell in with a group of young men who encouraged me to engage in any vice I wished. Fortunately, I was still a minor and news of my doings came pretty quickly to my father's attention. He decided to send me away. Banish me before I ruined the family name."

Marcus rubbed his face. "Covey, my groom, was the only servant who would accompany me. I was set to sail not many days after I'd left the Worthingtons. I drank heavily during that time. When Covey got me on board the ship, I was still half sprung and felt ill for a few days."

"Mal de mer?" Phoebe asked.

"No." He grinned. "It was, as my mother would say, my turn to pay the piper. When I started to feel better, I looked for something to do, something to occupy my time. The ship's captain, Grant was his name, took me under his wing and taught me to sail. By the time I'd arrived in Jamaica, I was looking forward to managing the estates, and discovering what life in the West Indies had to offer. I had only one regret."

"What was that?"

"You. What I said, what I did. Despite all else, my feelings for you were true and never changed. But I had to become deserving of you."

Phoebe glanced at her horses and the Serpentine. Whatever she'd expected, it was not that. And she did not know if she wanted to hear more. She forced herself to breathe. "I'm—I am glad you were able to turn your life around."

"Phoebe, I couldn't have done it without you."

She shook her head. "I don't understand."

He spoke in a low voice. "You told me to put others first and to treat people with respect. In Jamaica, no one knew me, I had a clean slate. I took your advice and prospered."

Other pieces of his story started to fall into place. Her throat tightened. "You knew you were being banished when you were at Lady W's?"

He closed his eyes, groaned and opened them again. "Yes. It was to be my last party in England. Phoebe, open your budget, what is it you wish to know?"

She brought the phaeton to a stop under a low hanging tree. Her mind in turmoil, it was impossible for her to drive and have this conversation. "I want to know why you did what you did to me that day."

"Why I tried to kiss you?" he asked.

She nodded. "Yes. Why you did all of it. Why you treated me in that horribly despicable fashion before you tried to kiss me. Acting as if I was some sort of . . ."

"Something cheap? Rather than something very precious?"

"Yes, that's it." Phoebe held his gaze, refusing to allow him to look away. What he'd done had haunted her for eight years.

Marcus's eyes darkened. He reached out with one finger and lightly caressed her cheek. When she tensed, he dropped his hand. "I was an imbecile. I did all of it because I knew I was sailing from England in ten days, for I knew not how long, and I was in love with you. I needed you, wanted you to accompany me. You tried to understand me, who I was as a man. No one else had ever taken the time to do that. I'd been so spoilt and cosseted by the women I had been with, under the influence of the brandy I drank for the courage to ask you, it never occurred to me you would turn me down. I refused to allow myself to consider your age or your quality. I convinced myself that you felt as I did. When I staggered and . . . touched you inappropriately, I passed through Heaven to Hell. I knew I'd lost you."

Phoebe couldn't bring herself to speak. She had heard many young men behaved strangely. But she'd always blamed herself, at least partly, for his actions that weekend. "I thought I'd done something to cause you to deport yourself in that way."

Marcus took her hand. "No. You are never to blame yourself for my shortcomings. I should not have done what I did, and the only person at fault is me for drinking so heavily and losing control. I've wished for years, I'd treated you as I should have, and I've never imbibed as much again. The cost was far too dear."

She felt as if a weight had been lifted from her shoulders. "I didn't know. I didn't understand. You frightened me so much."

Marcus had an oddly arrested expression on his face. "Would it have made a difference if you had understood? Phoebe, I had so many devils to deal with. You were only sixteen, as I was later to learn, and I was a fool. If you had responded favorably to me, I was fully prepared to take you to Gretna Green. Lord only knows how I would have treated you in Jamaica."

Phoebe's eyes opened in shock. Had he actually said that? "Marcus, you would not have done that. *Gretna Green? And then Jamaica?* Not to mention that I was fifteen."

"Oh, God. Fifteen?"

She nodded.

"I would have and your papa would have pilloried me," Marcus said. "It was a deemed good thing you knocked me down. It probably saved the both of us from years of my youthful stupidity."

What would have happened if he'd treated her differently? If he'd been the way he was now. But, of course, then he would not have been banished. "I would not have gone with you. I was aware you were interested in me, and I did feel something. But then you gave me such a disgust of you. The way you treated me, your lack of interest in almost anything other than yourself, how you expected to be treated with regard but did not return the respect of others, and you always seemed a trifle on the go."

She shook her head slowly. "There was nothing healthy or well about you. I knew something was wrong, though I had no idea you were such a loose fish."

Marcus's eyes danced as he pursed his lips primly. "And what, my lady, do *you* know of 'loose fish'? I know I have been away for a long time, but I had no idea it was proper for ladies to use cant terms."

Phoebe blushed. "You, *wretch,* our conversations betray me into saying the most shocking things. You know very well I should not have used that term."

He opened his mouth to respond, but she rushed in with questions regarding the West Indies estates and their management.

Marcus answered her queries and told her about the time pirates tried to capture his ship. "I've always thought St. Vincent could not have been a very *successful* pirate. We didn't have that hard of a time repulsing his attack and taking his boat. By the time we made port with both the vessels, mostly undamaged, my reputation as a pirate fighter was made."

His self-deprecating smile touched her heart, and she wondered if the adventure was as much fun as he made it sound.

"You've had a very interesting life since you left England," Phoebe replied wistfully. "Do you ever wish you had not been sent away?"

Marcus shook his head. "No, never. I don't want to think what I would have become. Nothing good." He said in a teasing tone, "Unless, of course, you'd married me."

Oh, the wicked devil. How different her life would have been. But no, she hadn't even wanted him to touch her all those years ago. "*I* have become much more reasonable than I was at fifteen. *You, sir,* would have been living under the cat's paw had we married then."

"Ah, but I would have loved it," he drawled languidly.

His eyes teased her and he smiled as her cheeks grew warm. She shouldn't be enjoying this as much as she was. "What a bouncer. You *are* right. It was a very good thing you were sent away." She stopped, surprised at her candor. "The things you make me say. I'm very . . ."

He put his hand over hers. "No, no, don't apologize. I

don't think I could have told another female what I've told you. Most of them, I dare say, would've had vapors. I've never met a woman whose ideas and views are so compatible with mine."

"You purposely tempt me to be indelicate."

"But I have to tempt you. It's the only thing I can do to get you to blush." Marcus grinned boyishly. "You look so adorable when you do."

Would her cheeks ever be cool again? "You, my lord, say the most *outrageous* things."

He placed a finger under her chin and tilted her head up. Was he going to kiss her here, in the Park? Fear rose within her and she froze.

"Phoebe, smile for me, please," he said, lowering his hand.

She gazed into his eyes and gave him a small smile.

"Thank you. I promise, I'll never hurt you again. I won't do anything you don't want me to do. I'm not that man anymore."

Marcus had sensed her skittishness when he'd tilted her head up. Even now, there was distrust and fear in her eyes. He never wanted to see that expression again when she looked at him. Phoebe reminded him of a wary colt. He'd done that to her. Somehow he had to find a way to repair the damage.

She started the horses. "We'd better go, before anyone sees us."

That stung his ego a bit, but he remained silent as they drove out of the Park. Phoebe gave him a sidelong glance. "My aunt and I are attending Lady Thornhill's drawing room this afternoon. Would you like to escort us?"

Relieved by the invitation, he replied, "There is nothing I'd like better, unfortunately, I have promised to escort my mother to the same event, but I shall see you at Lady Thornhill's."

"Yes, I think you will like it. There are poets and artists and all manner of people."

When Phoebe pulled up in front of St. Eth House, Marcus turned in the direction she was looking.

Two women were with Lady St. Eth. They were indistinguishable from each other and looked remarkably like Phoebe, having the same vivid blue eyes set under nicely arched brows. Their hair was not quite as red as Phoebe's, but Marcus had no doubt the ladies must be her sisters.

"Phoebe." One of them called to her.

"Hermione, Hester."

"Phoebe, you hoyden. Come down from there this instant. You cannot shout in Grosvenor Square. What will people think?" exclaimed the other, quite as loud as Phoebe.

Lady St. Eth shook her head. "Both of you are sad romps and will set tongues wagging." She pressed her lips firmly together but they still twitched. What would it be like to belong to such a close family?

The other sister stood next to Lady St. Eth, eyes alight, smiling widely.

Phoebe glanced at him, her eyes shining. "My sisters, Hester and Hermione."

Marcus helped Phoebe down from the phaeton as a groom took charge of the horses.

The ladies came forward, heartily embracing Phoebe.

One sister's curious gaze focused on him. "But we forget our manners."

"Ah yes," Phoebe said. "I would like to make Lord Marcus Finley known to you. Lord Marcus, my sisters Hermione, Countess of Fairport, and Lady Hester Caldecott."

Marcus bowed elegantly over their offered hands. The ladies had quickly hid their shock, but the cat was out of the bag now.

*   *   *

Hermione shot Phoebe a questioning look and Phoebe sighed. She wasn't ready to discuss Marcus with her sisters.

Hermione and Hester took charge and insisted Marcus join them for a few minutes. Each of them took an arm, escorting him into the house. Once all were ensconced in the morning room and tea had been brought, two pairs of very curious twin eyes focused on their quarry.

Phoebe opened her mouth and shut it. There was little use trying to stop them. All she could do was to sit back and observe how Marcus handled their inquisition.

"Lord Marcus." Hermione smiled. "I believe you are acquainted with my husband, Fairport."

"Yes, indeed," Marcus replied. "I've known Lord Fairport since Eton. He is a friend of my brother's. Howbeit, they have not seen much of each other of late."

"We've been told of your brother's illness," Hermione said sincerely. "I am so truly sorry for you and your family."

Marcus nodded. "Thank you for your kindness. It's interesting that Arthur seems to be dealing with his disease— and what we know are the consequences—far better than the rest of us."

Hester jumped in. "I've heard that you have spent the last several years in the West Indies. Tell me, how did you like it?"

"Very well indeed, though it was time to return to England."

Marcus stood up under their probing questions better than Phoebe thought he would, deftly deflecting any question he did not choose to answer. It was very much like watching a fencing match with verbal thrusts and parries. She almost expected one of her sisters to ask what he had for breakfast. Though he did not glance at Phoebe, she could tell that she was never far from his mind.

The interrogation continued until the door to the corridor opened and Uncle Henry entered. He opened his eyes as if shocked, and said in mock severity, "I wondered who was creating all the noise in the house. I could hear you in my study."

Phoebe grinned. Uncle Henry's study was located on the ground floor on the other side of the house.

Matching their uncle's tone, her sisters exclaimed as one, "That I would hear my noble uncle tell such a bouncer."

"I am surprised my aunt will allow you to be so untruthful," Hester said. "*I* certainly should not allow it."

Sufficiently chastised, Uncle Henry came forward, chuckling, to greet his wife, nieces, and Marcus. "Good morning, Lord Marcus. How come you to be in the middle of these bagpipes?"

Marcus assumed a bemused expression, but his eyes twinkled with merriment. "Well, sir, I think I was kidnapped. I'd just finished assisting Lady Phoebe from her carriage, when I was borne into the house and here you see me."

Hermione and Hester protested and Marcus responded, "No, no I am quite *happy* to have been captured. How else would I have come to be in such lively and, if I may say, delightful company?"

Phoebe kept silent. Marcus really was doing a good job charming her sisters and Uncle Henry. She glanced at Aunt Ester and though she'd not said much, she had an indulgent smile on her lips. Soon all the female members of her family would expect her answer concerning Marcus.

As her sisters and Ester began to converse, Uncle Henry engaged Marcus's attention. Finally, Marcus rose to leave, explaining his father had commanded his presence that morning and his mother in the afternoon.

Uncle Henry bid Marcus to give Lord Dunwood greetings. Once Marcus left, Henry returned to his study.

Phoebe eyed the door, but before she could slip out, the

twins, freed from the constraint of a visitor, turned to her as one.

Hermione raised a brow. "Well, Phoebe, consorting with the troll. How did that come about?"

Perhaps if she told them some of what happened, it would be enough to avoid an extensive interrogation and their meddling. Deciding that partial honesty was her best course, Phoebe told her sisters about her interaction with Marcus at the inn, followed by greatly abbreviated versions of what occurred in Bond Street and at the ball.

Her sisters asked pointed questions, but finally seemed to be satisfied they had the whole story.

Hester smoothed her skirts and took a sip of the tea that had arrived. "I must say, my dear, it doesn't appear as if there is anything wrong with him now. He is really quite handsome."

Phoebe forced herself to smile. She loved her sisters, but she did not want them involved in the courtship. "He's in much better looks than he was before. Indeed, I didn't recognize him."

She fiddled with the fringe on her shawl. "In any event, Lord Marcus assured me I was quite right to have planted him a facer *and* ring a peal over his head at Lady W's house party."

"He did not!" Hermione exclaimed. "A man admitted that?"

Phoebe sat up straighter. "Indeed, he did."

Hester tilted her head. "When was that, my dear?"

"Last evening at Lady Buxted's party," Phoebe replied without thought. "When we strolled on the terrace."

Her sisters' eyes widened and their jaws dropped open. Shutting their mouths in unison, they continued to study Phoebe closely.

Berating herself for being so stupid to have told them

anything, Phoebe attempted to feign indifference. Unfortunately she couldn't keep a slow blush from infusing her face, which was quite as telling as any admission she would have made.

"Phoebe," Hermione said after several moments. "What did you do? You never stroll terraces alone with gentlemen."

"I have not strolled *terraces* with *gentlemen,*" Phoebe retorted. "It happened one time."

"Hermione, you were not sufficiently specific." Hester went straight to the heart of the matter. "Phoebe, what were you doing on the terrace, alone, with Lord Marcus?"

Phoebe gathered what dignity she could under her sisters' penetrating stares. "We . . . conversed."

Hester's brows drew together. "Doing it much too brown, my dear. If you did nothing but 'converse,' why then is your face as red as a fire?"

Hester was definitely the better inquisitor. Phoebe's eyes narrowed. "Has anyone told you that you should have been a Jesuit? I am rather more than seven, I assure you, and I am in complete command of my actions."

She tried to wiggle out from under their disquisition and was beginning to feel as if she were a child again.

"Phoebe if you don't tell us, we will suspect the worst." Hester pressed her lips together. "We know better than anyone how up to snuff you may be on many issues. With men, however, you are still a green girl."

Phoebe threw her hands up. "We kissed. That was all."

"All?" her sisters said in unison. "On a terrace? At a public event?"

By the exasperated look on Hester's face, she obviously wasn't done. "Since when have you begun allowing gentlemen to kiss you?"

Phoebe rose, drawing herself up to her full height, which unfortunately was much shorter than her aunt and sisters.

"You are making much too much of this. It was *one* kiss with *one* gentleman. If he had done anything I didn't like, I would have stopped him."

Phoebe knew she hadn't helped herself. Kissing meant marrying, and she wasn't ready. Not yet, and possibly never.

She started to walk to the door, but stopped when her aunt spoke. "That, my dears, was only to be expected after the way they stood staring transfixed at each other in Bond Street. . . ."

Phoebe turned and glared at Aunt Ester, unable to believe she'd betrayed her.

Her sisters' amazed gazes once again focused on Phoebe.

"Do you plan to marry Lord Marcus?" Hermione asked.

"He hasn't asked me yet."

"Do not equivocate." Hester frowned. "He told you he wanted to marry you. Have you decided if you wish to marry him?"

"I don't know yet." Phoebe rubbed her forehead. "I know I must make a decision. I just require more time. I have spent far too long disliking him immensely to agree to marry him just because he brings out feelings I have never had before."

Hermione sighed, then came to Phoebe and put an arm around her shoulders. "My dear, dear sister, we do not do this to make you unhappy, but you cannot be kissing a gentleman and not plan to marry him. With these feelings you have for Lord Marcus, how far do you think you can take this without making a choice, or ruining your reputation in the process?"

"I don't know. I feel I'm being pulled in two directions."

Hermione searched Phoebe's face. "Tell me, my love, if his name was not Lord Marcus Finley, would you marry him?"

Phoebe thought back to the kiss in the library, about which she had told no one, the kisses on the terrace, waltzing with him, the warmth in his eyes when they rested on her, conversing with him, and the easy camaraderie they'd achieved when she was able to forget who he had been. "I think I might. I would be much closer to knowing my mind."

"So then," Hester said as she stood and briskly shook out her skirts, "it is only that you have discovered he used to be the troll. Although, in the now several times you have met, he has not been at all troll-like. Can you concede he may simply have matured over the years and is now quite different?"

"Perhaps." Phoebe worried her lip. "If I could just forget the other, if I knew I could trust him not to revert, I would like him very well indeed."

Phoebe waved her hand. "I must be certain that he'll never treat me that way again."

"Come then, we are making progress." Hermione led Phoebe back to the sofa. "What do you want from him? What assurances do you need?"

"I don't know." Phoebe covered her face with her hands and rubbed her temples. "I just don't know."

She was saved by Ferguson announcing luncheon.

"I had no idea it had become so late," Hester said.

Hermione rose. "I suppose we should be going."

"My ladies," Ferguson said. "Lord St. Eth sent messages round to your husbands asking that they join you here for luncheon. The gentlemen are all ready in with his lordship."

"What wonderful ideas Uncle Henry has," Hester exclaimed, her and Hermione's faces wreathed in smiles.

Phoebe hid her sigh of relief. Now maybe they'd leave her alone to work out her feelings without their help. She glanced at her sisters and aunt. No, most likely not. They would want a decision soon and Phoebe was not ready. Perhaps she should just stop kissing Marcus. Despair rose in her at the thought of what she'd miss. Phoebe gave herself a shake, she would have to get her emotions—and her body—back under control, then she could take all the time she wished.

Chapter Eleven

Lord Fairport and Mr. John Caldecott had promptly answered St. Eth's summons. Ferguson escorted them to the study. St. Eth motioned to them to sit, then came out from behind his desk to offer brandy or wine.

Once the glasses of wine were accepted, he took a place on the small sofa and studied them for a few moments. Both gentlemen had his full trust. "I've brought you here to discuss a family matter. I don't know how *au courante* the two of you are on Phoebe's courtship."

John, in the process of taking a sip from his glass, choked. "Phoebe's what?" he sputtered, his attention on St. Eth.

A slow, interested smile played on Fairport's lips. "I take it this has something to do with Lord Marcus Finley?"

St. Eth raised a brow. "You *are* well informed, if you know that."

"Fairport may be, but I am not at all," Caldecott complained. "All I have been told is that we are in Town to support Phoebe, in the eventuality she needs it."

St. Eth told him the story of Marcus and Phoebe, as he

knew it, and was interested to hear what Fairport had to add.

Caldecott, after having interjected questions to clarify certain aspects, looked from one to the other and, as was his wont, went straight to the point. "How many weeks has this 'courtship' been going on?"

When St. Eth thought of the time that had passed, he could do nothing but grimace. "Several. To no apparent avail. She'll drive out with him, only in her phaeton and only in the mornings, not during the fashionable hour. They meet at political balls and parties, where Phoebe is much in demand, and she holds court all evening, spending little time with Lord Marcus."

Caldecott took a sip of wine. "It sounds as if this woo is proceeding at a snail's pace. Now with her sisters here to keep an eye on her it will be even more difficult for him, because no matter her age they *will* look after her." He made a disgusted noise. "I don't understand this reticence on Phoebe's part. It doesn't fit her behavior in Bond Street or at the ball."

Fairport tapped his fingers on the chair arm. "John, remember, all of that was *before* she knew he was Finley. I think she's frightened and doesn't know what to do about it. This is the first time Phoebe has allowed any gentleman close to her, and it happens to be the one person she never wanted to meet again."

Fairport continued, "It appears, on Lord Marcus's part, he agreed to this wooing and dares not take control, lest she bolts, Lord, what a tangle."

St. Eth nodded thoughtfully. "I think you've hit it on the head. After having attended several party meetings with Lord Marcus and having an acquaintance with him, I've seen he is a man of integrity and strong convictions. I've been surprised he's not tried to wrest the reins from Phoebe."

"We all care for her and want to see her happy. Which I do not think she will be if she becomes a spinster," Fairport interpolated. "We'll need to try to move this courtship along. There is one other matter to consider as well."

St. Eth and John gave him their attention. "Phoebe mentioned to Hermione the possibility of setting up her own household. Phoebe seems to understand she's too young. Nonetheless, you know what she is once she has an idea floating around in her head."

Caldecott briefly closed his eyes as if in pain. "No, we cannot have her setting up her own household. She is far too young. As to her remaining single, fond as I am of Phoebe, having to chaperone her during the Season for the next few years, doesn't bear thinking of. She fags me to death." He took a sip of wine. "We worry about her as well. She needs a man who is up to her weight, but still sympathetic to her causes. Is Lord Marcus the one?"

St. Eth reviewed in his mind what he'd seen and heard of the man since Lord Marcus's return and nodded. "Yes, I believe he is just the gentleman I would like to see marry Phoebe."

Fairport glanced at Caldecott and St. Eth. "Right, are we agreed that we'll assist Finley to get her to the altar?"

Caldecott's lips thinned. "So long as he is leading her to marriage, I have no objections."

Edwin turned to St. Eth. "What about you, sir? You are the highest stickler of us all."

All he wanted was for Phoebe to find the happiness in marriage all of them had found. "It is clear to me Phoebe is in love with him and he with her. I do not want her to pass up her chance of marriage and children."

St. Eth stood and raised his glass. "Let's make it happen, gentlemen."

Edwin rose. "I'll go round to Dunwood House after luncheon."

* * *

"Fairport, this is a pleasant surprise," Marcus greeted him as his guest was shown into his private study. "Please have a seat. Would you like a brandy or a wine?"

Fairport shook his hand. "It is a little early for brandy, but a wine wouldn't go amiss."

After handing him a glass, Marcus took one for himself and wondered what this visit was about. They sat and discussed Arthur for a few minutes before Edwin came to the point. "I came to discuss Phoebe with you."

Marcus stiffened. The thought that he was going to be warned off her chilled him. "Indeed."

"Don't fly up into the boughs with me." Fairport grinned. "We, my brother-in-law, Caldecott, St. Eth, and I, have decided to offer you our help."

Marcus's tension drained only to be replaced by curiosity. This should be interesting. "Help, concerning Phoebe? Why?"

Edwin gazed at him steadily. "We have been given to understand you wish to marry her."

Returning his look, Marcus had to concede that her family had a right to know what he was about. "My *only* intention is to marry Phoebe."

"St. Eth has been taking an interest in your courtship." Fairport regarded Marcus evenly. "It appears to us—feel free to stop me if I have anything wrong—that Phoebe is in charge of this courtship of yours, and, as Caldecott put it, 'It's proceeding at a snail's pace.' "

Marcus blew out a frustrated breath. At least he wasn't the only one who'd had that thought. "That is an extremely accurate description."

Edwin nodded. "We've decided to offer our help in getting the two of you leg-shackled. Just so you understand our motives, we all have a horse in this race." He edged forward slightly. "If Phoebe doesn't marry, it will be up to us, and our wives, to chaperone her during the Season. We're all very fond of Phoebe. None of us, however, relishes having to take her to all her affairs. She is interested in attending most everything, which makes her most exhausting to be around—*and* we don't want her setting up her own household. The idea has crossed her mind, and she has the means, we're afraid she might try to do it."

Marcus had been leaning back in his chair with his legs crossed, but Fairport's last sentence caused him to sit up. "Lady Phoebe couldn't possibly be thinking of setting up her own house at her age."

"You've been courting the woman for how many weeks? Have you not yet discovered that Phoebe is nothing if not determined?" Fairport raised his brows. "Once she has decided upon a course, it is almost impossible to turn her from it. *In for a penny, in for a pound,* as the adage goes. I am not saying she *has* decided to do it, but the idea has entered her mind, and we don't want it to bear fruit."

Marcus covered his face and groaned. "What do you propose?"

After taking a sip of wine, Fairport said, "The first thing to do is to take your courtship out of Phoebe's hands. *That* is merely a matter of efficiency. Under normal circumstances, she's a very competent female, reminds me of a general. Nevertheless, she has never been wooed before and doesn't have the experience to control the matter." Edwin shot Marcus a glance over the rim of his glass. "Unless, of course, you like the pace at which you are proceeding?"

"Anything but. I'd hoped to have an engagement by now. Instead, I feel as if I am taking two steps forward and one back." Marcus grimaced. "At this rate, I'll be lucky to be married sometime next summer. However, my concern in taking more control is that she'll run shy, then I'll be back at the beginning. *That* doesn't bear thinking of."

"Goes to show how undecided she is. You'll have to take over with stealth and speed." Fairport looked up for a moment. "To-day, for example, you will be at a drawing room with her. You'll have no chance to spirit her off, but you can make a statement by spending your time next to her. Put her hand on your arm and stay there."

Edwin placed his glass on the table and his elbows on his knees. "Let the *ton*'s gossips know you're interested and mean to fix her attention. Drive with her in the Park *during the fashionable hour*." He narrowed his eyes in thought. "My brother-in-law's not much interested in politics. He and his wife generally go to affairs that are purely social in nature. It's always easy to find places to be alone at one of those events. Caldecott will tell me where and when they plan to take Phoebe with them. I'll tell you."

Fairport sat back as though this was a done deal. "Live in her pocket, m'boy. Be with her every chance you get. It's now the beginning of October. We'd like to have a betrothal announced by the end of October if not sooner."

A month? How did they imagine he could manage that? "It's taken me over three weeks to get this far."

Edwin smiled slowly. "Use the *Gorgons* of the *ton* to good effect. When they see you're serious, they'll be of a mind to help. There's not a matron in the *ton*, especially those with daughters to settle, who doesn't want to see Phoebe off the Marriage Mart."

After sipping his wine, Edwin said, "Bear in mind as well, you are the first gentleman to have come this far with her. The wagers will soon start in the clubs."

That Marcus knew, but the knowledge didn't stop him from scowling. "Fairport, have you thought that the idea of my future wife's name being bandied about in the clubs may not please me?"

Fairport's smile merely deepened. "Tie her up quickly then, and the problem is solved."

* * *

Later that evening, when Edwin and his wife discussed Marcus and Phoebe, Hermione surprised Edwin by saying, "Hester and I have decided we will attend all the parties at which Phoebe is present. It is too much to leave to Aunt Ester. Phoebe must not be allowed to be alone with Lord Marcus until they are betrothed."

"*Will* she marry him?" he asked.

"Well, she likes him, likes being with him. Phoebe almost as much as said if he were not Lord Marcus she would marry him. She just needs time to forget what he did when he was young."

Edwin decided not to tell Hermione what St. Eth, John, and he planned. Now in addition to helping Marcus find opportunities to be alone with Phoebe, they would have to keep their wives from queering their pitch.

Early the next morning, Edwin visited his brother-in-law to inform him what their ladies had planned and what his wife told him of Phoebe's feelings for Lord Marcus.

"It's as we suspected," Caldecott remarked. "As long as she doesn't think about the past, Phoebe is fine."

That wasn't a very helpful remark. "And how do you propose we stop her from thinking?" Edwin asked crossly.

Caldecott grinned. "That will be up to Lord Marcus. St. Eth did say his address was excellent. We must trust in him to carry the day."

Fairport had been right, Marcus thought in disgust, when he arrived at Lady Thornhill's drawing room. He'd not spirit Phoebe away in this company. It was all he could do to stay by her side, which he managed somehow. Upon his arrival, feigning blindness to the young ladies and their mothers trying to catch his attention, he went straight to Phoebe. He adroitly maneuvered aside the young man standing next to her and bowed. Taking her hand, Marcus kissed it and placed it on his arm.

Phoebe glanced at him curiously but left her hand where it was.

If he'd not been so focused on his goal, he would have acknowledged that he had a very good time. The conversation was varied and erudite, the other guests and his hostess interesting, and the furnishings unique.

Lady Thornhill favored bright lush fabrics and interesting pieces of furniture she'd brought back from her travels. Lord Thornhill was also present. Marcus noticed the easy way he and his wife related to one another. Frequent touches and glances between them showed them to still be very much in love after many years of marriage. He hoped that Phoebe and he would be like that one day.

After an hour or so, Lady St. Eth signed to Phoebe that she wanted to leave. Marcus stayed by her side as they excused themselves from their group. When they were about half-way to Lady St. Eth, he glanced down at Phoebe. "Shall we drive together to-morrow morning?"

She searched his face before answering. "Yes, if you'd like."

He delivered her to her aunt then joined his mother, who was conversing with one of the more well-known authors in London.

Returning home later that afternoon, Marcus found a package waiting for him on his desk. Using his penknife, he broke the seal and opened the documents concerning Lord Thaddeus Travenor.

According to his sources, Travenor had a reputation as a brutish man, always in need of money, and not particular as to how he came by it. The only women he'd been associated with were tavern wenches and common prostitutes.

His father had been held to have married far below his station to a very ungenteel woman. Thaddeus had been heir to his cousin, Baron Jonathan Travenor, until that gentleman's unexpected murder, upon which Thaddeus came into the title.

Despite the current Lord Travenor's dressing well, no person of quality, upon meeting him, would have thought him of their station.

Well, from what Marcus had witnessed, that was true.

Marcus turned to another report, which informed him that the current Lord Travenor was reported to have been involved in a scheme in the West Indies, five years previously, in which he lost all his funds.

From that time, until he inherited, he was suspected to have been involved in a few robberies, but there was never sufficient proof to bring him to trial.

Marcus remembered what Cranbourne said about Phoebe being held up and wondered if it could have been Travenor.

At any rate, Marcus now knew why Travenor didn't like him. Travenor must have been involved in the smuggling ring Marcus broke up when he did some work for the Foreign Office. Marcus had systematically hunted down the ships and confiscated the cargo. The backers of the scheme had escaped prison, but were financially devastated.

Should Travenor be one of those men, he was unscrupulous and dangerous. If he wanted to pay Marcus back, Travenor would have no hesitation using Phoebe to do it.

Marcus clenched his fist. He'd kill Travenor if necessary to protect Phoebe. The idea of his love in that blackguard's clutches sickened him. More than one of the women Travenor had used had been found beaten or dead. No charges had ever been brought.

After Phoebe and Marcus's drive the next morning, she took a deep breath and turned to him. "Will you come in so that we may continue our conversation?"

When he smiled, her heart jumped.

"Yes, I'd like that."

Ferguson bowed to them, Phoebe glanced back over her shoulder. "I shall be just a few minutes. Ferguson, please show Lord Marcus to the morning room."

"Yes, my lady."

Phoebe found a maid. "Sally, find Lady St. Eth and ask her to meet me in the morning room. Oh, and ask Rose to come to me."

Rose was already in Phoebe's dressing room when she arrived.

Removing her hat, she said, "Quickly. I must change."

She was soon dressed in one of her new day gowns, and her hair tidied. Within ten minutes, Phoebe entered the morning room, pleased to see her aunt in conversation with Marcus.

Her sisters were right, she had to make up her mind whether she would marry him or not and the only way to decide was to spend more time with him.

They passed the next hour discussing his time in the West Indies, including some of his work for the government, then moved on to issues both social and political. Uncle Henry joined them not long into their discussion and a lively debate ensued, with her uncle taking the contrary positions to spur the conversation.

Phoebe found that she and Marcus were so much in accord in their views on the issues, she was beginning to feel perfectly at ease with him. The conversation continued over the luncheon table.

"Finley, I have seen your interest in politics," Uncle Henry said shrewdly. "Where do you stand? Your family has traditionally been more conservative than some of us."

Before Marcus could answer, Phoebe said, "Uncle Henry, Lord Marcus's views are very forward thinking. Even more so than views I espouse."

Why had she felt the need to answer for him? Was she trying to protect Marcus and from what? He was doing quite well without her help.

Marcus glanced at her, his eyes warm. "Indeed, sir, I've found myself in concert with most of Lady Phoebe's ideas concerning, for example, the raising of children." A smile tugged at the corners of his mouth. "Daughters especially."

A slight bit of heat crept into Phoebe's face. He did that on purpose. This blushing would have to stop.

Uncle Henry asked, "Has Phoebe told you about the schools she formed for the children on Cranbourne's estates?"

"No." Marcus turned to her. "What kind of schools?"

"Some are for the younger children, to give them a basic education." Phoebe folded and refolded her serviette. What would he think about her schools? "Others are to help train the older ones, before they are apprenticed. Or, in the case of those who will remain on the farms, the classes give them information concerning agriculture."

"When did you begin them?" Marcus asked.

He seemed genuinely curious, and Phoebe relaxed. "Not long after I took over the house," she replied. "I'd already begun to learn about estate management when—when my parents died. Geoffrey, my brother, bade me continue and agreed to implement my suggestions."

She plucked a grape from the bunch on the table. "We also take local children if there is no school in the area. I've been very pleased with their success."

Phoebe couldn't keep the sadness from her tone, when she continued, "I planned to begin an orphan asylum, then Geoffrey married, and it would not have been proper for me to carry on in my role at the Place."

Marcus's gaze caught hers and was so sympathetic it caused her breathing to quicken.

"When I marry," he said, "I shall expect my wife to propose just such ideas as you have."

Even with Uncle Henry and Aunt Ester present, Marcus lowered his voice and spoke just to her. "I promise you I'd welcome not only the ideas, but encourage *my wife* to implement them as well, as an example to *our* daughters and *our* sons."

Phoebe's blood seemed to roar in her ears. How dare he be so bold with her aunt and uncle looking on? "Would you indeed, my lord? You must be expecting to marry a spirited lady."

Marcus lifted his glass of wine to her. "I plan to marry a valiant lady. A lady with spirit, daring, and courage."

He held Phoebe's eyes for a few more moments. "Will you drive with me this afternoon at five o'clock?"

The fashionable hour. Her first impulse was to say no, but before Phoebe could deny him, Uncle Henry interrupted.

"An excellent idea, my dear. You will be able to assess Lord Marcus's driving abilities."

Chapter Twelve

Rather than returning straight back to Dunwood House, Marcus entered the small park in the square. He thought over Fairport's offer of assistance. To-day was a perfect example of his halting progress. She'd seemed happy and at ease with him and then pulled back from taking the next step.

Marcus arrived at St. Eth House that afternoon with his usual promptitude and was gratified to see Phoebe descending the stairs as Ferguson admitted him. She was so beautiful she took Marcus's breath away. For eight long years, he'd waited for moments like this.

"Shall we be off?" he asked, taking the hand she'd offered. "I know you don't like keeping the horses waiting anymore than do I."

"Yes, let's." As they left the house, she grinned.

Marcus was relieved to see the smile reached her eyes. She hadn't wanted to drive with him, though St. Eth's intervention had left her with little choice but to accept. The extra persuasion was a godsend. Marcus liked his male in-laws already.

After handing Phoebe into his curricle, Marcus went to

the other side and climbed up. Covey was very properly on the perch in back.

About a block from the Park, Phoebe said, "I admire your bays. Very sweet goers."

Marcus had to make a concerted effort to pay attention to his horses and not her. "High praise, indeed, coming from you. I like my pair very well, but they don't compare to your blacks."

Her eyes shone with pride. "Ah, well, I was very fortunate to find them."

"So I've heard. Rumor has it that there were quite a few gentlemen who wanted them."

He'd asked Rutherford what he knew about Phoebe's team and was told that she had such a good reputation regarding horseflesh that Marbury, their former owner, had written Phoebe's brother asking if Phoebe would be interested in buying them. Marbury gave them to her for a good price as well.

Phoebe shrugged. "I must have gotten there first. You're an excellent whip. Have you thought about joining the Four-Horse Club?"

"I haven't had a chance to think about anything other than the estate and politics since I've been back." *And you*, he wanted to say but kept the thought to himself. "I've also tried to spend time with Arthur."

Phoebe glanced at Marcus with concern in her face. "It must be very sad to know one's brother is dying."

"It is," Marcus acknowledged. "But we're only allowed to be sad when we're not around Arthur. He's a great gun. Always cheerful and rallying us. The only thing that pulls him down is knowing he'll not see his daughters grow up, but Arthur won't let them pine. He spends as much time with them as possible and teaches them all manner of things that Priddy, their governess, cannot. He's made my father and me promise we'll continue."

Marcus flashed a glance at her. "I think he's the reason I've become so much more an advocate of women's rights than ever before. Unfortunately, my father is taking his time coming around. You'll like my nieces. They're sharp, intelligent girls, full of pluck. Arthur adores them. Losing him will devastate them." Thinking of his brother's death threatened to overwhelm Marcus. "I shall miss him."

Phoebe put her hand on his arm. "Tell me where your nieces live."

He kept an eye on the traffic as they entered the Park. "At Charteries, our principal estate in Sussex. That's where Arthur is, and Mother spends most of her time there as well."

"How is it that your main estate has a different name?"

That was a good question, and one not many people asked. He was glad Phoebe did. "Our original title is Viscomt du Charteries. The marquisate is only a couple of hundred years old. No one could bring themselves to change the estate's name. There is a Dunwood Hall, which is in the north, but it's a minor property compared with Charteries."

Phoebe nodded. "I like the name, Charteries. I can see why one wouldn't want to change it. Evesham, I take it, was the Earldom?"

Of course she'd figure it out quickly. "We came up through the ranks as it were."

Marcus turned onto Rotten Row, checking his pace to the slower traffic. As they made their way around the carriage path, he noticed that he and Phoebe were attracting the attention of many older ladies, leaders of the *ton*, whose barouches and landaus were pulled up on the verge. Some waved, others inclined their heads.

Phoebe and Marcus returned their greetings. She identified for him people he either didn't know or recognize.

The younger gentlemen and ladies strolling on the side of the path took note as well.

Marcus was hailed by Viscount Beaumont.

As Marcus pulled alongside to greet his friend, Robert was staring at Phoebe. He shot Marcus a sharp look and waited.

What the devil was Robert about? Marcus heaved a sigh and with poor grace, said, "Yes, all right. Lady Phoebe, please allow me to present Robert, Viscount Beaumont. Beaumont, Lady Phoebe Stanhope." Marcus had no intention of allowing Robert to interrupt his time with Phoebe. "Now that you've had your introduction, Robert, you may move along. She's not your type. Don't even think about asking her to walk with you because it ain't going to happen."

Phoebe's eyes sparkled with mirth. Smiling graciously at Robert, she extended her hand.

Ignoring Marcus, Robert took her hand and bowed extravagantly over it. "Lady Phoebe, I am delighted to make your acquaintance," he said seductively, before directing his attention back to Marcus. "What a paltry fellow you are, Finley. I can't believe you stole the march on me. I saw her first."

Glancing briefly at Phoebe, Marcus saw she was enjoying their exchange of insults and he didn't want to disappoint.

He raised his quizzing glass to observe his friend, something Robert hated, and asked in a languid drawl, "Beaumont, do you really wish to expose yourself to Lady Phoebe?"

"Finley," Robert retorted, "I have never been so insulted. I thought you were my friend. First you introduce me to a beautiful lady, and then you wave me away as if I am of no account. I am not quite nobody you know."

He turned his attention back to Phoebe. "Lady Phoebe, I ask you, is this fair of him? Shall you allow *him* to dictate to *you?* Why have I not met you before?"

Delightedly, Phoebe laughed and clapped her hands.

Marcus made a point of scowling. "*You* haven't met her, Beaumont, because *you* don't frequent the types of affairs that *Ladies* attend. Lady Phoebe, allow me to tell you that an acquaintance with Lord Beaumont will not at all add to your consequence. Hamhanded, my dear, that's what he is. You would not wish to be seen driving with him."

"Ham-handed am I?" Robert said indignantly. "I'll have you know I'm a member of the Four-Horse Club."

Marcus raised a brow. "Someone must have taken sympathy on you."

He turned the conversation away from Phoebe. Though Robert was probably harmless in this instance, there was no point in taking any chances. "What are you doing here, Robert? I've never known you to do the pretty in the Park. Decided to give yourself over to the dowagers and eligible young ladies?"

"If it comes to that," Robert spouted. "I've not seen you here before either. By the way, put that deemed quizzing glass away. You know I don't like 'em. I was attending my grandmother and have just now escaped," Robert said with brutal honesty. "Come now, have mercy on me, Marcus. Make Covey there come down, and take me up behind you. I need to leave before anyone else sees me."

Marcus grinned. The devil he would. He'd be damned if Beaumont was going to get in his curricle with Phoebe there. "If you think I'll give you an opportunity to flirt with Lady Phoebe, you must be all about in your head. Now we've got to be going as we're holding up traffic."

He waved to Lord Beaumont and drove off.

Phoebe giggled. "You were very hard on Lord Beaumont."

"Not at all," Marcus answered amiably. "He's one of my oldest friends. Were he in my place, he would have done the same to me. Although I probably do owe him a favor. I would not have known you were in Littleton if he hadn't seen you talking to the landlord."

Phoebe stopped giggling and asked with interest, "Did he?"

Marcus gave a sidelong glance. "Oh, yes, and he made a point to find out your name. When he described you, *I* knew in an instant it was you."

She was looking forward, deep in thought. "That was how you knew to rescue me."

Despite his attempt to remain calm, his voice was harsh. "Yes, when I heard that young fool at your door, knowing at the very least he was disturbing your sleep, and at the worst frightening you, I couldn't stand it."

Marcus took a large breath. "He reminded me so much of myself at that age I wanted to drag him away and give him a bit of home brew. As if I could punish myself by punishing him."

Phoebe's eyes were wide. "What did you do with him?"

"I took him down the stairs and out the door and told an ostler not to allow the fellow back into the inn. He was staying there, coincidentally."

"The ostler obeyed you?" she asked, fascinated.

Marcus tightened his jaw. "Of course. I am rather used to being obeyed. Why does that seem strange to you?"

She shrugged and shook her head. "I don't know. I suppose because you are never forceful around me."

"Would it help if I was?"

Phoebe scrunched her face. "Probably not."

"Harrumph. I'm also not stupid."

She peeped at him as he glanced over. "No, you're not stupid. Not in the slightest."

Perhaps they were finally getting somewhere, and he could be married before he was forty.

* * *

Marcus had received a note from Caldecott that he and his wife would chaperone Phoebe at the Covington ball, that evening. Upon entering the ballroom, Marcus saw Phoebe's sister Hester conversing with another lady. Sticking to the sides of the ballroom, he searched for Phoebe and found her already surrounded by her court.

Maneuvering his way through the crowd—for the Little Season was well and truly underway—Marcus adroitly edged out the man standing to Phoebe's left. He bowed, took the hand she'd absently offered, kissed it, and placed her hand on his arm.

Deep in a discussion with a gentleman and lady on her right, Phoebe acknowledged him without thought and didn't seem to notice her hand was no longer free.

Standing across from Marcus, Rutherford raised a brow as his lips curved up. Marcus slightly inclined his head and tried, but failed, to keep from grinning.

When she finished her conversation, Phoebe glanced from her hand on Marcus's arm to his face in bemusement.

Marcus refused to respond, acting as if it was the most normal thing in the world. Well it would be if he had his way.

She seemed a little surprised but, in the end, didn't object and turned to converse with another lady who had come upon their circle.

The violins readied themselves for a waltz and he cursed the person, probably a bitter old spinster, who decided he couldn't dance with her more than twice.

Speaking in a low voice, he asked, "Milady, may I call this waltz mine?"

Before Phoebe could answer, Lord Travenor came rushing up. "Lady Phoebe, I believe this is my set."

Marcus's jaw tightened, but he forced himself to answer

in a bored drawl, "You are quite out, Travenor. Lady Phoebe is promised to me for this waltz and the next."

Hatred flashed for a bare second in Travenor's eyes.

Marcus covered Phoebe's hand on his arm and strolled off with her to take their places on the dance floor.

His sense of protectiveness over her had taken control when Travenor appeared, but Marcus realized he didn't know how Phoebe would respond to his high-handed answer. "I apologize if you didn't like my speaking for you. Travenor is such a bore and his manners don't bear thinking of."

Phoebe smiled shyly. "What is the point of a lady having her own knight-errant, if not to protect her? I thought it was very well done, my lord. Very well done indeed. I have no wish to stand up with Lord Travenor."

They took their places and the music began. "I would wish to always be able to protect you."

Phoebe lifted her gaze to meet his, searching deeply for he knew not what, but said nothing.

Marcus held her tighter and just a little closer than he had before. The need to guard her from Travenor overcame every other thought.

As Marcus brought them to a stop, he glanced around. "Travenor is coming this way. I've saved you from the next waltz with him. Help me think of a way to save you from the other sets, when I'm only allowed to dance twice with you."

Phoebe tightened her hand on Marcus's arm. "We can take a stroll on the terrace. It's still warm enough."

He moved her away from the direction Travenor was coming. Near the terrace doors, Marcus stopped to look back. Travenor was glancing around confused, as if he didn't understand how Phoebe had escaped him. A cruel scowl darkened his face before he schooled his countenance. A chill of foreboding rippled up Marcus's spine. The man would bear watching.

"John, did you see their expressions?" Hester asked as her husband led her out of the turn.

"Whose?" he responded.

"Phoebe and Lord Marcus." His wife tightened her grip on his arm. "They seem to have eyes for no one but each other."

Time for evasive actions. John retorted, "How nice, I wish *my* dance partner had eyes for no one but me."

Hester's tone was impatient. "But, John . . ."

"No buts, my dear. Just what do you think they can do on the dance floor?"

When the waltz ended, Hester quickly moved to follow Phoebe and Marcus and walked into John, bouncing off his chest as he blocked her way. He took her hand and led her back to take their places in the next set.

"John, you don't understand. I cannot dance now," Hester said as they came together in the Roger de Coverley. "Phoebe has just walked onto the terrace with Lord Marcus."

The steps separated John and Hester and brought them together again.

"My dear, what I understand is that I wish to dance with you. Phoebe will be twenty-four in less than two weeks. She is well able to take care of herself."

"Only when she wants to," muttered his wife.

John smiled. With any luck, Lord Marcus would make even more progress with Phoebe this evening and a betrothal would be in the offing soon.

* * *

Marcus and Phoebe were one of very few couples on the terrace. Once again, he took her to a darkened area, half expecting her to protest. When she didn't, he leaned back against the stone wall of the house, cautioning himself to go slowly as he gradually tightened his arms around her.

When Phoebe's body was lightly touching his, he bent his lips to her already upturned face, kissing her softly at first. As she responded, he made his kiss more demanding, and Phoebe's ardor grew. "Phoebe, sweetheart, open your lips."

She opened them a little. He tantalizingly ran the tip of his tongue between them. Teasing her mouth, playing with her senses, caressing her lips, breaching her walls. He entered. She tasted like sweet nectar. Languidly, he caressed her tongue with his, waiting for her response.

Marcus's knees almost buckled when she reached up to put her arms around his neck, pulling him nearer. The feel of her generous breasts against his chest, her body completely pressed against his, was almost more than he could take.

He was fully aroused and she was, unwittingly, rubbing against his erection. *Dolt, concentrate on the kiss. Don't scare her.*

Canting his head, Marcus explored the sweet cavern of her mouth and stroked Phoebe's back from her nape down to her waist. She shivered under his touch. He needed to stop this before he did something that would frighten her, and they'd been gone long enough. He had no doubt her sister would know exactly how long Phoebe had been alone with him.

Gradually moving back from the kiss, Marcus began to lift his head. Her eyes were glazed, desire stirring their depths. *Desire for him.*

The sudden consciousness that her yearning was for

him, and only him, almost undid him, but he wanted more. He needed her love.

When their bodies parted, she asked, "Is kissing, always so—so intense?"

Marcus's voice was deep and gravelly. "No." He wanted to leave it at that, but she needed to know what he felt. "Only with you."

Her breath quickened and her eyes widened. "It is because you love me?"

Marcus groaned. Why were they having this conversation? "Yes, because I love you, my reactions are deeper, more profound."

Her forehead wrinkled. "Hmm, I have no one with whom to compare."

That was too much. The thought of her kissing anyone else pushed him over the edge. Marcus hauled her roughly into his arms and brought his mouth down hard on hers. When Phoebe opened her lips, he invaded, laying claim to her. This time one of his hands cupped her bottom, bringing her closer.

He could tell the moment Phoebe stopped thinking and gave herself to him. That was part of their problem. The *Damn Woman* thought too much. If he could only stop her from thinking long enough, he'd be married or at the very least betrothed.

A small kernel of an idea began to take form in his mind as he reluctantly set her feet back on the stone pavers of the terrace. He'd seduce Lady Phoebe into loving him. His lips lingered on hers, unwilling to give her up.

She opened her eyes and searched his face. "Of course, what I was going to say was I haven't wanted to kiss anyone else."

Marcus slumped back against the wall, taking her with him. As he laughed silently, his shoulders shook. He'd make damn sure she never would.

* * *

Phoebe rested her head on his chest. His deep laughter rumbled inside him, and his heartbeat was fast but steady. She'd been thrilled to be treated so passionately. Once, she'd seen her father kiss her mother like Marcus kissed her. The taste of his tongue, the feel of his palms stroking her back, sent shivers of sensation sliding through her body and stoked her flames higher. She hadn't wanted him to stop. She'd wanted more.

When he'd lifted his head, she'd felt bereft.

Meeting his eyes, Phoebe saw the heat smoldering in them and saw his desire for her flare. She suddenly knew how much control, how much strength he had exercised when he'd ended their kiss. Far more than she could have mustered, lost as she was in him.

She'd known, in an abstract sort of fashion, that he was physically powerful. His muscles, the animal-like grace in his movements and the way he'd lifted her like she weighed nothing proved his strength. But to her, strength of mind was even more important.

Phoebe remembered the hard tone of his voice when he'd removed the young man at the inn. He really was used to being in command. But with her, he was always warm, gentle, and patient, except for that passionate kiss.

He rested his cheek against hers. "We should go. I hear the next waltz beginning."

Phoebe sighed. "Yes, I suppose you're right."

His voice was a soft whisper against her ear. "My dance, I believe, my lady."

Trembling, she replied, "Yes, your dance, my lord."

After entering the ballroom they made their way to where the other couples were taking their places for the waltz.

Marcus's hand firmly held her waist, and his fingers clasped hers, spreading his warmth through her. This time he held her even tighter as if in an attempt to preserve the heat they'd felt during their kiss, and to her surprise, she did not pull away. He captured her gaze, holding her in his web.

"How long do you think it will be," she asked, their eyes still locked, "before people notice that we don't talk whilst waltzing?"

"We are talking." He smiled. "Do you care if they notice?"

"No, but my sister will." Strange, Phoebe had always observed the proprieties, now she did not worry so much.

"We can talk," he said so softly only Phoebe could hear him. "I can tell you that, more than anything else, I'd like to kiss you again."

"And I," Phoebe said, and licked her lips. "I can tell you that I want to wrap my arms around your neck so that my body is . . . pressed against yours."

Remembering the feel of her soft frame and voluptuous breasts pressed into him, he responded to her, hardening. Marcus nearly tripped, his blood pounded, and his breathing quickened. "Milady." She quivered under his hand.

"My darling, Phoebe," he said softly, "I think we need to stop talking."

Instead, in a low sultry voice, she whispered, "No, we shall make it a game. I can tell you I want to feel your hands stroke my back."

"Phoebe, do you know what you're doing? What you're asking?"

She brought her brows together. "Not entirely, but please don't stop. I feel an excitement and wonder I've never felt before."

Marcus didn't quite know what had changed, but clearly something had. Holding himself tightly in control he answered, "Very well. We'll play the game. I want to feel your tongue tangling with mine."

The fire between them flared hot.

By the time the dance ended, Marcus was ravaged. He'd known for a long time she was the only woman he could love or who would understand him. Now he knew she was the only woman who could satisfy his raging passions. He needed to convince her to marry him soon.

Supper was starting and Marcus looked for and found John. Their eyes met. By unspoken agreement they made their way down the stairs and sat at the same table.

Rutherford and his dance partner, Miss Anna Marsh, joined them as well. The ladies knew each other and immediately began chatting whilst the gentlemen fetched their champagne and selected from the delicacies on offer.

Marcus glanced at John and Rutherford. "Travenor is going to be a problem."

"I'll grant you he's an irritation," Rutherford drawled, selecting a canapé for Miss Marsh. "A problem is carrying it maybe a bit too far."

"Phoebe is well able to take care of herself. All the sisters are," John said dismissively.

"Travenor has accosted Phoebe once this evening and will do it again. The look I saw in his face when he was thwarted means trouble." Marcus's jaw tightened. "I've not a doubt he'll try to get Lady Phoebe alone somehow. All I ask is that for the time you're here this evening, you dance with her or keep her with you, if I cannot. You know she'll not wish to make a scene by refusing to stand up with him."

John frowned, but said, "Of course."

Rutherford followed suit and added, "Finley, if you're correct, the threat is not just for this evening."

Marcus nodded. "I am aware of that. I'll have to consult St. Eth and Fairport to insure she is protected."

Returning from the buffet table to the table where the ladies were waiting, Rutherford said quietly to John, "I can't imagine a threat for which Phoebe is not the equal."

John responded, "Nor I, but because of the expression in Finley's face and the way he obviously feels about Phoebe, I cannot deny him."

"I find a fine irony in all of this," Rutherford said.

John smiled. "I can see how you would."

Marcus grinned. So Rutherford had been on the receiving end of Phoebe's fist. It served him right.

After supper, Marcus tensed as they were returning to the ballroom and Travenor once again confronted Phoebe.

Chapter Thirteen

"Lady Phoebe, I believe you must now dance with me. I have been waiting all evening. You've stood up with Lord Marcus twice." Travenor puffed out his chest. "Under the rules, you may not dance with *him* again."

Marcus responded, "Travenor, you seem to be plagued with bad luck. Lord Rutherford here has just now been accepted as Lady Phoebe's partner."

"Rutherford?" Travenor spouted. "But, but—I heard him—he is to dance with Miss Marsh."

Miss Marsh smiled innocently. "Oh, no, Lord Travenor, you are mistaken. I am to stand up with Lord Marcus."

Very briefly, a black look of rage passed across Lord Travenor's face.

"You see, Travenor, *I* have not danced twice with Lady Phoebe," Rutherford said and leveled his quizzing glass at Travenor. "You, I think, are *de trope*. Shall I give you a hint? It is very bad *ton* to eavesdrop."

Lord Travenor opened his mouth to speak again.

Hester turned to John, saying clearly, "My dear, I believe after Phoebe has danced with Lord Rutherford, we should leave. I'm becoming fatigued, and we have a full day to-morrow."

Having had the wind taken out of his sails, Travenor finally left.

Hester narrowed her eyes, staring after him. "I would like to know how he came to think himself so important."

"What was that boorish behavior about? Who does he think he is?" Phoebe asked heatedly. "To talk about me as if I were a piece of property to which he has some rights. He—he is a *troll*."

As angry as Marcus was with Travenor for distressing Phoebe, Marcus knew he'd made substantial progress, and replied, "I will happily give up the name to him."

Phoebe's eyes flashed quickly to his and humor returned to her countenance. "Yes indeed. You've quite outgrown it."

Marcus turned to Miss Marsh. "Thank you, Miss Marsh, for being so quick-witted in offering your dance partner."

"It was my pleasure, my lord. I would gladly help any lady avoid dancing with"—she grinned at Phoebe—"a troll."

On her way home, Phoebe thought of nothing but the kisses and the waltzes she shared with Marcus. If she'd been alone in the coach, she would have touched her lips to see if they were still heated and swollen. She'd felt his physical response to her. It thrilled her she made him react that way. It was a power she'd never known before, or maybe never wanted to have over a man.

"I was very impressed by Lord Marcus," Hester said.

Phoebe glanced over at her sister, raising a brow.

"I mean that his manner is excellent, his conversation informed, and his—his . . . Well, no matter." She stopped. "Phoebe, are you any closer to knowing if you will accept him?"

"A little, I think." Phoebe glanced briefly at John. "I do not wish to discuss it right now."

Hester lapsed into silence.

Once at St. Eth House, Phoebe practically floated to her room. Her mind and senses were still focused on Marcus's kisses. Free to do so, she touched her mouth, remembering the feel of his lips brushing hers. The memory of the way he'd lifted her, holding her against his hard body, caused a strange tingle to arise in her, and she flushed with heat. She closed her eyes and sobered.

Her sisters were right. She couldn't go on this way much longer. Each time they were alone, she let him take more liberties with her person. Where would it stop? Any other man would have already pressed her to marry him—particularly after tonight.

But Marcus didn't press her, for that she was thankful, and his protectiveness felt right, as it should be between them. Phoebe sighed, snuggled down under the covers, and closed her eyes.

She was walking in a family picture gallery, sun lit half of it and a shadow moved from the doors at the end of the room. Phoebe woke punching her pillow. It was a few moments before she realized she was alone, safe in her bed.

Tearing open the bed hangings, she took large gulps of the cool night air. Was she deranged? No matter how she responded to Marcus when she was awake, that day still haunted her. Her mind and her body were at war with each other and her heart ached. How was she supposed to make a decision when she was so confused?

Afraid to return to sleep, she read until the hour or so before dawn, and then waited for Marcus to call. When he didn't, Phoebe wondered if he truly cared for her, or if the courtship was some game he was playing. She was certainly no longer in control.

* * *

The next day, when Marcus wanted to walk down the street to within a few feet of St. Eth House, he stopped himself. Ladies were usually tired after a late night, or early morning—and what if she did not wish to see him? Phoebe had not invited him to come and, surprisingly enough, there were no entertainments that evening.

By the following morning, Marcus could wait no longer. If he wasn't to go mad, he had to see Phoebe now. Marcus saddled his horse and arrived at St. Eth House at seven o'clock.

The door was opened by an astonished footman, who imparted the knowledge that Lady Phoebe had not yet come down, however, if his lordship wished, Ferguson would inquire if Lady Phoebe was awake.

Marcus was shown to a parlor.

Ferguson entered the room a few minutes later to inform him that Lady Phoebe would be down within fifteen minutes. Marcus settled in to wait. In his experience, no woman could be ready in under thirty minutes. She arrived ten minutes later.

He blinked at the radiant smile she gave him and wanted to take her in his arms.

"Good morning," she said. "What a lovely surprise this is. Ferguson tells me we are due for another warm day."

Returning her smile, Marcus took the hands she held out to him. It was the first time he had touched her bare fingers. He pressed his lips first to them.

Phoebe's cheeks turned a becoming shade of pink.

"Ah, Lady Phoebe, I've found another way to make you blush. Come, I hear your horse being brought round."

Pulling her by the hand, he started toward the hall until Phoebe stopped him. "What is it?"

Her tone was firm but kind. "Marcus, you may not hold hands with me through the house."

He gave her his best wide-eyed innocent expression. "Why can't I?" Before she could answer, he started walking toward the hall again.

Hearing her sigh behind him, Marcus grinned to himself.

"Very well," she conceded. "Just this once. It would not be very dignified to fight over it."

Phoebe removed her gloves from a pocket and was trying to fasten them as she walked through the door.

He took the gloves from her. "Allow me."

He held her hand, and though she gave him a surprised look, allowed him to fasten the buttons.

Her gaze searched his face. "Thank you," she said with a touch of confusion. Her mare whinnied when she saw Phoebe, and she used the excuse to regain her hand. "I've not had an opportunity to ride her in a few days."

Marcus admired the mare's points. She was as dainty a chestnut as he'd ever seen. Her bloodlines were obviously excellent.

Phoebe walked around his large roan. "Marcus, he is lovely. What is he, eighteen hands?"

"Yes." Marcus shook his head. "Is there anything you don't know about horses?"

She grinned. "Not much. What is his name?"

"Rufus. I bought him shortly after I returned."

When Marcus lifted Phoebe to the saddle, he heard her breath catch, and she glanced at him. He was pleased to see her as affected as he was. She had to know that their connection was growing, but she said nothing. Other than allowing him to kiss her and protect her, she'd given him no clue as to her feelings. How was he supposed to know if she loved him or would accept him?

Upon reaching the Park's gate, they urged their horses to a trot.

"I love to ride. How did you know?" she asked.

He kept pace with her as they headed toward Rotten Row. "Someone may have mentioned it to me the other evening."

"Ah," Phoebe said, smiling. "My sister or my brother-in-law?"

"Neither," Marcus responded. "Rutherford."

Phoebe put the mare through her paces. "Oh, Marcus, look at her. She's always so playful."

They reached the track on Rotten Row and Phoebe gave the horse her head.

Marcus admired Phoebe's seat and the light way she held her reins.

He pulled up behind her at the turn. "She's fast. I thought I'd catch you easily."

"She's like the wind, isn't she?" Phoebe's face glowed. "Uncle Henry said she had Thoroughbred in her line. She is wonderful."

"What is her name?"

"Lilly."

"Race you?" he asked.

Phoebe looked around and, seeing no one, she replied joyously, "Yes, why not!"

His heart swelled at the excitement on her face. My God, he loved her more every day.

They laughed and galloped back down the track. They were in no hurry. Breakfast would not be served for another three hours at least in either of their houses.

Phoebe had been so glad to see him this morning. More so than she thought she'd be. On horseback, she could study Marcus more easily than when driving her phaeton. His seat was excellent, and she was happy to see him so at ease with a horse he'd not had long. Rufus knew who was his master. Phoebe remembered what Marcus had said a few days ago about being used to having his orders obeyed. Now that she let herself, she could see it. Then it occurred to her that he was never on the go. Never smelled of brandy. His scent was more of leather, and the sea. His hands, when they touched hers, had been strong and slightly callused, as if he'd done manual work. She liked the feel of them.

As she urged Lilly to a trot, she realized he was letting her set the pace.

They were among a group of trees, when Marcus stopped. Phoebe reined in beside him, waiting.

He settled Rufus close to her then reached over to take her face to kiss her. Just at that moment, the horses decided to move apart. "Well, it was a good idea when I thought of it."

She laughed. It occurred to her that she'd wanted him to kiss her, even here, where anyone could ride past.

A low growl from her stomach caught her attention. "I'm famished."

Marcus nodded. "As am I. When I have a household of my own again, I'll order breakfast to be served early."

She turned Lilly toward the gate. "I'll wager if we go back to St. Eth House now, François, my uncle's chef, will find something to feed us."

"Lead on."

After they entered St. Eth House, Phoebe motioned to Marcus to follow her through the baize door leading to the kitchen.

With a brilliant smile on her face, she approached François, the St. Eth *chef de cuisine*. "François, we have been riding and are so very hungry. Will you feed us?"

He glanced from her to Marcus. *"Oui, milady. Naturellement."*

François gave them each a warm bun with honey before shooing them up the stairs to await their breakfast.

Phoebe took a place at the table and Marcus sat next to

her. Ferguson brought tea and she poured them each a cup. The buns were wonderful, tasting of honey and butter. She wondered what François would send up for the rest of their breakfast.

Marcus gave a satisfied sigh. "Phoebe, I can't thank you enough for the tea. I almost always have to have coffee at home."

That was very strange. Puzzled, she asked, "Why do you not ask for tea to be served if you don't like coffee?" It was the first time she'd ever seen him disgruntled.

"I asked for tea once, years ago, and my father gave me coffee. He was so adamant, I never asked again. I still feel like a guest at Dunwood House, as if I'll be returning to Jamaica. . . ."

She understood the feeling of not having a home. "As if you don't belong anymore?"

"Yes." He reached for her hands. "How did you know?"

Phoebe closed her fingers around his. "When Geoffrey married Amabel, I stayed just long enough to make sure she felt comfortable in her role and with our—their people. Now, although they both assure me it is still my home, I don't feel that bond anymore. It is no longer my place to make changes."

"Such as starting the orphan asylum?"

She smiled tightly. "Yes, that and other things. Responsibilities, which were mine for so many years, are now Amabel's. I have very little to do at the Place. No occupation to speak of. I am not used to being idle or superfluous."

Marcus studied her for a long time. Sensing the pain that loss caused her, he wanted more than anything to give her a home. But did he even have a home of his own to offer her? He made another vow. He'd find her a house to care for.

Phoebe slowly licked a bit of the honey from her lips, causing his body to spring into readiness. His breath seized and her gaze snapped to him as if she sensed his arousal.

She leaned toward him, and he stood, forgetting she would see evidence of his desire.

Phoebe rose and twined her arms around his neck, pulling him close until her body touched his.

Tilting her head up, he asked, "Are you sure?" She met him in a kiss.

She tasted like honey and her own citrus nectar. Marcus breathed deeply, taking in her scent. At his urging, Phoebe opened her mouth, and he allowed his tongue to caress hers. His hands seemed to move of their own accord, stroking down her supple back over her derrière, then up to gently skate over her breasts. Her nipples hardened, and at her soft cry of wonder, he drew her closer.

To his amazement, Phoebe moaned, pushing her breasts into his hands and her body as close to his as possible. She must love him. If only she'd say the words.

Footsteps shuffled outside the door. Marcus and Phoebe sprang apart in concord, then Marcus stepped forward, trying to shield her from sight.

The door opened. That was close. He'd be happy to declare them betrothed, but what would Phoebe think about that. No, as tempting as it was to end his slow torment, he would wait for her to make a decision. That was the only honorable path to a life with her, not that his recent actions fell into that sphere.

Ferguson and a footman brought in ham, baked eggs, cheese, fruit, and croissants.

Phoebe selected a croissant and handed it to Marcus. "Have you ever had croissants?"

"Yes, in Paris." Marcus's mouth watered as he bit into the flaky French confection. "These remind me of them."

Her eyes widened with surprise. "When were you in Paris?"

"Someday, I'll tell you." He fed a piece of croissant to

Phoebe, who in turn fed him forkfuls of ham and cheese. Lost each in the other, breakfast became a sensuous meal where the only touching allowed was the nourishing of the other.

Much laughter ensued. Marcus had never had so much fun at breakfast. They had begun to move closer to each other when the door opened and they sprang apart.

St. Eth walked in. His gaze focused first on Phoebe then on Marcus, but he remained ominously silent.

Marcus eyed St. Eth warily, knowing that if he'd been a few minutes later, her uncle would have interrupted more than them eating breakfast. Marcus bowed. "Good morning, my lord."

"Good morning, Uncle Henry," Phoebe added.

St. Eth walked to the table and said, "Good morning, my dear, Lord Marcus. Did you take the mare out this morning?"

Phoebe picked up her cup and held it tightly. "Yes, Lord Marcus came by to take me riding."

St. Eth moved his gaze to Marcus.

He opened his mouth, but Phoebe interrupted. "When we finished riding we were so hungry, and—and Lord Marcus said that breakfast wouldn't be ready at Dunwood House so then I thought . . . perhaps . . ."

Phoebe stopped as a slow blush rose to her cheeks.

"Yes, well, it was fortunate François was able to take care of you." Henry turned back toward the door. "Lord Marcus, if you've finished, I'll walk you out."

Marcus glanced at Phoebe. "I'll see you this afternoon at five?"

"Yes."

They all left the room together, and after a whispered,

"Good luck," Phoebe picked up the skirt of her habit, and swiftly climbed the stairs.

St. Eth said to Marcus, "Come with me."

St. Eth requested that his butler bring coffee. When they reached his study, he sat behind his desk, motioning Marcus to the chair in front of it.

But Marcus decided to remain standing. He wondered what St. Eth would say?

Once the coffee had been served and the door closed, Marcus said, "I assume, Lord St. Eth, you wish to know my intentions."

"Don't, I beg you, get on your high ropes with me. Please sit. I have no intention of thrashing you."

Marcus did as he was bade and waited. He had the distinct impression St. Eth was trying not to laugh.

After taking a sip of coffee, the marquis said, "I take it you have the same objectives toward Lady Phoebe you had when you spoke with Fairport."

"Yes, my lord, exactly the same."

"It looks to me as if progress is being made. I wanted to tell you that Lady Phoebe will be attending the Billingleys' ball this evening. You may accompany us."

Marcus stared in shock, unable to believe he wasn't going to be raked down.

"This," Henry continued, "is one of those occasions when we must decide whether it is better to take the carriage or walk, as it is just across the square. Lady Phoebe, I know, will wish to walk. She always does."

St. Eth motioned to the coffee-pot and other cup. Marcus shook his head and the older man went on. "Lady St. Eth will not decide until the last moment. I recommend you offer to escort Lady Phoebe on foot. I shall do my best to bundle Lady St. Eth into the carriage."

Marcus was stunned that St. Eth was still willing to help him.

St. Eth's tone became serious. "On another note, I received a message from Caldecott this morning. Lady Hester is concerned that you and Lady Phoebe will be found in a compromising position. Her fears are well founded, if what I witnessed in the breakfast room is any indication."

St. Eth waited, but Marcus remained silent. "Her main concern is if you are caught doing anything that would give rise to talk or, indeed, an immediate proposal of marriage, the *ton* will think you've offered for Lady Phoebe solely because you had no choice. That, as you must understand, would not be a comfortable position for either of you, or the families."

Marcus nodded. "Yes, sir."

"However," Henry said, "if you keep to your plan, the gossips should begin to notice you are being very particular in your attentions to Phoebe. That will stop any talk if something should happen."

St. Eth's brows lowered. "I depend upon *you* to insure you are not caught. It clearly isn't any good at all to rely on my niece to be discreet in this matter. She is, in general, a very sensible girl, quite up to snuff, but apparently not in this case."

He poured another cup of coffee. "Despite some of Lady Phoebe's independent starts, she has never set the gossips' tongues wagging. But, she is a babe in the woods when it comes to your courtship, and her usual good sense has gone begging. Though that might be to your advantage."

Henry fixed a stern gaze on Marcus. "Now as to your activities in my house . . . What the devil either of you thought you were doing in the breakfast room alone, not a servant in sight, *with the door closed,* is more than I can understand. You're very lucky it was I, and not Lady St. Eth, who came upon you."

Marcus had the grace to blush, something he had not

done in years. Neither he nor Phoebe had thought about the propriety of being alone in the breakfast room.

"Phoebe has agreed to drive with me again this afternoon at five o'clock. What time would you like me to arrive this evening?"

St. Eth smiled slowly. "You should dine with us. Lady St. Eth has a very good opinion of you, and you would be wise to cultivate it. We shall expect to see you at eight o'clock."

"My lord, there is something I wish to discuss with you," Marcus said gravely. "A fellow, Lord Travenor, who is apparently new to Town, at least no one I know knows him, has been very aggressive toward Lady Phoebe. Lady Hester and Caldecott were present the other evening when he accosted her. His behavior is such that we—Caldecott, Rutherford, and I—felt called upon to stop him. I would like your permission to protect her should the need arise."

St. Eth frowned. "If he does anything untoward when you are present, you have my permission."

"Thank you, sir. I don't think anyone recognizes how serious his threat may be to her." Marcus wanted to take St. Eth into his confidence, but if Phoebe found out Marcus was putting her in danger, she'd never agree to marry him. And he was so close to achieving his dream now. He couldn't allow anything or anyone to impede his progress.

Phoebe's mind was full of Marcus as she soaked in her warm bath. What did she feel about him now? It had taken her a long time to forgive him. No—not him—to forgive the young man he'd been.

She remembered that weekend as if it had just happened. What a wasted man she'd thought him. If she were perfectly honest with herself, she would not have been so angry with him or remained so angry if she hadn't felt something all those years ago. No other man had bothered her as he'd done.

Her thoughts were in a jumble. Why him? The question she had to answer, and soon, was did she want to marry him? She smiled as she remembered breakfast. They seemed to fit so well together. When she was with him riding or talking or in his arms, she had no doubts. He made her happy.

But if he came to make a formal offer . . . she sighed, still unsure.

Phoebe didn't think he was trying to trap her into marriage, but his touches this morning were so much more intimate. She'd been on fire. Who knows where it would have ended, if they hadn't been interrupted. Anyone could have walked in on them and then what? Why didn't she stop him? She chastened herself. *You liked it, that's why. You liked when he touched your breasts and put his hand on your derrière.* She'd never let any other man even kiss her before, and she was allowing Marcus to do as he pleased.

Her wanton body yearned for him, for his touch. What else would she permit him to do? The answer scared her. Anything. Then he could treat her as he wished, like he treated her before, because this time she would be a trollop.

He hadn't mentioned marriage again. Had Marcus decided he didn't need to wed her? That he could get everything he wanted without becoming a tenant for life? She put her head on her knees. *"What am I doing?"*

Phoebe attended an afternoon tea with her aunt and sisters at the home of Mrs. Waxsted, a friend of her aunt's and Phoebe's late mother. Mrs. Waxsted was a plump lady of medium height and light brown hair. She reminded Phoebe of nothing so much as a hen bustling around the room from chick to chick.

Miss Marsh waved, and Phoebe started to weave her way through the company to her friend sitting on a window seat.

"Lady Phoebe, my dear."

She turned to see Lady Worthington. Phoebe smiled. "Good day, my lady. How have you and your family been?"

"The girls are coming along nicely. I imagine you see more of my step-son than I do."

"Well, I have seen him at the political parties. I'm glad to see him taking an interest."

Lady Worthington's lips formed a slight *moue*. "I hear you have been seen in the company of Lord Marcus quite a bit lately."

Phoebe paused before answering. "Yes, I have been."

Lady Worthington took a breath, and said, "I have heard he has changed for the better, but I cannot help but advise you not to trust too easily. Sometimes change is not permanent."

Tension snaked up Phoebe's spine, but she kept the smile on her face. That is exactly what she feared most about Marcus, that he had not truly changed. "Thank you, my lady, for your concern."

Lady Worthington patted Phoebe's arm before moving away to speak with friends. When Phoebe finally reached Anna, her friend grinned and pulled Phoebe down to sit on the window seat. "Phoebe, how are you faring after *that man* was so rude the other evening?"

Phoebe had been thinking so much about Marcus, she'd almost forgotten about Lord Travenor. "Oh, I am quite well. Isn't it terrible of me to have so little sensibility? I'd forgotten all about the other gentleman—if one can, indeed, call him that. Thank you again for helping rescue me."

"Entirely my pleasure." Anna's eyes twinkled. "It gave me an opportunity to dance without worrying who would partner me. I am the only lady to have danced with Lord Marcus other than you this Season."

Phoebe chuckled. Anna Marsh was a very beautiful young lady of one and twenty years, with dark curling hair and a neat figure. Her manners were assured and her personality lively. She was never at a loss for a dance partner.

Anna's face became serious. "What will you do if Lord Travenor is so importuning as to approach you again? If the other evening's persistence is an example, it's unlikely he will soon take himself back to his county."

Phoebe closed her eyes briefly. "How I wish he would, yet if he doesn't, I shall have to rely on my friends to help me avoid him."

"What a bother for you." Anna lowered her voice so none but Phoebe could hear. "Now, I shall be impertinent. People are starting to notice that Lord Marcus Finley has become *very* particular in his attentions. He spends entire evenings dancing attendance on you, and I've just heard, when you were driving in the Park, he refused to allow you to walk with another gentleman."

If Phoebe had thought to prevaricate, the blush now infusing her cheeks would have told the truth.

"Aha, it is true," Anna said in a satisfied voice. "What a downcome for all those other ladies setting their caps at him."

Phoebe told her about Lord Beaumont. "Anna, I have never been so diverted. They have been friends for years, and it is so interesting to watch how men treat their favorite chums." She shook her head, remembering. "They are quite harsh with one another. If we hadn't been in the Park during the fashionable hour I would have gone into whoops."

Anna nodded. "Oh, I know what you mean. My brother and Lord Rutherford were forever saying the most awful things to one another, and they were fast friends. Men can be so different. Do you drive again with Lord Marcus?"

Phoebe grinned. "Yes, he is to drive me around the Park again this afternoon."

"Oh, how pleased I am for you, Phoebe," Anna said.

"Isn't this quite the first time you've allowed yourself to be driven at the fashionable hour? I have never seen you, but you are driving."

Phoebe stared at Anna. Was she right? When was the last time a gentleman drove her? "Do you know, I've never thought of it? It is the first time I've allowed a gentleman to drive me. But, tell me, *are* there ladies setting their caps at Lord Marcus?"

Anna looked at Phoebe as if she'd lost her mind. "Indeed they are. He's quite eligible you know."

"Oh?" She'd been so immersed in her own feelings she'd never thought that any other lady was interested in him. And now people were noticing the attention he was paying her. "I didn't realize . . ."

Anna took her hand. "Are you all right? You look a little pale."

"No, no, I'm fine. I just never expected to attract so much attention." Panic seized her. *Had* he been setting a trap? That would have been just like his old self. She had to get this courtship under control.

Chapter Fourteen

Phoebe stared at Anna.

"I have never known you to be such a pea goose!" Anna rebuked. "Lord Marcus Finley is the biggest catch on the Marriage Mart this Season."

None of this made sense. She'd admit he was well looking. Well, in all fairness, more than that, and was soon to be heir to a marquisate, but . . . "I wonder why he's so eligible."

Anna heaved a sigh and shook her head. "That's easy. Aside from his looks and prospects, he dresses fashionably, has a large personal fortune." She paused and glanced at Phoebe. "He has a quality about him. You should hear the romantic stories that are being put about concerning his time in the West Indies. He's every lady's current hero. A live Minerva Press hero."

Phoebe opened her eyes wide. "I've never thought about him that way. I didn't even know he had a personal fortune."

He did mention he'd been wealthy, but she thought . . . what had she thought?

"Oh dear, yes, why I've been told it is in the neighborhood of between forty to fifty thousand pounds a year."

Phoebe felt as if her breath had been taken away. "But, I

don't understand . . ." She seemed to be saying that a lot lately. "I've never seen any other ladies try to draw his attention."

Anna's eyes twinkled in amusement. "That is because he will look at no one but you. Every time he enters a room, he immediately searches for you, pretending blindness to all others until he's by your side. I cannot tell you the number of ladies who are waiting for you to knock him down so they'll have a chance."

Phoebe glanced around to insure no one was close and smiled. "Actually, I did knock him down once many years ago."

"Well, he must be the only one who didn't give up on you afterward," Anna replied sagely. "With you off the Marriage Mart, the rest of us will have more opportunity with the gentlemen left over. With Lord Marcus fixing his attentions, I know why I have been able to command so much of Lord Rutherford's time lately."

"Anna, what a bouncer!" Phoebe exclaimed. "You know very well Rutherford gave up on me long ago. He told me he could not marry a lady with a more punishing right than his."

Miss Marsh frowned. "Be that as it may, he has used you as an excuse for too long. One he will not have anymore, should you marry Lord Marcus."

Phoebe gave her friend a knowing look. "This Season promises to be more interesting than I first thought."

Lightly shrugging, Anna replied, "I don't know about that. Rutherford and I have known each other forever. If he has, indeed, decided to turn his attention to me, after having ignored me for so long, he will find he must earn the privilege."

Phoebe asked softly, "Have you loved him very long?"

Anna started to throw up her hands and stopped, as if remembering where she was. "Only all my life. I used to try to follow my brother Harry and him when I was just in pig-tails."

Anna's breath hitched and Phoebe remembered when her family had received word of Harry Marsh's death. He'd been killed in Badajoz during the Peninsular War. Anna's family's property was not entailed, and whomever she married would eventually own it.

"All funning aside," Anna said, "I need to know that he wants me for myself, and not for the property."

Phoebe knew how her friend felt. "Anna, you will know in your heart if he is sincere or not. But Rutherford, being Rutherford, it may take some time."

"I know, and I have time." Anna leaned toward Phoebe. "I don't need to marry to please anyone but myself. I take my example from you, my dear friend."

Phoebe laughed. "He'll have a hard road indeed. You know, Anna, if there is anything I can do to help, just ask."

"Yes, I will." She smiled. "But you will have a wedding to plan and a husband to care for and . . ."

"Lord Marcus hasn't offered yet." *He told me weeks ago he wanted to marry me, but he's never proposed.* "And, I am still not yet sure what my answer will be if he does ask."

"He will. Can you doubt it? The man is besotted." Anna gave Phoebe a knowing look. "If you do, you have not seen the way he gazes at you. And—well, never mind. It will all work out."

He hadn't told her he loved her recently. Would he renew his offer, and what would be her response? If only she could trust him.

That afternoon at five o'clock, Marcus glanced up as Phoebe descended the stairs. She was very fetching in a new carriage gown of royal blue with matching pelisse and a small hat with a feather that curled around her ear.

"How do you contrive to look more beautiful every time I see you?"

Phoebe smiled, but retorted, "Very pretty talking, my lord. You should know I don't like such flummery."

Taking her hand, he smiled into her eyes. "You wrong me, milady. Was a knight-errant ever so cruelly treated?" Marcus raised her hand, turned it over, and placed a kiss on her wrist. Phoebe blushed charmingly, just as he'd intended.

Once in the Park, he moved his curricle into the line of carriages crowding the path, and was pleased to note he and Phoebe were attracting even more attention than previously. They were halfway around their first circuit when they were hailed from a carriage pulled up onto the verge.

Giving Phoebe a speaking look, Marcus pulled his curricle to a halt beside the landau and greeted his mother and Lady Bellamny. Lately, his mother had not been in the way of joining the afternoon promenade and he wondered why she was doing so now.

"Mamma, Lady Bellamny, I didn't expect to see you here." Nor, Marcus thought, did he want to. He wasn't sure of Phoebe and didn't want to scare her off or raise his mother's hopes.

"Mamma, I believe you've met Lady Phoebe."

"Yes, of course, Marcus, your sister *is* married to her brother." Lady Dunwood addressed Phoebe. "My dear, I am very happy to see you again."

Marcus tried to stifle a groan. His mother glanced at him with narrowed eyes before turning back to Phoebe and smiling. "You are so far away. I cannot even shake your hand, my dear. Please come join us for a little. Marcus, help Lady Phoebe down. You may take a turn and fetch her when you come back around."

Even though Phoebe wished it, there was no avoiding this meeting. With good grace, Phoebe smiled politely at the two older women.

Once Marcus was gone, Lady Dunwood's conversation focused on Phoebe's life and views, in which she seemed genuinely interested.

Lady Bellamny, however, whom Phoebe had known since she was a child, was as disconcerting as ever. She was the perfect foil for Marcus's mother.

Taking advantage of their long relations, Lady Bellamny *did* ask her about Marcus, offering her advice and opinions. Between the two of them, Phoebe felt artfully interrogated.

She was relieved when Marcus maneuvered his curricle beside the landau. Saying all that was proper to the ladies and bidding them adieu, Phoebe changed carriages.

"I returned as soon as I could," Marcus said in apology. "I had trouble passing two landaus—one had pulled to the side, the other hadn't. They gave me such a look when I asked to pass."

"Your mother and Lady Bellamny probably planned it," Phoebe replied cynically.

His brow creased with worry. "Was it that bad?"

Phoebe pulled a face. "Not any worse than my sisters. Though if I had to lay a wager between your mother and Lady Bellamny against Wellington's Intelligencers, as far as interrogation skills, I would probably back the ladies."

He gave a low bark of laughter. "You poor thing."

Glancing at him, Phoebe replied, "Marcus, your mother is very lovely and astute. Lady Bellamny is, well, Lady Bellamny. She always could put me out of countenance. I just pray that they don't conspire with my sister, Hester. Hester ought to have run the Inquisition."

"I am sorry they put you through this on my account."

Phoebe mustered a tight smile. "It was not as bad as it could have been. Indeed, your mother is quite charming, and I am glad to have furthered my acquaintance with her. If you haven't spoken with her concerning our courtship, she no doubt wants to know what is between us."

The thrum of brittle tension running through Phoebe was palpable; she reminded him of a high-strung Thoroughbred, ready to bolt, and he prayed his mother and Lady Bellamny's collective curiosity had not set him back.

He covered Phoebe's hands with one of his. "I'll take you back to St. Eth House before anyone else decides to try to figure out what is going on."

Phoebe smiled gratefully. "Thank you, and thank you for not pressuring me. Most men would have done so by now. Especially after . . ."

They'd come to a brief stop in the traffic. Marcus captured her gaze and held it. "I will not use what is between us against you. I will not allow you to do anything that would stop you from marrying another man, should you decide you cannot marry me."

Phoebe's tone was a hoarse whisper. "Thank you. You are being very generous. I could not ask for more."

He'd kept his tone even and prayed she understood what it cost him to say those words. Just the thought of her marrying anyone else sent panic coursing through him. Did she even suspect that she held his heart in her small hands?

Rather than taking Phoebe straight back to St. Eth House, Marcus drove them out of the Park and around the streets until they were able to converse and joke normally again. When he escorted Phoebe to her door, he bowed. "I'll see you at eight. Your uncle invited me to dine with you and attend the Billingleys' ball in your company."

Her eyes widened. "He did? After this morning, I am surprised he didn't forbid me to see you. I played least in sight until I left to go shopping with my aunt and sisters."

Marcus grinned ruefully, but could share the jest with her. "Your uncle made the invitation and then raked me down. He blamed the whole situation on me. *You* he held completely innocent."

"I don't believe it." Phoebe made a disgusted face. "*I,* not responsible for my own behavior? He has always said I was quite up to snuff."

Marcus sat up straighter in mock consequence. "Ah, yes, but you have the benefit of being innocent of courtship. Whereas *I,* apparently, am not."

He shot her a glance. "Although, other than you, he suspects me of having courted, I assure you I have not the foggiest idea. *You*, on the other hand"—the ends of his lips curved up—" 'although quite up to snuff in the usual way, have allowed your good sense to go begging' when it comes to us."

"Uncle Henry did not say that?" she said, insulted.

"He did indeed, or something very like it. So, my love, I am the one to be held responsible if anything untoward occurs."

"What does he think could possibly happen?"

Marcus raised his brow and waited for her to remember this morning.

"Oh." Phoebe looked ridiculously guilty.

"Precisely."

She frowned. "Are we not to have breakfast together again?"

He couldn't help being pleased that she wanted to continue to break her fast with him. If only she'd give him a hint that she wanted to marry him. "Not unless there is a servant in the room and the door is left open."

Her hand flew to her head. "Oh, Marcus, I don't understand how I came to be so lost to propriety that I did neither of those things—"

"That, my delight, is what he meant when he said your wits had 'gone begging.' "

Her eyes widened. "What did you call me?"

Somehow, he had to move their courtship forward. He kept his tone even and caught her gaze. "I called you 'my love' and 'my delight.' Which is precisely what you are."

Phoebe glanced at him shyly. "No one has ever called me 'their delight' before."

Marcus wanted to crow, but tamped down his happiness and kissed her palm before closing her fingers.

He would ask her this evening. "Until tonight."

Phoebe dressed with care, wearing a new gown of rich brown with tiny translucent sleeves. The bodice, of pleated chiffon, formed a low neckline that framed the swell of her breasts. The heavier silk of the gown skimmed her figure. Her hair was dressed high in a tumble of curls, some of which were allowed to caress her shoulders. Pearl and amethyst drops adorned her ears, and a matching necklace encircled her throat. Rose draped a Norwich shawl over Phoebe's shoulders. An ornately carved fan and reticule completed her ensemble.

Marcus was in the parlor drawing room with Uncle Henry when Phoebe entered the room. She knew she looked well and was gratified to see the desire in Marcus's face as he watched her.

Phoebe walked toward him, smiling. For a moment their eyes caught. She almost forgot to greet her uncle first.

"Phoebe, my dear niece. I have never seen you in better looks."

"Thank you, Uncle Henry."

She raised her eyes to Marcus's, and her breath stopped at the look on his face. It was the same look he'd had when he kissed her.

Marcus took her hands and lifted one to his lips. "You are a *Vision*," he said, reminding her of the image he'd kept of her.

Henry cleared his throat.

Phoebe glanced around. "Oh dear . . ."

Both her aunt and uncle were staring at Marcus and her. "Good evening, Aunt Ester."

"Lady St. Eth, good evening." Marcus bowed.

Uncle Henry offered them sherry as the couples sat on the two love seats flanking the fireplace.

"Marcus, you must try this sherry," St. Eth said. "It is the best I've ever had."

Marcus took a sip and promptly agreed. "Sir, where did you find this? It is remarkable."

Henry smiled provocatively. "I've told Phoebe I will give some to her when she sets up her own house. However, Lady St. Eth tells me I'd do better to give it to her as a wedding present."

Phoebe gasped. How could he say that, when Marcus hadn't even offered for her?

Marcus regarded Henry, a grin dawning. "I daresay, sir, it would make a perfect wedding present. Do you think Lady Phoebe would insist on it being settled on her?"

Henry chuckled. "I wouldn't doubt it at all."

She glanced at her aunt, who had a perfectly benign look on her face, as if nothing untoward had been said. Was Phoebe the only one to think this conversation was strange?

Uncle Henry assisted Aunt Ester into the carriage and said, "Lord Marcus, I believe Lady Phoebe would rather walk. Wouldn't you, my dear? We will meet you at the Billingleys'."

She didn't know what to make of her uncle's deliberate action to allow Marcus and her time alone. In fact, both her aunt and uncle were behaving very strangely.

But Marcus started talking to her. As they strolled, they conversed in soft voices; Phoebe came to realize that she and Marcus were never at a loss for conversation. They had so many common areas of interest and were both curious about so many different subjects, the time passed all too quickly.

As they drew even with the St. Eth's carriage, which was very slowly moving up the queue to the door, Uncle Henry called to his coachman to stop. He climbed down and assisted Aunt Ester to descend.

Once their party entered the receiving line together, Marcus silently thanked St. Eth. Nothing could have made it clearer to those present, that Marcus's courtship had St. Eth's blessing.

"I see Miss Marsh and Rutherford," Phoebe said.

Marcus firmly entwined his arm with hers, and headed toward their friends.

Phoebe engaged Miss Marsh, and they were soon deep in conversation.

As Rutherford stood with Miss Marsh, her hand on his arm, Rutherford's hand over hers, Marcus had his question answered.

"As you see," Rutherford said.

Marcus grinned. "I wish you good luck. Have you seen Travenor?"

"No, and I don't wish to see him," his friend replied. "There is something very smoky about his manner. The other evening, I had the feeling Travenor wasn't who he presents himself to be."

Marcus responded, keeping his voice low, "He's not. I've received some information concerning his background, and I'm convinced he poses a danger to Phoebe."

"I agree." Rutherford nodded. "The man bears watching. Other than that, I don't know what else you can do. Speaking of Phoebe, I saw you arrived with the St. Eths. When may I expect to see an announcement?"

Marcus lowered his voice, again, so that it was barely above a whisper. "As soon as I convince her."

Rutherford's eyes lit with laughter. "More than willing to help you become a tenant for life. The conservatory here is considered to be quite a remarkable specimen."

Marcus acknowledged the hint, glad for the help. "Indeed? I'll have to visit it."

The strains of the violins began and he turned to Phoebe and asked if she would care to dance.

Marcus held her closer and more firmly than ever before, and she did not pull away, only stared at him intently. Their connection seemed to deepen and flare just that much more than the last time. He led them easily through the turns, holding her even nearer. His thigh touched hers and she trembled. Desire blazed in him, his muscles hardened and his blood heated.

Dragging her off the dance floor was out of the question. Talking might distract him. "It looks as though Rutherford means to offer for Miss Marsh."

Phoebe looked away, and it took her a moment to respond. "Yes, I had the same impression. Did he say anything to you?"

"Not in so many words. His actions made his intention clear."

"It would be a good match." Her tone was noncommittal, and she still wasn't looking at him.

Something was wrong. "At first, I thought he was dangling after you. That wasn't the case, was it? Do you think he had Miss Marsh in mind all along?"

Phoebe finally glanced at him. "How very perceptive you are. Other than during my first Season, when it seemed to be the fashion to fall in love with me," she said with self-deprecating asperity, "I believe you're right. Their families are very close, and they have known each other forever. Their lands march along one another's. I don't understand why he has waited so long."

Marcus shrugged. He could guess but would say nothing

to Phoebe. Rutherford needed to marry for the same reasons he did, but had been able to put it off as long as his mother thought he was interested in Phoebe. Since Marcus had shown his attentions so clearly, and Phoebe seemed to assent, Rutherford's mother, in addition to blaming him for not fixing his attentions sooner, began to tax him again to find a wife.

However, Marcus would not tell Phoebe. She, for some reason, had not realized how much as a couple she behaved with him. He would ask for her hand soon. He just wished he knew what Phoebe's answer would be.

Phoebe's sisters arrived about an hour after the St. Eths. Hester kept an eye out for Phoebe as she and Hermione ambled around the room, greeting their friends and acquaintances. Caldecott and Fairport joined Uncle Henry in conversation with some other gentlemen.

Ester smiled fondly at the twins as they joined her. Hester sat next to their aunt and Hermione took a chair next to the sofa.

"Aunt Ester, I have never heard such impertinence," Hester complained. "I don't know how many people have asked me if Phoebe and Lord Marcus will make a match of it. Of course, I said they would know if, and when, they saw an announcement in the *Morning Post*. I just wish *I* knew the answer."

"Indeed." Hermione pursed her lips. "They cannot go around smelling like April and May and not have people notice."

"Phoebe says she's still not made up her mind," said Ester grimly. "I think it more likely she won't admit it to herself."

Ester told them about the breakfast that morning and how taken they were with each other this evening. "Something must happen soon. At this rate, they will set the *ton* on their ears."

Whilst they'd been conversing, a series of country dances had played. When the beginning strands of a waltz were heard, the ladies' heads turned toward their husbands who immediately came to claim their dances. Coming together, the couples made their way to the set forming.

Marcus and Phoebe twirled down the floor as if in their own world.

"Look at them," Hester said to John. "They're hopeless. We need a betrothal, sooner rather than later, or there will be a scandal. Any ideas would be helpful."

After the supper dance, the couples made their way down the stairs. Determined not to say anything to Phoebe, Hester joined the lovers in the supper room. The ladies made gay conversation whilst the gentlemen fetched their refreshments.

The men were not so reticent. Marcus, sensing the mood, decided to steal the march on them. "I wish one of you will tell me if Phoebe has made up her mind. I don't know how much longer this can continue."

"Not much longer, I can tell you that." Fairport frowned. "We had every gossip in the room asking when they would see an announcement."

"Or trying to discover if there would be one," John added.

St. Eth shook his head. "If it were anyone but Phoebe, we would know her answer."

"I am open to any ideas to help her make her decision," Marcus said in exasperation.

"Let us think about it," St. Eth said thoughtfully. "We should be able to come up with at least one idea."

John grinned. "The conservatory."

Marcus turned to him. "That shall be my next endeavor."

As they finished eating, Marcus gently touched her shoulder. "Phoebe, have you seen the conservatory here? I am told it's remarkable."

Phoebe smiled. "Yes, it is. Very lovely. Come, I'll show you."

The conservatory was large for Town. It had winding paths, a fountain in the middle, and several benches tucked into arbors covered with tropical vines and other flowering plants.

"I have always been fascinated by the conservatory. I've never seen it in the evening before. Doesn't it look like a fairyland now, with the moon shining through?"

Marcus glanced at her. "It definitely looks like a fairyland. Do you know what these plants are?" he asked as they came upon some of the exotic flora he recognized from his travels.

"No, there should be a sign somewhere." She stooped down.

"No need." He helped her rise. "I'll tell you about them."

Meandering, Marcus led her down a path, pointing out plants and flowers as they walked.

She smiled brightly. "How wonderful. This is almost like an exploration."

At the end of one path, they came to a deep arbor covered in a sweet-smelling vine. Marcus led her into the arbor. Their eyes met once again. Her gaze dropped to his lips. He placed one long finger under her chin, tilted her head up, touching his mouth gently to hers.

He drew Phoebe closer, deepening the kiss. She opened to him with a soft breathy sigh, and he touched his tongue to hers. She melted into him, reaching her arms up around his neck and bringing her body against his. He groaned, and stroked her back, moving one hand down over her bottom, pulling her flush to him. Phoebe had to love him, to allow him to touch her like this. If she'd just admit it. He cursed himself for hurting her so long ago. If she married him, he'd spend the rest of his life making it up to her.

Marcus found her nipples already hard and tight and settled in to play. The fabric of her gown tightened across her swelling breasts. He applied more pressure, circling each nipple, encouraging her to arch against him. Her soft gasps and moans were music to his ears. Wanting her to pay attention to the sensations she was feeling, he lightened the kiss.

Phoebe gasped at his heat and the odd throbbing his touch caused between her legs. His hand caressed her as he had that morning. She struggled to keep up as he plundered her mouth. Her breasts ached, waiting for his touch again. Slowly his fingers slid up her sides until they reached her breasts. His thumbs caressed, skirting lightly over her furled nipples.

Phoebe shuddered as fissions of pleasure and desire shot through her.

"No," Phoebe protested when he removed his hands from her breasts back to her waist. "Leave them there." *What are you doing,* a part of her screamed. *Now you are encouraging him!*

"If I leave them there, I can't do this." Marcus cupped her derrière and drew her close.

Phoebe sighed when he pulled her back into the kiss, ignoring her conscience, she asked, "Can't you do both?"

Marcus gave a low chuckle. "I'll see what I can do to accommodate you." Holding her bottom in one hand he palmed one breast with the other. "Better?"

"Umm," she moaned.

Marcus whispered in her ear, "Phoebe, I want to ask you something."

Her breath came shorter. She was barely able to pay attention.

"Phoebe . . ."

She heard a light female voice and a deeper male one. "Marcus, someone is coming."

Quickly moving back, he twined his arm with hers.

Phoebe schooled her face into polite interest. Her body still shimmered with heat and desire. Guilt surged through her. Not only had she become a wanton, she had become abandoned as well, pretending nothing had occurred.

Just before the people came into view, Marcus pointed to a nearby trailing plant. "So you see, Lady Phoebe, that's the reason they call this the love vine."

Phoebe choked. Biting her lip, she glanced from the vine back to Marcus and met his eyes. The warm merriment in them almost undid her. She tried to control her voice. "That is very interesting, Lord Marcus. I had no idea you'd become such a botanist during your travels."

They inclined their heads to the couples who'd appeared on the path as Marcus steered them out of the arbor in the opposite direction as it circled back around to the door.

"Marcus, what we did . . . how I allowed you to touch me . . . Do you think I—I'm becoming a loose—"

He stopped her. "No, never. Nothing you decide to do would lessen my respect for you. Phoebe, haven't I shown you that?"

Later, she sat next to him in the carriage. Even though no part of him touched her, his heat penetrated her. Her body still thrummed with the feelings he evoked. She needed to think about Marcus and the way he made her feel, but could not concentrate when he was so near her. Who was she fooling? She looked forward to seeing him and enjoyed his company. With what he'd said tonight and before, she should be able to trust him. What was it that held her back?

Chapter Fifteen

The next morning turned to rain. Phoebe sat on her window seat, cursing the perversity of the weather, and hoped Marcus would make some excuse to call.

She went down to breakfast and toyed idly with her toast, while her tea grew cold. She wondered when it was that seeing Marcus in the morning had become so important to her existence.

She'd just resolved not to succumb to a fit of the blue devils when she heard the knock on the door and a low male voice. A few minutes later, Ferguson showed Marcus into the breakfast room.

Phoebe rose. Quickly walking toward him, her hands held out, she said, "I wondered if you'd come. I've been cursing the weather and oh, feeling so . . ."

"In the dismals?" He met her eyes and returned her smile with a charming one of his own. Marcus took her hands, holding them as Ferguson sent word to the kitchen and stationed a footman just inside the door.

"Yes, just that. Was it the same for you?" She searched his face.

"Exactly the same. I hoped you'd be up. I couldn't stay away. Not seeing you was making me maggoty-headed." Marcus's smile was slow and sensuous. "Besides, who else will serve me tea in the breakfast room?"

"Oh, you odious, odious man. Come get your tea." She laughed and poured him a cup. What would it be like to do this every morning? Without the footman standing guard, of course. Phoebe peeped over at Marcus, savoring the tea.

"Phoebe," he said, "this is very good. Is it your own blend?"

It surprised but pleased her that he'd noticed. But then again, she was beginning to realize he was different in so many ways. "Yes, it is. I'm glad you like it."

They ate their breakfast chatting about nothing and everything.

Uncle Henry entered the room, took his seat, greeting Marcus as if his presence at the table was normal, and asked for coffee. "What a change in the weather. It's been so fair, I'd forgotten that it is almost November."

Phoebe glanced at the window, watching rain-drops make paths down the pane. "It can't be almost November. My birthday comes before then, and it's not here yet."

Uncle Henry's voice was teasing. "Of course, how could I have forgotten? When is it?"

That was a good question. She turned to her uncle and stared. "What is the date?"

Uncle Henry rubbed his chin. "The thirteenth."

Already? "My birthday is this weekend. How could I have forgotten?"

"Phoebe, my dear," her uncle said, "you've become most scatterbrained lately. Would you like to take a small party and go to the manor house in Berkshire?"

"That would be perfect." She turned to Marcus as if it was the most normal thing in the world. "You'd like that wouldn't you?"

Marcus replied, "Indeed I would, if your uncle will allow it."

Sitting back, St. Eth grinned. "Delighted to have you join us, my boy."

Phoebe started to plan. A small party, her family and . . . "Marcus, we could also ask your parents if they'd like to join us, and Hester, Hermione, John, Edwin, and, of course all the children. Uncle Henry, is there anyone else you'd like to invite?"

"No, my dear," he said. "I think that'll be enough on such short notice. Ester will want to know our arrangements."

"Oh, yes, of course." Phoebe held out her hands to Marcus. "It's so unfair for the weather to have upset our ride. When do we meet again? Do you attend the Moreland ball this evening?"

Marcus smiled at her. "Yes, my delight, I'll be there."

"Will you join us?" she asked a little shyly.

"I'd like nothing better."

"I'll see you at nine o'clock." Phoebe took her leave and went in search of her aunt.

St. Eth shook his head. "Come with me." When they reached his study, he turned to Marcus. "When do you plan to ask her?"

"I tried last night, but we were interrupted." Marcus ran his hand through his hair, frustrated. "We are never alone long enough."

St. Eth was quiet for a few moments. "I'll arrange for you to have the time you need this weekend. *Do not* disappoint me."

Marcus nodded, but his most frequent fear prompted him to ask, "What if she won't accept me?"

St. Eth raised a brow. "You will just have to be persuasive."

* * *

Ester glanced up as Phoebe entered her parlor.

"Aunt Ester, Uncle Henry suggested we go to the manor house for my birthday. I think it's a wonderful idea. What do you think?"

Ester had already sent a note to the manor house staff and approved François's menus for the weekend. "Yes, my dear. I agree. Whom do you wish to invite?"

"Well, my sisters, of course, and I thought we could invite Lord Marcus . . . and his parents."

"That will be delightful." Ester entered into Phoebe's preparations with zeal. Ester sent notes to Hester and Hermione, who'd been forewarned, before penning a more formal invitation to Lord and Lady Dunwood.

Surely, Phoebe was contemplating accepting his proposal. "Phoebe, do you know yet if you will agree to marry Lord Marcus?" The look on her niece's face reminded her of a wild animal being cornered.

"I'll decide soon, I promise." Phoebe fled the room.

Ester sighed and rang for her dresser.

Later that morning, Henry joined her. "Have you spoken to Phoebe?"

"Yes," Ester said. "Phoebe still doesn't yet know if she will accept him."

"What in the name of God ails that girl?" Henry paced the room. "It's clear to anyone with eyes she's in love with him, and she's invited both Marcus and his parents to her birthday party. Doesn't she realize that is tantamount to an acceptance of his offer?"

"My dear." Ester closed her eyes for a moment. "For Phoebe, it is not that simple. She's waited all this time to find the right gentleman. All the prodding in the world from us will not bring her around. We must leave it to Lord Marcus to persuade her."

Henry stood thinking for a bit, and then, in a determined voice, said, "Ester, I want to insure they have time alone together this weekend. I've told Lord Marcus he must convince her. You know, as well as I, this state of affairs cannot go on without some sort of resolution. If she's not betrothed soon, she'll be labeled a flirt. Nothing could be more damaging to her reputation."

Ester sighed wearily. "My dear, the only one who doesn't seem to realize it is Phoebe. They'll have their time alone. I'll tell Hester and Hermione not to play gooseberry."

Phoebe fled up the stairs to her room and the comfort of her window seat. What was she to do? She had invited his parents. He'd have to offer soon, and she would need to have an answer. Pressing her head against the chill of the windowpane, she blinked back tears of frustration, loathing the unexpected burst of panic. She was being foolish beyond permission.

Maybe Aunt Ester was right and Phoebe should just look at who he is now. But could she?

Drawing her knees up, she hugged them to her. Could she live without Marcus? What would happen if she had another bad dream about him after they were married, and he saw her remembered fear of him? If she did not decide soon, it would be taken out of her hands. Perhaps that wouldn't be so bad.

Phoebe lowered her head to her knees.

That evening, Marcus kept her with him. Greeting friends and ignoring the calculating looks they received from the gossips, he strolled the room with her. Once again he and Phoebe formed a circle of friends, which included Lord Rutherford and Miss Marsh.

Having danced their two waltzes and gone down to supper together, the two couples decided to find Miss Marsh's mother and Lady St. Eth when Phoebe was once again confronted by Travenor.

Huffing up to her, he said belligerently, "Lady Phoebe, I demand you grant me this next waltz."

Phoebe's eyes narrowed. "You what?"

Every protective instinct in Marcus rose to her defense, and he pulled her closer. Travenor would never touch her, if Marcus had his say. His tone was icy when he said, "Travenor, I am escorting Lady Phoebe to her aunt. They are preparing to leave."

With Phoebe on his arm, Marcus took a step. Travenor stopped them by the expedient of moving in front of Phoebe. Marcus whisked Phoebe behind him, and clenched his hands into fists.

Marcus would have liked to have drawn Travenor's cork and would have, had they been in Jamaica. Instead, Marcus fixed Travenor with a hard look and pitched his voice in a low threatening growl. "Travenor, I don't know where you learned your manners, but I suggest you return for more lessons. I warn you, now. Do not attempt to approach Lady Phoebe again."

Travenor stood rooted in place, his mouth open, breathing heavily.

Not waiting for his response, Marcus turned to Phoebe, smiled to reassure her, then escorted her to her aunt.

Phoebe's voice shook in rage. "What a horrible man. Why does he persist?"

"Veritable troll," Marcus said.

He was relieved when Phoebe gave a small smile at his joke. If they were betrothed, then Phoebe could dance only with him. He'd have to find some way to make it happen.

*   *   *

Phoebe rushed to the window the next morning then chastised herself. Fine behavior for a lady of almost four and twenty. She could have been in her salad days for all her girlish impetuosity, but the weather was dry to-day, if not sunny, which meant she could ride.

Ringing for Rose, Phoebe washed and dressed quickly.

Lilly was being brought round just as Marcus rode up. He lifted Phoebe into her saddle, and her heart stopped as the now familiar sensation struck. The more he touched her the more she wanted him. Phoebe watched as he mounted Rufus in a single fluid movement and wished she hadn't met him until this Season.

An hour later saw them back at St. Eth House, once again asking François for breakfast. In François, the lovers had found a kindred spirit. He was a romantic, and his ability to further their romance appealed to the Frenchman's heart.

Ferguson once again stationed a footman inside the door to the breakfast room and left the door open.

Not long afterward, Henry took his seat as Ferguson poured him coffee. "Lord Marcus, it's rather last minute, but I think it would be a good idea if you were to drive down with us to-day, rather than waiting for the rest of the company to-morrow."

Uncle Henry took a sip of his coffee. "With the addition of the family and the children arriving then, it is likely to be pandemonium. The weather is fairly warm and dry. You may drive Phoebe in your curricle."

Marcus glanced at her, sitting next to him. "Phoebe?"

Her heart for some reason was lighter. "Yes, I think it's a wonderful idea. But I don't understand what the children have to do with anything." She waited, but neither Marcus nor Uncle Henry deigned to explain it to her.

Marcus leaned forward to see Uncle Henry. "Thank you,

my lord. I shall inform my parents. Do you still depart after luncheon?"

Henry nodded and took the plate Ferguson offered. "An early luncheon, yes. You may join us, if you're here at eleven o'clock. We'll leave immediately afterward."

She hadn't had an opportunity to drive the whole team for some time. The trip to the manor house would be a perfect opportunity to do it. "Marcus, let's take my blacks. We can take the whole team."

He'd taken a sip of tea and sputtered. "You know how to drive a team?"

Phoebe was perplexed by his reaction. "Well, of course, don't you?"

He shook his head slowly. "Other than making a very bad job of it on a stagecoach once, I've never done it. I'm very impressed that you can."

She narrowed her eyes and pressed her lips together. Was he actually saying what she thought he was? "You were one of those young men that got foxed and caused a wreck?"

Marcus flushed and nodded bashfully.

Phoebe opened her eyes wide in disbelief. "How could you have been so stupid?"

Henry choked, trying to hold back his laughter.

Marcus grimaced. "You do know that I was very wild in my youth."

Of course. She'd gotten into the habit, when near him, to think of Marcus only as he was now. But she could very well imagine him doing it before. "You wouldn't do so now would you?"

He crossed his fingers over his heart and grinned. "Absolutely not. On my honor. I am much older and wiser."

Satisfied he was telling her the truth, she said, "Well, then, I shall teach you. It's not that difficult. By the time we

arrive at the manor, I daresay, you shall be perfectly proficient."

Uncle Henry set down his cup. "Phoebe, my dear, I have
no wish to cast aspersions on Finley's abilities, but what
will happen if he doesn't pick it up quite as quickly as you
hope?"

She sat up straighter. "I shall drive, of course."

Henry raised both brows. "Not on a major post road. It
wouldn't do."

"Oh, you're right." Only someone like Lady Lade would
tool a carriage on a post road. Drat.

When Phoebe pulled a face, Marcus took her hand and
squeezed it.

"Phoebe, let's just take a pair. I can easily manage them,
and we may share the driving. You can teach me how to
drive the team later. I can't tell you how excited I am that
you'll trust me to handle your horses."

"Yes, I suppose that is the only thing to do."

That decided, they discussed the arrangements for their
trip to the manor. The curricle being a much faster conveyance than Uncle Henry's coach, Phoebe and Marcus
arranged to meet Henry and Ester at the Golden Ball, an
inn known to Phoebe and the St. Eths, for tea, before continuing on to the manor together.

Marcus raised Phoebe's hands one at a time to place a
light kiss on them. She wished she could kiss him and have
his strong arms around her. Phoebe stood, watching him as
he strode through the door and onto the walkway. Would
what she was feeling for him now last? She would give him
her decision this weekend.

Marcus found his father in the study and explained that
St. Eth wanted him to leave to-day. Lord Dunwood balked

at the change in plans, until his wife came into the room. Upon hearing of the invitation, she arched a brow at her husband and gave her full approval to the plan.

His father immediately agreed.

A few hours later, Marcus stood amazed and impressed at the large cavalcade in front of St. Eth House. One baggage coach, a carriage for the upper servants, another for the lower servants, who would augment the skeleton staff at the manor, and the elegant conveyance in which the St. Eths would ride.

Upon being assured by Phoebe this was very common for a four-day trip, Marcus laughed. "I've been away from England too long."

St. Eth glanced at him with an amused expression. "If you think this is extraordinary, you should see the twins when they set off with the children. Come to think of it, you will see them when they arrive to-morrow. Prepare yourself to be stunned. Their entourage is madness. Let's be on our way."

Marcus's curricle was brought up with Phoebe's blacks harnessed to it. That Phoebe would allow him to drive her horses had humbled him. In general, she did not allow anyone other than her coachman or her groom to handle her cattle.

As agreed, she tooled the curricle out of London, keeping the team well up to their bits as she maneuvered through the busy London streets. Once they reached the main toll road out of London, Marcus took the ribbons.

The day was fine and dry, the countryside interesting. They arrived at the Golden Ball to be greeted by the inn's landlord.

Phoebe, having visited many times before, greeted the landlord warmly. "Good afternoon, Mr. Bagwell. How are you and your family doing?"

The man flushed. "Good day to you, Lady Phoebe. We are very well, thank you for asking, m'lady. My rib being most particular glad you've come."

Phoebe introduced Marcus to the innkeeper.

The innkeeper led them to the parlor St. Eth had reserved. Taking off her gloves, Phoebe asked that tea be brought and informed Bagwell that her aunt and uncle should arrive within the half hour.

There was much to admire about the inn. Built in the Elizabethan era, the Golden Ball was mainly stick and waddle construction, with a rush roof and mullioned windows. The rooms were large but low, the ceiling in the parlor less than a foot over Marcus's head. Though the day was warm for October, the fire burning in the large hearth was welcome and gave the room a feeling of cozy comfort. Removing his gloves and drab sixteen-caped driving coat, he joined Phoebe at the fire where she warmed herself.

Alone for the first time that day, Marcus sighed as Phoebe walked into his arms. This is what he wanted, always, to hold her and keep her safe with him. Standing still and content, they embraced each other until a knock announced their tea.

Mrs. Bagwell and her daughter brought tea, wine, sherry, an assortment of sandwiches, small cakes, biscuits, bread, cheese, and fruit.

"My Lady Phoebe"—Mrs. Bagwell bobbed a curtsey, curiosity burning in her eyes—"Mr. Bagwell and me are very happy to see you. A sight for sore eyes you be, and that's a fact." She flushed. "You and your young lord here."

Phoebe introduced the landlady to Marcus. As he closed the door behind the innkeeper and his wife, Mrs. Bagwell said to her husband, "Mr. Bagwell, I believe Lady Phoebe is finally in love."

Marcus sincerely hoped that was the case. Otherwise, he didn't know what they were doing. He returned to Phoebe, drew her back into his arms, and kissed her. She responded eagerly and held on to him as he stroked her. When his hands reached her already swollen breasts she moaned, melting against him.

"I love the way you make me feel."

He heard the wheels of a coach crunch on the stone drive, and silently cursed. "Phoebe, your aunt and uncle are here."

"Oh, no."

Marcus opened the door and took a place at the table.

Phoebe was preparing the tea when Lord and Lady St. Eth entered. She glanced up. "There you are. Would you like tea or sherry?"

"I'll drink tea." Ester sat on the other side of Phoebe, eying her carefully.

"I'll have tea as well, my dear," Henry said. "How long have you been here?"

Pink tinged her cheeks. "Not long. Mr. and Mrs. Bagwell were happy to see us, and we exchanged pleasantries for a bit. I love this area. I don't know why I do not come more often."

While Phoebe poured, Marcus passed the dishes and asked St. Eth, "The house is not much further is it?"

"No," Henry said, as he finished his sandwich. "Shall we be on our way?"

Now that they were off the major roads and Phoebe could drive once more, Marcus settled back to enjoy watching her handle the ribbons. An hour later, she skillfully feathered the turn through the gates of a tree-lined road to the manor house, which ended in a circular drive around a flower bed of the same shape.

When they stopped at the house, Marcus admired the reflection of the sun on the many-paned, floor-to-ceiling windows butting out along the front, which, in earlier times, would have served as the main part of the building.

Most of the red brick and half-timber manor, he'd been told, dated from the Elizabethan times, with additions from later years.

Phoebe introduced him to Mr. and Mrs. Jenkins, the care-takers, when the couple came to greet them. Once inside, Mr. Jenkins escorted Marcus to his room. As the other coaches had not yet arrived, Mrs. Jenkins had the parlor maid bring warm water to Ester and Phoebe. They met again in the morning room, where Mrs. Jenkins had laid out tea.

Lady St. Eth groaned. "I never know if Mrs. Jenkins will decide to have tea for us or not. It is completely perverse. If I expect her to have tea ready, it is not. Yet, whenever we stop at the Golden Ball for tea, Mrs. Jenkins invariably serves it. With such old retainers, one does not wish to of-fend, yet I wish I knew the reason she cannot remember in-structions." Lady St. Eth gave an exasperated smile. "We must do our duty to at least some of this repast, or she will be insulted."

"Phoebe," St. Eth said, when they had finished eating, once again. "Take Lord Marcus around the house and grounds. Ester is feeling a little tired and plans to rest."

"Yes, do, my dear," her aunt urged. "There is no reason to waste such a lovely day. We'll not have many more left."

Phoebe stared at them both, bemused that they were en-couraging her to be alone with Marcus. Though since she wanted that as well . . . "That is a wonderful idea."

She rose and held her hand out to Marcus. The heated glance he flashed her, as he tucked her arm in his, caused a flutter in her stomach. "We shall see you later."

Chapter Sixteen

Phoebe's anticipation built as she led Marcus out through the front and around to the rose garden on the side of the house. Phoebe loved the house and was happy to show it to him. The outer wings had been extended and enclosed to form two inner courtyards. The front doors opened onto a huge room with an immense fireplace and stone floor. Carved beams decorated the high ceilings. Due to wings added during later periods, the house was larger than it looked. Fortunately it did not suffer, as did many houses, from later additions that detracted from the original style of the house and made it a warren of halls and unused rooms.

She took him on a quick survey of the ground floor and then out to the garden, complete with an original Elizabethan knot garden and a maze.

He drew her closer to him. "Do you like to garden?"

She gazed up and into his azure eyes and smiled. "I like the results, but I have more interest in the stables."

"Ah." He returned her smile and his arm circled her waist. "A good head gardener will be an essential to your house."

"Yes, I love the flowers." She placed her arm around him

as they continued to amble through an arch in the tall laurel hedge. His palm stroked over the swell of her hip and heat streaked through her. She caressed his back and turned to him.

His voice was low and warm. "Phoebe, my love."

Marcus caressed down over her derrière and back up to her breasts. She tilted her head up, and he covered her lips with his. His tongue teased her bottom lip, and she opened to let him in. Reaching up, she twined her fingers around his neck, enjoying the intimacy of his tongue exploring her mouth. She sighed, and returned his caress. Someone sneezed. Was there no place where they could be alone?

Marcus fluttered kisses from her lips to her ear, and whispered, "Shall we go in?"

She stole a glance at him, his eyes had darkened with desire. "If you'd like."

Re-entering the house through a parlor at the end of one wing, giving on to the terrace, Phoebe barely noticed the room had been recently cleaned and the fire lit.

Marcus came up behind her and placed his arms around her waist. After pulling her back against him, he dipped his head and, with the tip of his tongue, lightly traced the outer whorl of her ear. Phoebe loved how he touched her, and tilted her head to one side, encouraging him to continue. She sighed as his lips moved down to her jaw and on to her throat. She could stay like this forever. Reaching back, she touched his thighs; they flexed, growing hard as rock.

His thumbs stroked over her ribs, shivers of sensation rippled through her as his palms moved up her body and finally reached her breasts. Phoebe moaned, wanting more, wanting him. She arched against him as he found her nipples, already aching for him.

Marcus rolled them gently and intense rapture sliced through her. She sighed as Marcus pressed soft kisses caressingly down the line of her neck, while his hands teased her. Phoebe pushed into his hand, trying to gain relief from the feelings assailing her. She never tired of his touch. Her body throbbed with need. He could give her so much more, if she but dared. Phoebe was lost in the sensation of fire flowing through her body, the strange heat at her core.

He turned her toward him. Her eyes were closed as he bent his head, feathering his lips against hers. When she opened her mouth, he entered, kissing her deeply.

Phoebe breathed through him as the heat of his tongue played against hers. Tasting him, she returned his kisses more ardently than she ever had before. Her body melted into his as she slid her hands over his chest to his shoulders, wrapping them around his neck. His hands seared a path over her spine and down over her bottom then back up her sides to attend once more to her heavy breasts.

How could she think? She was drowning in his kisses, her body aflame under his hands. Her nipples were tight and so sensitive as he played with them.

His erection rode against her stomach, and she tried to move closer to him as she shuddered again. One hand left its breast and swept slowly down her back to caress her, then moved lower. There was no space left between them. Marcus held her more tightly, his hard thighs against her. Their kiss, ever deepening, caused the fire flaring through her body. All her concentration was on their kisses and his hands and his hard body, the heat between them. Marcus eased back. "Phoebe, darling, will you marry me?"

She gazed up at him and searched his face. Love, passion, and fear mingled as he looked down at her. This was it. She had to respond. If she didn't, he'd leave and that thought was unbearable.

Phoebe prayed she was making the right decision. "Yes, my love, I will marry you."

Marcus pulled her back into the kiss. His urgency showed as he ravaged her mouth. She opened her lips to welcome his plunder. His hands stroked harder, more possessively.

He swooped her into his arms and carried her to the daybed set between two long windows. He held her on his lap and her bodice and stays sagged.

Marcus touched the tip of his tongue and lips to her neck, moving slowly down to one breast. He licked her nipple, gently drawing it into his mouth. She gasped at the intense feelings and writhed against him.

Phoebe kissed him as if she could find the release she sought. He licked and suckled until she was in a frenzy. Marcus replaced his mouth with his hand and ministered to her other breast.

The strange pooling of warmth between her thighs intensified with a throbbing she'd never felt before. She lifted her hips and his hand moved from her stomach down to the place between her thighs.

Over the fabric of her gown he pressed his fingers between her legs, silently asking. Answering, she opened her thighs a little, and he pressed closer, deeper, until his hand was completely between her legs. His fingers played, making her more frantic than she'd thought possible. Her breath came in short pants as if she'd been running. She was unaware of anything other than the fire, the need, the sensations racing through her.

Thank God she had agreed to wed him. He could not have borne it if she'd refused. Marcus moved his hand to the hem of her skirts. His touch teased her inner thighs as it traveled slowly upward until he stopped at the apex between her legs and toyed with the wet curls of her mons. Fondling her, he reveled in her heat and the slick wetness. He may not be able to seek his release, but he'd show her some of the passion and love she would find in their marriage bed.

Marcus increased the pressure until she was sobbing and begging him. Slowly he inserted one long finger into her hot wet sheath.

He moved back from the kiss just enough to encourage her to focus on the feeling of his finger deep within her, to the pleasure he gave her. "Phoebe, feel me touching you, loving you."

She pressed against his hand and contracted, on the verge of release.

He tried not to think about how she'd feel tightening around his shaft.

Marcus's body was like a rock. His muscles bunched, his erection raged. He had to fight himself to keep to his path. Slow, he told himself. He needed to show her how much enjoyment he could give her.

He moved his palm over the small pearl of her mons, rubbing harder as his fingers found their rhythm, driving her higher and higher until she cried out in ecstasy.

Marcus held her gently. A smile played around her rosy, swollen lips. He shifted her closer to him. Enjoying her limp warmth, he knew a peace he'd never experienced before. He was glad the instructions St. Eth had given him to this room were so clear. Her uncle had told Marcus that he and Phoebe would be left alone so that Marcus could convince Phoebe to marry him.

She was his. His to love. His to protect, and protect her he must. Travenor might still be a problem. Marcus had wanted to tell her how dangerous the man was, *but Marcus couldn't take the chance that she'd refuse him because he was the reason she could be in peril.*

The sun was low in the sky, casting long shadows across the room, when she stirred. He met her eyes, searching them.

Phoebe smiled.

He kissed her. "I love you, Phoebe. I've always loved you."

Her lips lingered on his. "I love you too. I did at the house party as well. I think that was the reason I was so angry at you. The way you'd wasted what life had given you. Mamma was right," Phoebe said. "When I look at you, it's as if I've never truly seen a man before. Others don't exist for me anymore."

Tears started to burn Marcus's eyes, and he kissed her softly. "We'd better go. Someone will be looking for us soon. The other carriages should have already arrived."

He placed her on the floor and fastened her stays and bodice, wishing he didn't have to cover her perfect creamy mounds. "When do you want to tell your family about our news?"

Phoebe tried to shake the creases out of her skirts. "When we meet in the drawing room. I'll ask Ferguson to bring champagne, if we have it."

Marcus grinned. "I don't think you need worry. I am very sure St. Eth remembered to bring champagne or sherry, perhaps both."

Phoebe entered her room to find Rose pacing. "My lady, where have you been? I was about ready to start folks looking for you."

Phoebe smiled. It hardly seemed real, that she would wed Marcus, and she was glad about it. "Rose, you may wish me happy. I am to marry Lord Marcus."

Her brow furrowed. "If you're happy?"

Phoebe took her maid's hands. "I am, Rose. I detested him for years, and I let myself be tortured by it. I think the reason I was so hurt and so angry was that I cared for him and felt betrayed. That he would treat me so. We are lucky, I

think, to have found one another again and were able to
heal the wounds of the past."

"Then I do wish you happy, my lady," Rose said, adding
in a brisk voice, "and about time it is that he asked too."

Phoebe laughed as Rose set out her clothes.

Phoebe reached the top of the stairs just as Marcus came
out of the other wing. She glanced up at him, the man who
would be her husband, her lover.

He held out his hand and she took it. His gaze captured
hers just like it had the first time. When he looked at her
like that, all her doubts faded and she knew she did love
him.

Uncle Henry coughed. "Once you two have quite assured yourselves that the other is present and not part of
your imaginations, you may join us in the drawing room."

St. Eth descended the stairs with Aunt Ester on his arm.

Entering the drawing room, Ester, who had kept her lips
firmly together on the stairs, lost the battle and went into
whoops. "I believe the matter is settled. I have never seen
two people so enthralled."

Henry met her gaze, and grinned. "Were we ever such a
sad case?"

"I don't think so, my love, but like them, we wouldn't
have known. On the other hand, our love was simple and
straightforward. Theirs has been hard won."

Henry, who didn't think winning Ester had been at all
simple, had to, in fairness, acknowledge that Phoebe and
Marcus had had a much harder and longer road. "Are we to
act surprised when they announce their betrothal?"

"I think we can simply express our joy. *That* will not be
feigned." Ester wiped her eyes.

"No, it won't." Henry drew her to him. "Was it right
what I did—allowing Lord Marcus so much time alone
with Phoebe to persuade her?"

St. Eth's sense of propriety and his conscience had pricked him during the afternoon as he tried not to imagine what was going on. He'd insured Marcus knew where the room was and the staff was told to stay away.

"I think we'll know in a minute."

Phoebe and Marcus's voices were at the door. Releasing Ester, Henry said in an under voice, "I had no idea it took so long to descend our stairs. It is marvelous indeed."

Ester poked him in the ribs. "Hush."

Phoebe entered, looking radiant.

"I have asked Ferguson to bring champagne," Henry said.

Meeting his gaze she said simply, "Thank you, Uncle Henry. That would be especially appropriate."

Marcus added, "Did you, perchance, bring any of your special sherry?"

Henry turned to Marcus and shook his hand. "I take it this is your way of announcing your betrothal?"

Marcus took Phoebe's hand and raised it to his lips. "Lord and Lady St. Eth, Lady Phoebe and I have decided we should suit."

Ferguson brought in the champagne, sherry, and glasses. Before leaving, he turned to Phoebe. "Lady Phoebe, the staff would like to wish you happy. You as well, Lord Marcus."

"Thank you, Ferguson," she said, "and thank the staff for their good wishes."

François, stating he knew he would have a celebration that evening, had prepared a meal they would not soon forget. Since he'd brought delicacies from London, they were served a first course of turtle soup, roasted turbot and pheasant in mushroom sauce. The second course consisted of cauliflower, *haricot verts*, Brussels sprouts, buttered lobster, a haunch of venison, thin slices of ham, and a roasted goose stuffed with chestnuts. They enjoyed pastries, nuts, and fruit for the third course.

The gentlemen declined port in the dining room to join the ladies.

Henry poured the sherry, which reminded Phoebe of Henry's promise. "Dear Uncle Henry, let's discuss the sherry."

Henry assured her that he would indeed settle the sherry upon her.

Phoebe went to him and hugged him. "Thank you."

"Thank you, my dear, for finally deciding to marry."

Phoebe tried but failed to look offended. "Has it been so bad?"

"My dear, we all love you very much, but you are the most active, brilliant, exhausting person we know." Uncle Henry grimaced. "The idea of setting up your own household—which I have no doubt you would have done—acting as if it were the most natural thing in the world, *and* carrying it off in your high-handed manner, doesn't bear thinking of."

Marcus turned Phoebe to him. "My love, you wouldn't have, would you?"

Ester laughed. "Marcus, had you not come along when you did . . . well, I will only say that our Phoebe is equal to anything. I am very pleased she is marrying you." Ester turned to Phoebe. "After the way you looked at each other with such love, it is what we all wanted for you, my dear."

Phoebe fought tears. Was it true? Would she finally have the kind of love her sisters and aunt knew?

The family's bedchambers were located in the east wing of the house, the guest chambers in the west wing. The wings were connected by the original hall and the grand staircase, which led up to the first and second floors. Smaller stairs at the ends of each wing were used, for the most part, by the servants.

Phoebe lay in her large bed, the hangings drawn closed,

thinking of that afternoon in the parlor. A tremor of excitement ran through her, and the throbbing between her legs returned.

When she could stand it no longer, she rose and donned a day gown that fastened in the front, enabling her to dress herself. Moving silently, she stole across the hall to the main staircase then headed to the west wing.

Finding Marcus's room was easier than she thought it would be. A sliver of light shone through the bottom of the door. She stopped at the door, hesitating, when it opened.

He stood naked before her. "I knew it was you."

She stared at him. He took her breath away. Her betrothed was a magnificent combination of taut skin and muscle. Dark hair covered his chest.

He glanced down at himself and flushed. "I'm sorry, I can't get used to sleeping in a nightshirt again."

"You are perfect." She came into his arms. Rubbing her hands over the hard warmth of his back, feeling his strength, her mouth suddenly dried. She raised her face as he bent his head and kissed her.

Phoebe wasn't sure he would agree with her desire. She broke the kiss then whispered in his ear, much as he'd whispered in hers earlier, her voice low and sultry. "Marcus, make me your wife, tonight. Make me yours. I don't want to wait. I want you now. I want you to show me your love."

"Phoebe, I want you, God knows how much I want you," Marcus said, meeting her gaze. "Once this is done, you can't take it back, my love."

She had to make him understand. "Do you plan to back out on our betrothal, because I do not. When I told you I'd marry you, I gave myself to you then. Have you thought about how much trust I'm putting in you agreeing to wed? Under the law, you will have more control over me than my parents did, and I've been my own mistress for several years now. Don't you think it is up to me to decide when I give you my body, my maidenhead?"

Lines of concern etched his forehead. "What if I got you with child and something would happen to me?"

Pregnancy was a possibility, but they'd marry soon and she did not want to wait. "Then procure a special license when we return to London." She searched his eyes. "Marry me out of hand, but don't deny me the ability to make my decision about my virginity. I would rather gift it to you now, while it is still my choice."

He gazed back at her, uncertain. "You're sure you want to do this?"

"Yes."

"If you want to stop—"

"I won't, but thank you." She smiled at him. "You taught me kissing. Teach me this."

Marcus groaned, covering her lips with his into a deep kiss. He crushed her against his hard body. One hand moving down over her derrière, holding her into him, his other hand moved over her breast, finding the nipple under the thin muslin of her gown.

"Where does this gown fasten?" he asked urgently, breathing against her.

"In the front." Sensual flames shot through Phoebe's body, heating her, making her breasts throb and ache for his touch. She rubbed her hands over his muscular chest, reveling in the feel of the soft hair covering it. She desperately wanted to feel her body naked against his. "Take me now, Marcus, I need you."

Chapter Seventeen

Marcus stepped back a little to look at her. He'd not known her hair was so long, curling almost to her waist. He lifted it and twined his hands in it, then held her face as he kissed her again. She was so beautiful.

He worshiped her and devoured her with his eyes. He unfastened her gown and stays before untying the ribbons of her chemise. Caressing her silken skin, he pushed the garment over the swell of her hips until it fell softly to the floor. He lifted her into his arms and walked the few feet to the bed. Holding her close, he crawled onto the bed and stretched her out beside him.

Marcus needed to touch her, all of her. "Oh, God, Phoebe, you are beautiful."

She searched his face. "Am I? Even like this?"

"Especially like this." No woman could ever be more perfect.

He kissed the corner of her mouth and rubbed his thumbs over the light pink buds topping her breasts. She gasped, and arched, pushing the perfect peaks up toward him. He grazed her bottom lip with his teeth, before nibbling her chin and throat, then took one furled bud into his mouth and suckled, while rolling her other nipple between his fingers. She tasted of honey and woman. He switched to her other breast, and she moaned, low, anguished, and needy. He returned his lips to hers, drawing her into a kiss, while moving his palm over her stomach, down between her legs. He stroked, building her flames higher, urging her on until she opened her legs, and he eased one finger into her, then a second. His fingers' thrust matched his tongue's, as he played with the pearl nestled in her curls. He wanted to roar with pride when she cried out, convulsing around him.

He sat up onto his knees, holding her before him.

She glanced down at his erection and her eyes widened.

"Tell me if you want this."

She swallowed and nodded. "Yes. I want all of you."

"Then don't think." He nudged her head up and kissed her again. "Straddle me."

Lying on his back, Marcus arranged her legs so that she was on her knees over his hips. He brought her closer, and lifted her. His fingers found her again, sliding easily into her wetness, as he kissed her.

Phoebe slid her arms around his neck, holding on to him as he replaced his fingers with the head of his erection. She jerked slightly, startled by how large he felt.

He stroked her hair. "Tell me if you want me to stop."

"No. Don't stop."

"Try to relax."

He pushed in, stretching her. Phoebe tensed at his invasion. Her emotions ran rampant. Sudden uncertainty at what she was doing overcame her desperate passion and need for him.

As if he knew what she was thinking, he halted.

He caressed her back. "We'll take this slowly."

She willed herself to open to him as he gradually filled her part way. Then he moved deeper again, letting her feel more of him, more of his heat. A burgeoning need began to well within her. She tried to take control, make him go faster, but he held her to the languid, deliberate pace.

Phoebe's need grew as she became wetter, slicker with each slow, shallow thrust. Shivering, she kissed him ravenously, as if that would assuage her.

He whispered, "My love, this will hurt the first time. Do you want me to go on?"

The sensations were so overwhelming all she could do was nod, and move on him, telling him with her body what she had no breath to say aloud.

He drew her into a searing kiss and thrust up, burying himself deep within her.

The sharp pain made her tense and cry out, but he stopped and held her until the sting receded, and she began to relax.

Marcus murmured in her ear, "Shhh, my love. There is no hurry. You'll be all right now, it won't hurt again, I promise."

He caressed her until her tension ebbed. Finally she moved on her own, just a bit, body hardened, filling her more, but causing no pain. "Love me," she whispered.

"Always."

His muscles clenched as Marcus moved so excruciatingly slowly as if to avoid harming her again. Each time waiting until she was ready to take him in further. Soon he was so deep within her they could have been one.

Despite the dull throbbing inside her, at her core, their lovemaking felt so right, as if it was meant to be.

She opened her eyes, dazed. Marcus's countenance was hard, determined. His jaw clenched in control. Once Marcus was fully inside her, he rolled her beneath him. When he withdrew a little, she held on to him. "No."

Marcus pressed kisses on her hair and eyes. "Are you all right?"

This couldn't be all of it. Why was he stopping? "I don't want you to leave me. It finally feels good again."

He laughed. "I'm not going anywhere."

He captured her lips, running his tongue, exploring her mouth, as his body began a new rhythm within her.

"Wrap your legs around me."

This time, each stroke pushed her higher, made her need greater, until she tossed beneath him, gasping for breath. She knew now that the throbbing she'd felt earlier had been the primitive drive to feel him deep inside her, making her his.

She gave up thinking as he quickened his pace, thrusting deeper. Wave upon wave of sensation drove her, making her more and more frenzied until she felt as if the sun was exploding, and she cried out. He moved inside her, faster, deeper until he groaned, spilling his seed.

He rolled, drawing her to him, softly kissing her hair and her face. His fingers touched her swollen lips. "Phoebe?"

Her skin and the curls around her face were damp. "Yes, I'm all right."

"I love you," he whispered.

Tears of joy pricked her lids. She'd never known such deep happiness could exist. Snuggling into him, wanting to feel his strong, naked body against hers, she said, "I love you too."

Phoebe's dream became erotic, she was wet with desire. She spread her legs and dreamed Marcus was stroking her. Groaning with delicious delight, she shuddered as his fingers once again slipped inside her.

Waking fully, she realized that Marcus was behind her, touching her. He removed his fingers and thrust his shaft deep inside her. She gasped and pushed back against him, reveling in the fullness and trying to urge him deeper still. With one hand, he caressed her mons, while the other palm kneaded her breast.

This time their loving was softer, warmer. The tension she'd felt before bloomed and spread as wave upon wave of pleasure coursed through her. And he'd been right. There was no pain, only the love he gave her, and the deep satisfaction of having him inside her, bringing her such utter joy. This new passion was one she could grow used to.

After all the years of waiting, Marcus could barely believe he was making love to her. Phoebe was his. Nothing would ever separate them again. His need to protect her had grown exponentially, as had his need to reassure himself she was truly his.

He never knew he could feel this close to another being, that a connection could be so deep. She was a craving, an addiction.

"I love you." Soon she would be his wife.

"I love you, and thank you," she replied in a soft voice.

Thank you? After what she'd gifted to him? Marcus lifted himself on one arm and gazed at her. "For what?"

She turned her head toward him. "For being so gentle and taking it all so gradually. I saw how hard it was for you, how much it cost you." She caressed his cheek. "I want you to know how much your patience and tenderness means to me."

His throat tightened. She was the most generous woman he knew. "You gave me so much more. You entrusted me with not only your body, but your trust."

Phoebe smiled and gazed into his eyes. "I granted you my trust when I agreed to marry you, and you gave me *your* body as well."

He tried not to frown, but he didn't understand her at all. Was she trying to lessen her gift? "It's not the same. It wasn't my first time."

Phoebe tilted her head as if considering his words carefully. "Well, that is true. I think it's a good thing it was not your first time. What a mull you could have made of it. And as for it being my first time, well, that's expected." She patted his chest.

He shook his head. With luck, he'd have years to try to figure her out.

She relaxed back into his arms, and he held her safe against him until dawn stole through the drapes. He hated to let her go, but soon servants would be up.

After waking her and helping her dress, Marcus checked the hall. He didn't want to let her out of his sight and watched until she'd reached the hall leading to the grand staircase. When she was no longer in view, he closed the door.

He'd have to give much more thought to Travenor and how to keep her protected without letting Phoebe know. He couldn't lose her now.

When Phoebe returned to her room, she changed into her nightgown and climbed into her cold, empty bed. She'd never thought—and would not have believed—how powerful an intimacy the act of mating could be. A primal and fundamental sharing of bodies and souls.

When he'd entered her, she understood profoundly why it was called possession. She'd been helpless beneath him as he'd filled her, but she'd reveled in it because she'd made him hers as well.

Phoebe drifted back to sleep, dreaming of Marcus deep inside her, his hands roaming her body, his mouth hot on hers.

When she awoke, Rose had opened the bed hangings. The morning light streamed through the windows, and she heard the sound of water being poured into a tub set by the fire.

Phoebe moved, twinges and little pains where she'd never felt them before came upon her. As she stood, her legs wobbled a little, like jelly.

Marcus had cleaned her earlier, but she was thankful for this bath. She climbed into the tub and sank down, letting the warm water soothe her aches and caress her body. Bergamot flowers floated in the tub, their scent energizing her.

Would she and Marcus be able to be together tonight? Attempting to move, she wondered, ruefully, if she would be able to walk today. Ah, but what they'd done had been so amazing. She leaned back against the tub, remembering. The sensations she'd felt when he'd made love to her returned, and a tremor ran through her body. Her breasts felt full, and her nipples tightened as the now familiar throb beat at her core.

Phoebe searched her conscience for any lingering guilt or shame and was shocked to discover all she really wanted to do was return to bed with him.

Now she understood why married ladies didn't discuss certain things with unmarried ladies. Marriage had definitely become a more enticing proposition than when she'd accepted him. There must be some way for them to be together tonight.

Then she remembered that her sisters and his mother were arriving to-day. Phoebe groaned and put her head in her hands. A whole day and evening to wait with her sharp-eyed sisters and aunt, and his equally sharp-eyed mother. There would be altogether too many knowing women in this house. Somehow, Phoebe would find a way.

Later that morning, Phoebe held Marcus's hand as Hester, Hermione, and their cavalcade arrived. Before her sisters were able to descend from their coaches, Phoebe's older nieces and nephews piled out of the carriages and ran up to her.

Marcus laughed as Phoebe was surrounded by children, ranging in age from three to six, all of them chattering at the same time. He remembered she had always loved children. A warm feeling infused his heart. She would be the mother of his children. Hopefully soon.

The two older boys took her hands and the girls circled her with hugs. Phoebe smiled and greeted them all.

One little girl was trying to hurry her nursemaid and practically flew into Phoebe's arms.

"Oof, Mary! I almost dropped you," Phoebe exclaimed.

The child put her small hands on either side of Phoebe's face and kissed her. "No drop. Hold."

Her sisters, finally having descended, chuckled at the melee surrounding his betrothed.

"I don't know how you do it," the Countess of Fairport said. "You are like honey to their bees."

"Little heathens, all of them." Edwin came forward and held out his hand to Marcus. "How are you, Finley?"

"I'm well, Fairport." Marcus glanced back at the children. "Are they always like this?"

Fairport tried to remove the small girl from her limpet-like grip on Phoebe. "Only around Phoebe. We don't know what it is. Her mere presence sets them off."

Fairport's wife took his hand. "Leave Mary, Edwin. She will let go when the others have been taken away. It's the only way she can be part of this group without being trampled."

John Caldecott and his wife joined them. He shook his head. "Don't understand it. She turns them all into barbarians."

Marcus stood near while Phoebe listened to her nieces and nephews as they told her all their news, and she made the appropriate comments to each of them.

Motioning them in Marcus's direction, she said, "I want all of you to make your bows and curtseys to Lord Marcus, then go with your nurses. I am very sure Cook has something nice waiting for you in the nursery."

After they were properly introduced to Marcus, she handed Mary to Nurse and shook out her skirts.

Marcus and Phoebe joined her sisters and brothers-in-law as they all repaired to the morning room whilst their lady's maids and valets prepared their chambers.

Tea was waiting and Phoebe poured. Marcus's hands touched hers as he took the cups then handed them around. The sparks were still there, but seemed even more intimate. Was that because of their lovemaking?

Marcus grinned to himself as curious and interested eyes took in the picture of domesticity they presented.

Hester settled back against the sofa. "I take it we have our usual rooms?"

"Yes, I checked with Ferguson," Phoebe said. "There are no surprises."

Marcus glanced at her. Unless they found her sneaking to or from his room. Would she come to him?

When Lord and Lady St. Eth arrived, Phoebe served them, and the women settled down for a comfortable coze.

Marcus stood with the men, trying not to glance at Phoebe. The few times their eyes had met, they'd both looked away quickly before Phoebe's blush betrayed them. They'd agreed not to tell her sisters of their betrothal until his parents arrived, yet it was harder than Marcus believed to remain silent when he wanted to shout out their news.

Shortly after he rose, Marcus had sent the notice to the *Morning Post*. To-morrow was Phoebe's birthday, and plans had been made to drive out to the nearby abbey ruins in the morning. Afterward, a small party with a cake had been planned for the children whom, her sisters told Phoebe, had worked diligently on the gifts they'd made for her and were excited for her to see.

When the party finished luncheon, the twins retired to their chambers and the gentlemen to the billiards room, except for Marcus, who'd asked Phoebe if she'd like to walk in the gardens before his parents arrived.

Hands clasped, they ambled around the knot garden, which led through an arch cut into an old boxwood hedge surrounding the rose garden. Alone and hidden from the house, they strolled with their arms around the other's waist, stopping occasionally to look at the last bloom of some bush or another.

When they reached the hidden arbor at the end of one walk, Marcus enclosed her in his arms. "Phoebe, I need you, I never knew how much."

He stroked her back, easing her nearer, and she melted into him.

She slipped her arms around his neck, reached up and kissed him. "Marcus, you wouldn't believe the thoughts I've been having. They're quite wicked."

Her low, sultry voice made his member throb. "If they are anything like mine, I would say quite wicked indeed. I can't wait to have you naked in my bed again."

She shivered.

Marcus held her closer. "Cold?"

Phoebe's eyes widened. "No, it's my reaction to you."

He kissed her. Softly at first. She was intoxicating. His tongue danced with hers. His muscles hardened as he crushed her against him.

Phoebe stretched up and slid her fingers around the back of his neck and into his hair. When his hands moved to her breasts, she moaned.

She glanced around. "Can we do it here?"

Her eagerness was as unexpected as it was welcome. And

though it was a risk, he couldn't bring himself to deny either of them. "Yes. Are you able?"

"I think so. Marcus, I feel so wanton. I need to have you inside me."

Marcus kissed her ravenously. Sitting on the arbor bench, he lifted her skirts. His fingers stroked her already wet curls. "You must be sore. If it hurts, tell me, and I'll stop."

Sighing, she opened her legs wider as his fingers entered her, before moving over him. "Now, Marcus. I want you now." Phoebe kissed him deeply, voraciously, inviting him to join with her. He unfastened the buttons of his breeches and released his shaft, then brought her down slowly upon him, impaling her.

She gasped as he began lifting her up so that he was almost out of her then filled her again. Shuddering, Phoebe tried to help but had no purchase. She trembled with pleasure.

"Put your legs around me," Marcus whispered.

Doing as she was told, he filled her deeper still, and she gave herself up to the sensations of him being so far inside her he touched her heart. She clung to him and when the tension in her rose to an unbearable level and she opened her mouth to cry out, he covered her lips with his. She reached for the sun as his warmth filled her. They slumped against each other, their breathing ragged. The more they were together, the stronger their tie became.

Phoebe remembered where they were and laughed out loud. "What is it?" he asked.

"We've gone mad. Look at where we are. We're very fortunate we were not caught."

He kissed her. "I thought about that, but not for very long," he said ruefully. "We'll have to be more careful."

She pressed her lips against his temple. "Particularly now that both our families will be in residence."

They stayed until she heard the sound of coaches. "Marcus, I think your parents have arrived."

Quickly detangling themselves, they stood, straightened their clothing, and hurried to the front of the house, arm in arm, arriving just as his parents' carriage stopped.

"Mamma, Papa . . ." Marcus walked forward.

He was interrupted by a large carriage with the Cranbourne crest arriving on the heels of the Dunwoods' carriage. Marcus helped his mother alight as Phoebe walked forward to greet her brother.

"Geoffrey, what a wonderful surprise, and how delighted I am to see you," Phoebe said. "How did you get here so soon? How did you get here at all? There wasn't enough time."

Geoffrey hugged Phoebe before turning to assist Amabel from the carriage.

A footman came forward to aid Nurse and little Miles.

With long strides, Marcus walked to meet his sister. "Amabel, I didn't expect to see you here."

Uncle Henry and Aunt Ester came onto the front steps, followed by the others. Pandemonium reigned as the new arrivals were greeted and Miles cuddled and exclaimed over.

Amabel stood a little off to the side whilst the ladies admired her son. She glanced at Phoebe, her forehead wrinkled in concern.

The last thing Phoebe wanted was for her sister-in-law to feel estranged. She clasped Amabel's hands and hugged her.

Amabel clung to Phoebe. "I am so sorry—"

"No," Phoebe said, "you could not have known."

Shaking her head, Amabel replied, "No, it was very wrong of me to try to push him on you. Marcus told Geoffrey everything. If it hadn't come from Marcus himself, I would not have believed a brother of mine could have behaved so disgracefully. It is outside of enough to have done something like that at all, but to one so young."

"Marcus and I have discussed it," Phoebe said, patting her sister-in-law's arm. "It was very wrong of him and yes, disgraceful, but we've put it behind us, and you must as well."

Amabel's eyes searched Phoebe's face. "Have you, my dear? I don't know if I could."

She nodded. "Yes, indeed, else Marcus would not be here." Phoebe led Amabel toward the house. "Believe me when I tell you, if he were not the right man—the only man—for me, nothing in this world could make me accept him."

"You always said you would wait until you found . . ." She broke off and stared at Phoebe, amazement in her face, then smiled. "You accepted Marcus? I *am* glad. Knowing what he is like now, I was sure he would be perfect for you."

Phoebe raised a brow. "It was a very good thing I was not aware of who he was when I saw him in Bond Street. *That* was what started it all."

Amabel took Phoebe's arm and laughed. "Geoffrey mentioned something about it but I have not heard the whole. You must tell me. Was it very scandalous?"

"According to my aunt Ester, it was the most scandalous thing she'd ever seen in Bond Street." Phoebe grinned as she related the event.

Amabel replied in shocked tones, "Great heavens, Phoebe, what were you two thinking?"

Phoebe shook her head, but couldn't keep from smiling. "Quite honestly, Amabel, I don't think either of us was thinking. It was the most remarkable thing. I don't remember a thought running through my head, and Marcus doesn't either."

"Well," Amabel replied, "it is a very good thing you are marrying or we would have a scandal on our hands, and you know, my dear, how much that would displease Geoffrey."

Phoebe went into whoops. "I perfectly understand it would not do to upset Geoffrey. The poor dear has had enough to suffer being my guardian."

"He's not been your guardian for years now," Amabel said sternly, "and how *can* you say such a thing. Geoffrey has *always* said you have such superior sense."

"Only because I've left you both alone as much as I could," Phoebe retorted.

"Well, that may have had something to do with it," her sister-in-law admitted.

Once everyone was in the drawing room, Henry poured sherry and tea was served.

Phoebe turned to her brother. "Geoffrey, what brought you?"

"Well," he said, glancing at his brothers-in-law, "I've been receiving letters concerning what has been going on and, finally, one arrived summoning me here."

Phoebe frowned, not understanding. "What do you mean? What is going on?"

Geoffrey glanced pointedly at Phoebe and at Marcus standing next to her. "From what I hear, there have been some events verging on scandal."

Chapter Eighteen

"Oh, I see." Phoebe gazed up at Marcus, who gave her a questioning look. She nodded. "Now is as good a time as any."

Taking her arm, he addressed his parents. "Mamma, Papa." Waving his arm, Marcus included the rest of them. "I have the great pleasure to inform you that Lady Phoebe has done me the honor of agreeing to become my wife."

"That saved you," Geoffrey muttered, but his eyes were alight with laughter.

"It's about time," Edwin said as the rest of them converged on Marcus and Phoebe with their good wishes.

Phoebe whispered to Marcus, "Shall we bring down the children? They'll hear it from the staff, if we don't tell them first."

He grinned. "You're right, that wouldn't do at all."

Phoebe sat on the sofa with Marcus, when the children entered. She held out her arms and gathered her nieces and nephews to her, taking the younger ones in her lap and praying the children would take the news of her betrothal well. "My loves, I want to ask you to wish me happy. Lord Marcus and I are to be married."

Robert, Hester's eldest, and William, and Arabella, Hermione's eldest, exchanged glances, then bowed and curtseyed, regarding Marcus with deep consideration.

Marcus smiled at them, wondering if they'd accept him.

They turned their attention back to Phoebe.

"Will you still visit us?" asked Robert, the spokesman. "And play with us as you do now?"

"Yes, my dear, to be sure, and I'll have a home, where you will be able to visit me as well."

The cousins exchanged somewhat less tense glances, then Arabella asked Marcus, "Do you like children?"

Marcus held out his arms to her. "Yes, I do. Very much."

She went to him, taking his hand and tugging him down until she could kiss his cheek. William and Robert followed her lead, their demeanors grave as they shook hands with Marcus. Soon, the two younger ones climbed onto his lap, and he hugged and kissed them both.

When their treats were brought, the children gathered around the table.

Phoebe whispered to him, "It was easier getting over that fence than I expected."

Marcus was thankful it had been. He liked the idea of being part of her family. "I was always taught to get over heavy ground as lightly as possible."

Phoebe grinned. "Did I tell you that I am their favorite aunt?"

He widened his eyes in feigned surprise. "No, are you? I would never have guessed." He raised her hand to his lips and placed a kiss in her palm. "Meet me early in the drawing room. I have something special to show you."

*   *   *

Phoebe arrived to find Marcus staring out the window. He turned and drew her to him, before handing her a small box. "I meant to give you this yesterday."

She glanced up at him.

"Open it."

Sliding the top off the carved wooden box, she found, nestled in satin, an ancient ring of delicate gold filigree, set in the center with a large opal. The sides were decorated with smaller diamonds and amethysts.

Tears pricked her eyes. "Marcus, my love, I have never seen anything so beautiful. It looks quite old."

"It is. It belonged to a great-great-great-grandmother, and this ring has been waiting for another bride to wear it. Family legend has it that it may only be worn by a bride born in October, else it's bad luck. You are the only bride to have been born in October in so long my mother almost forgot about it."

Marcus slid the ring on her finger and lightly touched his lips to hers. "It's been waiting for you, as have I."

Phoebe reached up to embrace him.

The door opened and Edwin coughed. "I do hope you intend to marry quickly."

Marcus grinned. "As soon as possible."

After their families had gathered, Henry made the first toast. Lord Dunwood followed him. After that, the toasts became much funnier and a little ribald. Laughter and good humor persisted until Ferguson announced dinner. Leaving formality aside, they walked into the dining room as couples.

François once again rose to the occasion and dinner was even more stupendous than last evening's had been.

Marcus whispered to Phoebe, "Do you think we could entice him away from your uncle, or would that be bad form? I feel as if he assisted in our courtship."

"Maybe we could ask for him as a wedding present."

Marcus chuckled lightly and took her hand. "Will you come to me tonight?"

"If I am not discovered and made to turn back."

His lips tightened. "This is intolerable, to be sneaking around like this."

Phoebe nodded. Considering her new passion, the sooner they married the better. Yet more than that, now that she'd made a decision, she wanted her life with him to begin.

He pressed his knee against hers, and she glanced up and sighed.

Hermione caught Phoebe's eye and frowned. "We need to pick a date. One not very far off."

Amabel, who had been very quiet, said, "Yes, Mamma told me Arthur is not at all well. Marcus, Phoebe, if you are not to have to postpone the wedding because of his passing, you will be well-advised to marry soon."

The reminder of Arthur had a subduing effect on the rest of the group's frivolity, but gave Phoebe a sudden idea.

Uncle Henry exchanged a glance with Lord Dunwood, who motioned to her uncle to speak.

"We can procure a special license easily enough," Uncle Henry said. "Phoebe, when do you and Marcus wish to marry and what kind of wedding do you want?"

Phoebe took Marcus's hand. "After seeing what Hermione and Hester went through, I forswore a large wedding, but I have a thought. Marcus, have you a chapel at Charteries?"

"Yes."

"I would like to hold the wedding there, so that Arthur and his daughters are able to attend."

Marcus's eyes glistened as he squeezed her hand. "Thank you, my love. I'd like nothing better."

Lord Dunwood frowned. "Yes, my dear, but—"

His wife interrupted. "Phoebe, what a wonderful idea and how generous of you."

Phoebe shook her head. It was necessary. Families should

be together. "No, indeed, I am to be a member of your family. It's only right that everyone is able to attend."

She grinned. "I'm quite sure mine will gladly travel to see us married. I could probably have the wedding in Timbuktu, and they'd come, so happy they'd be."

Aunt Ester glanced with approval at Phoebe. "The where is settled. The next question is when."

"Next week?" Marcus suggested hopefully.

Every lady, with the sole exception of Phoebe, who thought it an excellent idea, narrowed their eyes.

His mother glanced at the ceiling and then at him. "My dear son, I understand you want this wedding to take place as soon as possible. However, Phoebe must have her gown made, and all sorts of other things as well."

Lady Dunwood smiled sympathetically. "If ten days is agreeable to everyone we can plan the wedding for then."

Phoebe gave a sigh of relief as they all agreed on ten days.

She and Marcus decided to forgo the trip to the ruins the next day in favor of having the settlement discussions. They had made an agreement between them that she thought her uncle would consent to, but Marcus wasn't sure about his father. Because she knew her aunt would insist on being present, Phoebe asked that Lady Dunwood attend as well.

After breakfast the next morning, everyone adjourned to Uncle Henry's study, where he handed her financial details to Lord Dunwood.

"Phoebe's fortune is substantial," Uncle Henry said. "She has been schooled as to her finances, and from which properties or investments her portion derives. To date, she has not shown any interest in personally managing her assets." He said to her, "My child, you will have to make a decision how you want it administered."

Phoebe glanced at the documents and pulled a face. She knew how to hold house and manage an estate, but investments didn't interest her. "I am perfectly happy to leave my funds to the expertise of my man of business."

"But, my dear . . ." Lord Dunwood said.

"I agree with you, my love," Marcus interrupted. "If you are happy to keep them there, that is where they shall remain. I will, of course, agree to all your property being settled on you."

His father frowned. "This is highly irregular."

Lady Dunwood smiled at Marcus. "I am very proud that you are being so modern."

His father glanced around the table. "I don't understand this at all."

Phoebe felt a little sorry for him and was about to explain, when Marcus fixed him with a firm look.

"Papa, Phoebe and I have discussed the settlements. I have no need for her money, and I believe that a wife should have her own funds."

"But she will have," Lord Dunwood sputtered. "You shall give her an allowance."

Phoebe watched with interest to see what Marcus would say.

His countenance hardened, and his tone held a note of command he rarely used around her. "Hear me out, Father. Certain of her portion will be set aside for our daughters and part of my private fortune will be settled on any younger sons. But I see no need for me to own what is hers, and I will not agree to any settlement that is contrary to the compact Phoebe and I have struck."

Phoebe finally had a glimpse into the man who'd defeated pirates and made such a name for himself in the West Indies. A thrill of delight coursed through her as he prepared to do battle on her behalf.

Then Uncle Henry turned to Lord Dunwood. "I know it seems radical to you, but it's what they want. I, for one, see no reason they should not have it as they wish. Phoebe's funds are already in trust. I'll arrange to have her personal possessions placed in the trust as well."

Uncle Henry paused a moment. "Do you have any real objections to their arrangements?"

Lord Dunwood's brows drew together and he said, "Merely that it is so unusual. Though I daresay I shall grow used to it. No, let them do as they will."

His wife patted his hand. "Indeed, my love, I think they will go on very well with the plans they've made. Let us continue."

Her husband stopped frowning, but still did not appear happy. "Marcus has his personal fortune as well as the expectancies from the earldom and eventually the marquisate."

Lord Dunwood also agreed to a significant allowance for the couple until such time as Marcus inherited.

Aunt Ester caught Phoebe's eye, then glanced at Marcus as well. "Phoebe, have you and Marcus decided where you will live?"

She shrugged. "No, I've not given it any thought."

Her aunt hesitated for a moment. "I ask because you will need to decide whether to reside with Lord and Lady Dunwood, or have your own home. Henry had a country estate given to the heir, but when in Town, we were expected to live with his parents." Aunt Ester glanced at her husband. "I will tell you it was not a happy experience. In the end, we bought a small townhouse."

Marcus listened with a furrowed brow. He'd spoken many times of having his own house and Phoebe needed a home of her own to manage. He would not have her remain in the position she was now. "Mamma, Papa, what do you wish?"

His father raised his brows. "The Dunwood heir has always lived at Charteries, our principal estate." Gazing at Marcus, he paused. "I would like to retire from managing the estate. In that respect, I think your mother and I agree. I propose we give over part of one wing of the house to you and Phoebe. Isabel, what say you?"

Her face lit up. "I would dearly love to give over the management of the Charteries to you, my dear Phoebe. We have been, for so long, tied to the estate due both to family and the war." Mamma glanced lovingly at her husband. "As the Corsican is now at Elba, I would like to travel a little."

Dunwood regarded Marcus and said gruffly, "You have made a very good start in becoming conversant with the estate and the political issues." Papa sighed. "I have no doubt you will be on the more progressive side of the party. Phoebe will be a great help to you."

Dunwood looked at his wife and back to Marcus. "I'll give you my proxy when I am not in Town for a vote."

His mother smiled. "The townhouse will also be left to your management, Phoebe, if you don't mind?"

Phoebe returned her future mother-in-law's smile. "I don't mind at all. Tell me, what are the plans for Arthur's daughters? Do you, ma'am, wish to raise them, or shall Marcus and I act *in loco parentis?* Who will be appointed guardian and trustee?"

Before his mother could reply, Marcus touched her shoulder. "Phoebe, my love, are you sure you want to care for two young girls?"

Phoebe took his hand. "Marcus, they will be both motherless and fatherless. How could I not want them?" She grinned. "Aside from that, you told me I should like them."

He nodded and his voice was low. "That was before I knew you so well. You will love them and they you."

Lady Dunwood's eyes swam in tears. "I love being their grandmother, but I think they need a younger woman as a mother and a model."

"Then that is settled. Marcus and I will treat them as our children," Phoebe replied.

Marcus did not know how he'd come to be so lucky. Perhaps the only good thing he'd done eight years ago was to fall in love with this remarkable woman.

That afternoon, the families celebrated Phoebe's birthday. She received the children's gifts, exclaiming delightedly over their handiwork. Pleased to have their presents admired so much, the children led the way to the birthday cake, holding Phoebe's hands and skirts. Afterward, their parents, Marcus, and she played games with the children, until her nieces and nephews were led away to the nursery.

The adults lounged in their chairs on the terrace, enjoying the rare warm afternoon. Tea and other refreshments arrived as Phoebe received gifts from her sisters.

Marcus handed her a long, thin, plainly wrapped package.

Phoebe glanced at him and wondered what it was.

He grinned. "You will have to open it to find out."

She found her fingers trembled a bit. Other than the ring, this was the first actual present he'd ever given her.

Inside the wrappings was a pretty but lethal-looking double-edged lady's dagger. It had an elegant bone handle decorated in gold wire that formed a swirling design and a small, flat, ornate pommel. The blade was about six inches long. She remembered their conversation and smiled broadly. "Marcus, thank you. It's beautiful."

John inspected the dagger. "Unless you'd visited Manton's or Tattersall's, you could not have selected a better gift for Phoebe."

Marcus looked at John gravely. "After seeing Phoebe's horses, I would not take it upon myself to choose for her. Now, a pistol I could probably manage."

Fairport lifted his glass. "Good decision. She always seems to have the best cattle in the family. Indeed, Marcus, you have now shown yourself to be worthy of a Stanhope bride. All wives deserve to be well armed."

"So I've heard," retorted Marcus, laughing as Fairport pulled a face, obviously remembering when he and Hermione had been waylaid, and she'd saved them with her own pistol.

Geoffrey had a wicked look in his eye. "Marcus, you'd better take care that she doesn't use it on you."

Amabel primly added, "You will have to be a model husband."

"My dear sister, that was never in question."

The older members of the party regarded them with amused grins.

Lord Dunwood shook his head. "I had no idea what a bloodthirsty family you were marrying into, my boy."

Geoffrey responded, "Not bloodthirsty, sir." He glanced at his sisters proudly. "Only well able to defend themselves."

Lord Dunwood's lips twitched. "Amabel, my girl, have they corrupted you as well?"

She glanced up demurely. "No, Papa. I shall rely upon my husband to defend me."

"In that case you'd better take lessons," Hester scoffed.

The twins ignored Geoffrey as he protested, but Phoebe grinned at her brother. "That reminds me. I don't think I ever thanked you for showing me that upper cut."

Narrowing his eyes at Geoffrey, Marcus said, "So you're who I have to thank for it, Cranbourne."

Geoffrey's eyes twinkled. "Indeed."

Hester and Hermione inspected the dagger and exclaimed over it.

Phoebe asked Marcus, "When will you teach me how to use it?"

"If no one minds, we can have your first lesson now if you wish."

"I don't think anyone will object." Phoebe waited and, as

she suspected, Hermione, Hester, and their aunt all agreed that they were extremely interested in learning this new form of combat.

Phoebe listened intently as Marcus first showed them the balance of the dagger without its scabbard. He gave it to her, and she held it, becoming used to the feel.

Then he explained the fine points of how a knife could be used to enter a body to cause the most damage. Some of what he'd said—such as how to avoid hitting a bone and how to assure that the knife isn't taken away by an opponent— Phoebe had learned when training with a short sword. When they began practicing, the most difficult move for her to remember was to press in with the knife, once the cut had been made, rather than jumping back as she did with a sword.

Her sisters and aunt cheered her on, before each had her turn.

Though very interested, Phoebe had trouble envisioning how one might employ it if attacked. "Marcus, when would one use a dagger?"

Marcus motioned to the knife. "Unlike a small sword or a pistol, a dagger can be concealed on one's person, making it readily accessible in the event of need." He glanced at her sisters. "A lady can strap a dagger to her leg and access it through a pocket slit in the skirts. Ladies who wear boots tuck them there. It takes some practice to draw the dagger out in a hurry, but, I've been told, it is well worth the effort."

Hester stared at the dagger still in Phoebe's hand and pursed her lips. "If we can have our maids alter at least one gown, we can practice to-morrow."

"But will it ruin the line of the gown?" Hermione frowned.

Phoebe grinned. Hermione had always been the most style conscious of the sisters.

Rising, Phoebe said, "We won't know until we try."

Excusing themselves and sending for their maids, the ladies left their men on the terrace.

Amabel, Lady St. Eth, and Lord and Lady Dunwood also decided to go inside. Marcus with his future brothers-in-law and St. Eth remained.

John scowled. "Finley, I take leave to inform you that, due to you, my wife will insist on having a dagger strapped to her leg at all times. Boadicea to the life. I sincerely hope she doesn't decide to use it on me."

Geoffrey gave a bark of laughter. "You're fortunate she is very sensible."

Edwin said, funning with Marcus, "*I* only hope Hermione decides it ruins the line of her gown." He took a sip of wine and asked, "What made you decide a dagger would be a good gift for Phoebe?"

Marcus really didn't want to tell them. Her protection was now his responsibility. Trying to pass it off lightly, he responded, "Geoffrey told me she liked self-defense. I'd mentioned to her that it was a good weapon, and she seemed interested."

Edwin and John lifted their brows.

Well that diversion didn't work. "Oh, very well. I have a feeling that won't leave me, that she may be in danger and need it." Marcus's jaw clenched. "I will tell you what I've discovered about Lord Travenor."

Their teasing stopped. Marcus related what his contacts discovered. "You know that his cousin was found murdered in one of the slums. As the baron's heir, some suspicion fell on Travenor, but nothing could be proved. His reputation is that of a rough man, much addicted to gaming and ready to sport his canvas. The women he's been with have not fared well."

Marcus walked to the cart and poured a glass of wine. "Before Travenor inherited, he never had a feather to fly with, but he always managed to come up with the money he needed. Although none of my contacts would venture a guess as to how he did it, one of them did say that for several years there were many reports of a gentleman highway robber around the Bristol area. He disappeared a few months ago, around the time of the baron's death."

Marcus made the decision to tell them the rest of it. "Travenor may very well blame me for his previous financial problems. Five years ago, I was instrumental in breaking up a smuggling gang. Travenor was one of the investors and lost everything. If he seeks to avenge himself on me, he could try to use Phoebe."

John rubbed his chin. "His upbringing and subsequent behavior would explain why we thought his manners very odd. Curst rum touch."

Geoffrey nodded. "He'll bear watching, if he is after Phoebe."

St. Eth glanced at Marcus. "Have you told her?"

"Not yet. I only recently received the information."

St. Eth's gaze was steady. "We'll leave it to you to discuss it with her."

Marcus nodded, understanding the implied command to do so quickly. The idea of telling Phoebe that due to him, Travenor could be a threat to her, didn't bear thinking of. He was terrified it would cause a wedge between them. She'd be, rightfully, upset that she was in danger. He'd promised to keep her safe, to protect her, and he would do just that.

Chapter Nineteen

Later that night, lying sated in Marcus's arms, Phoebe mulled over their future living arrangements. She cuddled closer to his warm body. "I think our housing arrangements will work. Do you?"

He heaved a sigh. "Yes. I had my doubts, but I believe my parents are in earnest. At least, I know Mamma is." Marcus nuzzled Phoebe's hair. "Mary, Arthur's wife, dying as she did, and now Arthur, have been a great strain on my mother. She tries not to show it, but she's exhausted. As to my father?" Marcus grimaced. "We'll see if he can give up his politics. It is his life's blood."

Phoebe twisted around to be able to see Marcus more clearly. "Would you be very disappointed if your father cannot?"

He drew her closer. "I don't know, my love. That wouldn't bother me so much. I am very used to my own house. Ever since I've returned to England, I've felt as if I were a guest in my father's homes. If that feeling continues, we shall buy a place of our own."

She nodded and lay back against him. "Yes, we would, of course."

Phoebe hesitated, she had felt a tension in Marcus since they'd met in the drawing room before dinner. "Is there something bothering you?"

He shook his head. "No. Why should there be?"

She frowned. "I don't know. I just feel as if there is something wrong. You'd tell me if there was, wouldn't you?"

"If you needed to know, of course."

Phoebe pushed herself up and speared him with a look. "No, not just if I need to know. You said we would be equal partners. If that is not truly what you had in mind . . ."

Torn, Marcus searched her worried eyes. Did he dare wait nine more days to confide in her? But God, he couldn't lose her. Not now, and not over Travenor. He held her close, feeling a desperate foreboding, and kissed her. "I do want a partnership with you. I want everything with you. It's nothing, really. Go to sleep, my love. Dawn comes too early."

"Marcus."

"I'm worried about Arthur, and the girls, and whether everything will work out as we hope. I love you."

She settled down in his arms again. His throat tightened. He'd waited so long to be with her, to call her his. For eight long years he'd feared each letter he received from family or friends would tell him she was either married or betrothed. Nothing would stand in the way of their marriage. He would be by her side, protecting her, every moment until he could tell Phoebe the truth. Nine more days.

Awakening before dawn, they made love, slowly and sweetly, with none of the frenzied passion that accompanied their nighttime lovemaking. Marcus slid slowly inside her, thrusting deeply. The tension grew as he kept to his path. He needed to bind her to him, brand her as his. To insure she'd never leave him. He heard her soft moans grow more desperate and reveled in her need and that he was the one to fill it.

His hands roamed possessively over her silky skin until she shuddered and her contractions brought him to completion.

He'd wanted her, loved her for so long; he'd thought his feelings couldn't grow any more profound. Yet each time they came together, each time she gave herself to him, his love deepened and his need to protect her became more acute.

He'd kill Travenor or anyone else who tried to hurt her.

Marcus was the only one in the breakfast room when Phoebe entered. He was already discussing his breakfast. He laughed at the amount of food she took from the dishes on the sideboard.

Phoebe glanced at her plate with a frown. "I don't know why it is that I am so hungry. It was the same yesterday."

He couldn't keep a wolfish smile from his face. "My love, have you really no idea what has caused you to have such an appetite?"

She blushed rosily. "Do you really think it's that?"

Happy to be the cause of her appetite, he said, "You'd better eat quickly if no one is to notice. I promise you, your sisters will very soon guess the reason."

She picked up a roll and eyed it as if she'd throw it at him. "Marcus, you wretch."

Seeing the look in her eye, he moved quickly to take her in his arms. Removing the roll, he bent his head to capture her lips.

Phoebe returned his kisses greedily. "What have you done to me?"

"Nothing more than what you've done to me." He drew her back to his lips.

She pulled back. "Will this craving lessen?"

Marcus groaned. "I hope not."

The door opened and the twins walked into the room. Phoebe and Marcus sprang apart a second too late. Hermione was the first to see them, followed closely by Hester. Phoebe glanced at her sisters.

Marcus stood silent, holding her hand. The twins looked at Phoebe's plate and moved their gazes to Phoebe, then him, and finally each other before shrugging in unison. Hermione said, "The special license was an excellent idea."

Both Marcus and Phoebe blushed. Geoffrey, Amabel, Fairport, and Caldecott entered the breakfast room shortly thereafter.

Hester sipped her tea. "We will need to begin the guest list." She tapped the table. "Marcus, can you give us a list of your friends you would like to invite? I think my aunt is discussing your parents' list with Lady Dunwood. If we can make a start now, there will not be so much to do after we return to Town."

Hester's gaze shifted to Phoebe. "When is Aunt Ester's ball? She's decided to make it in honor of your engagement."

"In three days' time. All the plans have been put into effect already. I have a gown I shall need to have fitted."

Hermione swallowed the toast she'd been munching. "My dear, I am more than happy to shop with you. You will have so much to do."

Phoebe spread jam on a roll. "I'd very much like that. I have my bride clothes to purchase, and other things as well."

"Oh, *definitely* other things," Hermione said.

"Have you decided if you will take a wedding trip?" Hester asked.

Marcus glanced at Phoebe for the first time since the others had arrived. He would love to take her off somewhere for a few weeks, but with Arthur dying, did he dare go?

Phoebe bit her lip. "We haven't even discussed it. Marcus, what do you think? Do you have a preference? *Should* we go anywhere?"

Amabel reached her hand out to him. "I think you should. Marcus, I know you are worried about Arthur, but once you take up your duties, both of you will be very busy. You with the estate, Phoebe with the children and the household, and both of you with politics. And *you*, my dear sister"—Amabel looked at Phoebe meaningfully—"will not be in the same position as *I* was. No one will offer to leave you alone with your husband."

Amabel had a point. Marcus needed to think of Phoebe now. "Amabel's right. Once we're at Charteries, you will become, in effect, mother to my nieces and will have to pick up the reins of the household."

Needing to touch Phoebe, he rubbed her shoulders. "And, if I am not mistaken, you have some plans you'd like to implement on the estates. If we are going to take a wedding trip, we should do it immediately after the wedding."

"Maybe several weeks in Paris?" Phoebe suggested. "Shopping there will lessen the amount I must do before we leave."

Some of the tension, he wasn't aware he'd been holding, drained from him. "Paris would be perfect, my love." They wouldn't be too far away in the event of Arthur's passing, and the distance might nullify Travenor as an immediate threat.

That night, Marcus took Phoebe into his arms after she entered his chamber.

He'd borrowed candelabras from the rooms next to him and his chamber was ablaze with light.

"Marcus, what . . ."

He caressed her. "It may be our last night together until we're married. I want to see you and I want you to see me."

Phoebe frowned. "Will we really have to wait until the wedding?"

He kissed her forehead, pleased that she didn't want to leave him any more than he wanted to leave her. "If we can contrive it, no. But if we cannot . . ."

She reached up to kiss him. "Then let's not waste the time we have."

She had worn only a day gown. The buttons were quickly undone. He pushed it down over her hips, letting it fall to the floor with a soft swoosh. It amazed Marcus that she'd never been embarrassed to be naked with him.

She touched his chest, then her hands moved down slowly over his taut stomach to his staff. Marcus groaned and stood perfectly still, allowing her to explore. The light was his idea. How could he have been so stupid as to forget her curiosity? He couldn't hurry her now, but he might be able to guide her. Taking her hand, he showed her how to stroke him, then decided he needed to distract her quickly.

He nibbled her neck and caressed her where she liked it the most, purposefully setting sensual fires burning in her body. Kissing her deeply, he picked her up, carried her to the bed, and tossed her onto it.

Phoebe bounced and laughed. "Come here, my love."

He slid in next to her and tilted her head back before moving his lips down her throat, sucking lightly, reveling in the heat rising from her skin. She sighed and ran her palms over his back and into his hair. His hands roamed as his mouth licked and teased until he reached her breasts. Paying homage to them, he moved lower over her soft stomach, stopping at the curls of her apex.

Phoebe gasped for breath as Marcus's hands and lips

pushed her desire higher than ever before. Her breasts ached. He soothed them. The throbbing between her legs made her push into him. She wanted the relief that only he could give, and she moaned as he placed light kisses and nibbles down her body. When his mouth covered her mons she stilled, but only for a moment. His tongue softly licking made her writhe. Phoebe grabbed his hair and urged him on. She arched up as his tongue entered. Her tension rose, and she reached for the intense pleasure that would come.

"Marcus, please, now."

Tremor upon tremor coursed through her as he drove into her, filling her. Crying out, she wrapped her legs around him, opening herself to him, to take, to conquer, as she flew apart into a million pieces; with a few more strokes, he spilled his seed into her womb.

Marcus collapsed, breathing heavily. She held onto him tightly. A tear slid down her cheek.

He touched the tear with the tip of his finger. "Phoebe, my love, what is it?"

"I don't know, I—I feel so close to you. As if my heart would rip apart if anything happened to you."

He gently turned her head and kissed her. "Nothing is going to happen to me. Not while I have your love."

They slept until dawn. Not wanting to part, she snuggled close to him, warm in his arms until they heard the servants moving around the house.

Phoebe reached her chamber without being seen and fell back asleep, thinking of ways she could be with Marcus after they returned to London.

She awoke to her maid bustling about the room packing.

Sunlight assailed Phoebe's eye as she peeped out of the bed hangings. "What time is it?"

Rose pulled back the bed hangings. "Time for you to be up. I've never known you to sleep this late. It must be all the excitement."

"Yes. Everything is exciting!" Famished, Phoebe rose quickly, to wash her face and dress.

Hester grinned as Phoebe entered the breakfast room and went directly to the dishes set out on the sideboard. "It is hungry work, is it not?"

Phoebe opened her mouth then shut it, preparing for a lecture. There were times being the youngest sister was not very much fun.

"Don't worry, my dear," Hester said. "Your secret is safe with me. Do you think that John and I waited? Not a bit of it."

Smiling, Phoebe filled her plate and took a seat. "You don't eat that much now."

"Children have an effect." Hester's brows drew together in thought. "And I suppose one just gets used to it. Don't expect to be able to continue this way once you arrive in Town."

Phoebe chewed and swallowed. "Well, I know it will be much more difficult."

Hester frowned. "There will be many more eyes upon you. What if you were to be caught?"

Phoebe sighed. "I would have much preferred to be married immediately. At the rate this is going, my wedding is going to be as much of a circus as yours and Hermione's were."

Hester glanced at Phoebe with an exasperated expression. "You cannot marry the heir to a marquisate and not expect to have a large wedding. Also you must consider that he is the biggest catch on the Marriage Mart this year, and you have been the same for years now."

Phoebe took a cup of tea, and they sat in silence for a few minutes. Anna had said the same thing about Marcus. Phoebe realized that she must have been the only one in the *ton* who had not thought of him as a "catch."

Her sister leaned over to hug Phoebe. "I've never seen you look so happy, so *radiant*. I am so very pleased you finally found the love you were meant to have."

Tears glistened in Hester's eyes. "You've no idea how worried Hermione and I have been that you would not know that kind of love. The idea that you would grow into an unmarried aunt . . . well"—Hester sniffed and pulled out her handkerchief—"it doesn't bear thinking of. He *is* everything you want, isn't he?"

"Yes, and you're going to make me cry as well." Phoebe chuckled wetly, searching for her own handkerchief. "Marcus is everything I want. Hester, you have no idea how very much the same are our beliefs, our desires. I had almost given up hope that I would find a man who could entice me to marry." She added wryly, "And I never thought it would be him."

Her sister nodded. "That was a bit of a surprise."

Phoebe took a bite of egg on her fork. "We've not had our first argument yet."

Hester raised her cup and laughed. "Arguments are only an excuse to make up. You'll have them as we all do. Well, maybe not Geoffrey, but really Amabel is so different from us."

Phoebe nodded. "He claims that he lives under the cat's paw, but he told me all men in love with their wives do."

Her sister smiled knowingly. "Geoffrey has finally become wise."

Phoebe glanced up just as Marcus came through the door. His eyes immediately focused on her as she flushed with heat. Had it been only a couple of hours since they'd been with each other last? It seemed like forever. There had to be a way they could be alone in London. Nine days was an eternity.

*   *   *

Thankful the weather would be good for their trip back to London, Marcus handed Phoebe into his curricle where she took the ribbons.

John ambled up to them. "Well, Marcus, how does it feel being driven by a female?"

Ignoring the double entendre, Marcus smiled proudly at Phoebe. "It's an experience I would not forego. I've rarely known a more excellent whip. My only wish is that she'd allow me to tool her phaeton."

Edwin raised a brow. "Consider yourself lucky. *I'm* surprised she's allowing you to handle her blacks."

Geoffrey shook his head sadly. "Ah, but Marcus, you didn't see her in her early days learning to drive."

Hermione came up behind him. "Geoff, I remember her taking the shine out of you when she was only twelve."

He glowered, but his lips twitched. "It's a hard thing to have sisters who remember all one's mistakes and don't hesitate to tell one."

The others continued teasing him until Henry strolled out of the house. "Let us all be off. You can talk once we are back in Town. We have a busy week ahead of us."

Marcus climbed onto the curricle, a moment before Sam let go of the blacks' heads and jumped on the back of the curricle as Phoebe set off at a smart pace.

Phoebe and Marcus arrived at St. Eth House well in advance of Lord and Lady St. Eth. Phoebe gave orders to have the curricle pulled around to Dunwood House.

"Come." Phoebe held out her hand. "We have some time to ourselves."

"But, my love, François is not yet here." Marcus smiled wolfishly, speculating whether St. Eth would still require a footman to be posted in the breakfast room.

She peeked coquettishly through her long lashes. "We don't always need François."

Phoebe led Marcus to the morning room, where they discussed the plans for their wedding trip until their tea arrived.

She set down her cup. "How much time do you think we have?"

His lips curved up. "A half an hour, maybe a little more."

She went to him, stretching her arms up around his neck. "That's what I think too, let's make it worth our wait."

He kissed her deeply. "You have become a wanton woman, my lady."

She smiled seductively. "You should know, my lord, you made me that way." She slid her hand over his erection. "And for that, I shall be eternally grateful."

He sucked in a sharp breath. "By God, you're not alone in that sentiment."

"No more talking, my lord. I want you now."

Chapter Twenty

A few minutes after Marcus left for Dunwood House, Phoebe walked around the back garden, reveling in the memory of their lovemaking on the daybed in the morning room. She'd just sat on the bench at the end of a path when she heard the crunch of boots on the gravel path. Hoping it was Marcus returned, she glanced up as a rough-looking man came around the hedge. He grinned and reached out for her.

She dodged his grasp but was trapped between the hedge and the outer wall, with no way to escape. He came closer and Phoebe climbed up onto the bench and screamed for help hoping someone was nearby.

"Won't do you no good, your ladyship. Ain't nowhere for you to go, and ain't no one to hear you."

His burly arm grabbed her around the waist as he hefted her and started toward the back gate. His bruising grip made it hard to breathe, giving her a desperate idea. Hoping he'd think she had fainted, she went limp in his arms. He lifted her higher.

Phoebe waited until they'd cleared the hedge and there was a direct view toward the terrace. Bracing herself, she took a deep breath and threw her head back, hitting the man's nose hard. He roared in pain, and his hold on her loosened enough for her to break away. Lifting her skirts, Phoebe bolted toward the house, yelling at the top of her lungs. She heard the man's harsh breathing coming ever closer behind her. Suddenly he stopped and ran in the other direction. Just ahead, Jim, the footman, came racing across the lawn to help her.

"A man tried to kidnap me in the garden," she said.

Pointing the way, she turned and ran back toward her attacker.

The villain reached the gate leading into the alley before they could catch him. Sounds of horses trotting reached them. Phoebe and Jim rushed into the small street and searched in both directions. About half-way to the end of the mews, a town coach was traveling faster than was safe in the narrow alley, toward the entrance to the street.

Phoebe halted, gasping for air. "He must be in that carriage. Can we alert anyone in time to stop him?"

"I'll head to the front, my lady," Jim said. "I might catch him before he reaches the main street."

Phoebe nodded. "Try it."

"Not until you're safe, my lady."

Glancing around, Phoebe saw two more footmen running to her. "They can guard me. Go now, I'll be fine. Be careful."

Jim dashed off around the side of the house. The other men helped her inspect the gate, which was always kept locked. The key was hanging in its usual place. The attacker must have picked the lock.

When Phoebe got back to the house, Uncle Henry and Aunt Ester had arrived. She told her uncle what had happened.

"Here? In my garden?" he bellowed. "When I find out who it is, I'll have them strung up!"

Her uncle sent Marcus an urgent summons to return to St. Eth House. When he arrived, Phoebe told him what happened.

Marcus trembled with rage, his blood pumped faster, even as he gathered Phoebe in his arms to comfort her. The kidnap attempt must be *Travenor's* doing. Guilt consumed Marcus. If he'd warned her, she would not have been alone or without her dagger and pistol. He'd tell her of the danger and what he'd thought he'd learned of Travenor. Perhaps it would be enough to put her on her guard.

Everyone met in St. Eth's study and discussed the attack. Jim returned to report that he'd seen the coach as it turned the corner onto the street, but once it left the alley, there was nothing to distinguish it from any other unmarked carriage on the street. He'd been too far away to see the occupants.

Phoebe gave an accurate description of the man who grabbed her, but Marcus doubted it would do them any good. Brutes like that could easily be found in London's slums.

He drew Phoebe a little aside. "I must tell you what I discovered about Travenor. I should have told you before. I had him investigated. He's much more dangerous than any of us thought. There have been abusive incidents with women. . . ."

When he'd completed his account, Marcus caught Phoebe's gaze. "And there is something else. Travenor was part of a smuggling scheme I helped to break up in the West Indies." Marcus took a breath. "Travenor may be after you to avenge himself against me. I can't shake the feeling he is behind this. I'm sorry if I'm the one who brought you to his attention."

Phoebe placed her small hand on Marcus's cheek. "You

have nothing to be sorry for. We are more than a match for him."

Ester pinched the bridge of her nose. "Be that as it may, knowing it was indeed Lord Travenor behind all this would be helpful. Since we are not certain, we must take a broader view to protect Phoebe."

Marcus took Phoebe's hands. "My love, please promise me you'll not go anywhere alone."

"Yes," she said. "I promise you that."

"Thank you."

Ester invited Marcus to dine with them, and later, whilst Marcus and Phoebe walked on the terrace, she glanced at him. "Was it what you'd discovered about Travenor that had you upset at the manor house?"

Marcus nodded. "To some extent. The rest is about my family. I'm sorry, I didn't mean to leave you out. I am just so used to keeping my own counsel."

She reached up and kissed him. "Marcus, I understand, but if we are to have a successful marriage, we must share the bad along with the good."

He raised both her hands and kissed the insides of her wrists. "I'm beginning to apprehend that. Ride with me to-morrow?"

She smiled gently. "Yes. We'll have breakfast afterward."

Marcus took her in his arms, holding her safe. "I can't allow anyone to hurt you."

"You do realize that I am able to take care of myself, especially now that I've been forewarned?"

He stifled a growl. She'd had to protect herself long enough. Now, it was his job, and he damn well meant to keep her safe.

Lord Travenor was in his study, a glass of brandy in his hand, when his groom, Figgins, entered.

"My lord. The attempt to kidnap Lady Phoebe failed."

Roaring, he threw the brandy glass against the fireplace. "*Bloody hell!* Can't anyone do a job right? Get rid of him. If he was seen, I can't have the bugger associated with me."

Figgins nodded. "I'm meeting him down by the docks tonight. He won't be talkin' to anyone after that."

"See that he doesn't." Travenor paced before the fireplace, seething with anger. Figgins would take care of it. He'd been with Travenor since he was a boy and would do anything for him.

Travenor snarled. "I want Lady Phoebe followed by at least two men. If there's a chance in hell to grab her, I want it done, and tell them I won't be bobbed. They'd better be rum about it. I can't afford to get caught."

"Yes, my lord. I'll make sure they know you don't take kindly to being disappointed."

Figgins bowed and left.

Curse Lord Marcus Finley for getting to her. Travenor hadn't seen the bloody betrothal notice, but he'd heard about it. It was the only thing the blasted Swells were talking about. He'd have to act swiftly if he were to capture Lady Phoebe. They'd already posted guards at her uncle's house so it wouldn't be there. Travenor would have to figure out another way.

Lady Phoebe would be his, and he'd set her straight. After which, it would be his pleasure to destroy Lord Marcus Finley.

The next morning dawned fine and crisp. Marcus and Phoebe, accompanied by one of St. Eth's grooms, rode to Rotten Row for a gallop, then trotted around the Park.

Upon returning to St. Eth House, wary of another attempt on Phoebe, Marcus saw a scruffy-looking man in the square watching the house. He had the groom escort her to the house. Once Ferguson opened the door, and Phoebe went inside, Marcus strode across the street toward the blackguard.

The watcher took off at a run, dodging in his way. Marcus gave chase through the square. If there was even a possibility that he knew his employer, Marcus would make the man talk. He was closing in on his quarry, but when they reached Upper Brook Street, the man darted into the traffic and hopped onto a wagon. He slipped, falling off the other side right into the path of a carriage. The pair of horses bore down on the watcher. The man screamed and the horses reared up in panic, hooves flailing and trampling the man. He went down in a bloody pulp. The nondescript, black coach rolled over the body, crushing it, and kept going. *Somehow Marcus knew the death was no accident.*

Marcus regained the house and joined Phoebe, still standing in the open door. "Marcus, what happened?"

He took her arm to lead her in the house. "The man watching the house is dead. I gave chase and a coach hit him."

Phoebe covered her mouth. "Oh, God."

Marcus held her tighter. "The coach could have stopped, but did not. It was murder."

They were both quiet as they entered the breakfast room and sat.

Phoebe's hand trembled slightly as she took a croissant and poured tea. "Do you believe he was observing the house because of me?"

Marcus accepted his cup. "Yes, and to see who comes and goes, determine the patterns of the servants and their masters." Marcus stared at her steadily. "Phoebe, one question we did not ask yesterday was how the thug knew you were in the garden. I now believe someone—or several people—have been watching this house and you. We need to ascertain their hiding places. How did you go out from the house to the garden yesterday?"

"Through the side door." Her eyes widened. "Oh, Marcus, if one were looking, the door can be seen through the gate."

Marcus pressed his lips together. "The villains were in place before we returned."

Phoebe fixed Marcus with a look. "If it is Travenor's doing, why is he so relentless?" Not waiting for his answer, she stood and started to pace. "What if he doesn't cease after we're married? He may follow us to Charteries, and we don't know why he wants me." She halted and turned to Marcus. "We must stop him."

Marcus took her in his arms. "We will, my love. I promise you, he'll not take you from me."

She peered up at Marcus. "I want more practice with the dagger."

"Very well, I'll work with you this afternoon."

"Rose has already fashioned a leg sheath and altered my gowns." Phoebe gave a small smile. "Perhaps I'll set a new fashion trend."

Marcus laughed.

Henry and Ester entered the breakfast room.

When Marcus told them the house was under surveillance, they were infuriated.

"We must," Phoebe said firmly, "discover, for a certainty, who he is and put an end to this."

Marcus nodded. "We need a way to draw him out."

Ester held her cup suspended between the table and her lips. "We can set out our people, in street clothing, footmen and grooms, to discover who is spying on the house."

Phoebe nodded. "I'm sure they would be willing."

They all glanced at Henry, who had been silent.

He raised his brows. "That might work." Henry met each of their eyes. "We have less than four days before we leave. If we're to do this, we must start immediately."

Hermione and Hester entered the room, stopped, and frowned.

"What's happened?" Hermione asked. "Why the long faces?"

Upon being told, the sisters immediately offered to help.

Hermione took a croissant and nibbled. "Since Phoebe has to go shopping, perhaps some of the men can go out now." Hermione glanced at Marcus. "We'll take two footmen to guard us."

Marcus caught Phoebe's eye. "I'll send Covey as well. Be careful, my love."

She bit her lip. "I will. It feels good to be taking action."

Phoebe grinned at Madame who came bustling forward to the front of the shop with effusive greetings. "*Bonjour,* Lady Phoebe. I believe I must wish you happy. You are to be married, *non?* And to the very fine-looking Lord Marcus Finley. *Bien,* it is as it should be. A beautiful lady marries a handsome man."

Phoebe laughed. "How do you know he's good-looking?"

"Ah, milady, I have heard of nothing but Lord Marcus Finley since the Little Season began. *Moi,* I think there are no other gentlemen in London. He is all *les jeune filles* speak of. Now, you are here for a gown for the wedding, no? *Mais dites moi,* when do you require it to be finished?"

Heat rose in her cheeks. "In three days."

Madame clapped her hands in delight. "Ah, the Lord Marcus loves you very much and cannot wait. *Moi, je comprends.* It is always the way with young men." Madame shook her head. "Come, you must have your ball gown fitted, and I shall make a drawing of the wedding gown. Do you make *un voyage de noces?* The mademoiselles of the *ton* shall weep with despair."

Phoebe blushed again as her sisters collapsed in chairs, struggling not to go into whoops. She didn't know what was so funny about Marcus being the focus of every young lady's attention and flashed them a quelling glance. "We shall travel to Paris."

Madame clapped her hands. "I can recommend to you a very good modiste in Paris. I shall send a letter of introduction. *Bien, allez, milady.*"

Madame sketched quickly while Phoebe stood for her final fitting. When Madame was finished, she showed the drawing to Phoebe and her sisters while an apprentice made the final alterations. The wedding gown Madame had sketched was simplicity itself. It had a high bodice cut low across Phoebe's bosom in a diaphanous material folded over several times, short sleeves—gathered rather than puffed— decorated with seed pearls, the skirts in a heavy silk with a train.

"Madame, it's beautiful," Phoebe said. "Are you sure it will be done in time?"

"Of course, it will be done. *Je le fais.*"

Hermione sat up, glanced at Phoebe, and turned to Madame. "Madame, Lady Phoebe will also need négligées, chemises, and petticoats."

Madame nodded. "*Oui, milady*, but she should purchase most of them in Paris. The styles of Paris are *trés chic,* and milord will like them very much. I assure you." Madame turned to Phoebe. "*Milady*, I shall send your ball gown to you in the morning, with the others you ordered, and anything you will need until you reach Paris."

As Phoebe and her sisters regained Bruton Street, they made surreptitious scans of the area.

Covey, whom Marcus had declared would be with her until the villain was caught, was looking into a window across the street. Jim, St. Eth's footman, who'd come to her aid during the kidnap attempt, was half-concealed in a doorway a few stores down. Phoebe was careful not to give away that she'd seen them.

As she walked, a sudden frisson of fear ran up her spine. She was being watched. She'd felt the same foreboding after leaving each store, but her adversary remained out of sight. The hunted feeling didn't lessen, but, finally, there was nothing to do but return to St. Eth House. The sense of being someone's prey did not abate.

That evening Marcus, Phoebe, and their families attended Lady Worth's ball. The families entered the ballroom together. After descending the stairs, the couples parted to find their particular friends. Phoebe and Marcus quickly found themselves besieged by well-wishers.

Marcus was unable to keep a smug smile from his face as he was congratulated for having convinced the elusive Lady Phoebe to finally marry. But he sensed Phoebe's agitation. He tilted his head closer to hers. "My love, what's wrong?"

Her lips formed a tight smile. "Nothing." She gave a slight shake of her head. "No, that's not true. I'd no idea you were such a big catch when we began all this. The arch looks I'm receiving imply I set my cap at you."

"No one could truly suspect you of being so vulgar. Come with me, my love." He whisked her through a door, down a hallway, and into a lit parlor. "You're still upset, what else did you hear?"

Phoebe's lips turned down. "That the wedding was set so soon because I was afraid you'd escape."

Marcus drew her into his arms. He wanted to smile, but she'd take it the wrong way. "No one who knows us would think that. Quite the opposite, in fact. You have my permission to tell them you led me a merry chase, for indeed, my love, you did."

When she gave him a half-hearted smile, he kissed the top of her head. "Where's my Valiant Lady, and since when do you care what some rude cats say?"

Phoebe sighed. "I suppose you're right."

"I'm right?" Marcus grinned. "I shall store those words in my heart. I've been told I won't hear them much after we're married."

She giggled. "Who told you that faradiddle?"

"You think it nonsense? I've been forewarned by every married man I know, including your brother and uncle." He smiled down at her, happy that her good mood had returned. His Phoebe was normally very even-tempered, but there'd been an underlying tenseness in her since they'd returned to London. He'd put it down to the attack and hoped it wasn't more than that.

Marcus kissed her softly. "I hear the violins tuning up for a waltz. Are you ready to go back in there and face the maddening horde?"

"Yes." She lifted her eyes to his. "Thank you."

He held her in his arms for a few moments longer. "My pleasure, my love."

They took their places for the dance. Waltzing with her was like entering his own magical world. She relaxed, her deep blue eyes soft.

"Have you realized we are no longer limited to two dances?"

"I have." Marcus held her tighter as he maneuvered them through the turn. "And woe to the man who tries to capture you for a set this evening. I plan to enjoy our new-found license to indulge."

She laughed lightly. "You've become very greedy, my lord."

He searched deep into her eyes. "Only with you. I would keep you in my arms forever. Do you mind?"

Phoebe's breath hitched. "No, not at all. I've no wish to stand up with anyone but you."

As Marcus and Phoebe were leaving the floor after their second waltz, her arm firmly fixed in his, Lord Travenor approached.

"Lady Phoebe, I would like to ask the pleasure of the next waltz. I see you have already danced with Lord Marcus twice."

Phoebe's grip tightened on his arm. He'd told her he suspected Travenor of being behind the attack, and, apparently, that had been enough to put her on her guard.

Marcus assumed a politely jaded expression, though his eyes were hard. He straightened and glanced down at his enemy. "Travenor, you are fast becoming a dead bore. Don't you read the *Morning Post*?" Marcus didn't wait for an answer. "Lady Phoebe is my affianced-*wife*. She will dance with none but me. Do not approach her again."

Marcus kept his cold gaze on Lord Travenor's reddening complexion. All evening, the other man had leered at Phoebe when he thought no one was looking, but Marcus had seen it and glimpsed the baron's lustful jealousy.

Now, Lord Travenor's expression showed his malevolent intentions all too clearly.

"Well, it seems I must wish you happy. Lady Phoebe, Lord Marcus." Travenor bowed and left them, but the anger emanating from him was palpable.

Phoebe smiled delightedly at Marcus. "I quite like having my own knight-errant."

He gave a brief laugh, but wanted to take Phoebe away from there. Travenor was a scoundrel of the worst sort and Marcus didn't trust him at all. They soon joined a group of

friends, including Lords Rutherford, Huntley, and Worthington, who called for champagne.

Worthington grinned. "I never would have believed I'd
see this day, but it seems as if fate has spoken."

After more well wishes, Marcus found himself next to
Rutherford. "I'd like to talk to you about the wedding."

His friend raised a brow.

"I'd like you to support me," Marcus said. "My brother
will be there as well, if he is able."

Rutherford's lips quirked up. "It would be my pleasure.
In fact, I wouldn't miss it." He glanced at Phoebe. "But tell
me. What was wrong with Phoebe earlier?"

Marcus frowned. "Someone started a rumor she set her
cap at me. If you hear anyone mention it, I'd take it as a
kindness if you'd set them straight and tell them what a
devil of a time I had convincing her to marry me."

Rutherford narrowed his eyes. "With pleasure. One
should not say the unassailable Lady Phoebe fell easily." His
mouth twisted into a rueful smile. "It would make the rest of
us look inept."

Rage infused Travenor as he watched Lord Marcus walk
around with Lady Phoebe on his arm. Lord Marcus, *that
spoiled fop,* had all but threatened him—a baron and true
man, not a milksop. Lord Marcus treated him as if he were
dirt under the great lord's feet. Lord Marcus might think
Lady Phoebe was his, but he'd learn the truth soon enough.

Travenor kept a mild look on his face, but his hatred
grew. Perhaps he'd let Lord Marcus have her *after* he was
finished with the woman. Soiled goods for his lordship.
The idea grew. If Travenor couldn't marry her, he'd make
damn sure Lord Marcus Finley would have a wife who
would cringe from his touch.

Travenor smiled. He'd enjoy himself with her ladyship and have his revenge. If he didn't get her in London, he'd go to where the wedding was being held and take her there. Later, after he'd laid them both to waste, perhaps, he'd just kill them.

Chapter Twenty-one

After riding with Phoebe that morning and breaking his fast with her, Marcus returned to his house to change, then strode back to St. Eth House hoping to find his betrothed alone.

Ferguson bowed him into the house. "Good morning, my lord."

"Good morning, Ferguson. I'm here to help prepare for the ball. Can you tell me where I might find Lady Phoebe?"

The butler directed Marcus to a parlor in the back of the house, where she was staring at something on a large table.

Catching her up into his arms, he kissed her soundly. "What can I do?"

"How is your handwriting?" she asked promptly.

He wondered why she wanted to know, but replied, "I am held to have an elegant hand."

She handed him a stack of cards for her aunt's dinner that evening. "You can start with these."

His jaw dropped. Playing scribe was not what he had in mind. "That'll teach me to ask. I thought you'd say there was nothing to do, and you wanted me to ravish you."

Phoebe laughed musically. "That sounds lovely, but there

is always *something* to do on the day of a ball. Be happy it's not the regular Season. I'd have you moving potted plants."

Marcus heaved a dramatic sigh. "I take it that after we are married I'll have to repair to my club on the day of a ball."

The narrow-eyed look she gave him made him laugh.

"I expect you, my lord, to attend to your business at home on the day of any ball we will hold," she said tartly.

"Business? Which business is that? The one where I keep you sated and happy?" He gave her his best wolfish look and caressed her from the wispy curls at her neck to her lush derrière.

Phoebe blushed and raised a haughty brow. "My lord, this is bad enough without *you* making it worse."

He sighed for real this time. Perhaps if they finished quickly, he could have some time alone with her. Sitting at the table, he applied himself diligently to his task. He sharpened his pen with the knife she'd handed him and worked steadily until all the cards for the table were written.

Though he would rather just make love to her, he decided he should discuss the threat Travenor posed to her first. Waiting until she'd stacked the seating cards, he said, "Phoebe, I need to speak with you."

She glanced up, alarmed. "Is something wrong, my love?"

"I wish to discuss your protection. You know I suspect Travenor of trying to abduct you . . ."

She nodded.

Marcus placed his hands on her small waist, and drew her to him. "The madness I saw in Travenor's face at the ball last evening concerns me more than before. Promise me you'll carry both your small pistol and dagger with you."

Phoebe bit her lip. "I promise. At this point, I am willing to be bait."

Oh God. That was the last thing he wanted. Marcus took her in his arms and buried his face in her hair. "No, my love, you cannot take the risk. If anything were to happen to you, if he were to hurt you, I wouldn't be able to stand it."

Her voice was strangely calm when she replied, "I know how you feel, my darling. But *I* don't want to be a target anymore. If someone were after you, what would you do?"

He searched her face and let out a low growl. He'd do the exact same thing she proposed. Yet his mind and his heart rebelled against the idea that she'd place herself in harm's way. "We can discuss this to-morrow."

Marcus pulled her roughly against him and wordlessly commanded her to open her lips to him. He poured all his fear and frustration into his kiss as he claimed her mouth, then showed Phoebe a more pleasurable use for the table than writing cards.

Damn it, it was his duty to protect her. He had to convince her to stay safe.

Phoebe saw Marcus standing at the bottom of the stairs staring up at her as she descended. His gaze roved her body and he sucked in a breath. His reaction was everything she'd hoped it would be.

Her ball gown was in a bronze-green silk over a bronze petticoat that was caught just under her breasts with a twisted cord. The skirts of the gown flattered her curves, and the fabric seemed to change colors when she moved. The bodice had tiny transparent sleeves, making her shoulders seem almost bare.

He held out his hand to her as she reached the last step. "My love, you are a *Vision*."

Phoebe had never been happier.

After the dinner, where their betrothal was announced, and the reception line, where they received more congratulations, Uncle Henry gave the signal for the orchestra to begin. The violins sounded the chords for a waltz.

Marcus led her onto the dance floor. Once in his arms, she gazed into his wonderful turquoise eyes and became lost in a world where just the two of them existed. She once again felt the heat of his hand on her waist as they twirled down the room, then the touch of his hard leg as he led them through the turn. Soon Phoebe's breath shortened, and she grew warmer. Tingles of desire shot through her and her nipples hardened and ached.

"Phoebe?" he asked. "Are you all right?"

"No. There must be a way to be with you."

Though she'd lived in St. Eth House during the Seasons for many years, it was the first time she required a discreet door to exit the room. "There is a door behind that palm. Once we've strolled a little and talked with all the guests, we'll be able to slip out."

Marcus gave his head a small shake. "Too dangerous. The servants are using it. We'd probably run into one of them. The terrace might be a safer choice. Which rooms lead out to it?"

"The back parlor would work. No one will look in there."

Phoebe relaxed once more into the dance, satisfied they'd be able to be alone together.

At the end of the set, she left the dance floor on Marcus's arm. They strolled the room, greeting their friends and families. Slowly—and she hoped, subtly—making their way to the terrace doors.

When she tried to quicken the pace, he held her back. "Patience, if we walk leisurely we're less likely to be noticed."

Soon, Marcus swept her out onto the terrace. Phoebe turned to the right. As they reached the doors to the back parlor, he opened it and pulled her in. He captured her lips.

She returned his kisses with hungry urgency.

Just as he reached back to close the door, footsteps sounded on the stone pavers.

Phoebe sighed and leaned against him. "Who is it?"

"Hermione and Edwin." Marcus released Phoebe and stepped back a little.

She groaned. This was so unfair. Their families wouldn't allow them to marry when they'd wanted to and now Phoebe couldn't even be alone with Marcus.

Hermione smiled, but said nothing, as she took Phoebe's arm and led her back toward the ballroom.

Edwin took Marcus's and chuckled. "There's no point in giving me a black look. The problem you have is that Phoebe has two older sisters who have gone before her. They know all the tricks."

Marcus glowered.

Edwin merely laughed. "Only a few days more. You'll make it, we did."

Once back at the entrance to the ballroom, Marcus was allowed to escort Phoebe in, but they were given no opportunity to slip away again.

Five more days; Phoebe wondered if Marcus's frustration matched her own.

As had become Marcus's habit, he met Phoebe to ride the next morning. When they returned to St. Eth House, he spotted a ragged boy lurking behind a tree in the square. Another watcher.

"Marcus!" Phoebe cried. "There is a plain black carriage at the corner. It looks to be creeping toward us. Could it be him?"

"I want you in the house. Now." After quickly dismounting, he lifted Phoebe from Lilly and threw the groom the reins. Two ruffians rushed out from the side of the house.

"My lord, watch out!" The groom shouted and started toward the thugs, but the horses shied and sidled in fear.

"Stay with the horses," Marcus ordered.

He reached for Phoebe to push her behind him when one of the thugs reached them and threw his first punch. Marcus's jaw exploded in pain.

Driving his fist into the man's face, Marcus yelled, "Phoebe, run. Get help from the house!"

His attacker came at him again and Marcus smashed his fist into the villain's nose. Bleeding, the blackguard fell to the ground.

He whirled to see Phoebe with her dagger out, warding off the second brute as he made another grab for her. Damn the woman. Why hadn't she done as he'd asked? Marcus hauled the man around, knocking him down with an uppercut to his chin.

Shaking with anger and a fear he'd never known before, he grasped her shoulders. "Why aren't you in the house?"

"It was two to one, and he'd blocked the path to the door."

He crushed her to him and heedless of propriety, kissed her ruthlessly.

A footman, who'd run from the house to give chase to the villains, came back panting. "My lord. They're gone," the servant gasped. "Picked up by a black coach. The driver had a muffler over part of his face."

Damn it to hell. They lost the thugs. Holding Phoebe again by the shoulders, he fought himself not to shake her. "I told you to run."

"I started to." She firmed her jaw. "But I saw you needed help."

"It's my duty to protect you, not yours to protect me."

She scowled. "I had my dagger and was doing fine. You should have trusted me. If you'd secured the first man, we'd have someone to question."

"And if *you'd* done as I said, we might have them both," Marcus growled.

Drat him. In their own way, they were both right. Phoebe's anger ebbed. They loved each other, why was this so difficult? She glanced back to him. A bruise was forming on his jaw and he had a cut on his cheek. She took his hand. It had been wounded as well. "We'll have to talk about this later. Right now, I need to attend to you."

Uncle Henry was in the hall when they entered. He called for water, soap, salve, and a raw beefsteak to be taken to the breakfast room. Phoebe attended to Marcus while he explained what happened to her uncle.

Her uncle slammed his fist on the table. "*Again?* This is intolerable."

"I *cannot* allow this to continue," Phoebe said. "We have no assurances it will ever stop, even when I am married." She paused and took a breath. "I propose we allow him to take me."

Henry stared at her. "*Take* you? Have you gone mad? Finley, talk some sense into her."

Marcus rubbed his hands over his face and winced. "I already tried. She won't listen to me. I don't like the idea at all. If you've a better one, I'd be happy to hear it."

Males, Phoebe thought bitterly. "I've been trained to defend myself. I have a *right* to help in my protection. I cannot believe that you and Marcus don't think me capable of helping end this."

Marcus frowned and his voice was more like a growling animal's. "It's not that. I know you're capable. But it's my responsibility, *my right* to protect you. I don't understand why you would foolishly put yourself in danger."

"Foolish?" She had not been so close to losing her temper in a long time. "If you think that, I wonder why you want to marry me."

Her uncle, who had been silent, lowered his brows. "Phoebe, Finley is right. It's his duty to protect and care for you."

Phoebe passed a hand over her brow. This didn't make any sense at all. "Uncle Henry, how can you take his side?"

The conversation was not going her way.

Fortunately, Aunt Ester entered the room. "Stop shouting. You can be heard all over the house. What is going on?"

Marcus and Uncle Henry opened their mouths. She silenced the two men with a look. "Phoebe, tell me what happened."

She told her aunt about the latest attempt, and what she proposed to do about it.

Henry and Marcus both began to speak but were once again silenced.

"If I understand you, my dear," Aunt Ester said, "you propose to allow yourself to be abducted, but have our people around to retrieve you before you are harmed. Do I have that right?"

Maybe Marcus and her uncle would finally listen to reason. "Yes, Aunt Ester."

Her aunt turned to the men. "Henry, Marcus, I understand you have objections. I would be astonished if you did not. However, my dear, before you state your reasons, do you have an alternative plan that would free Phoebe from this menace?"

Henry shook his head. "Marcus?"

He glowered from beneath his brows. "As I've said, I cannot like it."

Ester regarded each of them. "Can we—all of us, Hermione's and Hester's households included—provide

the protection Phoebe will need? Because"—Aunt Ester
glanced at her niece and met her gaze—"if we cannot, then
your plan would only place you in greater danger."

Silence reigned for several minutes as they thought over
the details.

Marcus was the first to speak. "May I call my man,
Covey, here?"

Aunt Ester inclined her head. "Of course."

Marcus's groom entered the breakfast room as Phoebe's
sisters and their husbands arrived.

Aunt Ester told them all about the attempt that morning.
They listened in grim silence until her aunt turned to Marcus and nodded.

He motioned for Covey, who was leaning against the
wall, to step up. "Did you see what occurred this morning?"

Covey narrowed his eyes. "I did at that, m'lord. Got a
good look at them toughs and at that black carriage that
picked them up. It were the one I seen afore. Iffen' I see it
again, I'll know it. Looked like the same man in it, but he's
sitn' too far back for me to get a good gander at him."

Marcus surveyed the group. "Ever since the first attempt, except when Phoebe's been with me, Covey has
been following her. He's made note of the persons who
have been keeping her under observation. He's seen the
carriage but the driver and occupant take great care not to
be recognized."

Marcus fixed his gaze on Phoebe. "The plan I had is that
if she were taken, Covey would stay on the back of the carriage and intervene if there was any sign of danger."

Aunt Ester's glance swept the room. "Well, what say
you all?"

Hester spoke first. "I think Phoebe is right. If this is to
end, she will need to allow herself to be abducted."

Edwin and John started to argue heatedly but were silenced by Aunt Ester. "I shall tell you both what I told St. Eth and Marcus. You may not like this plan, but, unless you have an alternative, nothing will be accomplished by merely expressing your disapproval. No one likes these circumstances."

They lapsed into silence.

Aunt Ester continued briskly, "Well then, we are—if not all happy about this arrangement—in agreement there is no better alternative. Let us discuss the details."

Geoffrey rubbed his chin. "I think when Phoebe and Marcus are married, the attempts will stop. I cannot see how taking her after the marriage would benefit the scoundrel."

"No," Marcus said firmly. "If it's Travenor, he won't stop. The man's obsessed."

Travenor seethed with impotent rage. "They missed taking her again? How did it happen?"

Figgins recounted the story. "Seems like that Lord Marcus is pretty handy with his fives."

Travenor had misjudged Lord Marcus. Who knew a fop could fight? One more thing to add to Travenor's account against the bastard who had made Travenor's life a living hell, stolen his treasure, and nearly ruined him. Lord Marcus would not get Lady Phoebe.

Travenor tossed off his tumbler of Blood and Thunder and slammed the glass down. He'd use Lady Phoebe to settle his score with Lord Marcus. If she didn't come around to his way of thinking and marry him, he'd make sure she'd never lie with another man. All gentlemen wanted a virgin to wife. He'd deliver a well-used one to Lord Marcus.

From now on, no more intermediaries; Travenor would take care of the problem himself.

Chapter Twenty-two

Phoebe and Aunt Ester had taken a coach to Bond Street. Phoebe took a deep breath and smiled, making her voice as calm as possible. "Aunt Ester, I am going to the glove maker. I'll be back in less than a half an hour."

Phoebe glanced at Rose, who dutifully followed behind Phoebe.

Covey had seen the black town coach in Bond Street and sent Jim, the footman, with the news that all was in place to begin the plan.

"We can do this," Phoebe insisted as she made her way down the street. Forcing herself not to look around as she walked, she kept her steps even. Rose would try to identify the villain and get away to inform the others.

Phoebe glanced down to fiddle with her gloves. She hoped that this dangerous ruse would make her unknown abductor show his hand. Finally, she'd know who was after her and why.

All was proceeding as planned. Marcus, her brother, uncle, and brothers-in-law, along with footmen and under grooms from their houses, and Covey, were watching from the street, inside shops, and from various conveyances. Phoebe touched the sheathed dagger for reassurance.

Last evening, the ladies had finally convinced Phoebe's recalcitrant male relatives she would need to go shopping, without a footman, if they hoped to enable her to be snatched. Thankfully, in the end, even Marcus agreed, though he was not at all happy about it.

This morning, he'd hovered over her, making sure she had her dagger and pistol, blaming himself. "If I'd not been such a scamp . . . If I'd returned years ago, you would never have had to protect yourself. I would have been there to do it."

She put her fingers over his lips. "Don't torture yourself. Let us just deal with what we have."

They were leaving in two days for Charteries. She would not be inured in the country, from which she could still be abducted, or be constantly on her guard in London—or any-where else.

Phoebe took a breath. This would end to-day.

The coach slowed to a crawl. Phoebe braced herself to be taken. Suddenly, it picked up speed again and continued on.

Phoebe stared after the vehicle in disbelief and motioned to Rose to continue walking, praying the scoundrel would do something. After several minutes, Phoebe and her maid turned back. She'd been so sure the blackguard would try to abduct her. Phoebe clenched her fist in frustration. She wanted, needed, this to be over, so she could start her life with Marcus.

Travenor had watched as Lady Phoebe and a female dressed as a lady's maid left the lending library. Before this, he'd never seen her without a footman. Wary, Travenor glanced around the street. More than the usual number of people lingered in doorways and looked in store windows.

One of the men took several surreptitious glances at Lady Phoebe.

Suspicious, Travenor approached her in his coach, slowing as he neared her. Her movement changed, her body tensing as if she was waiting for something to happen.

A damn trap! Furious, Travenor tapped twice on the roof of his carriage with his cane and it resumed its normal speed. He seethed all the way home, his anger escalating. Followed by his groom, Travenor entered the hall of his townhouse, tossed his hat and cane to a footman, before stalking to his study. He slammed the door open. Once he'd poured a glass of brandy and downed it, he scowled. "They must think I'm a bloody fool to fall for a trap like that. I'd be surprised if there was a servant left in St. Eth's House."

"What will you do now, my lord?" Figgins asked quietly.

Travenor splashed more brandy in the glass and tossed it off. It was clear whoever put the plan in motion thought Travenor would be easy to catch, but he'd waited a long time for Lady Phoebe and an even longer time to pay back Lord Marcus. Travenor sat in a large dark brown leather chair near the fireplace. He didn't get this far by being stupid. "Find where they're getting shackled, and send in a few people to the estate to question the servants. I want to know all the comings and goings."

Figgins screwed up his face in confusion as he refilled his master's glass. "When will you try again?"

"When they least expect it." Travenor drank his third brandy in one long pull. "Get me a woman, and make sure she's stronger than the last one."

"Where do you want me to go? That French madam said she'd not give you any more girls. Said you beat the last one too badly."

Travenor's groin twitched at the memory of the light-skirt from Madam Désirée's house, reddish-blond hair and fair skin. Her cries for mercy still made his groin twitch.

The only problem was the whore bruised too easily and was slow to recover. He'd had to pay for the days she missed work, and the French bitch wouldn't let him use the girl again. "Go to Betsy's. Tell her I want someone who likes it rough—very rough."

That evening, Phoebe tried to put their failure to catch her assailant out of her mind. Dressed in a simple aubergine silk evening gown, she descended the stairs. Marcus waited in the hall. When she reached the bottom tread, he took her hand, placed a kiss in her palm and closed it. Phoebe smiled. "It won't be long now. Three more days, and no one will part us, ever again."

In his gaze was his love for her, the same look she'd seen that day in Bond Street, but hadn't known what it meant. She vowed no one—not Lord Travenor, or anyone else it might be—would separate her from Marcus.

He wrapped his strong arm around her waist, and she placed one hand on his face, and whispered, "You are everything to me."

When Phoebe turned around, Hermione and Hester stood stock still, staring at Phoebe and Marcus from the drawing-room doorway.

Aunt Ester, who'd come down the stairs, chuckled. "That, my dears, was how they gazed at each other in Bond Street."

The twins turned quickly to their aunt, eyes wide.

Hester started to laugh. "I would have had them to church the very day."

Ester gave a wry grin and narrowed her eyes at Marcus. "Yes, well, that would have been a bit difficult. He would not give me his name."

Marcus flushed. "If I'd introduced myself, Phoebe might never have had anything to do with me."

Phoebe drew her brows together. It had only been a matter of weeks since they met in Bond Street. "It seems such a long time ago."

He twisted his lips as if in pain. "Too long for me, my lady."

The twins exclaimed that they'd never acted with such abandon and were instantly contradicted by Geoffrey, who'd wandered into the hall with Amabel. "Both of you were just as besotted. We put it down to youth."

Their brother's eyes held a mischievous twinkle. "Now *I,* on the other hand, behaved with remarkable propriety."

Everyone smiled as Amabel's blush grew, and he was made to retract his remarks.

"At least I didn't do it in Bond Street," he grumbled.

At dinner there seemed to be an unspoken decision not to discuss Travenor, which suited Phoebe. She never wanted to think of him again and prayed he'd decided to forget her, as well.

The talk turned to the wedding. Phoebe would have been happier to have been married in a small ceremony, shortly after her return from the manor house. She was impatient to begin life as Marcus's wife. Finally she'd have a house of her own, an estate to work on with her husband, and eventually children. Everything she'd always wanted. A warm glow of contentment settled over her.

Nothing would mar her happiness. "Marcus, could we make an early start to Charteries in the morning? We've so much to do before the wedding, and I'd like to meet with the senior staff."

He smiled. "As you wish, my love. Shall we take my curricle?"

Phoebe shook her head. "If you don't object, I would rather we take my traveling coach. We will need it after the wedding for the journey to Newhaven. Your curricle can be brought down later. I usually leave my phaeton in Town."

After tea, Marcus and Phoebe lingered in the hall, unwilling to part.

"Until morning." He kissed her hand.

She reached up and lightly brushed her lips against his. "Yes, until morning. When you will take me home."

The next day, Phoebe and Marcus set out, followed closely by Geoffrey and Amabel in their coach.

When Amabel had first come to live at Cranbourne Place, she'd described her former home in detail to Phoebe. After all this time, she would finally view it for herself. The estate was located midway between London and the coastal village of Newhaven.

Marcus tapped on the ceiling, addressing the driver. "Stop at the next rise." Turning to Phoebe, he said, "You'll have a better view of the house and some of the landscaping from there."

Phoebe stood on the top stair of the carriage and gazed over a lawn, with a lake, to the large rambling fortified house of light gray stone. The wings were canted out, somewhat like a bird's span, from the main house.

"The original parts of the house date back to the fourteenth century," Marcus said. "In the last century, the famous landscape designer Capability Brown was responsible for the expansive lawn leading to the large natural lake."

Phoebe couldn't wait to see the original wall, moat, and gate. She already loved Charteries, and it would be hers, her home. "Oh, Marcus, it looks like a castle. Like something from a fairy story. What a vastly pretty house."

"I've never thought of Charteries in quite those terms." He smiled. "I like seeing it through your eyes."

He put an arm around her. "My grandfather added the Georgian portico. My father made other improvements. We have bathing chambers in the main apartments and many of the older rooms have been enlarged," he said proudly. "I defy you to find a drafty window or smoking fireplace." Marcus gave Phoebe a loving look. "I hope you will like it."

"I already do."

When they drew up in front of the door, Geoffrey's coach was not far behind them. Lord and Lady Dunwood were on the steps, as were Marcus's nieces.

Lady Dunwood came forward as Phoebe alighted from the carriage and hugged her. "Welcome to your new home, my dear. We are all so happy to have you at Charteries."

"As am I to be here, my lady," Phoebe said, returning the warm embrace.

Lady Dunwood held Phoebe's shoulders. "Please, call me Isabel." She hesitated, flushing. "Perhaps someday you will call me Mamma."

Phoebe's throat hurt a bit and she blinked back tears of happiness. "Thank you, Isabel."

Lord Dunwood greeted Phoebe, as Isabel welcomed Marcus, Amabel, and Geoffrey.

Isabel led Phoebe up to the door, where Arthur's daughters waited to be introduced. "Lady Phoebe, may I make you known to Anne and Emily? Children, Lady Phoebe is to marry your uncle Marcus. Come and make your curtseys."

They were pretty girls of ten and eight, a little taller than usual, with dark brown curls and frank blue eyes the same shade as Marcus's.

Phoebe held her arms out to them. "Please call me Aunt Phoebe, for I shall be just that in no time at all."

She was pleased to find that—as with her other nieces and nephews—the girls were drawn to her. Phoebe held them both gently for several moments, whispering encouragement, before taking their hands in hers and entering the large, old marble-and-linen-paneled hall. Anne and Emily chattered excitedly, telling Phoebe all about themselves as they led her into a drawing room.

Marcus watched his betrothed, and his heart ached with love for her.

His mother glanced at him wide-eyed. "How does she do that? I was sure the girls would be shy of her. They don't meet many new people."

Marcus shrugged and cast a look at Amabel. "You would know better."

Amabel shrugged as well. "Marcus, there is no point asking me. I have no idea what magic Phoebe possesses over children." Amabel pursed her lips. "I can only tell you that Hester's and Hermione's broods are besotted with her. Caldecott and Fairport complain Phoebe turns them into heathens. I imagine, when Miles is older, he will be just as bad."

His sister paused for a moment and gazed into the doorway. "It is a good thing Phoebe does have that effect. Anne and Emily will need it."

Marcus gave a bark of laughter. "Not if Phoebe turns them into heathens."

Amabel punched him playfully. "No, it is just that all the children love her so much, they can't wait to have her attention. They really do behave well for her."

Marcus reached Phoebe and took her hand. "Come meet my brother."

Arthur, the Earl of Evesham, lay on a chaise covered by a blanket and propped up by pillows. Marcus cleared his throat, trying to get rid of the knot that had formed upon seeing Arthur's condition. He had the look of one who had hung on to the very end.

Marcus started to introduce them.

Phoebe interrupted, "Lord Evesham, we've met before. I am quite sure my brother-in-law, Fairport, introduced us some years ago. You were at Amabel and Geoffrey's wedding, though we only spoke a few words there."

Arthur struggled to sit. "Yes, how could I have forgotten? How have you been, Lady Phoebe?"

She placed a hand on his shoulder. "Don't move on my account and, please, call me Phoebe. You are to be my brother, after all."

Arthur, a gentle smile on his face, held out his hand to her.

Phoebe took it and drew him into an embrace. "I am very happy to meet you again. Marcus has told me so much about you. He said you were a very good influence on him."

Arthur gave a weak laugh, which turned into a coughing fit. Finally, he was able to say, "Not such a good influence that he wasn't shipped off."

Phoebe glanced at Marcus. "Yes, but, after all, it was for the best."

Marcus gripped his brother's hand. "Arthur, how are you?"

"I am well, stripling. I am well, and I will be as long as I am on earth."

Arthur motioned Phoebe to a nearby chair. After she'd settled and smoothed her skirts, Phoebe smiled brightly. "Arthur, Marcus told me you are educating the girls beyond what their governess is teaching them."

"Yes, I am," Arthur responded. "I've had a lot of time to read, and a couple of books written by Bentham came my way. The girls are studying the classics, as well as Latin, Greek, politics, and estate management."

"I'm impressed. My mother was a great proponent of Bentham, Wollstonecraft, and the Marquis de Condorcet. My sisters and I were all educated in the same fashion."

Arthur's eyes brightened with curiosity. "That's wonderful and very unusual."

Marcus glanced at Phoebe and then said to his brother, "Phoebe and her sisters were also taught self-defense and the use of arms."

Arthur's eyes grew wide. "Is this true?"

"Oh, yes." She laughed. "Much to my brother's dismay since we mostly sparred against him. My sisters did so more than I, as they are older, and I had them to practice with as well. Geoffrey taught me some very important boxing moves."

"Which weapons did you use?"

"We were taught to fight with the short sword. We also learned some boxing, wrestling, and to shoot." She took Marcus's hand. "Your brother recently taught me to use a dagger."

Geoffrey had joined them a few moments earlier. Arthur asked, "How good are your sisters at self-defense?"

Grinning proudly, Geoffrey responded, "Very."

Arthur was quiet for a moment before saying to Phoebe, "What an interesting idea. I should like the girls to be able to protect themselves, if the need arose. Would you be willing to teach Anne and Emily?"

"Yes, of course. If you allow it, that was my intent. My sisters arrive to-day. We can arrange to have a lesson to-morrow. It will be fun to have all of us here to begin your daughters' instruction."

Marcus accompanied Phoebe to the main staircase, amazed at her effortless gift of making others feel at ease in her company. Arthur had been drawn to her, much as his daughters had been, and, for that, Marcus was thankful. His brother would know now that she was the perfect woman to be a mother to Anne and Emily.

Isabel showed Phoebe to the room she would have until the wedding and loaned her the use of Tibbs, Isabel's dresser, until Phoebe's maid arrived.

"Before it is dark," Isabel said, "you must have Marcus

show you the gardens. If you'd like, Tibbs will escort you to the small morning room where Marcus can meet you."

After Phoebe assured Lady Dunwood that above all things she would like to see the gardens, Phoebe was left with the dresser, who brought her wash water and helped her change gowns before leading her to Marcus.

He placed her warm woolen shawl around her shoulders to guard against the cooler air before leading her outside. These gardens, Mr. Brown, the famous landscaper, hadn't touched, as they appeared very old. A path led from the terrace to a fountain, from which more garden paths guided visitors to different areas and a woodland beyond. The wood's leaves were already turning to bright yellows and oranges.

She nudged closer to Marcus. "It's beautiful. I understand now why Amabel loves it so much."

He smiled contentedly at Phoebe. "Having you here feels right."

"Yes, for me as well, as if this was always meant to be."

They walked toward the lake and a Grecian-style structure on the other side of a small bridge came into view. "A folly. May we go in?"

Marcus took her hand in his. "Yes."

When they reached the octagonal building, she realized it was larger than it first appeared, with views over the lake on one side, and the meadow on the other.

Marcus opened the door and stood aside as she entered.

Two fireplaces flanked the room at opposite ends. It was well furnished with couches, chairs, and a daybed. It was that last piece of furniture upon which her attention focused.

They gazed into each other's eyes until Phoebe's eyes dropped to Marcus's lips. "Dare we?"

"Yes." He bent his head, touching his lips gently to hers. She reached up, wrapping her arms around his neck and opened her mouth to his.

At first, there was no urgency, just peace in being with him. Marcus drew her tongue into his mouth and stroked it with his own. A flair of delight shot through her, and he swept her up into his arms and carried her to the daybed. After laying her on it, he stretched out beside her.

She wanted to make love with him, feel his bare skin against hers, but the room was too cold for them to remove their clothing.

Phoebe broke the kiss and looked to him for direction. He flipped up her skirts, being careful not to crush them, and unfastened the buttons of his pantaloons, releasing his fully engorged shaft. Spreading her legs, he covered her and entered.

Phoebe arched up, urging him on as he burrowed deeply within, then almost left her. The tension in her body rose higher with each stroke. Soon she was sobbing and trying to grab his hips to move him faster and deeper as she wrapped her legs around him. "Marcus, Marcus, please . . ." she cried out as she exploded into ecstasy.

"Phoebe, my love." After his release, he slumped beside her.

Holding her close, he pulled her shawl around them. That, and the heat from his body, kept her warm.

"Phoebe," he asked, "where is your chamber?"

"In the west wing."

"Where in the west wing?"

When she'd told him, he was so silent, she became concerned. "What is it?"

"You are housed as far away from me as is possible," he said ruefully, "and surrounded by everyone else."

Phoebe came up on one arm and gazed down at him. "They did it on purpose, didn't they?"

He pulled her to him. "They must have. I wonder how closely we'll be watched."

She sunk against him and groaned. "Two more days before the wedding. Perhaps we can slip out here again."

"We can certainly try. We'd best return before someone comes looking."

By the time they'd returned to the house, the rest of her family had arrived. Greeting them, they discovered her sisters' rooms were between her room and the upper hall to Marcus's apartments. They'd be watching Phoebe like Gorgons at the gate.

Phoebe exchanged a disgusted glance with him. The chance that she'd succeed in making it to his chamber and back again without notice had just decreased significantly.

The sun was sinking low in the sky when everyone retired to change for dinner.

Marcus escorted Phoebe to the hall. Her sisters lingered, talking outside of one of their rooms.

Marcus whispered, "Meet me in the drawing room early?"

Phoebe sighed. "It will be our only time alone together. Our friends will arrive in the morning, and the rest of the guests who are staying overnight are expected later in the afternoon."

Marcus grimaced. "We may well have to resign ourselves to abstinence until we are married."

Not if she had anything to say about it.

Covey was in Marcus's room as he entered his chamber to change for dinner.

"Well?" Marcus asked.

"There's been some strangers in the village askin' about work hereabouts."

Marcus frowned. "Men or women?"

"A couple o'men and a female." Covey scratched the side of his face. "Talk like Londoners."

"I don't like it," Marcus said. "I'll keep an eye on them."

Chapter Twenty-three

Phoebe spent a comfortable, if lonely, night in the pretty room she had been given and arose early the next morning. Rose hummed as she laid out her mistress's clothes.

Phoebe threw open the bed hangings and grabbed her wrapper. "How do you like it here?"

Rose grinned. "Tibbs, her ladyship's dresser, gave me a tour of the house and grounds, and I met the other senior staff. They seemed well trained. I think we'll be very happy here, my lady."

Phoebe padded to the washstand and made her ablutions. "Since you were shown around the house, can you give me directions to the breakfast room?"

"I was told the family will still eat in the small breakfast room." Rose shook out Phoebe's gown. "You go down the stairs and then take the corridor on the right until you reach another one. "

Phoebe found Marcus outside the door.

Taking her arm, he said, "I couldn't let you become lost."

She smiled. "I think I was in danger of doing so. I understand there are many twists and turns."

After going down two corridors toward the back of the house, they entered a bright yellow breakfast room, which overlooked the rose garden. Marcus led her to the polished cherry table. A corresponding sideboard was crammed with silver serving dishes. When the footman placed a pot of coffee on the table, she glanced around, but there was no corresponding tea-pot.

Phoebe wrinkled her nose, and Marcus grimaced. He *had* told her of his father's penchant for coffee over tea. The lack of tea in the morning was one of the chief things Marcus disliked about Dunwood House. At St. Eth House, Marcus could enjoy breakfast tea with her, but now? Humph. If they were to be happy at Charteries, this must change.

Phoebe decided to go on as she meant to do. After all, Lady Dunwood had said she would hand over the household to Phoebe.

Summoning the footman, Phoebe said, "Please have a pot of tea brought immediately."

She'd made her selections from the sideboard and turned back to the table only to find the footman rooted in the same spot, mouth agape.

Phoebe glanced at Marcus, who sat back in his chair, eyes sparkling as if he was prepared to be entertained.

She smiled politely at the footman. Coffee had been the only beverage his father allowed served in the family breakfast room for as long as Marcus could remember. "What is your name?"

"Tim—Timothy, my lady," he stuttered.

Keeping her tone even, Phoebe said, "Timothy, is there some reason you have not done as I've asked?"

He straightened a little, perhaps thinking himself on firmer ground. "My lady, tea's not served at the breakfast table."

Phoebe regarded him for a moment and said firmly,

"Nevertheless, I do not drink coffee, and I would like tea. Please see to it at once."

Timothy left the room, only to return a few moments later with Wallace, the Dunwood butler, who bowed to her. "Good morning, my lady. Timothy said you requested tea."

Phoebe maintained her smile, but exasperation colored her words. "Good morning, Wallace. Yes, I did."

When he stared at her as if not knowing what to do, she glanced up at the ceiling. "Really, Wallace, this is a ridiculous conversation. Do you intend to tell me that I may not have tea at the breakfast table? Because if you do, we shall be at outs. I do not take breakfast in my room, and I am determined to have my tea. I have no wish to offend the custom of the house, however, if need be, I will go to the kitchen myself and make it, then take this matter up with Lady Dunwood."

Lord Dunwood chose that moment to enter. He looked from Wallace to Phoebe. "You're up early, my dear. Is there something wrong?"

Wallace bowed. "My lord, Lady Phoebe has requested tea be served at the breakfast table."

Lord Dunwood turned to Phoebe and smiled. "Would you like coffee, my dear?"

From the corner of her eye, Phoebe saw Marcus put his hand over his mouth to stifle a laugh. That did not help. Phoebe tried to preserve her countenance. "No, thank you. My lord, I have no wish to be rude to one who is to shortly be my papa-in-law, nor do I wish to upset the custom of your house, however, I do not drink coffee. I would like my tea. My maid sent my own blend to the kitchen yesterday, so it is available."

Lord Dunwood stared at her, stunned, then said, "Wallace, why are you standing about? Bring Lady Phoebe her pot of tea."

Without betraying any bemusement, Wallace bowed and left the room.

Phoebe glanced at Marcus who saluted her and inclined his head. From his gesture, Phoebe realized she'd won a major battle in establishing her future supervision of the house.

A little while later, Marcus turned to his father. "Papa, why has there never been tea served here before?"

Lord Dunwood looked a little abashed. "My father would have nothing but tea served. I had become used to drinking coffee during a trip to the West Indies. One morning, after I returned, I asked for coffee. My father told me he would not allow that beverage to be served. When I became master I was determined to have my own way. I ordered that nothing but coffee be served."

He continued a little sheepishly, "The first argument I had with your mother was about tea. She breakfasts in her room because of it."

Lord Dunwood said to Phoebe, "I have been told the two of you like to break your fast together. I suppose, if that is to continue, you will have to command the meal as you like it. Particularly, as you are to have control of the household. I shall tell Wallace to insure the staff does as you request. I am sorry, my dear, my edict became such a problem."

Phoebe leaned forward to pat his arm. "If that is the worst problem we face, we will have done well, my lord. Perhaps Lady Dunwood will now join us?"

Dunwood smiled. "Perhaps she shall."

The rest of the morning was busy indeed. Phoebe, her sisters, brother, their spouses, and Marcus met with Anne and Emily in the courtyard to the side of the house to begin the girls' first lessons in fighting.

Afterward, Lady Dunwood arranged for Phoebe to

meet, later in the morning, with the housekeeper, Mrs. Armstrong. Until then, Marcus was told to escort Phoebe through the wing that would be theirs, and, if time permitted, other areas as well to familiarize her with her new home.

Most of their part of the house had been built in the previous century. As they walked down one corridor, she saw an old, arched wooden door. "Marcus, where does that lead?"

He stared at it for a moment, before saying, "One of the old towers, I believe. I'd forgotten all about it. Would you like to see it?"

"Yes. Cranbourne Place doesn't have anything like this."

When he pulled the door open, cool air rushed out. Spiral stairs lit by long narrow windows led the way to the next level. Phoebe held up her skirts to avoid getting dust on them. At the top of the stairs stood another old door. She tugged on it and it opened with a creak. "Marcus, a solar!"

Phoebe walked into the round chamber. The ancient floor-to-ceiling casement windows encircled the room, giving way only for a marble-carved fireplace with figures of scantily clad Grecian women. The half-timbered ceiling above them had carved beams. It was cold outside, yet, even with no fire, the room was sunny and warm.

She went back to Marcus. "I love this room. I've visited houses that had solars, but to find one here is beyond anything. May I have it as my parlor?"

He laughed and swung Phoebe around. "You may have anything you want. It will take some work to get it back in shape."

It *was* dirty, and had some broken bits of furniture, but nothing that a good clean wouldn't fix. She smiled. "It will be perfect. The repairs can be made while we're on our wedding trip."

The tour was almost completed, and Marcus was leading her purposefully toward their bedchamber when a footman arrived. "My lady, her ladyship says she's ready for you to meet the housekeeper, Mrs. Armstrong."

Marcus scowled. "Lady Phoebe will meet you at the head of the stairs."

The footman bowed and took off in a hurry.

"We should have started this deuced tour in the bedchamber."

Phoebe reached up and brushed her lips against Marcus's. "But I wouldn't have found my solar, or seen the rest of the wing. Our bedchamber will have to be a surprise to both of us on our wedding night."

While she was with the housekeeper, Phoebe received the message that their first guests, Miss Marsh and Lord Rutherford, had arrived.

Phoebe found Anna's room and joined her friend. "Anna, welcome to Charteries. I suppose I may say that now and not have to wait until to-morrow."

Anna grinned. "Indeed you may welcome me."

Phoebe hugged her. "How was your trip?"

"Much as expected. Phoebe, this is a wonderful old house. You don't have to tell me you're happy. You look it."

Phoebe blinked back tears. "Anna, I have never been so happy. I—I feel as if I have finally come home." Phoebe shook herself a little, unable to believe all her dreams were about to come true. "How goes it with Rutherford?"

Anna lowered her brows and said sternly, "Lord Rutherford has been spoiled by the matchmaking mamas and their daughters. He actually thought he could transfer his attentions from you to me, and I immediately would come to heel. He is finding I do not obey so easily."

Phoebe laughed. "When do you plan to be married?"

Consternation replaced the twinkle in Anna's eyes, and she pulled a face. "Oh, Phoebe, I don't know if we will marry. He pined for you for years and now this sudden change of course . . . I don't know if he loves me, or how to tell if he does."

"Anna, you know I've never believed him seriously interested in me." Phoebe frowned. Yes, with Rutherford, Anna would need to be certain, or he'd ride roughshod over her. "You have time to learn his true feelings. You've waited this long—a little longer won't hurt, and, indeed, may do a great deal of good. It would not do for you to enter into an unequal marriage, which is what would happen if you love him, and he does not return your affection."

Anna sighed. "I know, which is why he shall not get anything from me until he mends his ways."

A few minutes later, Phoebe and Miss Marsh entered the room to find Rutherford with Marcus.

Marcus greeted Phoebe and Miss Marsh, who glanced briefly at Rutherford.

"Phoebe, may I be shown around the gardens that are visible from my bedchamber?"

"Yes. We have time. Most everything has already been arranged." Phoebe looked at Marcus. "I ran into Rose and Covey ferrying our clothing to our new apartments. I hope Rose remembers to leave enough out for me to wear until after the wedding."

Marcus tugged the bell pull and asked the footman who answered to bring the ladies' shawls.

Rutherford cleared his throat. "When do you sail for France?"

"We expected to depart immediately after the wedding breakfast, but decided to wait until the next afternoon."

Miss Marsh smiled brightly at Phoebe. "I am so jealous. I've always wanted to see Paris."

Rutherford muttered, "If you'd marry me, I'd take you to Paris."

Miss Marsh was either ignoring him or hadn't heard, she continued. "How long do you expect to be gone and will you take the packet?"

Marcus grinned. Rutherford had quite a challenge in front of him. "I have a ship in Newhaven. We'll sail to Dieppe and travel to Paris. We expect to spend several weeks."

After the footmen arrived with the ladies' shawls, Marcus asked Phoebe, "May we join you?"

Phoebe glanced at Miss Marsh, who appeared none too happy about the prospect. "My love, if you wouldn't mind . . ."

"Of course not, Rutherford and I still have some things to discuss concerning his duties at the wedding."

Once the ladies had left, Marcus said, "She really is avoiding you."

"I have noticed," Rutherford replied glumly. "I just don't know what to do about it. I must have made a complete hash of it, but I've no clue how—or why."

"My lord," a footman said from the door. "Lady Dunwood wants to see you."

"Tell her I'll be right there." Marcus turned to Rutherford. "We can talk after dinner, if you'd like."

"Yes. Thank you."

Throughout the afternoon, the guests intending to remain overnight at Charteries arrived in a steady stream that filled the house with noise and gaiety.

Phoebe rejoined Marcus and they were in a drawing room with some newly arrived guests when a footman found them. "My lord, my lady, her ladyship has asked you to attend her in her parlor. It is urgent."

Marcus exchanged a glance with Phoebe and they excused themselves to their company.

Hurrying after the footman, Phoebe said in a soft voice, "I hope it is not Arthur."

Marcus nodded grimly.

They were led to his mother's parlor. When they entered the room, Marcus was taken aback to find not only his parents and sister, but Lord and Lady St. Eth, as well as the rest of Phoebe's family.

Sober faces met them.

"Arthur?" Marcus whispered.

Tears strangled his mother's voice. She could only nod.

Marcus's throat closed. "Is he . . . ?"

Papa shook his head. "No, but the doctor was just here. It will not be long. Arthur wants to speak to you both."

Phoebe squeezed Marcus's hand. "We'll go immediately."

Marcus strode swiftly down the hall to his brother's room, where Arthur's daughters, Anne and Emily, were with him. The girls' eyes were swimming in tears as they tried not to cry.

Arthur lay covered in blankets on a couch between the windows. Although the room was warm, his skin was alarmingly pale and clammy, his breathing labored. Marcus thought of all the years they'd spent apart and regretted every one of them.

Phoebe crossed quickly to Arthur. Sinking down on her knees, she took one of his hands. Marcus stood next to her.

"Tell us what you want." Her voice was rough with unshed tears.

Arthur smiled at them, so beautifully, Marcus blinked.

His brother called the girls closer to them. "I don't have much time. We've been saying that for a while, I know. This time it's true."

He raised his gaze to Marcus and Phoebe. "I want you both to promise me that if I die between now and then, you will marry as you have planned in the morning. Promise me you won't delay. Go to France. Everything will be here when you return."

Not trusting himself to speak, Marcus nodded tersely.

Arthur turned his daughters to face Phoebe. "Anne, Emily, I know you already love your aunt Phoebe."

They glanced at her, sadness in their eyes, and went into the arms she held out to them.

He nodded. "It is my desire that you treat her as you would a mother."

Silent tears rolled down their cheeks as they nodded.

"Marcus, you know my wishes concerning my daughters. When the time comes, our man of business will apprise you as to their portions and—"

Marcus held up his hand, stopping his brother. "I will treat them and love them as my daughters. Don't worry. We"—he squeezed Phoebe's shoulder—"will care for them as our children."

Arthur grabbed Marcus's other hand. "Mamma and Papa know my wishes, all of them. I'm a little tired now. Please call Nurse in to me."

Phoebe held the girls to her. "Send for me or come to my room if you need me."

Anne and Emily nodded.

Marcus helped Phoebe rise, before bending down to hug his brother. "We'll do as you wish."

Walking silently, hands clasped together, Marcus and Phoebe made their way back to his mother's parlor. He opened the door. Phoebe walked in, and he took his place beside her.

His eyes scanned the room and came to rest on his mother. "Have you told them of the change in Arthur's condition and what he wants us to do?"

"Yes." Fresh tears flowed down her cheeks.

Marcus addressed the others. "Arthur told us he wants us to marry no matter what may happen between now and the morning. We've promised to honor his wishes. Although it will not change our decision, we would like to know if any of you have an objection."

* * *

No one did. In the end, it was decided they would tell none of the guests how close to death Arthur stood. The rest of the day passed, if not in mirth—although there were moments—then at least in cordial equanimity. Quiet laughter could be heard here and there throughout the rooms.

At the end of the evening, before Phoebe's sisters accompanied Phoebe to her chamber, Marcus was given a few minutes alone with his future bride.

"What are they doing?" he asked as Hester and Hermione went into Phoebe's chamber, leaving the door ajar.

"There is an old Cranbourne family wedding tradition," she replied, "that I'd forgotten about. My sisters will spend the night with me."

Marcus kissed Phoebe deeply, longingly, wanting nothing more than to spend this night with her, vowing it would be the last time they were parted. After several minutes, her sisters gently pulled Phoebe away from Marcus. He was led off to the billiards room by Geoffrey, cursing under his breath as his brothers-in-law laughed uproariously.

Edwin clapped Marcus on his back. "Finley, stop complaining. We all survived it, and you will as well."

John added in speciously dulcet tones. "It will make the wedding night that much sweeter."

Marcus scowled at him.

Geoffrey was all good humor. "Marcus, you've been given enough time alone with Phoebe before the wedding. You can't complain now."

He could. The balls on the table were already set up. Entering the game with a purpose, he won several pounds from his new family members, and he was able to coax himself into a better mood. Until he discovered all his future brothers-in-law were to spend the night with him.

"From where," Marcus demanded, "did this damned custom spring?"

Geoffrey shook his head. "I don't remember."

John, the first of them to have married, said, as if remembering an event far in the past, "The old Earl told me it came from a spoiled marriage so long ago the time has been lost. The marriage had been arranged. The groom was not happy about it. The bride, a Cranbourne, was willing enough." John leaned his billiards stick against the table. "The couple had only met a few times before the wedding and then, only with chaperones. They'd never been left alone because the marriage contract stipulated the bride would be a virgin. As it usually was in those days—and these days as well, for the most part—the bride knew nothing of the stipulation."

"What happened?" Marcus asked.

John continued. "The night before the wedding, as the tale went, the groom found the bride's chamber and deflowered her. The next day, after the vows were made, he took her to bed and announced to his family that she was not a virgin. The bride argued, of course, that her defiler had been her husband. Fortunately, the bride's maid could produce blood on her mistress's bed linens, and the maid had witnessed the groom enter the chamber the night before. Since that time, all Cranbourne brides are kept guarded by the women of the family." John smiled. "Since Cranbourne women are a bit spirited, I imagine bridegrooms are guarded just to insure they don't run away."

The others laughed, but Marcus glowered. He would also like to run away, but this bridegroom would take his bride with him.

Chapter Twenty-four

Phoebe woke to the sun shining through the windows. Her sisters were gone, and Rose was preparing a bath.

Phoebe wondered if Arthur was still with them. "Rose, have you heard anything about Lord Evesham?"

"My lady, he's resting and sent his good wishes for the day. I'll have your breakfast set out soon."

Glancing at the clock, Phoebe was shocked to discover it was almost nine o'clock. The wedding was at eleven.

Phoebe jumped up, intending to apply herself to a number of chores she should attend to before she dressed for the ceremony.

"My lady, there is no point in hurrying," Rose said. "You are not allowed out of this area until Lord St. Eth comes to escort you to the chapel."

Phoebe sat back down on her bed. "What am I to do for two hours? It won't take me that long to dress."

Rose chuckled. "You could do what other ladies do and sleep some more, but I've no hope of that. After you've had your breakfast, your sisters and Lady St. Eth will come to help you dress."

Phoebe stared at her. "What did you say?"

Rose smiled. "More tradition."

For the first time in her life, Phoebe allowed herself to be pampered. Her bathwater had lemons, bergamot, and lavender. Her sisters left a cream to use on her skin. Her hair was washed and dried before the fire as all her attendants laid out her clothing.

Her sisters and aunt waited for Rose to finish Phoebe's hair in a high knot, with locks of curls flowing over Phoebe's shoulders.

Aunt Ester held out an antique comb of amethysts and pearls, which was set to hold the knot in place. "Phoebe, this is something borrowed and quite old. It has been passed down my family's female line to be worn by the bride on her wedding day."

Hester's eyes misted as she twisted a long strand of perfectly matched pearls interspersed with amethysts around Phoebe's neck to make three strands, and said, "Mamma left these to be worn for the first time on your wedding day."

Hermione took her right hand and slid a sapphire ring on the finger, which, until last night, had held the ring Marcus had given her. That ring would, in a short time, be her wedding ring. "And this," Hermione said, "is new, from Hester and me."

Hester handed Phoebe a handkerchief. "No, no, you are not allowed to cry. It will make your eyes red. What a goose you are, Phoebe."

"I'm not crying," Phoebe said untruthfully. "I just didn't know to-day would be so affecting. I thought I would wake up as I do every other day, but go to be married. I didn't realize ... my heart would . . ."

Aunt Ester hugged her. "No, of course you didn't, my dear. You were too young to be really involved in your sisters' weddings. Even *your* mother did not think it proper."

Phoebe reflected on the previous night's conversations with her sisters and agreed. She'd had no idea so much could take place between a man and a woman, and they'd given her some very exciting ideas of what she and Marcus could do.

Phoebe choked on a sob. "I wish Mamma were here."

Her aunt held her gently. "So do we all, and I think she is here in spirit. So smile and be happy you are marrying a man you love. She is overjoyed for you."

Aunt Ester straightened. "Come, it is past time we should be off. Your young man will think you have changed your mind."

Phoebe gave a watery smile. "Never, I am his."

Uncle Henry stood near the chapel door with Phoebe and said gravely, "You are sure this is what you want?"

She nodded. "Yes, Uncle Henry. This is exactly what I want."

He glanced down at her. "I am glad for you. My dear, you have never looked more beautiful, or happier."

She smiled and peeked down the short aisle to where Marcus stood speaking with Rutherford and Edwin. She thought to the day at the inn when all she could see was his back. Later he'd told her he knew she'd been looking at him because he could feel her.

He turned now and gazed at her like she was the only woman in the church. Her heart filled with love. "Thank you, Uncle Henry, for saying that. I feel beautiful."

Defying convention, all her nieces and nephews who were old enough to walk on their own had been made a part of the wedding.

The youngest boy and girls, scattering rose petals and green leaves on the stone floor, preceded her sisters who held the hands of Phoebe's newest nieces. Two older boys remained behind to hold the long detachable train of her gown.

Once the advance procession was completed, Phoebe, on Uncle Henry's arm, began her journey to meet her husband.

Marcus, flanked by Rutherford and Edwin, had turned when he felt her. He couldn't believe the vision she made as she walked down the old church aisle.

Rutherford leaned into him. "Finley, you are a lucky dog. She is the most exquisite thing I've ever seen."

Marcus nodded slightly. That was the word, *exquisite*. His wife, lover, and friend.

She arrived at the altar rail, and St. Eth placed her hand in Marcus's waiting one.

His smile matched hers as their gazes met before they turned together to face the rector.

Phoebe said her vows clearly, as did he. When they were pronounced man and wife, he threw caution and propriety to the wind and kissed her, a passionate kiss of long waiting and a new beginning. Then he took her arm and they began their walk out of the church to their new life.

As they passed Phoebe's aunt and uncle, Ester whispered to Henry, "It was a very good idea for them to marry here rather than in St. George's. They would have shocked the crowd if they'd decided to kiss, especially like that."

Phoebe and Marcus grinned the rest of the way down the aisle.

Arthur had his wish to hear of his brother and Phoebe's marriage.

Nurse stood in the back of the church and, after the vows were said, slipped out and brought him the news.

"I'm happy that the wedding was completed. Now my daughters are part of a new family."

"Yes, my lord. Now you rest."

He fell into a peaceful sleep.

Nurse continued tatting, until she realized Arthur was too quiet. She put her hand on his neck. He'd passed. Putting her tatting aside, she rose. "We'll have to tell them he's gone."

Arthur's valet, Timmons, stopped her. "You remember what his lordship said."

She sat back down, staring at the man she'd raised from a child. Tears flowed down her wrinkled cheeks. "Yes, Lord Marcus and Lady Phoebe are to enjoy their new beginning. The world has lost a sweet and wonderful man to-day."

Marcus and Phoebe led the short procession to the large ballroom where the wedding breakfast had been set for their guests. He introduced Phoebe to the local gentry and the few noble families residing in the neighboring area. She was already acquainted with some of them. They all promised bride visits upon the newlyweds' return from France.

In mid-afternoon, not long after the cake was cut, the guests began departing for their journeys home.

As the last carriage left, Timmons approached Marcus. "Lord Evesham."

Marcus had thought he was prepared, but his new title sounded strange to his ears. He stared at the valet seeing the sadness in his eyes. "Is Arthur . . . ?"

Timmons nodded. "Yes, his lordship, he passed a few hours ago."

Phoebe came up to him and Marcus put his arm around her, needing to touch her. "My love, may I present Timmons, Arthur's valet."

Timmons bowed. "I'm sorry, my lady."

She glanced at Marcus and bit her lip. "Arthur?"

Marcus's throat hurt and he had trouble getting the words out. "Yes. He's gone."

Marcus heard a gasp and realized Anne and Emily were standing close by. He and Phoebe gathered the sobbing girls in their arms. They held the girls until they were exhausted from crying.

Priddy, their governess, took them away.

Bereft, Marcus wanted to blame someone for not telling them sooner, but Arthur planned it so they should enjoy their wedding, and there was no one with whom to argue. Marcus sat on the sofa, his head in his hands, until Phoebe took one of them in hers.

He lifted his head and, through his fog of grief, stared at her. "Come." She urged him up. "It is time we were alone."

After bidding their families a good day, Marcus followed Phoebe to their apartments.

She opened the large, carved double doors into a hall, which in turn, led to their bedchamber, parlors, and dressing rooms. A bank of windows lined the wall of their bedchamber, giving a view facing the lake, and making the room light and airy.

The large four-poster bed was hung with cream-colored crewel curtains, decorated with myriad sizes and styles of flowers and vines in various hues. The window coverings were the same pattern. Turkey rugs covered most of the floor. Phoebe's nightgown was laid out on the bed.

Their new rooms were beautiful, but would have to be appreciated later. Right now, her husband was hurting and needed her comfort.

Marcus looked around. His voice was thick with emotion. "Do you like it?"

If he wanted to discuss the room, that's what she'd do. "Yes, it's lovely. As if someone knew exactly what I liked."

His breath hitched. "Well then, my lady, I'm glad it pleases you." Tears misted his eyes. "I can't believe Arthur's gone. I wanted more time with him. He died soon after our vows."

Phoebe reached up to put her arms around Marcus's neck and searched his face. "It is not as we wanted it to be.

But it is what we have. Your brother gave us a final gift of love. We will continue to honor his life."

Suddenly, as if a dam broke within him, he crushed her into his arms. "Oh, God, Phoebe, I don't know what I'd do without you."

He started sobbing. She cried softly and held him in her arms. Marcus told her how close he and Arthur had been until he'd been sent away. How guilty he felt that he'd not been there for his brother after the death of his wife and when he first became ill. "Phoebe, I can never lose you."

Ravenously, Marcus took her lips. Their first mating was hard and fast as Marcus poured his grief and fear into her, and she welcomed him into her body, soothing him with her love.

She must have slept because she came awake to his kisses. Wrapping her legs around him, she urged him inside, then deeper still, wanting him to claim her more fully. Phoebe gave herself up to the waves of pleasure he pressed upon her, and she took, bursting into a wild eruption of pleasure.

"Phoebe, my love, I need more," Marcus whispered, as he rolled her over onto her stomach.

Placing a pillow underneath her hips, he entered her again, drawing her to him.

She'd thought he could not be more deeply in her, but she was wrong. It was as if he was truly one with her. The sensual tension rose higher with each long, deep thrust until her contractions became uncontrollable and she fractured with delight, bringing him with her.

She knew, at that moment, she loved him with her whole heart. She could even, she thought, accept his possessiveness as an extension of his love, within reason.

* * *

Marcus rose and lit some candles. He stared down at the sleeping form of his wife, barely covered by a sheet, her hair wild and spread out over the pillows. God he loved her. She'd known just what to do to soothe him last night.

After grabbing a candle, he walked into the adjoining parlor where he found wine, lemonade, and various offerings of food left for them. He poured a glass of wine, tossing it off before taking the tray to her.

Phoebe stretched and sat up.

He set the platter on a small table next to her. "Look what they brought us."

Reaching out, she took one of the small sandwiches.

"Would you like lemonade or wine?" he asked.

Phoebe chewed and swallowed. "Lemonade, please. What time is it?"

Marcus glanced out the window. "Dark."

She shook her head, but grinned. "Indeed, I hadn't noticed. When do we leave for Newhaven?"

Smiling roguishly, Marcus's gaze roved her body. "Don't you remember? Not until after luncheon. We may *sleep* as long as we like."

Phoebe picked up her glass and drank deeply. "Umm, yes, *sleep* is what I need."

Marcus took the goblet from her, setting it on the tray. "You, my lady, have become a wanton."

Glancing up at him, Phoebe stretched out on the bed and wiggled. "How does it feel to have your very own wanton?"

He groaned. Abandoning the food and drink, he slid in next to her. "My very own? Hmm."

Meeting his gaze, Phoebe spread her palms over his chest. "Your very own. Come to me, my lord."

He gave thanks that she approached this part of their life with the same passion as she had for the rest of it. Especially now, when he needed her so much.

* * *

Phoebe awoke as dawn lit the room with a soft glow. She was cuddled into Marcus, her back to his chest, his arm holding her to him. She eased slowly and quietly away from the bed to slip behind the screen.

Phoebe stood next to the bed, devouring the last of the sandwiches, and glanced down at him. He was beautiful. He was long, lean lines and broad shoulders. The dark hair on his chest, that she loved to run her fingers through, narrowed to a thin line over his taut stomach, then down to the nest of curls between his legs and his virile member, as her sisters had called it. Phoebe licked her lips. Even in repose, his seemed large, though she had nothing with which to compare. It twitched and lengthened.

Lowering herself back onto the bed, she studied his member more closely, taking it in her hand and running her fingers over the soft skin. It was fascinating how it grew faster.

Phoebe glanced up to see Marcus grinning at her. "Do you plan to do anything with my shaft, or are you satisfied to just hold it?"

Shaft, another word for it. She wondered how many more words there were for it. "I don't know. It is amazing how it responds to my touch."

He grunted. "*It* has been responding to you since I first saw you."

Phoebe looked at his fully hardened shaft. "Really?"

"Really." He sat up and lifted her over him.

His shaft stood up against her stomach. Phoebe caressed it again.

His muscles clenched, and she wondered how long he'd allow her to explore. "I know it is also called a virile member. How many other names are there for it?"

A deep groan escaped him. "Phoebe, you're going to be

the death of me. It is also called a sword, and there are several words I will not tell you."

She frowned slightly. "Are they vulgar?"

"Extremely vulgar, and it would not please me to hear them on your lips."

Her sisters had told her some men liked dirty talking. Phoebe didn't think she would and was glad her husband didn't either.

Reaching further, she found his scrotum. The new words as well as the other things she'd learned last night from her sisters were helpful.

Marcus's voice was deeper and more gravelly. "Phoebe, my love, *please* tell me what you intend to do. You do have a plan?"

She glanced at him wickedly and wiggled down on his legs.

He blinked. "You couldn't know about . . ."

She bent over him, touching her tongue to his straining member, and took him into her mouth. Her lips closed around him. He tasted musky and salty, different but not unpleasant. He grew harder.

He collapsed back. "Your sisters. I had no idea ladies discussed such things."

Phoebe started to giggle, but found it was hard to laugh with him in her mouth.

Marcus's hands tangled in her hair as she licked and sucked. His breathing changed to panting. "Enough, please. Come to me."

She released him. Marcus lifted her up and slowly lowered her down onto his damp shaft.

Phoebe gasped as he filled her completely. She placed her hands on his chest, and he held her hips, moving her up and down until she moved herself and realized she could control the pace and the depth of his penetration.

He kneaded her swollen breasts, teasing her already

tight nipples, before taking one in his mouth and curling his tongue around it. He sucked as he gently squeezed the other. But it wasn't enough. "More, please. I can't . . ."

Her voice trailed off as Marcus put his hand in her curls and rubbed. The familiar tension sluiced through her and waves of warmth roiled deep inside. Finally, she arched back in an ecstatic cry and came. Marcus followed.

Marcus fell back against the pillows, taking her with him. She closed her eyes, about ready to sink back asleep when a sudden thought occurred to her. She was going to have her courses this week, and was glad it had held off. Strangely, she didn't feel the discomfort she usually did and wondered if having intimate relations with Marcus was medicinal. If so, she would have to have them more often.

When next Marcus woke, it was fully light. Sounds of clinking china came from the next room.

"Is that food?" Phoebe asked, throwing the covers aside. "I'm hungry."

Marcus stilled her. "Wait here. I'll see what we have."

He shrugged into his dressing gown and peeked into the parlor. Phoebe donned her wrapper and came up behind him.

Rose and Covey were setting up a table with rolls, butter, crumpets, and preserves.

Marcus cleared his throat to let them know he was present.

Rose glanced toward the door and blushed vividly, before turning away.

Covey grinned. "Yes, should have left it all to me. I tried to tell you his lordship wouldn't be dressed, but you wouldn't believe me. Iffen' you're plannin' to set up the table for them . . ."

As Marcus was trying to decide how to handle what was

obviously a potential *contretemps,* Phoebe entered the room, smiling widely.

"Rose, how kind of you. Thank you so much for thinking of this."

Her maid's flush faded under Phoebe's approbation.

His wife's smile faded a bit when she addressed Covey. "And Covey, how nice of you to assist."

Well, this was not a good start.

Raising her chin, Rose said, "My lady, I thought you might be awake soon. Shall I fetch your tea?"

Phoebe smiled again. "Yes, please do, and I think his lordship would like something a little more substantial to eat." She paused. "Come to think of it, so do I."

Rose bobbed a curtsey and left the room.

Marcus caught Covey's eye. "We'll leave after luncheon. I'd like to get to Newhaven while it is still light enough for Lady Evesham to stroll around the village. But first, you can help Rose bring the rest of breakfast and see to our bathwater."

Covey mumbled something under his breath, bowed, and left.

"Oh dear." Phoebe frowned. "Do you think we are going to have problems between the two of them?"

Marcus rubbed his forehead. It was much too early to have this discussion. "I certainly hope not. Covey has been with me forever, through thick and thin."

His beloved's chin firmed. "I understand what you mean. Rose has been with me since I was fifteen. They'll just have to learn to work together."

She shrugged lightly. "You speak with Covey. I'll do the same with Rose."

Marcus opened his mouth and closed it. The devil. He would not have his first argument with his wife over the servants. Particularly as it appeared Covey had started it.

"Marcus."

"Yes, my love."

"I think we should put off our trip for a week or so, I would like to be here for Arthur's burial, and you should insure all is in order with the guardianship."

He drew her into his arms. "You're right. We'll delay our travel."

As much as he wanted her all to himself, he could not deny his responsibilities. One of which was to give his brother a proper farewell and make certain all was well with his nieces.

Later that morning, Phoebe took her sisters and aunt aside and told them she and Marcus would remain at Charteries for a week or so.

"You must order mourning clothes as well, my dear," Aunt Ester said. "No one will expect you to wear them in Paris, but in England they will be necessary."

"I'll send a letter to Madame Lisette."

Hester and Hermione glanced at one another, and Hester said, "If you'd like, we'll remain here with you for a while longer."

Phoebe released the breath she'd been holding. Having her family here, with the children, would be a great comfort. "Thank you. I would like you to stay."

Aunt Ester smiled. "We shall delay our departure as well."

"There," Phoebe said. "That's settled."

A few days after Arthur's funeral, as she was hurrying to her apartments, a strong arm grabbed her around the waist. Phoebe gave a small shriek, before she recognized her husband's scent and broad chest.

He kissed her temple. "You're in a rush."

"Yes, I promised Emily and Anne that my sisters and I would practice shooting this afternoon."

His lips left a trail of open-mouthed kisses down her neck. "Do you mind if I come with you?"

Phoebe turned in his arms. "Not at all."

"My lord!" Covey said, striding rapidly down the corridor. "We've got a problem."

Chapter Twenty-five

Marcus pulled Phoebe to his side. "Covey, what is it?"
Covey glanced at Phoebe and back to Marcus. "I'll
let the groom who was at the bawdy house tell ye."

"Bawdy house?" Phoebe asked, confused.

Marcus rubbed a hand over his face. Oh, God. How to
explain this to her? "I didn't know we had one around
here."

"We do now." Covey's mouth twisted into a humorless
smile. "That woman I told ye about? She set herself up in
the tavern and's been givin' special rates to any of our servants. Asking a lot of questions, too."

"Travenor," Marcus said.

"That'd be my guess. I told ye, men like him don't give
up. Got gnats in his head, that one."

Phoebe's gaze had been going back and forth between
Covey and Marcus. "What is going on, and what is a bawdy
house?"

He glared at his groom. "You would have to mention
that." She was bound to put herself in the thick of things.
"My love, let me take care of this. You have enough to do
without getting involved as well."

Her face flushed, and she opened her mouth.

He rushed on before she could speak. "It is nothing a gently nurtured lady should be aware of."

For a minute, Marcus thought she'd throw a punch. "I am now a *married* woman, and there is no reason for you to keep secrets from me. If it's like a brothel, just say it. You're not going to shock me. Tell me what's happening now!"

Marcus tried and failed to think of a way out of this. Short of ordering her to obey him, which he had no reliance on her doing, he'd have to tell her. He grabbed her hand and started striding down the corridor. "Come on, I'll explain on the way. We think Travenor has had a woman in the village getting information from our servants."

"Like a spy?"

"Yes. To keep track of us as he did in London. Covey discovered new people in the area. The only reason I didn't mention it was because . . . quite frankly, I forgot."

"I understand. It's been a difficult time." Phoebe had to trot to keep up with him. She'd heard about brothels, and a bawdy house was just another term. Knowing French spies sometimes used men's carnal needs against them, she was not surprised that the prostitute had easily gained information from some of the male staff. Her stomach flipped, making her feel ill. It wasn't over; Travenor, or whoever, was just biding his time to strike when she and Marcus were unawares. As they were passing through the stable yard, she called to have her sisters summoned.

When they reached the stables, two grooms and three footmen were on the floor being guarded by some of the other male servants.

Marcus addressed Turner, the head groom. "Have they talked?"

Turner methodically hit his hand with a horsewhip. "They'll tell, or be sorry for it."

Marcus stood with his fists on his hips. "I don't believe we'll need that."

He turned to the men on the floor. "One at a time, tell me what you told the woman."

Shards of light pierced the gloom of the stables, small motes of dust floated in the air. Phoebe stood in the shadow so the men would speak freely, but the silence was thick with tension until one of the footmen finally spoke. "She asked me about who comes and goes, and what time deliveries are made. Am I going to lose my position, my lord?"

Marcus shook his head. "No. You had no way of knowing it wasn't just curiosity on her part, but there is danger afoot. This woman is part of it. I need all the information, and, if there is a next time, you'll know not to be so trusting."

He crouched and talked with the men, questioning them closely about the prostitute and any strangers she associated with. Phoebe finally understood how he'd become so successful. He examined each piece of information and formed a whole. One she was not happy to know existed. Someone, probably Travenor, was making a schedule, and determining the size of the property and house, and they'd been smart about it. Only the local servants, those least likely to suspect anything was amiss, had been approached with the special offer.

Her sisters entered and listened as well. Phoebe half expected them to have their own questions or comments, but the twins remained still, until Hester pulled Phoebe outside.

Phoebe went, but once they'd reached the end of the stables, said, "I wanted to stay to help Marcus."

Hester gave a small smile. "Phoebe, Marcus is a man, and you have to allow him to be just that."

Phoebe shook her head. Her sister was wrong. "You don't understand. We agreed to a partnership."

"Nevertheless, my dear," Hermione said, "there are times when Marcus needs to take the lead. He would not be the type of gentleman you wanted to marry if he did not."

Phoebe regarded her sisters. "But Hermione, you bested the highwaymen."

"Yes," she said. "I did what was necessary to save my husband and dependents, but I prefer to allow Edwin to show his strength. No man wants to feel unneeded."

Phoebe was about to respond when her husband strode up. "Marcus, my love, what will you do now that you know Travenor is here, somewhere?"

Marcus put his arm around her waist and held her possessively. "We'll question the woman. With any luck, we'll discover enough to stop any attack. The rest of the servants, as well as my parents and your family, must be informed there is someone gathering information."

"What is your plan?"

Marcus kissed her temple. "Wait until he strikes. We don't have enough evidence for a trial in the Lords." He took her chin between two fingers and tilted up her head. "Remember your promise, you'll not go outside alone, and you'll wear your dagger and pistol."

Phoebe shuddered. Just the idea of Travenor touching her made her skin crawl as if an eel had touched her. Phoebe stepped closer to her husband. "As you wish. I have no desire to end up in that madman's hands."

Marcus ushered Phoebe and her sisters inside. "We must gather everyone and alert them to this new danger."

He left it to Wallace, his father's butler, to deal with the servants. Once her family and Marcus's were gathered in the morning room, he took command. His voice was deeper and harder as he explained what had been discovered and pieced together.

Phoebe saw the respect her husband was given.

Even Uncle Henry listened to Marcus and agreed with him, and, although he'd told her he'd been in charge of many men under sometimes difficult circumstances, she'd never seen it or felt it before. Perhaps her sisters were right, Phoebe should learn to allow him to protect her.

Ten days had turned into more than a fortnight, and Phoebe's courses still had not come. She pressed her hand to her stomach, wanting it to hold a child. Finally, she went to Hermione's room and knocked.

"Come in."

Phoebe opened the door and made her way over to the window seat. "May I talk to you about something?"

Hermione put her book down and smiled. "Naturally."

Phoebe swallowed. "How did you know you were breeding?"

Her sister's smile broadened. "Well, we are all so regular that Papa told Mamma he knew just when another estate needed to be visited, or when he needed to make a bolt to Town. How late are you?"

Warmth rose in Phoebe's face. "Almost two weeks."

Hermione sat back. "The manor house."

Phoebe nodded ruefully. "Probably the first night."

"Well, it is early days. Let's see what the next two weeks brings. This is always the most dangerous time."

Phoebe stared at her hands twisting the fringe of her shawl. "Should I tell Marcus?"

Hermione laughed in delight. "My dear, any man used to breeding animals knows how to figure it out. We cannot hide having or not having our courses."

Phoebe stood and hugged her sister. "Thank you. I want a child so badly."

"Most of us do. Children are our greatest delight. Don't

quack yourself, but I know you won't, and don't allow Marcus to wrap you in cotton-wool. Men become impossible when we are increasing."

Phoebe grinned. "I remember Hester threatening to leave John if he didn't stop trying to wrap her in cotton-wool."

Hermione shook her head. "He would have followed, and Edwin refused to have them both in the house for six months."

That night, Marcus slipped into bed, placed his hand over her stomach, and searched her face. "Is there a chance you're breeding?"

"Possibly. I'm late."

He kissed her. "Shall we practice some more?"

They made love gently, as if he was afraid he'd hurt her. Later, they lay in each other's arms, and Phoebe did not ever want to be anywhere else.

Marcus nuzzled her hair with his lips. "As far as we can tell, there are no more spies in the village. Would you like to depart for Paris the day after to-morrow?"

"If you think it's safe to leave. It will be nice for us to be alone."

The evening before they were due to depart, Phoebe's family and Isabel—Lord Dunwood had returned to Town with Uncle Henry's proxy for an important vote—were lingering over sweets after dinner, when the girls' governess, Priddy, entered the room with Anne. "My ladies, Anne has something she would like to tell you."

Phoebe smiled and held out her hand to her niece. "What is it, my dear?"

Anne took Phoebe's hand. "When we were outside to-day, I saw a man in the woods. He was standing very close to a tree, as if he was trying to hide, and he was watching us. I didn't recognize him so he couldn't work here because I know everyone, and he didn't look like he was from around here."

Phoebe nodded. "That's very good. Can you describe him, love?"

Anne screwed up her face. "I didn't get a good look at his features, but his clothes were strange. He wore a great long coat with a red scarf tied around his neck and a hat with a wide brim."

Phoebe hugged her. "That's a very good description. If you see him—or anyone you don't recognize again—come to us right away. Tell Emily as well. Priddy, thank you."

Once Anne and Priddy had gone, Marcus rubbed a hand over his face. "Do we delay our travel plans again?"

"No," Phoebe said. "Let him come after us. I will not hide anymore. We can take precautions."

Marcus drew his brows together, but nodded. "Very well. Tomorrow it is. With luck, this situation will end."

The next morning, Marcus regarded the two traveling coaches standing in the drive with displeasure. "I thought we'd travel with only our personal servants. I didn't realize she'd planned to bring the carriages."

St. Eth gave a bark of laughter. "You are traveling with your personal servants. But Phoebe has three to your one."

He slapped Marcus on the back. "Never fear, my boy, by the time you return you'll be lucky you don't have another coach and horses, if she finds some she likes." St. Eth had an irritating grin on his face. "Ester tells me Phoebe's modiste has given her a letter of introduction to one in Paris."

Marcus closed his eyes and shuddered. "This is an aspect of married life I hadn't contemplated."

St. Eth chuckled. "No, none of us do."

By this time, they'd been joined by Edwin, John, and Geoffrey, who were all smiling infuriatingly. He tried not to scowl. "Does she always travel like this?"

Geoffrey grinned. "Always, unless she is fleeing you. Never saw her travel so light before."

"At least she leaves the furniture," John said. "I had a great-grandmother who took half her house when she traveled."

Phoebe came up to them and placed her hand on Marcus's arm. "What is it? Is there something wrong?"

He couldn't remain angry at her. He just wanted to get away quickly. "No, it's just that I didn't comprehend we'd be taking the coaches."

"Aha." She nodded wisely. "I've been reliably informed that with all the English flocking to the Continent, it is difficult to find proper conveyances. I understand the situation with horses is not as bad." Her lovely lips formed a *moue*. "Though I am perfectly prepared to buy horses if need be, I don't want to commission a coach unless I must."

Marcus raised a brow. "Excuse me?"

She flushed. "Oh, I suppose I should have said *we* will not want to commission a coach. I'm sorry, my love. I've been so used to ordering my travel as I see fit, I forgot I should now consider you as well. I expect I'll become used to it. In the meantime, *if* I become *too* managing, you will have to tell me."

He smiled at her, keeping his thoughts to himself. *How am I to do that?* "Shall we go?"

"Give me a few minutes." She squeezed his arm.

While Phoebe said farewell to the ladies, Marcus made sure the outriders were ready. There was only one good way to reach the main road to the coast, and it was a very narrow lane, not even wide enough to turn the coach, lined by woods on both sides. He wanted to make sure Phoebe was protected if they were attacked.

Thirty minutes later, their coaches started down the drive. Phoebe's leave-taking had been mostly for naught. Her sisters, brother, and their spouses escorted them to the main road.

"The ship will sail on the early morning tide. When we get to Newhaven, I'll point her out."

She'd had her neck tilted at an odd angle when she looked up at him and rubbed it.

Marcus lifted her onto his lap.

"That's much better," she said. "I can see you when we talk."

He grinned and kissed her. "What is in the basket?"

"I think I see a bottle of port, other than that, I don't know. We can look."

"Later."

Marcus closed the shades. Phoebe was soft and warm against him. This position was much better. Only a few minutes later, the coach slowed. He knocked on the roof and John Coachman opened the hatch. "There's something in the path. We'll have it clear in no time."

A chill crawled up Marcus's spine. "It's a trap. Send one of the outriders to tell the other carriage to halt, and then ride to Charteries for help. Tell everyone else to be on alert."

"Do we move it, my lord? We can't go forward with it there, and the road's too narrow to turn the coach."

"Behave as naturally as you can. Covey will keep watch."

"Marcus," Phoebe said, "he cannot. He's with Rose in the other carriage."

Marcus swore softly under his breath. "He'll know to take the coach out of sight and double back. In the meantime, we should have enough men to hold off an attack."

She pulled out her pistol. "I can help."

"You," he growled, "you are his target. Stay here with the shades down and fastened, and the door locked."

The coach had been made to Phoebe's specifications. That in itself was not remarkable, but the interior was. There were lights, a folding table occupied the place a second set of doors would be located, and the carriage had a strong lock. However, from the outside, the coach appeared as if there were doors on each side. Leather roll-down shades covered glass windows. The shades were thick enough to provide protection if the windows broke.

Phoebe threw her arms around his neck. "Marcus, if anything were to happen to you, my life would not be worth living."

He kissed her hard and fast. "You are carrying our child. That is something to live for, but if I lost you both, I'd have nothing. You have the coach pistol and your own. Don't be afraid to use them. My love, this time, you must shoot to kill, and if you hear guns being fired, get down on the floor."

Phoebe's eyes filled with tears, but she nodded.

He jumped down to the verge, waited until he heard the lock click, then turned to the coachman. "What's in the road?"

"A dead cow, my lord," John Coachman replied. "Right in the middle so's there's no way to go around."

"Hell. It will take at least three men to move it. They'll be unarmed. That's when Travenor will strike."

"Yes, my lord. Should we just sit—"

There was a loud shot and a ball whizzed over Marcus's head.

Chapter Twenty-six

"*D*own!" Marcus shouted. He glanced around to make sure no one had been injured, before crouching down and trying to make out where the shot had come from. The coachman had gone to the horses to try to stop them from bolting with the carriage. Their outriders ranged behind the coach, pistols out. One, a Baker rifle.

A group of men emerged from the wood on the opposite side of the road. Most of their weapons were trained on the carriage, the rest on Marcus and his men. They were outnumbered. He called to the horsemen, "What is it you want?"

A muffler concealed the face of the man who spurred his horse forward. When he pulled the scarf down, his smile was pure evil. *Travenor*. "Simple, my lord. Your life, or your wife."

Rage filled Marcus. He wanted to kill the bastard, but if he showed the pistol concealed in the folds of his greatcoat, the men guarding him would fire, possibly hitting Phoebe. He made a show of calmly rubbing his jaw while rapidly reviewing his options. Using a languid drawl, he replied, "Not a good enough offer."

Travenor reddened, his horse sidestepped uneasily. "Perhaps I should talk to Lady Phoebe and offer her your life in exchange for coming with me. The last time I stopped her coach, she got away. This time, I intend to have her."

Blackguard. "No."

Marcus fired. Travenor's horse shied at the last second and the shot pierced Travenor's arm instead of his heart.

Shots rang out, and a ball grazed Marcus's temple. He stumbled and grabbed the side of the coach, steadying himself. He couldn't see everything that was happening on the other side of the vehicle, but he heard groaning. At least one man had been hit, but whose?

Travenor gloated. "I think I'd gain a good deal of pleasure, my lord, from making you watch me take your wife before I kill you. You needn't worry about her though. I'll keep her in good health as long as she satisfies me."

Phoebe gasped. Marcus willed her to stay in the coach. "You'll never lay your filthy, ill-bred hands on my wife."

"That so, my lord? Then neither will you. Shoot her."

A shot ripped through the carriage. Phoebe screamed, then went silent. Marcus froze as a dark red liquid seeped under the coach door. *God, Phoebe!* He ripped the door open. The contents of their lunch basket were strewn across the floor, the bottle of port shattered, and Phoebe was gone.

"We got 'er, my lord," one of Travenor's men called.

"Unhand me now." Phoebe's voice was furious.

Thank God she was alive. Marcus had forgotten about the trapdoor.

Rocks and dirt flew out from under the coach as Phoebe fought the man pulling her from beneath the carriage.

Travenor laughed. "Bring her to me."

Marcus grabbed the second coach pistol, slipping it in his pocket. He straightened and turned back to Travenor. One of the thugs kept a pistol on Marcus as Travenor dismounted.

He held Phoebe against his chest and rammed a pistol against her head. Marcus's men drew closer, but there was nothing they could do while Travenor held Phoebe. He wondered where his footman with the Baker rifle was and hoped he had a clear shot.

Travenor stroked Phoebe's cheek with the weapon. "Shall I take her here, so everyone gets a view?"

Marcus clenched his teeth. Every muscle in his body tensed to attack as he was forced to watch his wife in Travenor's hands. "You won't live to be hanged."

Marcus met Phoebe's frightened but determined gaze. Seconds later, her hand slipped carefully down her skirt and disappeared for a moment, then a sliver of silver flashed.

Travenor roared like a bull being castrated, doubling over long enough for Phoebe to jerk free, her dagger in her hand. Blood flowed from between Travenor's legs. She dropped to the ground and rolled away to the side of the road.

Travenor leveled his gun at Phoebe and Marcus's heart stopped. He'd only get one chance to save her. Raising his pistol, he fired, shooting Travenor through the side of his head. The blackguard's mouth opened in shock, and his gun fell to the ground.

Pandemonium broke out. Shots were fired. One of his footmen fell. White smoke and the acrid smell of sulfur filled the air, it was like being on a battlefield. Marcus bolted to Phoebe, who was lying on the ground, blood covering her back. Then the shooting stopped. The ground trembled as Travenor's men fled down the road.

Marcus ran his hand down her back, searching for a wound, but there was nothing. He scooped her up into his arms. "Phoebe, Phoebe, my love, are you all right?"

She held on to him tightly. "I'm fine, but you've been hit. Marcus, there's so much blood!"

His throat closed. She was safe. His head started to

pound like a horse had stepped on it. "It's just a scrape. I'm a hard person to kill."

Phoebe's hand moved to her stomach. Marcus's heart lurched. "Is the baby all right?"

She remained silent for a moment, focusing her attention inward, then smiled. "Yes, I believe so. Survival must run in the family."

He held her closer. "From now on, it will be a tradition."

Phoebe gave a watery chuckle, and he kissed her, gently, as he willed his love to enfold her and their child.

"Are you two going to wallow in the dirt all day," Hermione asked, "or do you have a plan for what happens next?"

Holding Phoebe against him, he scanned what he could see of the area. Horses milled about and bodies lay in the lane. He glanced up at Covey. "How many did we lose?"

"One dead, my lord, and two wounded on our side," Covey said. "Five, not countin' Travenor, on the other side." Covey grinned. "Their ladyships made a good showing, one dead, the other wounded, my lord, as did our former soldier. He accounted for two dead."

Hermione glanced smugly at Hester. "Well, we know which of us is in need of shooting practice."

Hester replied shamefaced, "Yes, well, I have to admit I have not made the time. Clearly, that must change."

They were joined by their husbands, and the two couples looked at Marcus and Phoebe.

"He'll get used to it eventually," Edwin said. "I did."

"Leave them alone," his wife said. "He's had quite a scare today. At least when we were held up I was not breeding."

Edwin met her gaze. "No, you're right, my love, I would have behaved very differently if you had been." He opened the coach door and took out some napkins and poured water on them. "Marcus, let's get you cleaned up a bit. You go back looking like that and your mother will have apoplexy. By the way, that's the last time I give you a good bottle of port."

Phoebe took the cloths and cleaned the side of his head. He flinched at her touch, and tried to keep his thoughts on something else until she was done. "We'll need to move the cow."

Hermione frowned. "Cow? Is that what's in the road?"

Phoebe sighed. "Lord Travenor killed the poor thing and left it to block the path." She glanced at her sister. "How did you know to come?"

Hester laughed and handed a heavy gold ring to Marcus. "Lady Dunwood remembered that Lord Dunwood had forgotten to give Marcus the signet ring. We were trying to catch up to you when the outrider found us. Just in time, I'd say."

"I'll agree," Marcus said. "Thank you. We need to get the dead and wounded back to Charteries."

"One of the outriders went back. He'll bring a cart," Hester said.

It didn't seem like they'd been waiting long at all before two wagons arrived. The dead were loaded in one and the wounded in the other. Phoebe grabbed onto Marcus as he stumbled when he tried to rise.

"I've got him," Edwin said.

She glanced inside her coach. What a mess. "We'll take the baggage coach back to Charteries."

Lady Dunwood rushed forward as Phoebe descended from the carriage. Isabel's eyes widened. "Marcus. Get in the house right away."

A footman rushed over to help.

She linked her arm with Phoebe's. "Oh, my dear, what a dreadful thing to have happen."

Phoebe summoned a smile. "Yes, I feel most sad for the

man who died, and those wounded. We must do something for their families."

"Of course, we will. How brave of you."

"I? No. I did what I had to. It was the others who sacrificed. I think Marcus will agree with me."

"Phoebe is right. Our first concern is to take care of the family of the man who died."

A few days later, all of Charteries attended the burial of the one outrider they'd lost. Lord Dunwood agreed that the family should be allowed to remain in their cottage and given an annuity. The villains were buried in the paupers' field.

One of the men who had been wounded became feverish, and for a few days, they thought they'd lose him too, but he finally pulled through.

The night before the inquest, Phoebe was at a long table in the library searching through *Debrett's Peerage* and a book on the families of England, when Marcus entered.

"What are you doing?"

"Looking to see who Travenor's heir is." She put the book down and drew her brows together. "I found him. He's a vicar."

Marcus sat on the chair next to her. "If Travenor's misdoings are exposed, it will make it difficult for the new Lord Travenor and his family, if he has one."

Phoebe rubbed her forehead. "He'll never survive it. The scandal will be too much."

Marcus nodded slowly. "I'll tell my father. No one wants to harm innocents. He'll just have to find that the attack was by persons unknown and Travenor died as a result."

Phoebe put the tome down and kissed her husband. "It's a good thing your father is the magistrate."

A few days later, Marcus found her in the solar. "I've had your coach repaired."

That was good news. She smiled and wrapped her arms around his neck. "When do you want to leave?"

"To-morrow, if it's all right with you."

"To-morrow is wonderful."

Phoebe and Marcus arrived in Newhaven in mid-afternoon. Marcus greeted the inn's landlord as an old friend and introduced Phoebe. After conferring with her, Marcus ordered their dinner for an hour hence, and they set off to see the village and the port.

Phoebe gave a small skip. "I've never visited a port or seen ships."

He pointed out the different types of vessels to her. Leading her to the end of the pier, he pointed. "Look straight across from the lighthouse. Do you see the yacht at anchor?"

After a moment she nodded. "Yes."

She was tight against his side, and he rubbed her arm. "That is the *Lady Phoebe*."

Phoebe turned into his arms. "*Lady Phoebe?* How long have you had her?"

A flush rose in his neck. "About five years now."

She gasped, gazed up at him. "Five years? You were still in the West Indies then. What would have happened if we hadn't married?"

Marcus didn't care who was watching, he crushed her to him. "I love you. I never allowed myself to even consider the possibility that you wouldn't be my wife."

Marcus glanced around. This area was far too public for his needs. "Let's go back to the inn."

"Let's." She started to walk. "It must be quite an honor to have a ship named after one."

If only she knew how much of an honor. A small grin played around his mouth. "You could say that."

Phoebe turned the new information over in her mind, until her musings were interrupted by a ribald shout.

"Ahoy there, me lord," an old sailor shouted. "Are ye goin' to be having a name changin'? Bad luck if ye don't do it proper, and with plenty of rum."

A name changing? What was that?

Marcus's grin widened into a smile. "You'll have to find your rum elsewhere. I married my Lady Phoebe."

They'd come abreast of the old man who'd yelled.

"My love," Marcus said. "Allow me to introduce Mr. Hawkins."

His face broke into an almost toothless smile. "Well it took ye long enough." He bowed to Phoebe. "Milady, ye've got a right one there. Loyal as the day is long."

"Yes, I am very fortunate. Tell me. What is so bad about changing a ship's name?"

"Sailor's superstition," Marcus answered. "If the least scrap of the old appellation remains, it's dangerous to the ship and crew. Most sailors won't work on a ship that's been renamed."

Her eyes widened, finally understanding what he'd done. "So a ship's name *is* quite a commitment."

"Yes."

Phoebe was stunned. During the entire eight years, he really had wanted to marry her, and he never truly knew if she would even speak to him again. Phoebe smiled and blinked back her tears. "Thank you."

Marcus tilted her chin up and kissed her. "Phoebe, I've loved you since the first moment I saw you. Though you didn't know it at the time, my first commitment was changing my life, the second was my ship, the third, our marriage. For the past eight years, and for the rest of my life, you are the only woman I will ever love."

She stood on tiptoe and wrapped her arms around his neck. "And you are the only man I will ever love."

The old sailor cackled. "This calls for rum."

Epilogue

Phoebe's sisters and aunt arrived at Charteries the first week of July. Aunt Ester informed Uncle Henry that unless he joined her at Charteries, he would have to do without her until after the birth of Phoebe's child.

Aunt Ester arrived with three traveling coaches, bringing with her all the clothing, furniture, and accoutrements she thought she and Phoebe would need, in addition to several servants so as not to be a burden on the Charteries household.

Phoebe woke up with contractions two weeks later. "Marcus, get my aunt."

He rolled over, his eyes heavy with sleep. "What are you doing awake."

She put her hand on her stomach as another contraction came. "Get Aunt Ester, now!"

He jumped up. "Now? The baby's coming now?"

"Yes. Call for the doctor and midwife as well."

Marcus tried to light a candle, swore, and tugged the bell pull. Not long afterward, her aunt, sisters, and mother-in-law entered the room.

"Marcus," Isabel said. "Go wait for the doctor and show him up when he arrives."

He scowled. "Fine, but I'm coming back up here."

Aunt Ester and Isabel had everything ready by the time the doctor arrived.

He bowed to Phoebe. "Let's see how far along you are, my lady."

After his examination, he said, "Not too much longer."

That was good. Her sisters gave her sips of water and broth. Once, when Rose entered, Phoebe caught a glimpse of Marcus pacing the corridor. All of a sudden she felt like she was breaking in two and screamed.

Marcus burst into the room.

"Here, my lord," the doctor said. "You need to wait outside. I'll call if you're needed."

"I'm staying right here," Marcus growled.

The doctor muttered to himself, something about it not being a good idea, but said nothing more.

Phoebe was glad Marcus was there, holding her hand and trying to soothe her.

Finally, the doctor ordered her to push.

Tears of joy and relief showed in Marcus's eyes when he took the screaming body of their son from the doctor. He handed the baby to Phoebe, and then promptly fainted.

Aunt Ester regarded Marcus's recumbent form. "That is the reason husbands should not be allowed in the room during the lying in."

"Indeed," Hermione and Hester agreed.

"I wonder if this will be another thing Marcus will decide I should not do again," Phoebe mused, cuddling the baby.

The ladies looked at her questioningly.

"In order to protect me."

Isabel glanced down at him. "He always was a difficult child."

Dear Reader,

When the image of a woman in Regency dress furiously pacing the floor first started playing in my mind, I knew I had to write it down. Lady Phoebe Stanhope arrived fully named, gowned, and with a hero she didn't want. I didn't realize at the time of her story, THE SEDUCTION OF LADY PHOEBE, that it would be the beginning of my first series, THE MARRIAGE GAME. Yet as Phoebe and Marcus's love story developed, it turned out that they had friends whose stories also needed to be told.

When the plot for THE SECRET LIFE OF MISS ANNA MARSH, the second book in the series, first came to me, I honestly thought it would be a nice story about a young woman who has loved her dead brother's friend all her life, but is miffed with him for not proposing sooner. Boy was I surprised when I discovered Anna was keeping a secret from everyone, even Phoebe. Anna turns out to be anything but the prim and proper lady she seemed to be. Not only that, but the most interesting characters started to show up.

Anna and Rutherford's story was actually the third book I wrote. For reasons that will become clear when you get to know him, Robert, Viscount Beaumont, insisted his book be next. Robert tends to be a wee bit autocratic. However in THE TEMPTATION OF LADY SERENA, he quickly discovers trying to compromise Serena into marriage and getting her to the altar are not as easy as he thought. I particularly love the Dowager Lady Beaumont, Robert's grandmother, who helps Serena escape to Paris.

There are at least four more books, in THE MARRIAGE GAME and a second series, currently entitled THE WORTHINGTONS, underway. I hope you have as much fun reading the books as I had writing them.

A list of the books can be found on my website, www.ellaquinn author.com, where you can find excerpts, blurbs, and news. You can also be the first to see covers, get release dates, know about contests, etc., and sign up for my newsletter.

I'd love it if you join me on Facebook at www.face book.com/EllaQuinnAuthor where I discuss all sorts of things including the trials and tribulations of my characters, and enjoy interacting with my friends. I blog twice a week, always posting an excerpt on Mondays and hosting guest authors on Fridays at www.ellaquinnauthor.word press.com, and I'm on Twitter daily at www.twitter.com/ EllaQuinnAuthor.

Happy Reading!
Ella Quinn

Please turn the page for an exciting sneak peek of
Ella Quinn's
THE SECRET LIFE OF MISS ANNA MARSH,
now on sale wherever eBooks are sold!

Prologue

October 23, 1814, London

L ord Florian Iswell, the fifth son of the Marquis of Wig-
more, entered his rooms on Jermyn Street after eating
dinner at his club in the convivial company of some old
school friends. He spied a sealed letter propped up on the
fireplace mantel.

His heart thudded painfully. It had been months since
he'd seen his name in that bold scrawl. Gingerly, he reached
out his trembling hand. Using two fingers, he plucked the
missive up as if merely touching it might harm him, and
broke the unadorned seal.

As he read the note, his stomach roiled. He should have
never eaten the lobster patties.

> *My Dear Florian,*
> *Meet me at the Cock and Crow at eleven o'clock*
> *this evening. Do not, my friend, be late. We have mat-*
> *ters of Great Urgency to discuss.*
>
> G

"Envill," Florian bellowed to his valet, "when did this arrive?"

"About an hour ago, my lord."

Florian shook the letter. "Why did you not send for me? I'll barely make the meeting as it is."

"I'm sorry, my lord, I told him you were out. He didn't say it was urgent."

Forty-five minutes later, dressed in a shabby brown frieze coat and well-used hat, Florian entered the dingy tap of the Whitecastle Inn a few minutes before the appointed time. The pungent smell of unwashed bodies, gin, and ale made him wish he could hold his handkerchief to his nose.

He glanced around the room. A man, indistinguishable from the other patrons, sat in the far corner, nursing an ale. From this distance, he was very like Florian, not much above average height, medium brown hair, and a forgettable face, though in the man's case, it was a ruse. Florian should have seen about killing Georges long ago.

Trying to maintain a casual appearance, Florian walked to the table and assumed a polite smile. "Georges, how are you?"

The man motioned to the chair opposite him. "I'm glad you could meet with me."

After so many years in England, Georges's French accent was almost nonexistent.

"I didn't know I had a choice," Florian said, dryly, eying the seat with disgust. Who knew what was on it.

The smile on the other man's lips didn't reach his dark eyes. "You did not. I merely thought to be pleasant."

Florian ordered a tankard of ale and sat. "What's all this about? I thought we were finished."

"Yes? Many thought the same," Georges said. "One must not underestimate the Corsican."

Sweat broke out on Florian's forehead. Napoleon? He was in exile on Elba. "I take it some small changes are expected?"

"How perceptive you always are," Georges said and took a pull of his ale. "Then again, it runs in the family, does it not?"

"You would know." Florian's stomach clenched. Between the smells and the unwelcome news, he was starting to feel ill. "Tell me what I can do for you."

Georges leaned forward and lowered his voice. "We need to bring in some rather large packages. Your part is to contact the sort of people who can be helpful to the endeavor."

Tightening his lips into a thin line, Florian asked, "Do you have any particular area in mind?"

"We," Georges said, grinning wickedly, "rather like the cliffs of Dover and further east along the coast."

Florian nodded. "I can't go anywhere until the week's end. I'll contact you when I return."

"My dear cousin," Georges said, his cold gaze bore through Florian. "I knew I could count on you."

Only because of the mistake he'd once made in trusting the wrong people. "I want this to be over. If I get caught . . . the scandal."

"You should have thought of that before." Georges stood. "I shall await word from you."

"Yes, of course."

Georges left the tavern. Florian waited a few minutes before quitting the place himself. Bile rose in Florian's throat. He was to have been done with this. Where to find a smuggling gang? There was only one he knew of he might approach. What if they balked? No, they'd help bring the French spies in, or he'd threaten to expose them to the Home Office. He had too much at stake now to be caught.

If his father found out, Florian would be cut off without a penny.

Despite what he'd told Georges, Florian decided to leave for Thanport to-morrow, after he made arrangements to rid himself of his demanding cousin.

Chapter One

October 25, 1814, Marsh House, London

Miss Anna Marsh was in her parlor reading, when her maid, Lizzy, entered and held out a grubby piece of paper.

"Came from my brother, Kev, this morning," Lizzy said.

Anna nodded, took the note, and opened it. She perused the contents then closed her eyes. "I'm going to have to find a way to convince Mamma to allow me to remove to Marsh Hill before the Little Season has ended. Though I cannot do anything until after Lady Phoebe's wedding."

"That bad, miss?" her maid asked, screwing up her face. "You might have a time of it. I heard Lady Marsh was planning to go to some country house next week."

Anna sighed. Ever since her brother Harry's death, Mamma had become difficult. "She probably expects me to go with her." Anna shrugged. "Well I cannot. Someone has been sniffing around Thanport. I don't like the sound of it." Anna rose and walked over to her mahogany writing desk. She opened a drawer. Eschewing the neat stack of elegant pressed paper, she pulled out a piece of the distinctly rougher type. "I'll write Kev and tell him to lay low until I can get there."

> K
> *No information exchanged or meetings scheduled until I arrive.*
>
>   A

She sealed the message and handed it to Lizzy. "Make sure this goes out to-day, even if you have to take it yourself."

"Yes, miss."

Anna pinched her upper nose. "I do hope this is not going to make our lives even more complicated."

"What do you think that other man wants?" Lizzy asked.

"I don't know." Anna shook her head. "But I have a feeling whatever it is will do us no good. I'm going to Mamma and try to talk her around. I do wish she and Papa could settle their differences."

Lizzy nodded. "It does make things a bit more difficult."

"That it does," Anna said, smiling grimly.

A few minutes later, she knocked briefly on the door to the morning room in the back of the house, and tripped in only to stop. The gentleman sitting on a chair next to her mother's chaise rose. Anna curtseyed.

Sebastian, Baron Rutherford, bowed. Anna fought the urge to smile. He was tall and rangy. The cut of his coat molded to his broad shoulders, and his pantaloons clung to his muscular legs. He had hair the color of a hazelnut and impossibly gray eyes. When he was angry, they shone like molten silver. Anna frequently made him angry.

She'd loved him since she was a child. If he'd asked for her hand when she'd first come out, she would have accepted him. Now, at one and twenty, she was wiser.

Sebastian—he hated his given name—had spent the last

few years dangling after Anna's best friend, Phoebe, who was now marrying Lord Marcus Finley. With no more cover and his mother nagging at him to wed, he'd turned to Anna. Yet, the past two years had made it impossible for her to marry him unless he truly loved her and all she was. She wasn't sure they even knew each other anymore.

Anna met his gaze coolly. "Lord Rutherford, pray, what brings you here?"

"Oh, Anna dear," her mother said. "Lord Rutherford has very kindly offered to help by escorting you to Charteries for Lady Phoebe's wedding."

Anna raised a brow and stared at Sebastian for a moment before turning to address her mother. Lady Marsh reminded Anna of a wraith. Her mother's dark brown hair was still unmarked by silver. She always dressed in flowing gowns and draped gauzy shawls around her shoulders, giving the impression she would blow away if one breathed hard enough. Mamma desperately wanted Anna married and could not understand how it was she'd reached the age of one and twenty still single.

As objecting to Sebastian's escort would do her no good, Anna kept the smile on her face. "Yes, Mamma, very kind of him." She glanced at him and thought she saw the remnants of a smug look on his face. "How do you think of these ideas?" she asked sweetly.

His lips twitched slightly. "I really couldn't tell you, Miss Marsh, it just popped into my head. We are both attending the wedding after all."

It did not auger well for him that he had used her mother to get his way. "Yes, we do have that in common."

"Well, my dear," Mamma said, apparently oblivious to the tension between Anna and her guest. "Lord Rutherford would like to leave fairly early. He is to stand up with Lord Marcus, you know."

Anna's expression didn't change, nor did her dulcet tones.

"Indeed? How interesting. I trust you're not doing it for the practice, my lord."

The innocent expression in Miss Marsh's large blue eyes belied the stubborn set of her lips. Rutherford turned his choking laughter into a cough and looked down so she couldn't see his expression.

When he raised his head, she was in negotiations about something with Lady Marsh. He took the time to admire her. As always, Anna was elegantly attired. She wore a day gown in printed mulberry, and he could make out the lean lines of her slender figure. Lately, his fingers had itched to touch her in ways they never had before.

Gleaming chestnut curls were allowed to escape the loose knot held by combs at the back of her head. During the past year, her heart-shaped face had lost much of its youthful roundness. When she stood, the top of her head was below his collar-bone. Rutherford had kicked himself at least a dozen times in the last few weeks for not having made a move to engage her affections sooner.

He simply always just assumed she'd be available when he was ready, but he couldn't have been more wrong. To his chagrin, after Anna made it very clear he'd have to win her heart, he'd noticed other gentlemen of his ilk also vying for her hand. He wished she'd go home to Kent where he'd have a better chance. At least he'd have her alone. The only other gentleman of marriageable age living in their area was that insufferable pup, Percy Blanchard. Rutherford had nothing to fear on that score.

"But, Mamma," Anna said reasonably, "the Season is almost over. There are only two weeks left, and it will be terribly flat with Phoebe gone. Papa is at March Hill and so is Aunt Lillian. I'll be perfectly fine. I can leave from the wedding. If we take the coast roads from Sussex . . ."

"Anna," her mother interrupted, "I will not hear of you

taking that route, it is too dangerous. You will stay on the highway where it's safer."

"Yes, Mamma. Of course, you're right. Should I take everything with me or will you send it by courier?"

Rutherford frowned slightly. Anna had just won the argument and had really made no concessions at all.

"You will never fit all your baggage in the coach," Lady Marsh said. "Have your maid pack your trunks, and I shall send them."

"Thank you, Mamma. I can make the arrangements. There is no need to put yourself out over it." Anna bent and kissed her mother's cheek.

"Very well, my dear. Thank you."

Rutherford wanted to shake his head. When he'd proposed last week, and she'd refused, he thought it was out of pique that he hadn't asked earlier. It had been clear she was no longer a scruffy little girl in pigtails wearing grown-up clothes, but in fact ready to take on the role of his wife.

Was something else going on?

"Lord Rutherford," Anna said. "I shall be ready to leave when you are. I'll see you in the morning."

He watched her walk out of the room and a sense that she had walked out of his life passed over him. *Drat the girl.* She was up to something, and he needed to find out what it was. Perhaps he should have been spending more time with Anna and less hiding behind Lady Phoebe's skirts. He was being ridiculous. He'd known Anna since her birth. That was one of the reasons he wanted to marry her. During the past few years his life had been complicated enough. With her, there would be no surprises.

He almost offered to escort her to Kent, but he'd received a message from the Home Office to hold himself ready, so he needed to return to London after the wedding.

He bowed to Lady Marsh. "My lady, I trust I shall see you in the morning. I am glad I could be of service."

"My dear, Lord Rutherford, I cannot thank you enough for offering to keep an eye on my poor little Anna."

Rutherford gave her his most charming smile. "Not at all, my lady, it will be my pleasure."

He took his leave. Poor little Anna, indeed. The minx. What could she be up to that necessitated an early return to Kent?

Rutherford arrived at his townhouse in Berkeley Square to find a letter waiting for him asking him to attend Lord Jamison of the Home Office. He immediately set out again. Whatever it was, it had to be important for them to contact him after he'd sold out.

Twenty minutes later he entered Jamison's chamber.

Jamison stood and motioned Rutherford to a seat. "Glad you could come."

He regarded the large, buff, fair-haired gentleman with a sapient eye. "What is it you need me to do?"

"We think we've a bit of a problem in your area of Kent." Jamison glanced through some documents on his desk. "All along the coast actually. You're not the only one we're calling in." His bushy brows drew together. "We've heard rumors out of France that some of Napoleon's former officers might take up his cause. I've no doubt they'll be trying to run information through the smuggling gangs. That's where you come in." Jamison put his elbows on his desk and leaned forward. "Harry Marsh used to keep track of the smugglers in your area. You'll have to do it now."

Rutherford frowned. "I thought they'd disbanded. That was the reason Harry could leave to work elsewhere."

Jamison shook his large head. "No, my boy. Harry had gotten someone else to take them over. Never told us who it was. All he'd said was the man was responsible and would have good control over them. After all, it was only to have been for a few months."

Rutherford leaned back in his chair and blew out a breath. "I wonder who? I'll have to scout around and try to find out who their head man is. Harry always took the lead with them. I went a few times, but I'm not even sure they'd remember me." Rutherford sat up and scowled. "I wish to hell he'd stayed and not gone over to France."

Jamison nodded. "He was a good man. Reckless, but good. A shame his family can't be told the truth about his death."

"I've no idea how they'd feel about him being an Intelligencer. Better to let them think he died in Badajoz rather than on a mission." Most Englishmen thought spying the lowest form of vocation. If they only knew the military could not have won without its spies and the information they gathered.

"I'll be able to travel to Kent in a couple of days." Rutherford stood. "I've a good friend getting married. I'll go after the wedding."

Jamison rose and held out his hand. "Thank you. I know you don't have to do this."

Rutherford shook his former chief's hand and smiled. "I'll accept your thanks. You're likely the only one to offer it."

"Rutherford," Jamison said, "let me know if you need reinforcements."

"You can be sure that I will."

Damn Harry Marsh for going off and getting himself killed. Who the devil did he find to take his place? A mental review of the men in his area capable of handling the task came up with nothing. Two years ago, they were either all too young, gone off doing other things, or incompetent.

The only good thing to come of this was that he would be able to escort Anna home after the wedding ceremony.

He wondered how she'd take that bit of news, and decided not to tell her until they were already at Marcus's family's estate.

Anna entered her bedchamber to find Lizzy packing. "Did you send the note off?"

"Yes, miss, I had a footman take it," Lizzy said. "Told him it was a letter from me to home."

"Good. We'll be traveling home after the wedding." Anna looked at the clothes spread around the room. "You've no time to lose. Everything must be packed this afternoon. I shall make arrangements for the courier to pick the trunks up in the morning."

"Yes, miss. I have to say, I'll be glad to be home."

For the first time that day, Anna relaxed. "Yes, it will be good to be back in Kent again. Do you want me to help you?"

Lizzy grinned. "No offense, miss, but you're no hand at folding. I'll have it done in a trice."

"Very well, then," Anna replied. "If you're sure you don't need my help, I have some shopping I should complete."

"No, miss." Her maid shook out a gown. "You go on."

Anna found a footman to accompany her, left a message for her mother with the butler, and walked out the door in the direction of Bond Street. She had several items of clothing she needed to fetch and a new hat to buy, as well as silk stockings and other small items she'd not find anywhere closer than Dover.

Two hours later, pleased that she'd found all she needed in such a short amount of time, she returned to Marsh House in time for tea.

Her mother handed her a cup and Anna helped herself to some of the various biscuits as well as a scone with clotted cream and jam. "I've finished my shopping and Lizzy is packing. The carter will pick up my trunks in the morning."

"I hope you have a wonderful time at the wedding, my dear," Lady Marsh said. "I was so pleased to hear that Lady Phoebe is finally marrying. She certainly has taken her time settling on someone."

"Yes, Mamma. We are all delighted for Phoebe." Mamma had in no way approved of the license Phoebe had been given and could not fathom any lady waiting for a love match. Mamma's match had been arranged and she and Papa had got along very well until Harry died. Then it all seemed to fall apart.

Lady Marsh frowned. "I don't understand why Lady Phoebe had to pick the most eligible gentleman available this Season. Really, Anna, I think you could have done something more to interest him."

Anna valiantly forbore sighing. Lord Marcus Finley, Phoebe's intended, had been the topic of conversation since early September. "Mamma, I've told you. He formed an attachment for Phoebe years ago," Anna said. "The only reason he danced with me, that one time, was to aid her. I never had a chance, and I would have looked ridiculous trying to set my cap at him."

"Please do not use that vulgar term," her mother replied. "There *is* Rutherford, my love. He is very eligible, and his mother told me that since he didn't do a good job attaching Lady Phoebe . . ."

"Mamma," Anna interrupted. "Phoebe had no interest in Rutherford. They are friends. That is all."

"As I was saying, my dear, Lord Rutherford is free and in need of a wife. I am sure, if you would only make yourself *agreeable* to him, he'd be happy to make you an offer."

Anna resisted the urge to cast her eyes upward. She missed the intimacy she'd had with her mother before Harry's death. Everything was so different now. Anna cer-

tainly wasn't going to tell her mother Sebastian had proposed. Trying to turn the conversation away from marriage,
Anna said, "Mamma, why do you call him Lord Rutherford, when you've known him all his life?"

"That is what we do, my dear. You would be well ad-
vised to remember he is no longer a schoolboy, but rather a
very eligible gentleman."

"Yes, Mamma," Anna replied meekly and rose. "I must
check on Lizzy. She has a lot to pack and not much time. I
shall see you at dinner."

"Oh, my dear, I forgot to tell you, I am dining with Lady
Worthington. I do not plan to make a late evening of it, but
if you have retired by the time I come home, I shall see you
in the morning before you leave."

"Please give Lady Worthington my best wishes and
enjoy yourself." Anna kissed her mother's cheek and left
the room.

Anna walked to the library. If she was to spend the better part of two days in a coach, she'd need books. After
searching the shelves, she selected a novel she hadn't seen
before. She looked more closely at the cover, opened it,
and tilted her head. The pages were full of pictures of
naked couples doing the most shocking things *and* directions as to how to do them. She shut the book, then opened
it up again, fascinated by the pictures.

Oh my, Mamma certainly didn't buy this book! It must
have been Harry's. Anna put it back on the shelf, and tears
filled her eyes. She wished Harry were here. He'd know
how to help her. Even though he was ten years older than
she, they had always been close. She remembered him
holding her when she was very young. He was always the
first one to arrive when she awoke terrified at night.

Even when she was five and he was fifteen, although he
didn't really want her following him and Sebastian around,
Harry never tried to stop her. When he'd left, Harry had

made her responsible for the smugglers he'd led. Granted he had thought it would only be for a few months, but he'd taught her well. Anna had held the group together for almost three years without mishap, and she would continue to lead them.

She wondered briefly how Sebastian would take that part of her life. The secret part. Only Lizzy and her brother, Kev, knew Anna's identity and that she was female. Her position in the smuggling gang was one of the many reasons Sebastian must be in love with her before she could agree to marry him. He'd have to accept her as she is now.

Anna remained in the library curled up in a chair. When she was ten years old, she had decided to marry Sebastian. That he was twenty hadn't bothered her a bit. That he might wed someone else never entered her mind. Even now, marriage to someone else wasn't a consideration. She'd marry him or no one. Unfortunately, no one was now a real possibility. Anna stared into the fire trying to envision her future without him and got absolutely nowhere. He was such an integral part of her past.

A footman came in, closed the drapes against the late afternoon gloom, and lit the wall sconces and candelabras.

"Please ask Cook if dinner can be served earlier."

"Yes, miss."

He came back a few minutes later, to assure her Cook would be happy to bring dinner forward.

Once the footman left, she got up and went back to the bookshelf. Anna found a couple of novels before leaving the room and, after some hesitation, took Harry's book as well. If nothing else, it would make her feel closer to him.

October 26, 1814, London

Rutherford decided not to tell either Anna or Lady Marsh he would accompany Anna to Marsh Hill. She'd accepted his escort, albeit unwillingly, to Charteries, Marcus's family's estate. Rutherford had no desire to push his luck any further until he had to. Miss Marsh would discover he intended to escort her to Kent when he did not turn off the post road to London, and by then it would be too late for her to object.

Arriving the next morning shortly after eight o'clock, he discovered that early was a relative term. Anna was ready at eight o'clock. Lady Marsh had not yet come down.

He paced the entry hall and checked his pocket watch, again, before addressing Anna, "Do you think she'll be much longer?"

"I'll send someone to fetch her. It's not good to keep the horses waiting like this." Anna hailed a maid and gave her instructions.

Thirty minutes later, Lady Marsh appeared on the stairs. "Good morning, Lord Rutherford. I do hope I have not kept you waiting."

He took the offered hand and bowed. "No, my lady. Not at all."

Anna glanced up at the ceiling. "Mamma, we must depart if we are to reach Charteries by noon."

Lady Marsh fluttered over Anna like a hen over a chick. "Do you have everything you need?"

"Yes, Mamma."

Anna turned to go out the front door and her mother embraced her. "My dear child. How I will miss you."

Anna returned the hug. "I will miss you as well. We must leave."

Tears sprung into Lady Marsh's eyes. "Yes, of course. How silly of me."

She stood in the door weeping and mopping her eyes with a lace-edged handkerchief as Rutherford helped Anna into the coach. You'd think Anna was going to Russia and

Lady Marsh would never see her daughter again. "I don't remember your mother being like this."

Anna frowned slightly. "Ever since Harry died she has been."

"Lady Marsh has never recovered?"

"No. Not really," Anna said sadly.

Rutherford couldn't imagine how painful losing a child would be. The death of his friend had been hard enough to bear. Rutherford closed the door and gave the coachman the signal to start. He mounted his horse, waiting until the outriders Lady Marsh had hired flanked the carriage, before following after them. They made their way through London's morning traffic, then on to the post road without incident.

The trip would take approximately three hours. They stopped midway to refresh themselves. It would be a good time to start getting back into Anna's good graces.

He handed her down from the coach. "I've reserved a private parlor, if you'd like it?"

She glanced around. "Thank you, but I think I'd prefer to stand for a while."

"Very understandable. Would you like hot cider?"

"Yes, please."

He found a servant to bring their drinks. "Anna, it's occurred to me that I could have been of more help since Harry died. I'm sorry I was not."

She glanced suddenly at him, her brows drawn together. "It wasn't your fault you kept being called away to your other estates."

"I might have left it in my steward's hands." He should have quit going on missions and paid more attention to Anna.

"That is never the answer. You owe a duty to your dependents."

This conversation was not going at all how he wanted it to. While he was trying to think of what else to say, the coachman came up.

"Miss, it's time we were going again."

Anna put her cup down on a bench. "I'll be right there."

When Rutherford and Anna arrived at Charteries, Lord Marcus Finley, second son of the Marquis of Dunwood, met them. Rutherford had known Marcus since Eton and could think of no one better to confide in regarding his problems with Miss Marsh, particularly since he'd managed to bring Lady Phoebe up to scratch after her six years on the Marriage Mart.

"Welcome to Charteries." Marcus handed Anna down from the coach. "Phoebe will be with you directly. I've sent a message to her."

Anna smiled. "Thank you, my lord. If you'll have someone show me to my chamber, I'll be ready for her."

Marcus addressed his butler. "Wilson, please have Miss Marsh and her maid escorted to her room."

Rutherford dismounted and greeted his friend. "I'd like to have a word with you if I could."

Marcus raised a brow. "Yes, of course. Wash your dirt off and meet me in the morning room."

Rutherford shook his hand. "Thank you."

A half an hour later, Marcus handed Rutherford a glass of wine. "Please have a seat, what do you wish to discuss?"

Rutherford heaved a sigh. "Finley, you're getting leg-shackled. Can you tell me how to do it?"

Marcus laughed.

Rutherford grinned ruefully. "Yes, I know. That I, of all people, should be asking that question, but Finley, I am quite serious."

Marcus struggled to regain his countenance. "What in God's name has brought this about? I thought you were sure of Miss Marsh?"

"I thought so as well," Rutherford said, chagrined. "However, it turns out she is not coming round as I'd hoped. Sometimes it seems as if she's avoiding me."

Marcus dropped into a chair. "I suppose you'd better tell me about it."

"I thought she would just accept me," Rutherford said.

"Are you telling me"—Marcus leaned forward, with an incredulous look on his face—"you expected her to accept you, when you'd been dancing attendance on Phoebe for years and then gave Miss Marsh no reason why she should marry you?"

Rutherford wouldn't have put it quite like that. "Well, you see," he said, then paused, trying to find the words. "I've known her all her life. I thought she was already in a fair way to being in love with me, or at least liking me a good deal. It never occurred to me . . ."

"Never occurred to you," Marcus retorted, "she might not appreciate being treated as a sure thing?"

Rutherford heaved a sigh. "I suppose I didn't think of it in those terms."

Marcus shook his head. "What a sapskull. I don't know Miss Marsh that intimately, but I know her well enough to expect she'd bridle at that sort of arrogant behavior."

Perhaps Marcus had a point. "I thought I'd leave well enough alone until I needed to marry, or until I thought she might be forming an attachment for someone else." Something seemed to lodge in his throat and he coughed. "She was very young and as long as her heart wasn't otherwise engaged . . ."

"Rutherford," Marcus said. "You've rushed your fences and taken a fall. It appears to me you need to start over. You, my friend, will have to undergo the humiliating experience of courting the woman you could probably have had without effort three or more years ago, when she was not so knowledgeable."

Rutherford remembered Anna smiling at him and then accepting another gentleman's offer to dance, or to escort her to supper. He couldn't believe he'd been so blind. "Now that you've said it, it all makes sense." He groaned. "The way she's hung back from me and kept me at arm's length. She plans to go home to Kent when she leaves here. I shall accompany her, but I don't intend to tell her."

Marcus asked, "Are you sure she is the one for you?"

"Of course she is. Despite her recent behavior, I've known her all her life. Marriage with her would be comfortable. There'd be no surprises." Rutherford picked up his glass and twirled the wine before taking a sip. "She's poised and fits well into Polite Society. I've heard that since her brother's death, she's assumed all the household responsibilities at her home. I'm sure we'll have our little disagreements from time to time, but she is used to taking her lead from me." Rutherford nodded his head. "Yes, I believe she is now ready to take her position as Lady Rutherford."

In fact, he couldn't imagine his life without her. For years he'd resisted the lures thrown out by other ladies as he waited for Anna to mature. Then lately, there were the less chaste desires he'd been having about her as well. He wanted to spear his fingers through her dusky curls and run his tongue down her supple neck. Somehow he had to convince her to marry him.

Marcus regarded him dubiously. "I wish you luck."

He stopped himself from running his finger under his neckcloth. "It may take a little time, but I'm sure she'll come around."